10 -

The Ghosts of Ukuthula

By Rick McBee

Editors: Melissa Meeks & Lisa Pottgen of Black, White and Read
Author Services: http://bwrtours.net

Cover Art: Gigi McBee
Map Art: Rick McBee

Published through CreateSpace: an on demand publisher for
independent publishers, a part of the Amazon Group.

ISBN-13: 978-1532995347 (CreateSpace-Assigned)
ISBN-10: 1532995342
BISAC: Fiction / Action & Adventure

Other Books by Rick McBee (Richard H. McBee Jr.)

Fiction:
Kalahari © 1995
Non-fiction:
Rough Enough © 2013
Beachcomber Seashells of the Caribbean © 2014

<u>Dedication:</u>

The Zulu word, *ukuthula,* means peace. This novel is dedicated to the life of Nelson Mandela and his leadership in the African liberation movement from the 1960s through the 1990s. Mandela actively supported universal liberty and equality in the Republic of South Africa at a time when espousing these views was a matter of life and death. He and others like him, tried to achieve this goal initially through peaceful measures. They failed. This led to another thirty years of armed conflict and personal suffering under an oppressive government of white apartheid rule. To his great credit, after being released from his incarceration, Mandela and other black African leaders managed to refocus the vision of how the Republic of South Africa should be ruled. This vision helped foster a new order throughout much of southern Africa, one engendering nations that espouse multiracial unity, democratic leadership and peace (ukuthula).

Additionally, this book is dedicated to the thousands of women and men working behind the scenes of that African liberation movement. Clergy, missionaries, intelligence personnel and ordinary citizens sacrificed portions and sometimes all of their lives to move this goal forward over a period of fifty years. Without their moderating influence, the guerilla warfare which began in Mozambique and Rhodesia, then spread to Angola, Namibia and the Republic of South Africa would have escalated into genocide. Without them, Nelson Mandela would not have become the man to set an example of leadership for that section of the world which continues to move toward the still unfulfilled goals of unity, prosperity and democracy.

For
My wife Jill.
Without your loving support of my creativity,
I would never have finished this book.

Southern Africa

Introduction

When police cadet Dirk Van Zyl stepped out of the armored police van on that cold wet August night, he had no idea that the black man they were detaining would one day become the leader of his nation. Dirk's two uniformed mentors dragged the African, disguised as a chauffeur, from the sedan. Roughing him up with slaps and pushes, they handcuffed him and threw him into the back of the paddy wagon. When he had the audacity to ask for a lawyer, they laughed in his face, pulled him from the wagon and beat him soundly with their truncheons. Van Zyl helped his two superiors throw their now bloodied, semi-conscious captive into the back of the van. The three discussed in detail how they would write up their reports about the man resisting arrest as they drove back into Pretoria.

At the jail, the man was quickly identified as one of the most wanted members of the outlawed African National Congress, Nelson Mandela. He was booked on charges of resisting arrest, treasonous activities and the recruitment of terrorists.

The supervisor took the three officers into his office, shook their hands and congratulated them for their service to the nation. Then they stood by as he placed a call to the American Embassy, thanking them for information from a CIA mole. Information leading to Mandela's capture and arrest.

That evening as Mr. Mandela was being tortured, the three men sat in a pub and drank to their successful day. One which would undoubtedly lead to future promotions.

Several months later Dirk Van Zyl, now a fully-fledged police officer in dress uniform, sat in the audience of the highest court in the Republic of South Africa as the forty-four year old Mandela faced the South African High Court Justice in a final plea to avoid the death penalty for treason. He would never forget the words spoken by Mandela, which inflamed the hearts of black African peoples to continue to rebel against apartheid while hardening the hearts of those dedicated to preserving a country thriving on racial separation and abject black slavery.

"During my lifetime I have dedicated my life to this struggle of the African people. I have fought against white domination and I have fought against black domination. I have cherished the ideal of a democratic and free society in which all persons will live together in harmony and with equal opportunities. It is an ideal for which I hope to live and to see realized. But, my Lord, if it needs be, it is an ideal for which I am prepared to die."

Following that address, Nelson Mandela was sentenced to life imprisonment. He was immediately incarcerated, tortured and began his inmate life at the nefarious Robben's Island Prison off the coast of South Africa.

It would be thirty two years before Nelson Mandela finally regained his freedom. During that same period, the career of Dirk Van Zyl prospered. He entered the ranks of the elite South African secret police intelligence organization, BOSS, as a colonel. He became a member of the inner circle of the right wing apartheid hardliner organization, Weerstandbeweging. He was assigned as a liaison to the US Embassy in Pretoria. This position allowed him to work closely with CIA operatives; a perfect position for subverting newly organized US operations now assisting in the dismantling of the South African apartheid system. Fortunately, as a Colonel, Dirk Van Zyl could now do something to thwart what he regarded as treasonous governmental changes.

Chapter 1
Durban, South Africa, October, 1989

It was a perfect day to be walking through the Durban Botanical Gardens. Spring was in the air. School had not yet broken for summer holidays. The park has many wide open spaces and Monday is always a slow day for visitors. A perfect mid-morning site for clandestine conversations between disparate intelligence agencies.

Dirk Van Zyl smoothed back his salt and pepper hair with both hands as he passed the giant water fountain and gazed beyond the blooming cherry trees toward the long reflecting pool where the tall, broad shouldered figure of his contact waited. The figure mimicked his gesture, although Dirk knew the man's sandy haircut would be a Soviet military white sidewalls crew cut in length. He kept walking, finally reaching the round lily pad pool covered with a splendor of purple and yellow blossoms jutting above its surface. Settling onto a bench, he unrolled his newspaper and tried to calm his nerves while he awaited the arrival of his counterpart in this operation, Colonel Mikhail Petrov, Russian Foreign Intelligence.

"A good day for taking the sun," the shadow of the Russian fell across Dirk's paper, startling him from behind.

"Still spring, so we have no need for suntan lotion yet," Dirk replied, conscious that he had twitched in surprise.

"May I join you? I have news from the Kremlin."

"Of course, General Breytenbach is anxious to know how we can work together."

"Excellent. I think the plan your general needs to approve will go a long way to solving his problems with the new liberal government proposed by your president, Mr. Botha."

"We want nothing overt that can be traced back to us."

"Certainly," the big man smiled, leaning back in an attitude of relaxation while unfolding his own newspaper. "I'll fill you in verbally and leave additional details that your general will want to know in the usual drop box. He and I have already had extensive conversations."

"Fine," Dirk ran one hand through his hair, brushing the micro switch that activated his recorder. "Tell me."

"The plan will take approximately a year to complete. We understand that's the period of time Mr. Botha's government has set for getting ready to begin transferring power."

"Yes, President Botha has set next September as the date for the release of all the imprisoned black leaders. He will then begin incorporating them into his coalition government in 1991."

"So our goal must be to disrupt that process."

"Yes, we need to have enough tension and conflict between the tribes within our black community so that negotiations for any coalition of black tribal leaders will break down along tribal lines. This will prevent the president from putting together a new government."

"I think what I have in mind will do just that. It will also incite anger against the Republic from surrounding front line nations like Zimbabwe and Botswana so that international pressures force South Africa to take some military actions that will incite the international community against them. It may mean a reinstatement of the U.N. sanctions."

"Anything that will..," Dirk looked up at the approaching black gardener picking up leaves and small pieces of trash left from Sunday's visitors. His voice rang out sharply.

"Hey, boy! Leave us in peace!"

"Sa?" The young man looked at the two white men sharply and appeared about to say something else.

"You heard me! Boy!" Dirk made as if to rise, his face turning beet red.

"Yes! Sa!" replied the young man, giving a mock salute and sauntering off, leaving his waste bin and broom only yards away.

"Damn impudence." His brown eyes shifted back to focus on the hard visage and piercing blue eyes of his counterpart.

"You were saying?" prompted Petrov, his impassive face giving no hint of any opinion about the outburst.

"Ah, yes. I was saying…," Dirk paused momentarily, collecting his thoughts. "Anything that will give the hard line conservatives in our government more ammunition to persuade the president that now is not the time to give governmental powers to a bunch of savages is good for our system and will be good for you as well."

"Good. I will be starting with things on the outside of your country. There will be international incidents in Botswana and in several wavering front line states. We need to bring people into line with our thinking and harden everyone's hearts against your country. But before then, you will need to coordinate directly with General Breytenbach on ways of neutralizing the intelligence operations of the American CIA in your country. They know far too much about your work with me and your contacts."

"You're asking me to organize taking out a CIA operation?" Dirk shook his head and doubt showed in his eyes.

"Not just any CIA operation," clarified Petrov in a harsh voice. "I mean you need to take out the entire CIA unit in Pretoria. I don't want any survivors."

"But…"

"Are you with us or not?" Petrov's voice cut him short. "Our goal," he continued, "is to bring this country to near anarchy. By next August your black and white citizens need to be right at each other's throats. The Zulu, Xhosa, Sotho and other tribes need to have their old hatreds rekindled. Talks of coalition can no longer be on the table."

"We are orchestrating kidnappings, gang incidents and desecrations of grave yards. Does that sound like what you were expecting?" Dirk now clearly understood who was in charge.

"Perfect. Just make sure you build the tension and anger, slowly and steadily, so the country is ready to explode with the final trigger by the end of next August."

"What will you do to set it off?"

"I am working on that already with your General Breytenbach. He will inform you when the time comes." Petrov's voice had taken on a tone of command. "Until then I suggest you concentrate on the CIA problem. You need to accomplish that mission within the next month, Colonel Van Zyl." Petrov rose, gave a slight bow and turned away.

"Yes, Colonel Petrov." Dirk Van Zyl said to himself, watching the powerful man stride away past the trash container.

"The trash container! Holy shit!"

Dirk dashed toward the refuse container, grabbing it and dumping its contents out onto the grass. His meaty hands tore the wires of the exposed microphone from the container. His heel ground the tiny transmitter to powder on the sidewalk.

An hour after the two men had departed, the black gardener stashed his recording of the two men's conversations in a hollow of the Banyan tree and went to collect his trash bin. What he saw made him hit his beeper, alerting his backup. He stuffed the wires into his pants pocket and headed out the front gate.

The incriminating wires were still in his pocket as convicting evidence of espionage when Colonel Van Zyl's silenced pistol shot him dead moments later in the nearby street.

As per unit procedures the gardener's backup man had departed the scene at the sound of the beeper. He returned to the Banyan tree two days later, collected the recording and sent a quick email. When he found out three days later that all his contacts were dead, he ditched the incriminating recordings in the duck pond, fled to Mozambique and requested political asylum.

Chapter 2
Pretoria, South Africa, November, 1989

Even spies can find things to perk up a glum Monday morning. Jacob Nkwe entered the office of Southern Hemisphere Marine Insurance (SHMI) at nine that morning and logged onto his secure CIA email. What he read brought a smile to his face.

"Got the bastard at last! Van Zyl, you are one dead man!"

He encrypted a new message, writing it out longhand on his yellow tablet. Then typing it into his computer, he saved it to his mini CD drive and began to put together an email to Washington.

"Jacob, don't forget it's Kathy's birthday," his secretary peeked in the door with a smile on her face. "It's twenty minutes to ten!"

"Oh! Almost forgot!" he jumped up from his computer, popped the CD out, slipping the mini disc it into a padded holder on a lanyard around his neck. He hit close on his files and headed for the door.

This wasn't just any birthday that made this important, it was payback for the hell of the weekend they had all just been through. The tension in the unit needed to be damped down.

He replayed scenes from the weekend in his head as he waited for the elevator to the ground floor.

It had all started with the news of a plane carrying several high level African leaders going down in the northern section of the Drakensburg Mountains early Saturday morning. The crash killed all on board. Jacob's team had spent the entire rest of the weekend working out the plane's flight plan and the identities of its occupants. He had already briefed his US embassy contact this morning.

"How could they get that far off course?" The red haired man shook his head in disbelief as he heard the news.

"Beats me," Jacob's finger had traced the flight plan route from Maputo in Mozambique to Lilongwe, Malawi, on the wall map. "He should have been headed due north, not west."

"Instrument failure?"

"Nothing out yet. The South African Army is investigating it. So far as we can tell there was no distress call or any indication that the pilot thought anything was wrong."

"What about bad weather?"

"It was overcast and he was flying through the blanket of clouds which covers most of southern Mozambique this time of the year. Nothing out of the ordinary that would screw with his instrument readings like that."

"What's your best guess?"

"I'd say some kind of sabotage to the plane's instruments. Russian Tupolev TU 134A planes are excellent for these small countries and have a great safety record." Jacob turned away from the map and stared out the window of SHMI at the morning sky. "Have you had any reaction or feedback yet on your end?"

"Not a thing when I checked in but you can bet it will be coming. You don't lose the top two leaders of a moderate African nation without fingers pointing at someone, somewhere."

The tall red haired man had stubbed out his cigarette and stood up to leave. "We'll keep you posted. I'll want your reaction to anything we find out that might throw a monkey wrench into this country's talks on forming a coalition government. They are in a very sensitive stage right now." He held out his hand.

"Nobody trusts the other side." Jacob's dark hand held the other man briefly and met his eyes. "We'll keep our ears open on all channels. If it was a set-up, we'll hear about it." He watched as the other man departed.

Of course this morning, it had all blown up, right in South Africa's face. Statements out of Zambia made direct accusations of a South African Army attack on a defenseless civilian aircraft. The Russian Embassies in South Africa and Zambia sent out press releases as to the airworthiness of the Tupolev. They denied the possibility of a navigation error unless there had been sabotage.

In the end, the world could only come to one conclusion. The Republic of South Africa had everything to gain and apparently nothing to lose by getting rid of these two men. The fact of Russian tampering with the plane's navigation equipment wouldn't come out for months. But of course, by then the damage would already have been done.

This morning, the early news also had a report that a South African armored car full of policemen had shot two young black men at a soccer match in Soweto. This had only made things worse. Gangs of angry young men had stormed from the ghettos this morning, wielding knobkerries at shop windows and car hoods. There were rumors that the negotiations on forming a new multiracial government in South Africa had broken down. Jacob and his entire team were exhausted just trying to keep up with the news. Until this morning's email there had been no positive information that they could use to help South Africa fight back against the disruptions of the secret third force which was bent on destroying their country.

There was a crowd at the front entrance so he ducked back into the elevator and exited in the parking lot one story below. From there it was a brisk walk to the bakery. It was good to feel the warm sun and escape the stuffy tenth story office building. Rush hour traffic had disappeared, the noise of the central city was punctuated by occasional busses, helicopters and distant police sirens. He cut across the double lane street and turned the corner, disappearing into the sweet smelling interior of the Blue Bakery a block farther down the street.

While he waited for the pretty young girl to fill his pastry box, he scarfed a jelly filled croissant and sipped a steaming cup of coffee. His fingers crept to his throat as he remembered the CD hanging around his neck.

"I could get in trouble for taking this out of the office. Guess I'll just go back inside as if nothing has happened."

Ten minutes later he was back on the street. One hand balancing the box of doughnuts and the other nursing the remainder of his coffee. In the distance he heard what sounded like an old truck or bus giving a loud backfire.

He was halfway across the traffic light at the corner when his cell phone buzzed. He skipped to the sidewalk, placed his box of goodies on the hood of the nearest car, snapped open the receiver and poked the green answering button. The line appeared to be open for a moment and then his secretary's voice came through clearly, shouting,

"Broken Spear! Broken Spe…"

The sound of a second distant backfire, this time recognized as an explosion hit his ear simultaneously through the air and his phone. Then the phone noise was punctuated by screams, the crackle of gunfire and more explosions. The line went dead.

The doughnuts were forgotten. Jacob broke into a run, tossing his paper cup into the gutter. Rounding the corner he looked up toward a column of black smoke spewing from the smashed picture window of the SHMI office. Beyond, a helicopter was lifting from the top of the building.

"My God! We've been hit! Got to go! Now!"

His instinct was to race toward the building and scene of the disaster. His training told him otherwise. He did an about face, turning from the heart wrenching scenes he knew would await police and firemen. Sirens were approaching already. The encrypted information on his data dusc was now all important. Escape and the preservation or destruction of secure data was everything.

Jacob knew the disaster protocol by heart. His secretary would have been pressing the auto-destruct button, even as she spoke her final message. With one stroke of the finger, all his unit's work had been turned into vapor and ashes. Only one copy remained and that was dangling around his neck. He reached up and fingered it.

"A year's hard work in an attempt to bring down Petrov's third force network and his plot to destroy the peaceful transfer of power to black majority rule in South Africa."

A bus slowed at the kiosk only yards away. He ran forward, caught the closing door and paid his fare. Then with cold sweat beading on his brow, he slumped into a seat labeled "Swart" at the back of the bus. The bus pulled away before a second running man could reach the door. Jacob watched as the man pulled a phone from his jacket and punched in a number. He settled deeper into the chair, mind racing.

"Only minutes before they have a tail on this bus. Got to get off. Petrov's plan to destroy any peaceful transfer of power is working. I've got to preserve this data to take his unit out."

He was out of his seat and first through the door at the next stop. Pulling off his suit jacket, he slung it over an arm and hailed a taxi. Opening the door he slid into the rear seat.

"How much to Johannesburg. I've got to get to Soweto."

"Sorry mate," the Indian driver shook his head, "I'm not licensed to go out of Pretoria. You'll do best to take a bus. I can take you to the depot." The cab began to move.

"No, wait, it's for a family funeral. I'll try another cab." Jacob opened the door.

"You'll be lucky to find someone to take you that far unless it's a white man," replied the driver, "You know a white man won't go near Soweto. Best to take the bus."

"Sorry I bothered you," Jacob handed him a one Rand note and was back out on the street. Another bus was pulling to a stop. He jumped aboard taking the back row seat once more.

"Damn! He'll remember me. They'll be checking the bus terminals. This was planned with government authorization. My picture will be with every policeman all over Pretoria in an hour."

Three bus changes later he was out of the center of Pretoria and into the "Colored" section of the city. It was a short walk to a small branch of Barkley's Bank which held his safe deposit box. Along the way he ditched his phone down a sewer drain. Once inside it only took a minute to verify his identity using his South African worker's ID. His heart rate dropped as he opened the safe deposit box in a secluded booth and extracted his Namibian passport, money and a set of undated travel papers. Carefully printing the date in the space next to the official seal, he smiled, slipped everything into his trousers pocket and exited the building.

He crossed the street, reached the corner and looked back to see a black limousine with flashing blue light pull up in front of the bank. Three men got out and entered the building.

"Jesus! They are fast. Got to keep moving. No taxis. Got to ditch these clothes."

He flagged down a light passenger van and traveled deeper into the slum area looking for a used clothing store. Half an hour later, no longer in his smart inner city work suit, white shirt and patent leather shoes, he emerged carrying a worn shoulder bag, wearing an off color brown jacket with baggy trousers and feet enshrined in worn tennis shoes. A battered brown fedora now shaded his face.

It was already mid-afternoon. Walking through the township, he now blended well with other working men.

"Too late to catch transport at the central train terminal. The word is out. Petrov or the government is hunting me."

The dingy bus terminal with busses for the homelands was crowded and smelled of the unwashed lower class members of society. He mingled in their midst, conscious that he had just dropped from the privileged elite into the gutters with those who keep the city of Pretoria cleaned and preened for the wealthy, serving the government. No ID was required to purchase a commuter ticket for passage into the poverty ridden separate states required for these lower class citizens.

"Bophutatswana! Bophutatswana! Bus for Mmabatho!" Came the intercom call for the capitol of the homeland nearest the Botswana border.

Night had fallen, when after four hours of rocking through every little village or town the bus finally pulled into the last station and they disembarked. Jacob joined a group of men around a fire in the thorn bush thicket outside the depot.

"How far to the train station for Botswana?" he asked a wizened old man.

"Two miles down Malabedi road over there," he pointed at a track running off through village huts.

"You know the train times to Botswana?"

"No but there's one every night that goes from Mafeking to Gaborone and on to Francistown and Bulawayo. It goes through here about midnight, you might catch it if you hurry."

"Thanks," Jacob was already striding away into the dimly lighted village shadows.

"Watch out for thieves," the man's voice followed him into the darkness.

Jacob was halfway to the station when the three men accosted him, emerging from their den of shadows like three black panthers. The dim streetlight was behind him. He watched them approach, noting their sizes and trying to get a glimpse of any weapons that might be in their hands. He faced them squarely, glad for the jacket's protection and the baggy pants giving free leg movement. The largest of the three spoke first.

"Traveling?"

"I'll be on the train tonight." Jacob kept his voice level, showing no emotion. He noted the way the two smaller men moved to the sides slightly flanking him. The larger man's height easily matched his own.

"We need some help for our mother. She is ill here in the village," the larger man continued his approach. "Give us your money and you won't get hurt."

The broad shouldered man was obviously not going to stop. He strode directly toward Jacob, muscular shoulders slightly hunched, his arms half spread indicating his intention to use a brawler's bear-hug while his accomplices worked Jacob's pockets from the sides.

Jacob stepped to meet him, left hand parrying the encircling right arm while his right hand hit the man's Adam's apple with a sharp knife-edge hand blow. He then twisted to the left, following his parrying motion to plant his elbow on the big man's chin. The leader's legs crumpled beneath him. He went down flailing, trying to overcome the effects of simultaneous breathing paralysis and a partial concussion.

The two sidekicks continued to move in. Jacob felt their hands touching his body as he continued to twist and follow through with his two hundred pounds of inertia. Instead of hitting the closest man with his hands, Jacob kept his arms in and planted his right knee just beneath the man's rib cage. Pivoting his upper body completely around on his left leg, he gave a roundhouse slap to the ear of the third man's head. Both men went down but struggled back to their feet and circled warily. The kneed man gave a groan of pain as he touched his ribs.

"I don't have money for your mother or anyone else in this town," he said, turning slowly, keeping both men in view. "If you bother me any more you'll need attention at your local clinic."

The smaller of the two men who'd been bowled over with the slap produced a knife and moved in at an angle.

"Chaka!" Jacob shouted, jumping vertically and turning to land in a fighting stance in front of the man.

The smaller man flinched, jabbing ineffectively, leaving his arm outstretched a moment too long.

Jacob grabbed the outstretched hand at the wrist, stepped underneath the arm, twisting it and then breaking it as it came up behind the man's back. Whirling, he met the charge of the other man with a solid punch to the nose that left him groveling in the dirt.

"I warned you," he said, turning to go.

The big man, having regained his feet, charged across the sandy path. The urge to kill shown in his eyes.

Jacob dropped his center of gravity to a crouch, spinning to the right and stepped backward. Using the other man's momentum against him, he lifted the big man's extended right arm, placed his elbow in the exposed arm pit and stood up violently, throwing him in a heap ten feet away. Running toward the man as he struggled to rise, Jacob jumped and drove the man back into the ground using both knees as battering rams against the man's rib cage. There was an audible cracking sound. The big man lay gasping in pain. Jacob rolled to his feet and faced the man holding his broken nose.

"You need to get them to the clinic. Next time be more careful who you try to rob."

He turned away and began jogging toward the railway station.

"You're blowing it, Jacob! That's just the kind of incident someone will remember. You're leaving a trail."

An hour later, ticket in hand, he found a space on the already crowded fourth class bench aboard the train for Botswana. The lights stayed on all night and the crush of humanity made it impossible to sleep. After the conductor had punched his ticket, Jacob found a vacant double seat where he could stretch out. He had just managed to go to drop off, when the train stopped at the border. Everyone had to disembark and pass through the customs gates out of South Africa and into Botswana.

"Here's where I find out how far their net has spread," he thought, passing his Namibian passport and exit papers to the South African agent.

"You were working in the gold mines, boy?" The agent's eyes bored into him.

"Yes Sir, Anglo-Gold Ashanti." Jacob replied, speaking slowly as if struggling with the language.

"Going home?" Again the eyes. Jacob avoided staring back.

"Don't give any hint of dominance, aggression or intelligence to the 'man'."

"Yes Sir, I finished my contract."

"How long?"

"Six years, sir," he could feel the sweat beginning to form on his brow.

The man flipped through his pages. He looked up one last time. Momentarily the blue eyes met lion yellow orbs before Jacob glanced down in appropriate submission.

"Move along, boy."

The agent's fist pounded the exit stamp onto Jacob's passport.

Chapter 3:
Washington D. C., November, 1989

Jim Collins, director of the Africa Special Branch in the state department, felt like banging his head on the wall and screaming.

"Look at this pile of shit!" His finger jabbing toward the long work table covered with piles of newspapers from all over the world. "Do you see any patterns in the massacre?" He stormed around the room to where his assistant, Abe Miller, sat in front of a yellow tablet.

"Sure, I see lots of patterns but not what you want if I get your drift."

"Tell me what you see?"

"It's all 'spin'. Our politicians use it all the time. It isn't about what really happened, it's about saying your special version of blaming the other guy often enough so that everyone believes your story no matter how outrageous. Spin makes you quit looking for the truth of what really happened."

"Fine!" snapped his boss, "so here we have a whole pile of spin about a bombing, none of which makes sense. Is that what you're saying?"

"Perfectly." Abe held up a sheaf of papers. Here are a whole bunch I'd label as South African xenophobic attacks made by the reigning government and their friends, blasting the ANC, the liberation armies in Zimbabwe and Zambia and our CIA." He set them down and moved to another section of the table.

"Now over here," Miller continued, "we have our home grown pundits and the Europeans writing that this is just the internal xenophobic Broderbund wing of the South African government hitting a liberal corporation that hires a lot of blacks, to get things riled up and make the transition talks fall apart."

"I get your point," replied Collins, picking up other South African papers. "The Inkatha Freedom Party here has picked out the ANC as the culprit. Classic intertribal strife for power between the Zulu and Xhosa nations in the formation of the next government. Right?"

"Right."

"Most of the employees for Southern Hemisphere were Zulu?"

"No, they were mostly Tswana people not affiliated with either the IFP or the ANC but what the hell, spin is spin. You say it enough and your people will believe it. All that counts is if your party, idea or side wins."

"Then tell me this," Jim Collins leaned over the table toward Abe, "If everyone has picked out the culprit as being their favorite enemy. Who done it? All this work looks like we've just been plowing through a ton of crap! What's the truth here, Miller?"

"The truth is, our whole operation in South Africa, under Jacob Nkwe whose code name you will remember is Zulu, just got blown away. You know the details, I don't. What was Zulu involved in to bring this kind of crap down on us."

"Let's walk down to my office. I need some coffee." Collins turned and walked out of the room without saying another word. Miller followed on his heels.

Minutes later in his secure, copper lined office, Collins poured out two mugs of coffee. Flopping into his creaky office rocker, he leaned back, savoring the smell. Miller took a similar chair opposite him, cupping his hands around the drink as if in need of warmth.

"Let me explain more fully about Zulu's little project, Collins began, sipping carefully on the scalding liquid. Some interesting things are beginning to show up."

"In the news?"

"It's what's not in those newspapers that really intrigues me."

"How so?"

"You remember when we put the Zulu thing together, it was an open ended project."

"Sure, find out if there was anything to the rumor of a third force manipulating the final move to a new constitution and black majority rule in South Africa."

"Exactly, rumors were rampant but no real evidence or pattern. We sent Zulu in to build a team to find that pattern and trace it to its source. If it existed, then we needed to squash it before it triggered a major backlash in this democratization of the government."

"Right," Collins toyed with his pen, "like an incident bringing a massive crackdown by the white controlled military and police on all black Africans. Something that would set the country back eighty years or send it into genocidal civil war."

"Did Zulu find that?"

"I think so. Those newspapers are nothing but political spin. Where is Russia? It bugs me that we've known about the Soviet Union influence in African politics since back in the late 1950s and 1960s. Where did all that Soviet KGB influence and political manipulation go after Glasnost?"

"It just disappeared with the demise of the Soviet Union," Miller snagged a cookie out of the jar on Collins' desk.

"Just like that?" Collins snapped his fingers. "Poof! Everything they worked on for so many years just went up in smoke because the USSR no longer exists? Hogwash!"

"That's the party line."

"We're not paid to believe the party line, Abe. We're paid to see through the crap and the spin."

"So Gorbachev didn't really dismantle all of the old guard of the Soviet Union?"

"Look at his background. He grew up as the most successful of all leaders in the communist party. You think he wasn't in cahoots with the KGB? He was so powerful he could afford to take down the Berlin Wall. He could afford to give up trying to govern all of the old Soviet Union. You don't think he had to stomp on some toes to change some minds?"

"So you really think they're still out there?" Miller countered with a question.

"I think," Collins looked him straight in the eyes, "that Soviet KGB intelligence morphed into the current Russian SRV, the Russian Foreign Intelligence." He lowered his voice and tapped his cup in emphasis as he spoke. "I think a section of the SRV, with connections to Russian military intelligence, is on the ground in South Africa right now. I think that's what Zulu found out…"

"…and it got Zulu and his unit wiped out," Miller concluded his sentence.

"Not Zulu. There was no trace of Zulu's remains in the rubble."

"Disappeared? Captured?"

"Gone ghost," I think. "We may not hear from him for a year."

"The dead drops are closed, standard ops in a SNAFU. He can't contact us."

"We'll wait. He'll find a way, if he's alive."

"So, do you have an idea of who's behind this?"

Jim Collins laced his fingers through his white locks, tipped back in his chair and looked at the ceiling while focusing on some distant place and time.

"I think we're dealing with an old friend of mine who started in this business back when I did during the Biafra War.....Viktor Mikhail Petrov. He runs S1RIUS, Section One of Russian Infiltration and Unconventional Sabotage." Collins pronounced the acronym as if it spelled the star name, Sirius.

"He's bad news anywhere in the world. I think we're going to have our work cut out for us to find Zulu before he does."

Chapter 4:
Lusaka, Zambia, January, 1990

It was just after the New Year. All the festivities and celebrations had finally leveled off. Colonel Viktor Mikhail Petrov sat quietly in the situation room of the Zambian Russian Embassy. On the wall was a map of southern Africa with notes, arrows, and photographs, detailing his plans for revolution on the continent. Business in Zambia and the war of liberation could finally get back on track.

Petrov listened to the voice of the Russian Consul coming from the room next door. The man was addressing a VIP group of front line African leaders. The men whose countries had a vested interest in overthrowing the South African government.

Out the window he watched Lusaka's bustling open market three stories below. A scene flowing before his eyes. The main branches splitting off into ever smaller streams. Shoppers pushed their way through the market stalls, everyone going about their normal everyday business.

He watched the design below flow and change as larger strands of humanity split repeatedly until they disappeared into a mass of moving color. It was a living mosaic, formed by the human masses, tables of bush medicines, rows of canned goods, wood carvings, stolen auto parts, books, green malachite trinkets and colorful clothes… on and on.

"From a distance we are nothing but human ants. Crawling about, seeking food, shelter, reproductive success, all searching for a purposeful existence. You are all waiting for someone like me to direct the flow of life. Someone to set a new mission for the course of Africa!"

He looked down at his own immaculate dress uniform decked with miniature medals from a dozen campaigns in as many countries on the black continent. He relaxed and smiled as the square-faced, sweat dripping, fat Russian Consul appeared in the doorway.

"They are ready for you Comrade Colonel."

Petrov began his presentation to the group with a statement. Something he knew they wanted to hear from a military man. His deep command voice rang out.

"Zimbabwe is ours!"

A murmur of approval.

"With this conquest we now hold a horseshoe of countries encircling the Republic of South Africa. From now on, my friends, we can concentrate on bringing apartheid to its knees."

"Tell us your plan, Colonel. When will we attack them directly?" the voice came from a tall thin African with whipcord muscular arms. A man comfortable with carrying weapons.

"Ah, Comrade Moises, so you think we should attack directly?" The disdainful tone of the Russian told the others what he thought of the man and his ideas.

"Yes."

"Let me show you a chart of our military strength as compared to that of South Africa." He removed the cover from a draped board, revealing a map covered with pictographic tanks and troops. His laser pointer flitted across the numbers of troops, tanks, rockets and aircraft owned by each country.

"This should make it clear that a direct assault on South Africa is impossible. We don't want to give South Africa any excuse for declaring war on us. You might want to think of our situation as similar to the power disparity in Europe in 1938. South Africa is like the all-powerful German nation at that time, as you are like Germany's weak neighbors, Poland, France and so on. South Africa would crush you into the stone-age with a direct confrontation."

"But if we attack, won't Russia and China help us?"

"We can supply you with small weapons but not with troops. If we bring our troops then the old colonial powers and the imperialist United States will send troops to help the South Africans. You would all be destroyed in any large scale war." He paused, looking out over his audience, judging their receptivity.

"Additionally," he continued, "let me remind you that South Africa still has cultures of live Small Pox virus. "Your unvaccinated populations would be wiped out by that disease."

Again a murmur rippled through his audience.

"We also believe they have nuclear weapons," his voice was harsh, "no need for me to compare the destruction of Hiroshima or Nagasaki to wiping out your capital cities."

He could see from their postures and the widening of their eyes that this information made them uncomfortable.

"So, are you saying we can't do anything to cause the downfall of this great white devil of a nation?" interjected a small African wearing glasses and an immaculate business suit.

"No, not at all, Mr. Ngambe," replied Petrov, smiling broadly. "Time is on our side. Within a year they will be falling apart from internal decay which we will facilitate. You see, they are corrupt to the very core. The poor people are a smoldering fuse of revolution. We will light that fuse and fan it to burn rapidly."

The Zambian Vice President raised his hand, coal black eyes gleaming. "So, Colonel, tell us what to do. It worked in Zimbabwe, so how will it now work in South Africa?"

"Our plan is to harden the heart of Pharaoh! The way Ian Smith's heart was hardened in Rhodesia before Zimbabwe became free. We must make the South African government crackdown hard with the boot and the whip on their own people. When they are pushed to the limits of tolerance their anger will overflow into outright rebellion. Once the dam breaks, we have people in place to whom you will be able to give your stockpiles of guns. After that, there will be no stopping the revolution."

"What can you do to make them this angry?" Skepticism tainted the voice of the delegate from Mozambique.

"We have people in the secret police who will begin taking political prisoners in the months to come. They will kidnap influential people in the ghettos. This will cause demonstrations and violence in the white sections of the cities. The police and military will move in to stop the violence but they will do this by shooting people in the streets. When this happens, the black anger will spiral out of control. There will be no backing down for either side."

"But are we all united on this common front?" inquired the Zimbabwean who wore a brightly colored African print shirt. "What happens if one country decides to feed information to the South Africans?"

"Comrades," interjected Petrov, coldly, "you all know the watch words of our cause. Please stand up and repeat them with me!"

His laser pointer flicked to the banner on the wall and they raised their hands while shouting in unison.

"IF YOU ARE NOT FOR US, THEN YOU ARE AGAINST US!"

"Absolutely my comrades, we all understand our cause. It is a pact that none can break without betraying all of us who have worked so hard to bring liberation to southern Africa. The final stage must be completed. I will continue to supply you with weapons through our channels. Your governments will work to let our operatives pass through your territories. We will work together to pull down the fascist apartheid government and establish a new order. The end will not be long in coming."

"When you say, "Not long," does that mean less than a year?" inquired the young Defense attaché from Botswana.

"Let me just say, that in Tswana you would say it will come before the *Maru a Pula,* the rains of next year. Does that satisfy you?"

"Excellent," smiled the tall attaché in full military uniform.

"One more final thing for all of you to remember," smiled Colonel Petrov. "In case you are thinking of not staying with our motto, let me refresh your memories on two historical items. First," he held up a finger, "how many of you remember what happened on October 19, 1986 only three years ago?"

The room fell silent. Only the roar of the AC could be heard. All their eyes were upon him. A murmur came from within the group.

"Comrade Samora Machel died in an airplane crash." The voice of the Zimbabwean was full of emotion.

"Exactly," smiled Petrov. "He was a man who fought on our side valiantly but then after achieving his goal, sought détente with South Africa. He died with three members of his government on that day. It was a terrible tragedy for Mozambique."

He walked to the front of the room and pointed to the map. "How many of you remember what happened only two weeks ago over in the mountains of South Africa?"

Again a complete silence enveloped the group.

"Ah Yes, I see that you all remember that tragic airplane crash also caused by the South Africans, killing another group of our comrades. I believe the South Africans have found a way to disrupt our navigation systems. Many of you use Tupolev aircraft in your government fleets. I would therefore caution you not to allow any untrusted person who might have had contact with the South Africans to work on them or even go near them. It appears to be a very unhealthy decision."

He paused and gazed at the men in the group, watching the dawning expressions on some of their faces. A waxy pallor was also emerging on the faces of several leaders he had long suspected of playing both sides of the liberation game. His voice became less harsh as he continued.

"It is fortunate for us all that the world now recognizes that South Africa is willing to kill off the leaders of other African nations. Therefore, they will begin to support our cause more readily in the future."

The leaders before him relaxed visibly in their seats.

"Let me reassure all of you here today," now he smiled and his tone became friendly, "our plans for the future of Africa include all of you in leadership roles. That is why we trained you for so many months in Russia a number of years ago."

He saw their heads nodding and knew he had won, either through reason or intimidation, it didn't really matter.

Chapter 5:

Washington, D. C., February, 1990

"Quitting time, Sir," Jim Collins' gray haired secretary poked her head in the door as he was turning on the African section of the BBC news.

"Thanks, Julie. Yes, I know. I have an evening engagement. Just have to listen to the latest news to see if anything new has cropped up overnight there."

"Alright, I'll see you at the Botswana Ambassador's get together tonight."

"Fine. Collins leaned back in his chair as the familiar BBC tones rang through his office. He leaned forward as the announcer related the latest news on the spreading racial violence in South Africa.

"Following a weekend crackdown by South African troops on mining townships outside Pretoria and Johannesburg, rioting continued today between Zulu and Xhosa factions. More than two hundred persons were injured or killed today when troops opened fire on two demonstrations led by members of the outlawed radical arm of the ANC, Umkhonto We Sizwe, also known as The Spear of the Nation.

The riots initially began when Xhosa tribesmen attacked a Zulu ghetto shopping center after one of their members had been kidnapped in a nighttime raid by a Zulu gang. Authorities say they have found no trace of the kidnapped man, a prominent Xhosa civic leader.

Governmental authorities say they are contemplating a reinstitution of the requirement for a special pass to be carried by all black Africans in order to move about freely and travel within the country. Leaders of all the surrounding black South African homelands have stated emphatically that they will not tolerate such action by the central government, and that it will lead to further violence and bloodshed within the country..."

Collins flipped off the news, stowed the documents from his desk in the open safe and twirled the dials. He was looking forward to the evening at the Botswana embassy, an island of sanity and peace within the cyclone of racism, terrorism, tribal conflict and radical governments in southern Africa.

It was seven thirty exactly when he arrived at the unimposing, three story, gray terrace house on New Hampshire Avenue; the site of the Botswana Embassy. A valet met him and drove his BMW away to a secure parking lot. The Ambassador and his wife greeted him at the door. He was immediately ushered through into the finely decorated reception room where he signed the guest register and took a glass of bubbly from the proffered tray. The hors d'oeuvres were excellent.

Half an hour later they were seated at the long dinner table enjoying superbly prepared medallions of filet, mushroom sauce, mashed potatoes and steamed vegetables. Seated between the Ambassador's pretty wife and the military attaché of the fledgling Botswana army, Jim found the evening to be light, amusing and informative. The attaché was full of himself and stories about the workings of Botswana's tiny army. After hearing the history of the origins and progress of the small force almost to the point of boredom, Jim finally asked a seemingly innocent question.

"I heard you were the Botswana delegate to a recent meeting in Lusaka, Zambia. Quite an honor wasn't it?"

"Yes," the young man smiled, swelling with pride. "I was chosen because of my rank and superior ratings in my military studies both in the United States and in Russia"

"Quite an honor to have been able to live in both Russia and the US at your age. You must speak Russian quite well. Is it as good as your English?"

"No, I was only there for four years. We study English all the way through our schooling, that and Tswana. In high school we may get a chance to study French or perhaps German or Afrikaans if we are near the borders of South Africa or Namibia. I was good enough to take both French and Afrikaans in my high school."

"Quite a linguist then. I presume your conference in Lusaka was in English?"

"Yes, even the visits to the Russian Embassy were in English because many African leaders don't speak Russian. They came from all over southern Africa, Malawi, Mozambique and even Angola."

"What about Zimbabwe? Were they invited?"

"Oh, yes, they came as well and some members of other groups hoping to eventually establish official governments in Namibia and South Africa."

"Wonderful, like a conference of all the southern African nations then."

"Exactly. We had a kind of wish list of when black governments would be able to take over in Namibia and South Africa. The Russians say it will happen by the time the rains come next year in Botswana."

"Oh," Collins feigned ignorance of the seasons in that part of the world. "Does that mean by Easter? That's when our big rains come in the spring. That would be soon!"

"Not at all," laughed the young man, "Our seasons are reversed because we're south of the equator. What we call the *Maru a Pula,* the clouds with rain, come in late September most years. I would expect things to work out before then."

"Yes, I hope talks go well too," Collins leaned back in his chair and stretched, "If all goes well, I would think they might reach a draft agreement by then, although I thought the plan was for a year from this coming January. The first of January, 1991."

"The colonel I spoke to seemed to think his program would be finalized for completion before the *Maru a Pula.* Those were his exact words to me."

"Well, I suppose he might be a part of the overall longer plan. I wish him and his program luck. Perhaps we'll have a chance to meet again over at one of the State Department parties later this year. I'd love to have an update as to how you think the colonel's program is coming along."

"Unfortunately, I won't be in contact with those people again," the young officer frowned, "my posting here in Washington takes priority,"

"Well, I'll check back with you just in any case," Collins pushed his chair back. "It looks like the Ambassador is about to propose the final toast for the evening. Then I better get going. I've got another party this evening. You know how the diplomatic channels work even on a Monday."

"Yes, sir," replied the young man, as they raised their glasses in the final toast.

"What are you so cheerful about this evening?" Julie was waiting at the exit as he came out whistling softly to himself."

"You need a ride home? I'll give you an update for a night cap."

"I came in a taxi, so the answer is yes," she tossed her silver hair which, in the streetlight, matched exactly her blue and gray sweater. "I'd love to hear something happy for a change."

Chapter 6:
Johannesburg, South Africa, April, 1990

Evening had fallen over Johannesburg leaving red and gold traces of the sun's passing in the clouds streaking the sky. The afterglow of evening filled the street near the Voortrekker Bar. Patrons sat outside enjoying the long Easter weekend, many having already spent a part of the day in Good Friday services. Inside, the lights were being turned up and the regulars were already ordering their pints, steak pies and chips. The arrival of the two South African Security Forces men made no dent on the gab and noise. They were regular faces who glanced around very briefly at their usual booth while ordering up pints.

Colonel Dirk van Zyl was already seated in the shadows with his back to the wall observing their entry. His muscular frame sported more heft than the men approaching him with their brimming mugs. The two took their seats opposite him and raised their glasses.

"Cheers Colonel," said the more senior of the two sergeants.

"Cheers Sergeants Potschef and Simon," replied their commander, leaning back in his seat and taking in half of the liter mug in his first draught.

"How are the plans for this evenings' escapade going?" He looked at both of them expectantly.

"We're ready," replied Potschef. "We'll be at the warehouse by midnight and be dressed and ready to move out by two. Simon here is our driver. He's been over the route several times in the past week."

"I could do it with my eyes closed," volunteered the blond trooper.

"Excellent, that's the kind of planning I like to hear." The Colonel waved at the waiter carrying a large tray of steak pies and chips. "Another three Heineken, boy," he stated, lifting his order from the tray and watching the others take theirs.

"What about police patrols in the area?" the driver asked.

"All taken care of," replied Van Zyl. "I've given full details of the operation to the chiefs of all the sections you pass through. Those patrols will know you're on an operation and when you should be passing through their areas. You'll have free passage."

The three ate in silence, watching the darts game some fifteen feet away.

"The skinny guy is good," noted Potschef. "See how he kind of rocks his head back and forth and keeps his elbow stable as he aims? Even the drinks don't seem to muddle his game."

"It's a knack of the world champs," said Simon. "They say the more they have to drink the more stable they are in their stance. Unusual for a fellow so small to be able to throw that well. Usually the really good ones have some beef on them."

We'll find out how good you are, bean pole, right after dinner," said Potschef. "I've booked the board for seven thirty."

"I won't be staying with the two of you for that long," said Van Zyl. "I've got some business to finish up before we go out."

"Will this operation have the kind of effect we expect?" Simon asked.

"Absolutely," responded the Colonel, "this man is one of the best known Xhosa lawyers. He's been a thorn in the government's side for years and has been very outspoken about the Zulu opposition party trying to get more than their fair share of seats in the new parliament when it forms. He's a known target."

"Do we expect any guards on his house?" Potschef asked.

"Our intelligence says that normally we might expect one man out guarding the house at night but this is Good Friday evening. Everyone is home getting ready for Holy Week and a chance to relax for the next three days. It will be feast time on Easter and no one goes back to work until Tuesday. Van Zyl chuckled, "It will be quiet until you stir up the hornet's nest. After that, we'll see what happens. I expect it to be dramatic."

"More demonstrations and gang fights?"

"The worst yet, I'd say," Colonel Van Zyl finished off his plate, washed it down with the last of his beer and rose. "I'll see you men with the unit at midnight." Bar flies made way for his impressive hulk as he departed the bar.

"This will be better than last week's fun. I'm looking forward to it," Potschef rose and headed toward the dart board. "Let's play."

"They thought the street fires would stop us," Simon laughed. "They didn't know how easily those old gutted cars can be pushed away by the armored personnel carriers.

"Ignorant bastards," agreed the older man nodding his head.

He remembered how his lead vehicle had slammed into one of the derelict car bodies throwing it up in the air and opening a passage around the billowing flames of the burning tires. When the demonstrators ran, the army vehicles herded them toward an open football pitch surrounded by a chain link fence. Stones had bounced off the Plexiglas faceplate of his helmet.

Simon's voice broke into his reverie, "They didn't think we'd open fire, did they?" He threw his first dart, hitting the double twenty but missed with the other two.

"You'll have to do better than that," Potschef smiled, then called out to the waiter, "Hey! Boy!" His first three darts all hit triples. "Two more beers, boy, make them Lions this time."

"Yes, Boss!" The red-jacketed, black waiter dashed off across the room.

Chapter 7:
Johannesburg, South Africa, April, 1990

Five hours later, the two men arrived at an apparently abandoned government warehouse to the south of Jo'burg. It was just after midnight. Colonel Dirk Van Zyl was there waiting for them.

"I trust none of you have had too much to drink within the last four hours. Company rules you know."

"No Sir!" both men responded.

"Fine, the others are in the back room getting dressed. Snap to it." His gloved hand reached out, across the antique oak desk, to pick up the receiver of an old telephone. He dialed a number.

Somewhere else in the city another gloved hand picked up the ringing receiver and a familiar voice on the other end of the line simply said, "Ya?"

"All present and accounted for, Sir," was all Van Zyl needed to say. The line clicked and went dead.

"Move-out time is thirty minutes, fellows. Get it on!" he shouted out to the men in the next room.

He walked over to see Potschef, inspecting himself in front of a mirror next to a desk. He was applying camouflage grease paint to his face.

"Our man is home and settled in for the night. We'll be hitting his house around two in the morning. We've got an hour's drive ahead of us before we stir up the locals." He smiled. The emergency lights were hardly enough for him to make out the faces of his handpicked team. No more lighting than necessary in case the building had holes to the outside.

The other seven men laughed at his words, continued dressing and smearing their faces, arms and hands with camouflage paint. In no time at all it would be hard to tell they were white men. Exactly as they wanted it.

"Make sure you have someone check your back and armpits," Potschef reminded the men. "No white beacons out there tonight. We want this to look as authentic as possible so look sharp in those black skins." He laughed and finished his own face in the mirror.

"Hey, Simon," he said to the driver, "Make sure you wear some shades. I don't want those blue eyes of yours popping out of your black skull. The last thing we want is for this operation to start rumors that it was done by a bunch of white men. We want to incite a bit of intertribal conflict so we can bring in added security measures. After tonight, we will be able to roll in with armored personnel carriers or bring troops with dogs and they'll see us as their protectors not as oppressors. Got it?"

"Got it," came Simon's answer from across the room. He was surveying part of his garb, a faux leopard skin draped over his shoulders.

"The same goes for you Potschef," said Van Zyl to his sergeant, "pull that curly wig down over those curls and put a piece of black tape across your nose. It sticks out so much."

"Hey, rat face," retorted Potschef, "look who's talking."

"That's why I put on the hairnet mask over all that make-up," replied his commander. "We've got to look like authentic black thugs."

When finished, they all stood for inspection. In addition to complete camouflage, each man wore pieces of Zulu warrior garb including lion mane ruffs, leopard skin shoulder drapes and ostrich feathers over their motley street clothing.

To complete the disguise each man now selected a knobkerrie or short spear. Finally, Potschef issued each man with a cut-down dance replica of an African shield. On the inner side of the shield were pockets holding small Molotov cocktails, flash bang stun grenades and a small flare pistol.

"How would we look as a portion of a Zulu *impi*?" shouted the lean boned Simon as he cavorted around the warehouse brandishing his short spear.

"A bit puny on your part," spoke up a thick necked warrior who could have easily played professional rugby or American football. He carried a club the size of a baseball bat.

"Don't forget the flare pistol is your first weapon if you run into heavy resistance. It's got bird shot in the chamber. The last resort is your pistol. Make sure it's got one sixteen round magazine in it and another secured to your shield. If we run into something nasty we'll shoot our way out," reminded Van Zyl.

"Just like the *Induna,* chief," said Potschef looking at his hefty commander. His own muscles bulging under arm ruffs. His European features completely masked beneath a red and white striped nylon balaclava.

"Let's go! Into the van!" shouted Simon, "I've got to drive you guys to the party!"

Van Zyl dialed the number of his contact, and spoke into the receiver, "Warrior band on the move." Then jumped to his feet following his men.

A door on the side of the building rolled upward. The rusty battered van was soon speeding through back streets into the heart of the Xhosa tribal section of the township. Its careening path dodged potholes, derelict vehicles and occasional smoldering trash fires.

"Remember your mission and keep to your targets, men," reminded Dirk. "This is our party, no one else's. We should be in and out before they know what hit them. I don't want any of you hurt. Another thing, remember, complete vocal silence. You may look like blacks but your Zulu won't sound like blacks. Simon has a tape he'll play at the end."

An hour later, the driver drove them past the target house. It was a well painted older house with a tin roof, sandwiched between several more dilapidated homes. Speeding on for another block, he pulled to the side, flipped a 'U' turn and stopped.

"Here we are boys," Dirk said cheerfully. "You know the drill. Teams 'B', 'C' and 'D' hit several houses on both sides of the street so it looks a bit random. Keep an eye out in case something goes wrong. Back each other up. Team 'A' will concentrate on the target house. Everybody hit your targets hard and fast. We don't want our special passenger to have time to get away."

"I'll be half a block down the other end of the street," reminded Simon. "No dilly dallying when time is called. This show is timed to last only ten minutes. Don't keep Daddy waiting!"

The side and back doors of the van slid open disgorging the eight warriors who immediately took off at a run up the street toward their target houses. The vehicle moved up the street and parked. Simon emerged, crouched and turned to survey the street in all directions. His short barreled Uzi was flipped to automatic, ready for any unexpected flare-up.

Van Zyl heard a door kicked in across the street. He and Potschef raced up the steps of the house next to the prime target. The big man's heavy shoulder and metal ram took the door completely off its hinges. Van Zyl snapped open his lighter, lit the Molotov cocktail and flipped it into the interior. Then they were off, before flames leaped toward the tinder dry boards. As they passed a car, Dirk's iron tipped club shattered the windshield.

The other teams converged on their targets. Two more bottles crashed through windows and sent flames leaping. The shouts and screams of the awakened occupants reached their ears. Two large Africans charged out of one house onto the street. Their shouts of anger turned to screams as the clubs of the attacking secret police rose and fell in the flickering fire light.

The "A" team focused their attention on the well-built target house. Leaping the side fence, they swept around the side of the building to the back. They arrived just in time to collar the fleeing black lawyer, as he rushed out the back door.

Muscular arms lashed his hands and feet with tape and gagged his mouth. His wife lay on her back in the middle of the sidewalk where a club had felled her, blood welling from a scalp wound. Two wide-eyed youngsters cowered and watched in silence as their father was bodily carried over the fence on the shoulder of one muscular giant. He disappeared into the blackness of the night. Flames emerged from the windows of the house, torching the curtains which flapped out through the broken panes before they too ignited.

People were beginning to emerge from the surrounding houses as the two men with their human burden dashed up the street toward the van. The six remaining warriors fanned out, slashing and clubbing anyone who dared come near.

With their quarry inside the vehicle, the final six paused long enough to throw two more Molotov cocktails which burst and drove back any possible pursuers. They reached the van and turned back, facing the growing mass of onlookers. Their shields rang with the thumps of their clubs or spear butts. From the two loud-speakers on the top of the van came a loud cacophony of sounds that carried the message to the surrounding ghetto in deep African voices:

Thump, Thump, "Chaka!" Thump, Thump, "Zulu!"
Thump, Thump, "Chaka!" Thump, Thump, "Zulu!"
Thump, Thump, "Chaka!" Thump, Thump, "Zulu!"

The men vaulted into the van. Spinning rear wheels squealed and spit gravel as it surged forward and sped off into the night.

The buzz of a single bullet from a zip gun whizzed past the van. Angry shouts and waving fists signaled the pent-up anger. It would be futile for any to try and pursue the Zulu gang.

On board the van, Van Zyl still panting from the exertion, flipped off the speakers and the chant. His cursing voice carried to the others.

"Don't break with the plan! Dammit! You buggers bloody well know that this stopping to beat the shields is pushing the limit! We have a time factor on these raids. Breaking the rules could get one of us killed! I heard that shot as we took off!"

Simon chimed in, supporting him, "I almost had to 'off' one old man who came blubbering up and asked me to call the security forces. You guys! Keep to the schedule or get a new driver!"

They all laughed as he fell silent and concentrated on driving the return route. It was devoid of patrol cars as planned. The van swerved recklessly through the outskirts of the ghetto and then slowed as they entered the main streets of Johannesburg. Van Zyl opened a can of Lion beer and took a long swig. The others passed around the crate, quaffing beers, laughing and talking rapidly about their exploits.

Potschef happened to look down and see the whites of their captive's eyes as he watched each blackened face.

"Hey," he shouted, "This guy's awake and listening. He'll remember us."

"Not to worry, mate," Van Zyl's tone was almost jovial as he kicked the trussed man's head. "This guy's been inciting the black community to riot. By the time the General's men get through with him on Robben Island, he'll be wishing for a hole in the ground."

Chapter 8:
Washington D.C., April, 1990

It wasn't going to be one of those balmy, sleep-in mornings with your secretary cuddled up next to you. Jim Collins had been rousted out at six in the morning by the ambassador to South Africa. Julie had barely opened her eyes then dropped off as Collins scrambled for his code book in the locked cabinet under the phone and groggily flipped to the correct page.

"Bad news," were the first two words out of Abe Miller's mouth after he had properly identified himself to Collins with the code of the day.

"Don't tell me," the fuzziness was pushed aside completely by adrenaline surging into his veins. "We've got more trouble in the ghettos."

"You're damn right we do. A gang of Zulu went into Xhosa territory last night and kidnapped Maurice Amakwayi, the most important Xhosa civil rights lawyer. All hell is going to break loose here if he doesn't turn up."

"Why Amakwayi? Has he pissed off some of the Zulu bigwigs?"

"He's pushed for representation of the Xhosa peoples as separate from the Zulu peoples in the new government. It ensures that the Xhosa don't get swallowed up by the larger Zulu nation when it comes to getting representation."

"He doesn't want the Xhosa to be gerrymandered into oblivion, if I understand you correctly in stateside terms."

"That's a Roger."

"Any leads?" Collins was out of bed pacing the floor of the bedroom. Julie stirred and he walked through into the living room so as not to wake her.

"Not a one. The witnesses say it went like a clockwork operation. Van pulls up, eight big guys storm a bunch of buildings, setting fires and beating up any opposition. In the confusion, they grab this one lawyer fellow and are gone in less than ten minutes."

"Doesn't sound African to me." Collins slumped in a chair.

Julie came out of the bedroom, flipped on the coffee maker and started to putter around the kitchen fixing breakfast.

"That was my first conclusion," Abe replied. "I think your third force is coming out in a strong move to upset the whole constitutional applecart and even the transition to a multiracial government."

"You're expecting a Xhosa backlash?"

"Absolutely. If it doesn't begin today, we'll see it within the next week. I'm afraid it's going to be bad."

"Like bad enough for the hardliners in the South African government to force a military crack-down?

"I'm afraid so. You'll want to keep on top of it."

"This wasn't supposed to hit the fan until the *Maru a Pula* according to the Botswana attaché."

"I think this is part of the warm-up. If your third force is really planning something big, then it will make this little feud between the Zulu and Xhosa look like peanuts in comparison."

"Foreplay with the big climax still down the road." Collins was pacing again. The smell of fried eggs tickled his nose.

"Yep, I've got to go now. Just wanted to give you a heads-up."

"Thanks, I'll return the favor when I can. Play the hand close." Collins hung up, grabbed a cup of coffee and sauntered off to change.

Thirty minutes later having left Julie to clean up the dishes, he was out the door and headed to the office. He tuned the car radio into the BBC.

... at ten AM, violence overflowed into the center of Johannesburg when a bomb exploded in a popular shopping center of that city. Casualties appear to have been small. All blacks have been ordered off the streets and the Army is patrolling the central area and townships.

The British Prime Minister deplored the violent actions, apparently a power struggle between Zulu and Xhosa tribes, and called for reconciliation. He stated that radical forces within the country appear determined to throw a monkey wrench into liberal government plans to form a joint government with both black and white...,"

"Dammit! Petrov's third force is running circles around us. Where in the hell have you disappeared to, Zulu?" Collins snapped off the radio, handed his ID to the guard at the gate and pulled through into his parking spot. It was going to be another long week.

Namibia

Chapter 9
Windhoek, Namibia, April, 1990

Easter Monday, a slow day at work. Jacob Nkwe strode down the hillside path below his apartment toward the main office buildings of the Klipspringer Game Park. A neat pattern of rondavels and campsites spread out below him where guests stayed. He snapped his fingers, hummed a tune and gazed out toward the brown thorn bush covered hills surrounding the resort area.

"You lit on your feet, old man!"

He smiled to himself, remembering his meeting with the park manager last Friday evening when he had been informed of his promotion.

"Jacob, I've decided to make you the head steward here at the park," said the good looking, middle aged, white woman, Debbie Kotzee. She was an outsider who had only recently taken over the managerial position. The rumor was that the previous manager had been siphoning off profits. It was going to end up in a big court case eventually.

"I'm honored to be chosen for the job," Jacob had replied, standing at attention in front of her desk.

"Good, then I suggest you sit down over there at the table and read through all your responsibilities. I'll give you a copy and next week I want you to make sure you check out every nook and cranny of this place. I need a list of anything that doesn't appear to be up to snuff." She smiled and stared deeply into his eyes.

Those had been the marching orders and he intended to poke through everything. The previous head steward had been summarily fired because of testimony by his former boss. With a new boss, that person needed someone they felt they could trust completely. A black head steward was the white boss's set of eyes and ears on the job. He could and would hear things that no underling would ever tell the boss, yet those things might be crucial to the organization. It was the head steward's job to filter out the crap, solve as many problems as he could and bother the boss with only the most necessary of information."

It was an ideal cover for what he needed to accomplish in the next six months if he were to stop Petrov's third force from destroying everything he had worked so hard for in South Africa.

He started with the camp swimming pool, having the maintenance man run him through everything he did on a daily basis. He learned how to check the temperature, pH, chlorination and filters. Then he examined the log of how many swimmers were in the pool each day at what times, the schedule for washing and drying the guest swimming towels and even how much detergent was used in each load of washing. By lunch time his tablet was full of tidbits of information about room cleaning, the maintenance of the resort's van, even the times and schedule for sweeping the walk ways and maintaining the trails.

By evening time he was worn out but happy to see that most things were running the way they should be. After a light meal in his apartment he went out to jog through the maze of trails that covered the camp's vast acreage. It kept him in shape and also gave him a complete understanding of the trail system, should it be important to escape a police raid looking for him. He was halfway up to the top of the largest overlooking hill when he heard the sounds of running feet. He stepped off to the side and was surprised to see Debbie, his manager, jogging toward him.

"Jacob, what a surprise. Do you come up here often?" She stopped, smiled and questioned him while catching her breath.

"Yes, Miss Kotzee," he replied, "I usually come up here to get some exercise in the evenings."

"I've just started coming out, kind of for the same reason. It also helps me get rid of the day's tensions and the evening sunsets are so beautiful." She stepped closer to him.

"Yes, Miss," Jacob found himself unable to take a step backward because of a stone behind his heels. He could see the perspiration running down her neck into the cleavage between her shapely breasts. The scent of her sandalwood perfume drifted to his nostrils on the evening breeze.

"Oh, sorry Jacob, I shouldn't be butting up against you so closely." She smiled, noting his embarrassment and stepped back slightly. "You may call me Debbie instead of Miss Kotzee. We are going to be working closely together, so we should at least be on first name terms when we aren't in public." She smiled again and brushed her dark golden hair back with her two hands, pulling it backward to adjust the tie holding her ponytail. In the process her breasts jutted forward again alluringly.

"Yes, Miss Debbie," he replied, watching her closely. If this had been in the United States, he would have taken her actions as a come-on. Here, one had to be very careful about any impropriety. The laws were inflexible as far as black and white sexual fraternization. It was always the black man's fault!

The tinkle of her laughter accompanied her reply, "You can drop the Miss too. I'll call you Jacob, you call me Debbie."

"Yes Miss Debbie," he said it again.

She laughed again, turned and set off down the trail at a jog once more, saying, "You'll get used to it."

He watched the curves of her body until she disappeared down the trail, then turned and ran all the way to the top of the knoll where he sat down gasping for breath. *"Oh, boy! Watch out! This could lead somewhere you don't want it to go."*

Over the next week he avoided her except at their office meetings to go through the work schedules and any changes in routine. At each meeting she would walk around and look over his notes while leaning down beside him onto the desk. Her closeness made him aware of every curve in her body although she was very careful not to actually touch him.

On Friday, laundry day, he checked that the camp van was clean then drove from building to building as the cleaning girls loaded their bundles of sheets, pillowcases and towels into the back. His greeting to each lady was cheerful and they responded to his banter and relaxed manner with them.

The fact that he was a good looking guy had not hindered his work ethic for the company. He was tall, lean and quick witted. All these traits had enhanced his ability to work with the staff and visitors to the game park. He certainly wasn't going to let his love life interfere with the job. It demanded six full days of work to complete all his tasks.

He drove the van to the main gate. His thoughts turned briefly to Debbie as he passed her window. He knew she still went out running in the hills each evening. Fortunately she took the same trail every time so he was able to get his own exercise on alternative pathways. She smiled and waved, touching two fingers to her pursed lips. It was obvious to him now that she would not avoid his advances. The real question was, *"Do I want to get in that deep with my supervisor? It's extremely dangerous."*

The watchman raised the bar across the drive, allowing him to exit onto the highway. Turning eastward, he sped off toward Windhoek. Accelerating along the twisting road that led through the acacia covered hills, Jacob thought about Debbie. She had athletic beauty, was bright and had an adventurous streak that took her off running in the nearby hills. The two of them were being drawn like two moths attracted to a deadly candle flame.

"It took too much pain and anguish to get where you are right now. Hold on to it."

During the half hour drive into Windhoek his thoughts drifted back over the fearful days of escaping from South Africa and traveling across Botswana.

After the tension of leaving South Africa, followed by the casual entry into Botswana, Jacob had again boarded the train and found a fourth class niche. At last, the conductor having made his final pass through the cars, Jacob slumped into fitful sleep, thoughts flashing through his mind:

"A helicopter? Petrov must have high up contacts in the South African government."

"I would be dead or on the way to Robben Island by now if they had caught me."

"Can't go to an embassy. A black man with no papers would take weeks to check out and Petrov would be watching. By the time they cleared me, I'd be dead."

"Keep to your plan. Go 'Ghost'. You have a year to come in after an operation blows up.

"You can still stop Petrov's third force."

He'd awakened in a semi-state of starvation. Two sweetened puff-puff biscuits from an old woman at the Molepolole station stop did the trick. He ate the hot sugar-coated, deep-fried, dough while sipping a scalding cup of sugared tea from a tin cup sold by another lady. Then it was back on the train for another five hours of rocking slowly along the old tracks. The train stopped at every little station.

"Where can I find a place to spend the night?" Jacob asked an Indian man, also descending at the Francistown station.

"Blue Town," the man pointed down the main street.

"Expensive?"

"When you get into Blue Town ask for the missionary people. They have the best rates."

The walk past the Grand Hotel educated him quickly about his drop in life style. Black and white businessmen frequented the Victorian style building with a red tile roof. A doorman wearing a red fez gave him further directions.

"The missionaries live a mile down that side street," he pointed. "They run a clean place. It was a camp for black Rhodesian refugees during the war of independence. Now they keep it open for travelers like yourself. It doesn't cost much. They have communal meals. Hard plank bunks." He turned away to open the door for patrons of the hotel, letting Jacob wander off.

The missionary man walked him out to the men's dormitory area.

"I'm sorry we don't have mattresses," he apologized, handing Jacob a clean blanket. "When the war was over, we let the people going home to Zimbabwe take what bedding they needed. We're trying to replace everything. The women's dormitory is almost complete. Then we'll do the men's."

"Not to worry," replied Jacob, accepting the blanket and setting his small bag down on the bare planks of the bunk. "I've had to sleep on much worse."

"We start serving breakfast at six. If you want to catch the bus to Maun, you need to be one of the first in line. It's a long walk to the lorry park." The missionary left him to doze off.

When he finally woke up it was five in the morning. He splashed cold water from the outside pump on his face. An hour later, standing in line for a dollop of corn meal mush, sugar and a cup of hot milky tea, he glanced down at his dusty rumpled suit.

"What a change forty-eight hours can make. No need to worry about not looking the part of an itinerant workman."

He had asked the missionary about church connections in Namibia, sharing enough of his cover story so that the man knew he was educated, could hold down a regular job, but was fleeing persecution in South Africa and going home.

"When you get to Windhoek look for a blind man near the post office selling pencils," he said. "He's a member of the church. Give him this note. He knows where to find Nathan. He's worked with the refugee situation there for a number of years." He scribbled a short note, lit a bar of sealing wax and made a round molten spot on the center of the paper. Into this droplet he impressed what appeared to be a denominational ring. He handed the slip of paper to Jacob.

"Nathan knows my writing. He'll be your best bet at finding a decent job. Windhoek is inundated with refugees trying to get away from the Angolan border."

The note had been painfully brief. Jacob didn't put too much store in its worth after reading the contents, but he stuck it in his thin billfold.

"Nathan, Jacob is a friend of ours in Christ. I send him to you for refuge. He is well educated and able bodied. The Peace of the Lord be with you. Tom"

His daydreaming mind picked up the looming bulk of a truck. Reflex action by his hands on the wheel took over and he swerved just in time to avoid a collision. The return to reality and the winding road into Windhoek was abrupt. He willed his clenched hands to relax, loosening his vice grip on the wheel. Inhaling deeply, he shook his head as if to clear a fog. Then slowing at the city limits, he turned the van off the main highway, following a narrow street down the steep hill to the edge of the black ghetto.

His eyes briefly swept upward to the mansions on the tops of the hills

"One day, we will be living alongside you in those mansions. Your choice. Share or lose it all. We're going to take Africa away from its colonial masters. Step aside gracefully, we'll let you stay. Fight us and we'll drive you out."

Pulling the van to a stop directly in front of the small laundry, he got out and began unloading dirty bundles. A young boy came out taking each bundle and carrying it inside. On his return a moment later he carried a load of sparkling clean sheets and towels. Once the laundry tags were all checked and the clean bundles loaded, Jacob left the van and walked to Tjeetjo's Café.

Chapter 10:
Windhoek, Namibia, April, 1990

As it had turned out, the missionary's note had been a lot more help than Jacob could have ever imagined. Upon arriving in Windhoek he had sought out the blind man selling pencils outside the main post office. The blind man had taken him to the missionary who was the headmaster of a small church school. The man had listened to Jacob's fabrication of fleeing South Africa for political reasons. Then he opened one of the doors of a small servant's quarters building.

"We'll put you in here until you find a more suitable place to stay and have a job. I have several members of the church who are always looking for good people to hire. I'll put your name out. Until we find you something, though, you must report to the employment office daily and take whatever work you are assigned to do. Your rent for this room will be half of what you earn daily and the rest you should spend on food. We provide blankets for the bed and basic eating and cooking utensils."

Jacob had been speechless. The man had left him on the step, saying, "We are so glad to be able to help those who are fighting for the liberation from apartheid."

In the days that followed, Jacob had dug ditches, swept streets, carried sacks of grain and become a day laborer along with masses of other men, all seeking jobs. Along with the work came local social contacts which eventually led him to an association with persons working for the liberation of Namibia from apartheid. And that was how he came to Tjeetjo's Café.

Tjeetjo's Café and Sports Bar was an anachronism. Named for some Herero tribesman who had originally started the cafe back when the Herero tribe operated a number of Windhoek's businesses, the place was now operated by an Ovambo tribesman.

The new owner had left the Herero name on the sagging yellow billboard over the door. In part to keep his old customers and in part to associate himself with a group that was not under suspicion of being involved with the liberation movement. Inquisitive white eyes were much more interested in the Ovambo tribal power movement than in the cattle herding Herero peoples. It was a lot easier to run a business when inspectors assumed you were not associated with a tribe involved in the armed liberation movement.

Jacob swept back the curtains hanging across the door and entered the shaded interior. Inside Tjeetjo's were three small rooms, each starkly bare except for rickety metal frame tables surrounded by hard drab-brown Masonite backed metal chairs. Numerous red and green "Lion" beer coasters indicated the number of clients at night. A large ghetto blaster radio sat on a side shelf and there was an eighteen inch TV hanging high up the wall of the second room. This latter object was sandwiched between posters of Brazil's iconic Pele and Argentina's current God of the soccer pitches, Maradona. The room was plastered with old soccer billboard signs from every African country including Cameroon's world cup game against Argentina in 1990. The TV was positioned so that when the room was overflowing with inebriated soccer fans, observers from the two side rooms could still see an occasional goal.

The rhythm of African music blared from the ghetto blaster setting up a sympathetic vibration in the walls of the entire building. Jacob passed through the first two rooms, eyes dropping momentarily to the exposed brown calf and thigh of a professional lady straddling a stool. She leaned forward revealingly across one of the small tables. The perspiring drinker seated opposite her was completely enthralled by her wares. In the corner, two couples swayed to the music in close embraces, oblivious to his passage.

Jacob gave a negative wave of the hand toward the bar tender, ducked through the green curtains and entered the back room. The noon time meeting had not yet begun.

The vibration and drumming noise from the front room music muffled the low voices in this important meeting room. The Ovambo leader, Michael Shanika, and his body guard, Walter, were already seated. Several others stood in the corner conversing in low tones. Maria, the fat waitress, made an appearance to take food orders as several others of the group arrived.

"The samp is just made, Jacob," she assured him. "I promise you the pepper sauce will do wonderful things to your tongue."

"Thanks, Maria," Jacob replied, smiling, "but I think I'll stick with the corn meal, the *bogobe,* as long as it comes with that same delightful sauce." He remembered how the hominy like corn dish, called samp, could congeal in one's bowels for several days.

"Of course, sir," her musical voice bubbled. "I'll bring it right away. Would you like a beer?" The question was rhetorical, the top was already popping off his beverage.

"Absolutely!" he took a seat and grasped the cool bottle between both hands. The first swig sent an orgasmic chill rippling through his hot body.

The late comers pulled several small tables together forming a circular arrangement. Walter went into the other room to ensure that the sound level of the music stayed just a few decibels below the pain threshold. Jacob watched as Maria set a circle of dew covered beer bottles in the center of each of the tables while taking more orders. No one would go away thirsty.

"Can't afford to be slack about the sound when we know spies are listening everywhere," Walter said, plumping down in a chair and taking a dew covered beer from the line-up.

They all sipped their beers silently, watching the last of the members trickle in. When all were present Shanika outlined the latest developments.

"Welcome, comrades," Shanika said, "I called this meeting to give you an update on the arrangements we are making with our friends in Zambia." He looked around the room, making eye contact with each man. "The liberation army will supply us with the weapons, but they want us to pay for them in diamonds."

Jacob could almost hear several of the executive members of the group groan at the mention of paying in diamonds.

Shanika hurried on, explaining. "Normally the diamond supply would be good this time of the year, but after the police captured one of our diamond runners and made him talk, we had to close down the whole operation. Until we get things reestablished, we can't afford the weapons. So I am proposing that we put Jacob in charge of the diamond operation." Turning toward Jacob he asked, "How much do you know about our current diamond running business?"

"I've picked some things up from my brother. He's been out on several collecting runs."

"Do you think you and he could handle the logistics of finding a new route and getting the collecting runs operating again for the organization?"

"Why yes, of course I can," replied Jacob, jumping at the promotion. "I hadn't heard that there was any kind of a problem. Why isn't James doing it anymore?"

"James has a new position in the south of the country. The police came looking for him so we sent him away. We can't jeopardize our organization and plans by keeping him here."

"Oh, I'm sorry," Jacob fell silent, waiting to hear more.

"That's all I can tell you about his assignment," said Shanika. "I want you to work with your brother to find a new route into the diamond fields. We know of some good places for picking but without a new route your men will be sitting ducks for the police. If we have many more caught, it will only be a matter of time before they get onto our whole group. Then everything will fall apart."

"I'll need a place to meet with my brother. I can't have him coming to the game park very often or they will get suspicious.

"We've arranged with the missionary group that helped you find your job to give your brother a room. It will be safe. The missionaries are tight lipped about the things they do to help us."

"Fine, I'll contact him through the blind man and begin working on things immediately. How soon do we need to be able to have the diamonds all together to exchange for the weapons?"

"We want to make the exchange in August or September. You'll have to work fast to get it all done in six months."

"We'll be ready."

"Fine, then I'll let you get back to your duties."

Jacob felt like he was flying on a cloud as he headed back to the game park with the clean laundry. The rest of the day was spent distributing the clean bundles and supervising minor repairs on doors and windows in two of the guest bedrooms.

When he arrived back at his apartment it was already dusk. He cooked up a small meal, ate and read before deciding that he could turn in early. When he opened the medicine cabinet over the bathroom sink a small note fell out. He opened it with trembling fingers and read.

"Come to my house after dark. D."

"Oh! Oh! This could be trouble."

His mind raced, trying to think of an out that would not upset her. In the end he decided it was best to face the situation directly. Putting on his dark sweater to better blend into the shadows, he walked up the hill to her darkened house. He was about to raise his hand to knock on the door when it opened.

She stood there in the faint light of the stars. He could see she wore nothing but a thin nightgown. Her voice was husky as she took his hand and walked him into the candle lit living room.

"I thought it was time for us to get to know each other a bit better."

He could see the bottle of wine, the half-filled glasses and a wedge of cheese on the small table next to the sofa. When she turned to face him he could feel her body brushing against him. Then, as his heart began to race, her hands lightly drifted down his sides encircling his waist. As their lips met, she pulled him down onto the soft cushions.

<u>Botswana</u>

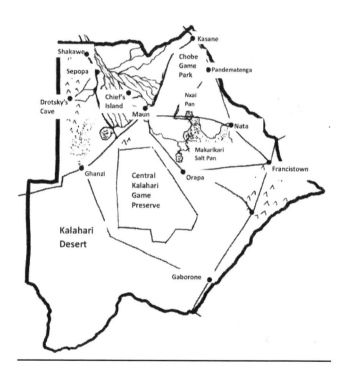

Chapter 11:
The Eastern Border of Botswana, June, 1990

Almost two months later far to the east of Namibia, near the border into Botswana, the moon was casting silver shafts through a glade of tall Mopani trees. A slim black hand released its hold from the stock of a 7.62mm FN FAL rifle and reached upward into the wing shaped Mopani leaves, plucking one and placing it on his tongue.

"Ah! *Sukiri*, Sugar" the man said, turning to his companions, "Look my friends, Bushman candy*, Sukiri ya Mosarwa.*"

He plucked another oval leaf coated with the white secretion of tiny scale insects and sucked it briefly for the sugary residue. The other military men clustered around him sampling the treat. Eleven grease painted faces each glistened faintly in places where the sweat of a forced march had removed the camouflage. The stop gave each the chance to briefly think of something other than the mission ahead and the accompanying white man.

Colonel Petrov stood apart from the group, leaning casually against a tree, watching this departure from normal rigid patrol discipline. His own preferred rifle, a lighter 5.56mm South African R4 with 35 round magazine, was cradled in the crook of one arm. A faint smile creased his thin lips. What would the cocky black training officer in Zambia have said to this elite group of hardened fighters if they had broken ranks like this?

"If you could see your crack troops now," he thought derisively, watching them begin to whisper. Voices carried a long way in this midnight quiet.

"Let's go!" Petrov said softly. Immediately they were back on task and under his control.

They moved out single file down the cattle trail following their two guides. Every man, dressed in South African Army bush uniform was armed with a South African FN – FAL rifle. Per the objective of their mission, in another hour they would be crossing the border of south eastern Zimbabwe and entering Botswana. They glided through the grotesque thorn bush and twisted Mopani woodlands - a band of silent, deadly, shadows.

Except for the two guides, his men were all South African in origin. They had left families and homes for a variety of reasons and come north voluntarily to join the liberation army. They had completed their training and participated in a number of missions. They knew what to expect and were confirmed hardened killers.

As for the two guides walking point, Petrov watched them closely. He trusted neither of them. They were Botswanan mercenaries with their own agendas for being in this war. Incriminating information about the two had reached his ears in Zambia. For the moment he could afford to keep them. Their intimate knowledge of these cow paths could mean the success or failure of tonight's mission. Punishment for other crimes would come later. He had read their dossiers very carefully. Especially that of the apparent leader of the two, Motsumi.

Motsumi had been a herd boy just a few years back. His father had been a big cattle owner in a small village just outside of Ramaquebane on the Botswana side of the Rhodesian border. As the son of the boss man, Motsumi's job had been to drive the cattle to market and bargain for the best prices. Because of the breakdown of farming within Rhodesia during the war, the nearly starving people were eager to buy meat at any price. Thus, Motsumi had made a fortune for his family by dodging Rhodesian army patrols and selling his cattle across the border.

What had started as a boy's game of dodging patrols had turned into a very lucrative business. So lucrative in fact that the Rhodesian army had begun to supplement their own meager wages by rustling the herds to sell for their own profit. They tended to shoot any herders first and ask questions later. In this war of smugglers two of Motsumi's friends had disappeared. Their bloated bodies left for the hyenas.

As the smuggling of cattle dried up, Motsumi had found an even more lucrative business - smuggling refugees fleeing the anarchy of the Zimbabwe/Rhodesian war. In the process he became a very rich man, even richer than his father. That was until the Rhodesian Security Forces placed him on their wanted list.

One night, the security forces paid a visit to his sister's home near Francistown. They left a battered suitcase filled with dynamite outside the door. When it was opened, the blast rocked Blue Town, killing Motsumi's younger sister and mother instantly. They missed Motsumi because he had just departed to collect another group of refugees.

The next day, Motsumi walked to Zambia and enlisted with the Zimbabwe freedom fighters. He didn't care about their ideology, he was only looking for revenge. Over the next few years he led raids to terrorize, kill, torture and maim as many whites as possible, deeming them responsible for the death of his family.

At the end of the Zimbabwe/Rhodesian War, Motsumi had become totally addicted to the adrenaline rush of a firefight. He tried to find the same high with drugs back in Botswana but the 'high' was always missing something. Something that could only be fed by hunting and killing other humans.

As always, Africa obliged him as the liberation movement in South Africa intensified. In a short while he was again employed as a mercenary. Now living safely in Zambia, he guided border crossings, assisted the escape of refugees and as with this mission, guided guerrilla units.

This patrol would be his last official work for the ANC. When it was finished, he and some friends were going to branch out into another lucrative field of killing. The weapons of human war were about to be turned to the collection of elephant ivory and rhino horn for the insatiable oriental aphrodisiac market. Soon he was going to be a very, very wealthy man.

"Fsst!" Petrov heard the warning snake hiss. He saw the downward motion of Motsumi's hand and dropped. The men behind, seeing their motion, dropped as well. They waited in absolute silence as the slight swish of clothing on tree branches and crackling of a twig underfoot told them the location of another band of humans. They waited like crouching panthers as a line of shadows materialized and passed across their intended pathway.

Petrov's index finger itched for the trigger of his automatic rifle. Not more than fifty feet in front of them was a group of twelve men silently crossing a moonlit opening. They were walking in single file, an occasional moonbeam reflecting from their rifles. Their mission was very different from his own. This was a real South African border patrol also in the no-man's land between Zimbabwe and Botswana.

There could be no contact with this patrol. Their objective was miles ahead, well within the international boundary of Botswana. A firefight here would destroy the entire mission. In several hours they would see plenty of action. He watched the last man in the patrol disappear from sight and concentrated on reviewing his true objective, while waiting for the all clear sign.

Their plan was to attack a Botswanan military camp near the border. The impact of the attack and the evidence they would leave behind would implicate the South Africans. It would make the Botswana government a bit more standoffish to the South Africans. The rebels needed to keep Botswana sympathetic to their liberation movement so they could smuggle weapons to the Namibians.

Fifteen minutes later, having waited sufficient time for the patrol to pass, Petrov's gang of intruders slipped across the border into Botswana.

Three hours later, a glimpse of light towers through the trees ahead brought them to full alert. Just ahead lay a newly completed army training camp. Over five hundred soldiers in varying degrees of readiness for combat were inside the barracks. Petrov watched as his men fanned out toward their predetermined positions. Then he settled into his own position and waited.

"A peaceful country, a peaceful night, a time to make sure that the cordial agreements between Botswana and South Africa are severed by a unilateral act of aggression."

The Army post in front of them was laid out to perfection. New barracks, parade ground, rifle ranges, obstacle courses and the best mess hall in all of Botswana. Nothing had been spared in preparing Botswana's future army for the defense of the country. But of course who would want to attack Botswana?

Inside the compound, the Sergeant at Arms on midnight watch understood the peaceful nature of the country and its neighbors. He sat tilted back in his swivel chair, head lolling to one side, spit polished boot toes angled obliquely outward. His cap was placed strategically, to shield his closed eyes from the glaring night light. A slight snore rose from his lips. Peaceful sleep in a very peaceful country.

"Comrade Petrov," a whispered question from his Sergeant. "Is it time?"

"Only a few minutes," came the Russian's soft reply.

The men had now worked their way forward through the shadows of the camp to assigned positions. Skilled hands attached plastic explosive devices beneath the petrol tanks of the two land rovers. A spring-loaded detonator wire was inserted in the ground and secured with a nail. Any movement of the vehicle would detonate the explosion. The infiltrators then wormed their way back out into the tall grass and waited for the prearranged signal.

Motsumi lay at one end of the camp next to his friend Boipela. The two men were in cahoots as far as this being their final mission and then branching off together into the poaching business. They had already recruited over a hundred men for their new gang.

"Are you still coming with me back to Francistown after this action?" whispered Motsumi.

"Of course," replied the former shop keeper, peering through tall strands of grass. "I've had enough of this white man and his puppets. We should kill him and take the men who want to join us. The extra weapons would be useful."

"That is what I think. Why do you think he came along?"

"I'm not sure. The Sergeant said he was going to go on to some other mission."

"Fat chance he can navigate the cattle paths without us. Keep an eye on him. He's too crafty."

"One false move and I'll cut him in half," replied the shopkeeper, fingering the safety on his weapon.

"Good, I have some men meeting us in Ramaquebane with clothing. We'll keep these weapons for our arsenal."

A shrill whistle cut through the silence of the night.

Without another word the two men and their comrades sighted in on prearranged targets, laying down a stream of automatic fire on the walls and windows of the barracks.

Their orders had been very specific. "Shoot high so we avoid killing a lot of the men. The explosive charges on the water tower and land rovers will produce sufficient casualties and get the effect we want. We want to incite the Botswanans and others into taking political, not military, action against South Africa."

Inside the barracks, pandemonium reigned! Men in upper bunks screamed as a few were hit and wounded or killed instantly. Black bodies leapt from their bunks and more casualties were added from men not smart enough to hit the deck. Screams pierced the night as concussion rifle-grenades burst windows and sent shards of flying glass into confused men, and onto the floor where they chewed into bare feet.

Within seconds the main fighting force for the entire country of Botswana had been routed. Black bodies hugged the floor amid expanding pools of blood. Other men burst out the opposite side of the building and ran, stark naked, into the bush.

In the entire camp only four men remained cool. It cost two of them their lives.

Lt. Col. Roger McFeeters, of Her Majesty's Army, was assigned as an advisor to train Botswana's fledgling army. He awoke with a start, rolled from his bunk with reflexes developed while leading Australian patrols in Vietnam. The F.N. carbine inside his locker was already loaded. His command voice carried above the rattle of gunfire and screams of his men.

"What the bloody God-damned hell? Molife! Tau! Motsa! Get in here!" he bellowed.

The three N.C.O.'s picked themselves up off the floor of the next room and appeared almost as one man.

Tau, you and Molife get the two land rovers from behind the supply shed. Bring them around here! Motsa, open the armory, load up some rifles, and hand them out to anyone who has the sense to appear when you call out! Then I want you to direct fire toward the incoming rounds."

Carbine in hand he was already out the back door worming his way to a corner of the building. His experienced eye noted the tracers mixed in with the regular rounds coming from the trees and brush less than one hundred yards away.

"Tracers? What the hell are you boys up to? You're shooting way too high to be very effective," he observed casually to himself as he picked out targets. "I may only have forty rounds, but I will definitely bring some pee onto your hairy asses." With that he brought his rifle to bear in the prone position, picked out the nearest tracer groups and fired for effect in short bursts until his magazine was empty.

Immediately a blue flare arched across the sky. The firing ceased as abruptly as it had begun.

McFeeters dashed toward the weapons room. He heard the two land rovers gun to life. Then through a side window he saw two mushroom-like clouds of flame erupt from behind the supply shed. He turned his head in time to see the flash of explosives on the water tower. Then he watched the massive two thousand gallon water tank plummet thirty feet and explode on impact.

"Oh Crikey!" was all he could manage to say as one of the blazing rovers jerked into view. Behind the steering wheel, he could see what was left of the dying driver jerking in life's final spasms.

Petrov's men regrouped rapidly within the trees. One man was missing. Two more had flesh wounds compounded by the action of the small 7.62mm slugs, which tend to tumble on entry into flesh. One of the men was minus a fist sized chunk of thigh muscle and had crawled to the rendezvous. The other was already wheezing and blowing small flecks of blood from his nose and mouth. A bullet had fractured his upper arm, and then somehow followed the bone up into his chest cavity.

The sergeant tried to staunch the leg wound, but the man soon slumped into unconsciousness. Nothing could be done for the man with the chest injury, although he seemed to still be able to walk.

"You made it this far," the Russian said to him, "start walking back and try to keep up." He turned his back on the man and walked off, saying, "A bit of blood on the grass won't hurt anything."

As they started back along the trail, Petrov reminded them all, "You all know the rules. We can't go back and search for Willy. We have to presume that he's dead. If a man falls out we must leave him. Nothing can compromise this mission. That's why we are all wearing South African Uniforms. The blame for this needs to fall on the white South African government."

Chapter 12
Washington, D. C., June, 1990

It was nearly midnight. Abe Miller rushed out of the Crypto room clutching three sheets of printout. A flush of excitement shown from his tired face. The Halls of the special branch were empty. No one saw him burst into Jim Collin's office. His action startled his superior, who was hunched over a pile of Cosmic Top Secret documents dealing with African uranium and Russian warheads.

"What the…?" Jim nearly jumped out of his chair.

"We just got this!" Abe thrust the papers into his boss's hands. "More trouble in the South Africa Theater!"

"What are you talking about?" Collins perused the secure message from the American Embassy in Botswana. "Shit! An invasion into Botswana? An Army base? What's going on?"

"That's the word. They're sending trackers out to follow the trail of the invaders back to their source. I expect we'll see some ramifications of this all over the continent and even at the UN level."

"What's your take?"

"Either the far right is setting the pace and they're out to sink any coalition government or our third force has a lot more power than we thought." Abe shook his head, "I can't believe the South Africans are this dumb or aggressive."

"So it's our third force again." Collins stood up and stretched. "What's done is done. Not much we can do about it but pick up the pieces and anticipate their next move. It's Friday night so we have a bit of respite. Monday's going to be a hell of a long day. Let's go home and get some sleep."

Half-way across the world, the Saturday morning sun's first glow was producing a false dawn over eastern Botswana. Colonel Petrov called a rest stop along a well beaten cattle track.

"We've reached the border. The route back to the landing zone for the helicopter is only a few miles away. I expect you will be there in another hour as planned and arrive back in Zambia by the time anyone comes looking for us. Hopefully they will already have drawn their conclusions about the raid based on the uniforms and weapons of our unfortunate casualties." He looked around at the men, now minus three of their original members. "I'll be leaving you here as I have another mission to organize."

Motsumi removed an envelope from inside his shirt and stepped toward Petrov and the sergeant. "Comrades," he announced, "Our comrade Boipela and I have also received orders for a special mission here in Botswana. You have the sergeant and Richard to guide you back to the pick-up point."

Petrov, noting the stance of the second man with finger near the trigger housing of his rifle, stepped forward, to take the papers from Motsumi's hand. In doing so, he moved so that he was partially shielded by the other soldier.

He perused the document. Looking up with a disarming smile, he said, "I see that you and Zimbabwe's General Mubabe are working on a new project. I had heard a bit about it before we came on this mission and have a note that will ensure you are properly decorated when you return to Zambia." He unbuttoned his shirt pocket and pulled out two official looking envelopes.

"These are your commendation letters," Petrov continued, stretching out his hand with one envelop for Motsumi. He then stepped past the surprised young man, the smile still creasing his face with the other letter outstretched for his comrade.

Taken by surprise, the young man dropped one hand from his rifle and reached out to accept the packet. As he did so, Petrov stepped closer, producing a small silenced pistol which he aimed directly at the man's chest. The sergeant, seeing Petrov's move, stepped forward and pressed the muzzle of his carbine in Motsumi's stomach.

"Whaa...?" An expression of surprise spread across Motsumi's face.

"As I said," stated Petrov, "these letters have commendations in them. They come from the highest authorities in the South African army. They also contain maps and special notes telling how this patrol is preparing the way for South Africa to invade Botswana."

Petrov's weapon made a snapping hiss. The 9 mm dum-dum bullet ripped through Boipela's heart, leaving a gaping hole out his back. Almost before the man fell, Petrov bent down, plucked the envelope from the ground and thrust it inside the dying man's shirt.

"You still have a choice to make," Petrov said, turning toward Motsumi. "We know all about your poaching scheme. We also know about your cache of weapons. The sergeant and men will take you back to Zambia. You will be a witness at General Mubabe's trial. You helped him divert important weapons from our revolutionary cause."

"No!" shouted Motsumi, spitting at the Russian. "I spit on your revolution! Africa is for Africans!" He leapt toward the white man.

Petrov's weapon hissed a second time. His forearm blocked the impact of the flying man, knocking his body to one side. The Sergeant wiped a spatter of blood and flesh from his own face.

"You did have a choice," Petrov stated coldly, looking down at the corpse at his feet. Then turning to the rest of the men, still frozen in place, he said, "I suggest you move quickly now. A border patrol may have heard something and be along soon."

He bent down again, placing the incriminating evidence inside the second dead man's shirt as well. Then taking a well-worn cattle track, he turned away from the group heading northwest and stepped out quickly for the next half hour. Along another cow path he stripped, burying his weapons, uniform and pack sack. Donning a light tan safari suit with long knee socks and suede desert boots, he headed for the main road just to the west of the Plum Tree border crossing. On the Botswana side of the border he hitched a ride with a farmer going into Francistown.

Checking into the Grand Hotel, he sent a brief message to Horst Grobler, his weapons courier, before relaxing with the locals in the bar.

Chapter 13:
Washington D. C., June, 1990

By Monday morning, Washington was well into an early spring heat wave and the politics of Africa looked to be heading in the same direction. Collins pushed back from his desk as Abe entered the office.

"More bad news I take it?" said Abe.

"Yep, listen to this. The BBC is just repeating the headlines." Collins turned down the volume slightly as Abe plunked into a chair.

"*... Seven black evangelists were found dead from smoke inhalation in a church outside Pretoria. The cause appeared to be the deliberate burning of the church in which they were sleeping. Firemen fighting the blaze found that the doors of the church had been nailed shut from the outside. Upon removing the victims, they were unable to resuscitate them. Police investigating the incident say the responsibility may lie with a white ultra-extremist group, the Wit Wolves. The group has advocated for complete racial segregation and are diametrically opposed to any softening of the apartheid rules by the current South African government...*"

"Don't these people ever learn?" asked Abe.

"It appears not. Oh wait, here's the one I'm even more worried about."

"On the international front, the tiny country of Botswana, this morning, introduced a resolution in the general assembly of the UN to increase the international sanctions against the Republic of South Africa following what they called an unprovoked, malicious attack by South African Special Forces on a Botswanan army training camp Friday night. Three enlisted men in the Botswanan army were killed and at least fifteen wounded in the attack according to initial reports. The raiders left behind two dead near the camp and another three were found on their escape route to the border of Botswana with Zimbabwe. Two bodies carried intelligence and maps of the incursion. Informants within the Botswana government say that all five of the dead men were wearing uniforms of the South African army."

"A pretty poor kill ratio for the South African army, I'd say," snorted Abe. "

"Exactly my thinking. Since when do you decide to pick on your most peaceful neighbor, take them by complete surprise, lose nearly half your unit, not take away your dead and wounded, then leave copies of all your plans behind for everyone to see ?"

"The South Africans aren't that stupid."

"Unless," Collins shook his head, "someone is trying to set them up and they weren't really professional South African Special Forces."

"Wow! Is the rest of the world that stupid to believe this scenario?"

"We love to hear evidence that indicates what we're doing is right. Many people would love to hear just how nasty South Africa is, so they can turn the heat up a bit."

"By increasing sanctions? Just when the country is about to achieve black majority rule?"

"Yep, Someone in South Africa is profiting from this, big time!" Collins snapped off the radio.

"The hard liners. The ones who want to hold onto the past. They want to tighten the reins of apartheid and keep blacks in their proper position."

"Right, so if this raid was done by our third force, they must be working with the hard liners."

"But the third force is Russian controlled, they're communist. The hard liners are more like fascists. They hate each other's guts."

"Ever hear of Hitler and Stalin?" Jim Collins leaned back, stared at the ceiling and scratched his white hair. "Two groups can profit from the same scenario of chaos even if their goals are widely different."

"Jesus! They both think their side is going to win the next battle."

"Precisely, no matter what the South Africans say about the incident, they're going to get hammered both internally and internationally. Frankly it's the internal stuff that I'm most worried about. A few more burnings of churches, a few more shootings into peaceful demonstrations and the whole country disintegrates. If it was orchestrated by our third force, meaning Colonel Petrov, then he's done a superb job of shifting world opinion against South Africa. Unless we have a miracle, we're headed for a big racial and tribal blow-up in the Republic of South Africa. We've got to know what Zulu knows and get ahead of things in order to cool this situation down."

He paused, looked at his watch, stood and picked up his brief case. "I'm late for my meeting in the Pentagon on the Libya situation. See you about five." He rushed out the door.

Abe scribbled a couple of notes and got up to go.

"Don't lock it!" Julie came down the hall. "I'll just straighten things up and wash out his coffee cup. He's so rushed off his feet with these crises at the moment. He doesn't take care of himself properly."

"Thanks, Julie, I'll be in the research library checking things out. If he comes in before you take off at five, give me a buzz." Abe ambled off down the hallway.

Chapter 14
Francistown, Botswana, June, 1990

The Grand Hotel was one of the few luxuries Petrov permitted himself while in Botswana. After the excitement of the raid, he'd slept well. Now his business was strictly the mundane organizational matter of setting up the next weapons run through Botswana in exchange for diamonds from Namibia. He left another message to be sent to Horst Grobler, and read the Botswana Times while he waited. Four hours later Petrov watched the big man's arrival from his discreet corner table in the noisy, open air patio of the Tati Concession Bar.

"You're late," he said as Grobler settled his heavy, body into the chair. The metal supports squeaked in agony. The hovering waiter dropped a half dozen cans of Lion beer on the table. Grobler picked one up and cradled it in his massive hands.

"My boss arrived with a list of chores a mile long in preparation for our next animal collecting trip. Why the visit?"

"I've got a project for you. That's presuming you can make the arrangements in your busy schedule," Petrov said.

"I'm generally only busy when I need to be at the moment," Grobler said, ignoring the sarcasm and popping the tabs off two Lion beers. He finished them both in as many gigantic swallows. "The animal collecting business is almost dead. Jacques won't be in business by this time next year if the drought doesn't break. I'm free whenever you need me."

"Good, I want you up on the Chobe River next week. There's a shipment coming across west of Kasane. It needs to be delivered for safekeeping to some of our friends near Pandematenga." Petrov leaned back into the shadows and took a long pull on his Heineken.

"A different site to our last shipment, I hope? That was too exposed on both sides of the river. It's a wonder the patrols didn't catch us."

"This one's different," Petrov slid a folded sheet of paper across the table. "The times and recognition codes are on the map. Don't be late."

"Not a chance," Grobler smiled, cracking another beer and chugging half. He unfolded the map, glanced at it and grunted in approval. "Fine, I know the place. Good cover and easy access to the bush tracks. I can use the return through Pandematenga to scout out some ostrich chick sites in case we get an order." He stuffed the paper into his shirt pocket and buttoned the flap.

"Fine. We'll store the weapons there for a few months until our clients are ready. Then we'll do a delivery. Questions?"

"Payment?"

"The usual," Petrov removed an envelope from his safari suit pocket. "This is your down payment. The rest will go into your account in Pretoria, once I get confirmation of delivery."

Grobler's thick fingers thumbed open the envelope to reveal the sheaf of banknotes. His dark hooded eyes met Petrov's icy stare. "I'll want to talk with you next time about increasing the fee. Things look to be getting more dangerous since that South African raid last week." He took another drink."

"We'll talk about that when the time comes," Petrov said, holding the other man's gaze until Grobler dropped his eyes. "For the time being, we'll continue as we have agreed. Is that acceptable?"

"Yes, I'm your man." Grobler's smile was thin. He tossed back the last of his beers, rose and strode toward the archway leading to the street.

Petrov's eyes followed the big man, "I'm going to have trouble with you one of these days, I can see it already," he said under his breath as he reached out and took another sip of his single Heineken from its green bottle.

Chapter 15
Northern Botswana, June, 1990

A section of Mopani tree woodland extends almost to the southern edge of the Chobe River, half-way between the towns of Kasane and Ngoma. The tall, almost majestic trees have been broken, mangled and pruned by countless herds of elephant to give the forest a hedge-like appearance. The hedge forms an impenetrable strip, ten miles wide along twenty miles of crocodile and hippo infested shores of the meandering Chobe River. It is here that smugglers have operated for centuries and it's an ideal place for a cache of weapons to be moved from Zambia, through the Caprivi Strip, into Botswana.

Grobler drove his battered brown land rover off the tourist sand track near the river and entered the labyrinth of elephant trails. Reaching a high point where he could observe both shores of the river, he scanned the far shore through high powered binoculars.

As the light faded into darkness, the casual movements of elephant herds, watering buffalo and lounging hippo satisfied him that no patrols were active in the area. He popped open a can of beer and watched the last light fade from the sky. It was going to be at least an hour's wait before he could expect any activity on the opposite shore.

Over two hours later, a laser flash from the opposite bank alerted him to the location of the smugglers. He flashed his headlights twice and when the laser answered, returned their confirmation with his own laser beam. It would take them another four hours to cross the swampy, croc infested, papyrus covered waters in their low lying canoes filled with rifles and ammunition. All he could do was wait. If they didn't make it for some reason, he would just fade away into the darkness.

Another three hours passed, during which time, two motorized patrol boats passed along the river channels sweeping their searchlights across the waters. There was still no sign of any movement of the smugglers' boats across the water.

At the four hour mark he started the land rover and slowly crept down the slope until he was out of the brush onto the river's edge. A quick adjustment of three long poles extending from his canopy spread a camouflage net over the vehicle. He flashed his laser once again out onto the black waters. The closeness of the responding flash surprised him. Moments later, the first of three low canoes was pulled ashore and black shadows, each hauling a hundred pound sack of contraband, approached him.

They dropped their loads and each returned to stagger back under three more bags while Grobler stood by the rear of the vehicle checking each weapon or case of ammunition and packing it in his own boxes. The process took nearly half an hour, the most dangerous part of the transfer.

When, with sweat drenching his clothing, he finally closed the back of the vehicle, he felt a wave of relief sweep across his body. He quickly handed each man a packet of money, flicking on his flashlight long enough so they could riffle through the bills and see they were genuine. Then he watched them evaporate like smoke into the night air, leaving their empty canoes hidden for another day.

An hour later, he was back on a tarred road. Bypassing the cutoff leading to the Peha Gate of the Chobe game park, he took the sand track to the Mokororo Pan. From there the sand tracks circled south, hitting the main track leading back toward Pandematenga and Francistown. The morning sun was just beginning to turn the eastern sky pink when he finally pulled off into the bush, threw his bedding on the roof of the land rover and collapsed into an exhausted sleep.

It was nearly noon the next day when he drove out of the maze of bush tracks into the village of Pandematenga. Children's faces peered from grass thatched huts as he stopped in front of the blue painted medical dispensary. Two young boys coming out to watch his arrival, disappeared instantly into nearby bushes at the sight of his white face. Grobler laughed at them. White men were usually doctors. Doctors gave shots whenever they came to the village. Nobody wanted another shot in the arm or rear.

An old man's voice greeted him from the shade.

"*Dumela,* Mr. Grobler, welcome to our village. I haven't seen you up this way for quite some time. What brings you here?" The aged man rose from his chair and stepped forward to shake hands.

"*Dumela,* Baruti," replied the white man, smiling and taking the other's hand. "I've come for two things. I think you can help me."

"Tell me," said the old man, resuming his seat and pointing to the vacant chair nearby.

"I'm probably going to be on a big collecting trip for Jacques later in the year. One of the items will be a clutch of ostrich chicks for a client in the United States. Do you know where they nest?"

"An easy question, my friend," replied the old man pouring him a large cup of the thick brown native beer. "I know several places. They're creatures of habit. It's no trouble finding a nest or two. But watch out for the adults. They guard the eggs well."

"I know," replied Grobler, sipping the brown liquid and chewing the softened grain. "There was a Peace Corps Volunteer in Maun who was nearly killed by a big male guarding a nest. Everyone thought he was joking until he took off his shirt. He had giant bruises, big as grapefruits, all over his chest and back where the male kicked him. Damned lucky he wasn't killed."

"Good eating too, those big legs," the African smacked his lips.

"So, I think you are in agreement to go out with me this evening and show me a nest or two. Right?"

"Yes, I'll come."

"Good, I have to set up my camp first. I'll be back in about that time." He said, pointing off to the west at an angle indicating that the sun would be just above the horizon.

"I'll be here waiting. Now, what was your other question about?"

"I need to find the camp of some Mashona soldiers off to the east toward the Zimbabwe border. Their leader goes by the name of Makwatsine."

"Humph, I know about him and his men. They're bad people," Baruti shook his head. "I don't want to go anywhere near them."

"What's the problem?"

"They have guns and no women. Sometimes they shoot our cattle when they get bored. We complained, but when the police come, they disappeared into Zimbabwe. Then, after the police left, they came back and threatened us. Now we just stay away from them."

"I understand. Unfortunately they have guns and that makes them the boss in this part of Africa. Take me near their camp so I can find it myself."

"I don't want them to know who I am."

"Fine. I'll drop you once we get near their camp and then swing back to pick you up later" said Grobler, finishing his drink and heading toward his vehicle.

He drove north out of the village and found a small water hole. Several large Mangosteen trees overhead provided shade from the midday sun. Baboons leapt from the trees as he arrived, barking their anger at being disturbed.

Parking the land rover close under one large tree, he proceeded to erect his large military surplus tent with window and door screens made from a porous Kevlar-like material. He then set about cooking his evening meal on a propane stove. As the sun began to swell red in the west, he checked his watch and headed out to collect Baruti.

The evening drive took a circuitous route from Pandematenga along old cattle roads that disappeared into two magnificent flat pans dotted with acacias. Baruti's finger pointed toward a clump of palms. "They will be over there."

Minutes later they spied a female ostrich settled on its nest with the big male standing guard off to one side.

"Aha! The chicks are still small. They'll still be that way in a couple of months. They freeze when frightened rather than running away," he fixed the location in his mind.

Within minutes they saw three more pairs of ostrich on their nests.

"That's plenty. Now show me Makwatsine's camp."

"Just follow this track. When we see a big Baobab tree, you can stop and I'll explain how to find them. Be very careful with those men, they shoot at our people."

"Don't worry about me, they know I'm coming. We have business."

The two men drove in silence. Night was falling rapidly.

"There it is! There it is!" Baruti said, pointing.

"Hmm, quite a long way off. Is the camp right there?"

"When you reach that tree the guards will take you to the camp."

Grobler stopped the vehicle.

"You better take my big flashlight. It will be dark soon. I've seen lion tracks on the road. I'll pick you up on my way back."

"I'll be fine with the light. The lions have plenty of game to eat around here. They won't bother a man with a light." Baruti took the large flashlight and climbed out of the vehicle.

Grobler had nearly reached the big tree when a man with an automatic rifle stepped into his headlights. Two other shadowy figures appeared by the sides of his vehicle. Grobler didn't have to look behind him to know that several other men were probably following up the rear as well. He could feel the hairs on the back of his neck pricking upward in fear. He was surrounded.

"Get out!" A voice called from the shadows.

He stepped from the cab, hands raised. Looking toward the firelight he could see two large three-legged stewing pots on the coals. A group of men dressed in tiger camouflage outfits stood nearby. Everyone was armed.

"Keep your hands high so I can see them," the voice spoke again.

He raised his arms higher.

A giant man, nearly a full head taller than Grobler himself, stepped into the light of the fire and approached.

"You have business with me?" the threat in the deep tone was clear.

"Yes, I have a message for Makwatsine from our commander of the third force," Grobler spoke quickly, knowing that his life depended on establishing his business connection. The men appeared to be itching to shoot something.

"Tell me your message," said the man, stepping forward.

"I am Prometheus, the one who will take fire to Namibia."

"Fire as of old?" came the response from the huge man.

"No, the fire power of independence," replied Grobler. "The weapons to rain fire on the white men who hold the people hostage."

"Excellent," the big man chuckled as he waved the gunmen off. "I hope you see the irony in having a white man deliver weapons to kill his own people. We would consider you a traitor."

Grobler nodded his head in affirmation, knowing better than to argue with a man who held all the cards.

"Welcome to our humble camp, Prometheus. I enjoy using literature in my passwords. I was actually a literature teacher over on the Umtali side of Rhodesia before the war...." He stepped even closer to the white man.

"And now?" Grobler asked.

The big man's bass voice sank almost to a choking whisper as he said, "Now, I only know how to kill." His black eyes shown in the firelight like two infernal glowing coals.

"The weapons are from Zambia. Our leader commands you to guard them until I bring final payment."

"We will do that, provided a payment is made in advance."

"I have that for you," replied Grobler.

"Good, then we'll unload here."

"I need to make an itemized list of what you take."

"That's fine," replied the giant man, pulling a small notebook from his fatigue jacket

Moments later, Grobler was handing the weapons down a conga line of men. The arms and ammunition vanished in the shadows. Their leader jotted notes. When they were finished, he handed the sheet to Grobler.

"This sheet needs to come back with you when you return to pick up the weapons. My men will pull them from our cache even if I am not here."

"One of our group will be back in about four months," replied Grobler, handing him a cash filled envelope.

"Fine. We will be waiting. Now I think it is time for you to go. My men have been fighting white men for too many years in Zimbabwe. I can hear their talk over by the next fire. They don't like any white man. If they were to decide to kill you, I wouldn't be able to stop them." He raised his eyebrows and laughed in a booming fashion.

Grobler wiped the cold sweat from his brow as he drove back toward the Baobab tree and on to the main road where Baruti waited. He dropped him in the village and drove back to camp. The evening air was cool so he walked down the sandy road to the village bar a mile away.

He could hear the throbbing music long before he saw the lone neon light of the bar shining through the mud brick rondavels and thatched roofs. Settling himself near the bar, he relaxed, watching several young men and their girls dancing to a blaring South African band.

His first two beers barely slaked the day's thirst as he focused on the rhythm and movement of the dancers. By the time he reached the serious drinking stage, the bar tender had turned on the nighttime mood lights; a multicolored collection of old Christmas tree lights which were strung above the bar.

Grobler ordered a steak and when it came, washed down the tough leathery meat and a pile of fries with a bottle of wine. He was halfway through a second bottle when he found out the bar owner was from Ghanzi.

"I grew up in Ghanzi myself," said Grobler, leaning across the table and peering at the scrawny yellow-skinned man.

"I thought I recognized you," answered the owner, eager to hear news of his home country. "Your father was that big man, the owner of the cattle post just southwest of the Kuke fence. Am I right?"

"That's where I grew up," replied Grobler.

"How long is it since you visited your family?"

The inebriated man took a long drink from his bottle, looked at the blurry image of the thin man in front of him and thought for a moment. His brain, addled by alcohol, mixed the images of his former life in Uganda with his childhood past in Ghanzi and the present. He shook his head trying to make sense of the thoughts flooding his brain.

"I left home when I was fifteen," he replied. "My father sent me to live with my uncle over in the Tati Concession. I never went back. Too many bad memories. All I know is that the farm was sold to strangers."

"Ah, family problems," a look of disappointment showed on the barman's solicitous face.

"No," Grobler replied, struggling to speak coherently, "the family was fine. They're all gone now anyway. I had to leave home because my best friend, a boy named Mosa, was murdered by a wizard."

"You mean a *Moloi?* A wizard murdered him?" The surprise in the bartender's voice carried above the noise of the music. A hush fell over the bar as others tried to listen in, through the din of the music.

"Yes, it was just before Christmas time."

"Ah, I remember those times," interjected the bar tender. "We were all warned not to go out alone at night around Christmas. Even the adults."

"Yes, there was at least one ritual murder around Christmas every year. It was supposed to bring fertility to the new crops."

"It had to do with the old religion before Christianity came to Botswana. Some things never died out."

Grobler took another long drink from his wine bottle before continuing. Someone turned down the riotous music. The listeners drew closer.

"Mosa and I had been out hunting springhare one evening," said Grobler. "We used my flashlight and his bow. You know how springhare freeze when a light hits their eyes? It's the perfect boys' game. A target that stays frozen long enough for you to shoot it." He smiled thinking of the fun of boyhood.

"I never tried that," said the barkeep, "go on."

"We got two nice springhares and were walking back home in the dark. It was almost midnight. Mosa wanted to stay away from the main path because of the danger. I told him there wasn't a problem because they never bothered white people. Then, when we were about half a mile from home, a group of men came out of a clump of trees. They grabbed both of us and covered our mouths. We didn't have time to shout for help."

Sweat had appeared on the big man's brow. He wiped it away with his hands. His eyes were glassy and staring.

"I was a big boy and very strong. I broke away and started to run off. Then Mosa called out to me, so I ran back to help." Again Grobler shook his head as if trying to throw off the horrible memories.

"They took a knife and killed him instantly, right in front of me." His voice had risen, "They tied me up but because I was white I was useless for their ceremony. They just gagged me and made me watch while they... cut him up."

His breathing was coming in gasps, his eyes were wide open, yet seeing scenes of the past. It was a flashback to a time of terror, death and the worst of human atrocities.

Not a sound disturbed the tale as the surrounding members of the bar watched and listened. He described every detail as he told them how the *Moloi* had cursed him and then mutilated Mosa, his best friend.

"The men finally let me go. They told me never to tell anyone or the curse would come back to kill me. I ran all the way home. When I got there I had some kind of a fit while trying to tell my parents what had happened. I lay like a corpse for nearly a week, stiff and cold and unable to speak. The village organized a search party. They found Mosa's mutilated body but they never found the men who did it. I was sent away to live with my uncle in the Tati Concession near the border with South Africa. I never went back."

With a gigantic sigh, almost as if a weight had been lifted off his shoulders, the heavy set man lurched to his feet. His massive body knocked over a chair as he made his way through the door and drunkenly staggered along the road toward his camp.

"He'll sleep it off tonight," stated the bar man to his audience. "Tomorrow he won't remember a thing. I've seen a lot of men in that kind of alcoholic stupor. They recount horrible experiences and the next day don't even remember they were in the bar."

Grobler's plodding feet led him out of the village. Instinct guided him toward camp. Although his ears heard the distant roar of a lion and the cackling hyenas on the garbage heaps, his mind registered nothing. He continued talking to himself, shuffling along the road, ignoring the looks of passersby. At last he turned onto the small trail leading to his camp.

"Mosa, I was actually glad they killed you," he muttered. "I was always so jealous of you being better than me. You were a faster runner, better with the short bow and spear, better at killing springhare. Oh how I hated to have to lie to my mother that they were my springhare when I got home. You even outdid me in classes, math, history, English... even in English. I was a native speaker, yet you were always far ahead of me. A black must learn his place in society. Whites are superior."

The glazed eyes picked out the approaching small form of a ten year old boy on the road ahead.

"Mosa," he spoke directly at the uncomprehending boy, "Why are you always so much better than me? Why do you make me feel like a fool in English class?"

His huge hand gripped the shoulder of the small boy, preventing his escape.

"Didn't you ever learn your place in life? Aren't you afraid of me now?"

The boy's whimpers carried through the night air for brief seconds. He struggled in vain against the giant man's grip. Then he squirmed, struggled, kicked, and bit at the relentlessly squeezing calloused hands encircling his neck.

The demented man giggled insanely as he heaved the limp body onto a nearby garbage dump, "Now, the hyenas will make sure that you never beat me again on a school exam."

His measured paces guided his blank brain back to his bush camp. Behind him, the squeals and laughter of the hyena garbage eaters rose to new heights as they fought and tore at their new, grisly feast.

Inside the tent Grobler fell comatose onto his sleeping pad. His sleep deadened ears didn't hear the soft footsteps of a woman creeping past, stunned by the horror she had just witnessed while relieving herself in the nearby bushes.

Chapter 16
Maun, Botswana, August, 1990

Nearly two months later, a dilapidated red and green passenger bus pulled up to the main petrol point on the southwest side of Maun. The tall thin Kalanga woman from Pandematenga gave the white station owner a furtive look as she got off. Hurrying across the road, disappearing into a maze of small brick with tin roofed huts.

Moments later, she knocked on the door of one of the few remaining mud brick, grass thatched rondavel huts. A woman opened the door revealing a clean room with seats, much like a waiting room. The room was connected to another mud hut, but separated from it by a heavy door. The woman opened the door and called into the back room. Moments later a wizened yellow skinned man poked his head through the opening.

"Hello, Madam, How are you this afternoon? *Dumela, Mma, O tlotse jaang?*" he said, smiling brightly at the lady.

"Hello Wizard, I am here. *Dumela Moloi, ke teng,*" she nodded her head downward.

"Come in, and sit down. *Tsenang, y nna fatse,*" he pointed to the bench while stepping into the room.

In the tearful rush of words that followed, the lady blurted out what she had seen several months previously, on the road outside Pandematenga.

"He killed him! *O lo bolaile!*" she exclaimed, weeping. "I was afraid of his size. I hid in the bushes. The police wouldn't listen to me even though they found a small piece of the boy's body. They said the hyenas had destroyed too much evidence. I know it was him, the big white man who collects animals. I keep dreaming about it and finally I had to do something. The boy was my nephew."

The old man listened quietly, occasionally nodding and making sounds that prompted her to continue. At last, when she had finished, he rose and took her through the door into the back room. Numerous skins, fetishes, masks, cymbals and small drums hung on the walls.

"What did you say the boy's family totem was?" he asked quietly, trying not to upset her as she rolled her eyes, looking at the instruments of his wizardry.

"*Mboma,* the python," she whispered in fear.

"Hmm," the old man crossed the room and fingered the rolled, tanned skin of a giant python. "*Mboma,* the one who walks at morning time. The one who tastes the air with his tongue and hears through his ribs on the ground," he murmured softly, stroking the skin. "It will take perhaps a month. I will have to consult with the ancient ones to see what they can do about this man. Do you want to stay the night?"

"Oh, no! Please! I must go back to Pandematenga tonight. I only brought payment from his family. They want you to solve the problem. I don't want to know anything more about this. It was too horrible!" She put her face in her hands and sobbed.

"I understand," the wizened man's claw like hand took the small bag of coins. "I will do everything in my power to right this terrible wrong. Go tell the boy's family. I hope they will be happy with the result."

"I am going now *Moloi,*" the woman backed from the room, her hands in a prayer like attitude before her face, her fear filling the hut.

"Travel well with Jesus our Lord, mother. *Tsamaya sentle le Jesu, Morena wa rona, Mma.*" The old man nodded his head as she disappeared through the curtain.

"Yes, my wizard. *Ehee, Moloi wa me.*" She closed the outer door of the hut, crossing herself repeatedly and praying volubly all the way back to the bus stop. There she waited to catch the next transport bus back to Pandematenga.

Chapter 17
Windhoek, Namibia, August, 1990

The alarm buzzed in the small apartment. Jacob's arm reached out across his pillow toward the offending sound. His forearm brushed across the velvet soft skin of Debbie's back. She rolled over slowly then suddenly jerked upright, her eyes popping open, wide awake.

"Oh! My Gosh!" she said, twisting sideways, planting her feet on the floor to stand erect. "I went to sleep! What's the time! I've got to get out of here!"

"You're fine," Jacob said, smiling as he snapped on the tiny light to reveal her naked body. He punched the alarm, stopping its shrill notes. "It's only four in the morning. Nobody else is up until five thirty. You have plenty of time. I set this just for you."

"Oh! All I remember was having so much fun. Now, here I am. How did I get into bed?!" She leaned forward, draping her nude body across the bed, staring at him."

"You actually pulled me in here," he said, taking her hand, caressing the palm.

"Do you know what the police would do to you?"

"That's why I set the alarm. I wanted you to have plenty of time to get out of here. Yes, I know exactly what would happen. They'd probably kill me. You'd lose your job." He sat up, rolled out of bed and walked into the tiny kitchen to turn on the gas burner under the tea kettle. "I'll make some tea. Have a quick drink and then you can run up the hill."

"Expecting anyone who sees me to think I've just been out for a morning run?" she laughed, fastening her bra and pulling on her t-shirt. "Get real!"

"Let's just hope no one sees you. This place is like a sieve for secrets."

"Agreed. We've got to back off from each other for a bit. This is exciting, but it's getting to be too dangerous."

"That's what I said a week ago," he reminded her.

"I know. I must have lost control last night. We've got to be more careful."

"From now on, only up on the mountain. It's safer. The workers don't go out on the paths at night."

The kettle boiled. It took her only a moment to swig down the cup of warm, milky tea. She kissed him and was out the back door.

"Stay off to the left as you go up the hill so the night watchman won't see you," Jacob said. "He doesn't leave his hut at night but he might be awake and the window looks right down the road."

"Don't worry."

He watched her disappear into the darkness. Glancing around at the nearby maid and worker's apartment windows.

"Was that a movement in that curtain? No, you're just imagining things."

He shut the door and looked around his bachelor pad. The sink was still piled high with last night's empty glasses and beer bottles from the party with Debbie.

"You're getting in way too deep!"

It was laundry day again. By noon Jacob was at Tjeetjo's café in the group meeting with Shanika and the other members of the Namibian liberation underground.

"How's the diamond running project going?" asked Shanika.

"We've located an amazing place for pick-ups. The new route took a long time to set up but it's safer than the old one and crosses new territory."

"Tell us some more about it. I understand you don't try to reach the diamond fields by going south from Walvis Bay anymore."

"No, after we lost people on that route a year ago, we had to find a new route. This one goes toward Walvis Bay but the hunters jump off their transport at the dry bed of the Kuisaab River. The old river bed is easy to follow. During the rains it actually has wet spots where we can dig for water if necessary. Water is the biggest problem but Matias is part Bushman. He persuaded us to bury water in plastic bottles at various places along the route. That means it takes more time to set up and maintain the runs but we can stay out there longer because we don't have to carry water for the return trip. The men simply dig up the jugs, drink what they need and move on."

"What do you mean by an amazing place for pickups?"

"Matias is our most experienced diamond hunter. He located a new alluvial wash that's never been picked over. It's a place where an ancient river ran into the ocean very rapidly over rocks that were like riffles. The winds had blown sand over the riffles, covering them and then the freak rains we got last season washed away enough to reveal the stones. It's a perfect place for diamonds because they're heavier than the rest of the rocks and collect in the cracks. Close to the shore the storms of winter bring in new sand and gravel each year. The action of the waves on the rocks does the sorting for us. A couple of the finds have been fabulous!"

"Does that mean we'll have enough to purchase the weapons in Botswana?"

"Yes," Jacob smiled, seeing their rapt attention, "we're going to send out one more group this week. It should take them no more than two weeks to complete the run. We'll have more than enough diamonds to buy our weapons."

"Good. You've done an excellent job for our mission this past six months. We can start planning our next moves. Did you see the newspaper headlines this morning from South Africa?" Shanika removed a section of newspaper from his jacket pocket and read it aloud...

"Last night terrorists detonated a bomb in the local National Party headquarters in Nylstroom. Other terrorists, acting at a similar time, blew up a party propaganda vehicle in the town of Cullinan. Whether these terrorists were white or black is unknown but they point to the escalating unrest within the country. The hard line right wing of the government seems likely to gain control of parliament if they call for a vote of no-confidence for the president..."

Shanika slapped the paper on the table and glared around at his colleagues.

"We know the ANC is not perpetrating these acts of violence against the government. There is some other force attempting to increase terrorism and bring back the hard line apartheid government. We need to be ready to act in the coming months. We need those weapons!"

He focused again on Jacob.

"Bring me those diamonds!" He rose from his seat, effectively ending the meeting.

Jacob nodded.

"If you only knew. I've got to get a message back to Washington and get out of here if we're going to have a chance to stop Petrov."

Chapter 18
Washington D.C., August 1990

Halfway around the world another man was thinking similar thoughts as the day's heat built up for another scorcher in Washington D.C.

"My God! When will this summer be over," Jim Collins said to no one as he ran his fingers through white locks, trying to let the breeze from the fan do its job.

He tilted back in his oak swivel chair, wiped another bead of sweat from one temple and clasped his hands behind his head. An insipid trickle of dampness crawled down the center of his back.

The draft caught the corner of a yellow slip of paper pinned to his bulletin board. It waved in a beckoning manner each time the fan swept back and forth across the office.

"Zulu has got to be alive," he muttered, leaning forward, half rising to grasp the smudged yellow slip. He slumped back down, the hinges in his chair giving a warning creak. He read the cryptic message for the umpteenth time.

"The indaba is over. Plot thickens, Petrov's plan is ready. Big play coming before the Maru a Pula."

He re-read the statement, shook his head and punched the intercom button.

"Hey Abe, come in here a second!"

He heard a creak from the next office and the sweating red face of his second in command appeared through the door.

"Whew! It's hot for this time of the year," Abe said, moving in front of the cooling stream of air. "What's up?"

"First get the hell out of my breeze," snapped his superior. "You'll get that eighteen inch fan when I retire."

"Do you think they might give me an upgrade? This one doesn't look like it's going to hold together much longer. Mine wails like a banshee, dangerously so!"

"We'll see what the next budget cycle brings in." His boss held out the bedraggled slip of paper. "You've seen this before. Our man, Zulu."

The bright look of expectancy disappeared from his lieutenant's face. A furrow of doubt creased his forehead.

"Are you kidding me?" The tone of exasperation was clear in his voice. "He sent you that nine months ago, just after Petrov blew his operation to smithereens. We expected conclusive evidence of a Russian third force meddling in the South African peace process. He was going to expose their whole plot. After all this time we still have nothing. He's got to be dead!"

"Whoa! Let's not fly off the handle," said Collins. "Yes, I did say he was dead. We know something's being hatched by Petrov's third force. We need Zulu's evidence." He thrust the yellow slip toward his partner.

"I think our friend Colonel Petrov has a plan he's going to hatch before the *Maru a Pula*."

"Before the rainy season which starts in late September or early October. Right?"

"Right, and that means we're running out of time. We read about Petrov's successes every day with the shootings, police brutality, bombings and plane crashes. We need to do something or roll over and play dead."

"Desperate measures?"

"Yep."

"Where do you actually think Zulu is?"

"I think he went 'ghost'. I think he reverted to his true African identity. I think Jacob Nkwe went home."

"You think he's back in Namibia?"

"He grew up in a Namibian village near the Botswana border. Why not go where he has papers, passport and friends?

"And live in a rondavel out in the bush? What a comedown for a university trained guy whose life has been espionage."

"I doubt he'd go to his village. Tsumkwe is too small. There would be too many questions. He'd attract some busybody and have his cover blown. I think he's someplace like Windhoek. A place where there are jobs and he can check the old drops."

"What good does that do him? We cleaned up everything. That's the rule. An op goes sour, we clean up and then set up a whole new system. We never go back."

"That's right, we cleaned up but we didn't start anything new. Petrov's operation apparently knew enough to want him dead. We figured they might be playing Zulu in hopes that we'd try making contact. Petrov would then clean us out of Africa all together."

"So going 'ghost' was his only option. Ok, but if a lone person can disappear here in the US with no trace, why not in Africa?"

"Humph! Bodies in Africa are a lot harder to get rid of than one might think. They rot and stink. The continent is not exactly unpopulated. Here in America, people avoid bad smells. In Africa you go out and investigate bad smells. Americans don't want to see something dead. A local person in Africa walks up to the bad smell. If they find a hyena chewed corpse, they go to the police. Rotting death is part of life's processes to them."

"Maybe Zulu was in an accident. You know, maybe they tried to ID the body but with refugees running all over the damn place he's just another John Doe. With no refrigeration they probably just buried him."

"Abe, that's hogwash! He's one of us! You don't think South African security has his prints? You darn well know they do. So does Petrov. If Zulu's pinky turned up in some remote district of the Kalahari they'd ID him."

"OK, OK, you're right. So?"

"So, we need to expose Petrov's links to the South African government. We need to know who the traitors are and get them executed. We need Zulu's information. If we don't get it then we know for sure that Petrov's end game is coming with the rainy season. Without Zulu's data, anarchy will rule South Africa before Christmas."

"So you want me to open up the drops?"

"Yep. I want the drops in Windhoek open from now until the end of September. I know it's dangerous. All we need is one message from Zulu."

"I'm on it! Zulu must have a routine that allows him to watch at least one drop every few days. We open them all and if we're lucky we get a hit. If not, then we close up tight and forget it. Right?"

"Yep," smiled Jim. The only downside is that once Zulu is in the open, he'll be visible to everyone, the vultures included."

"We could also lose a drop man, chief," Abe reminded him.

"That's a chance we have to take…, Oh one more thing, you noted the language?"

"Sure, looks like Northern Sotho or Tswana."

"We're going to need to pull Zulu out. How would you like to get out of this humidity?"

"Anything to get out of D.C. if you're implying what I think," Abe's face lit up.

"Don't jump to any conclusions yet," Jim smiled. "You get started on the drops, I'll handle the paperwork."

"They have nice cool nights this time of the year," Abe's voice sounded as if he were in a trance, "deep throated rumblings of the lion…"

"Shut up and get on with it man or nobody goes anywhere," snapped his boss. "Now get the hell out of the way of my fan!"

Chapter 19
Windhoek, Namibia, August, 1990

"They've been gone nearly two weeks now. I expect them back any day," Jacob was addressing another noon meeting in Tjeetjo's café. He could see the skeptical looks in the eyes of several of the group.

"You saw the headlines in the newspaper this morning?" asked Shanika, the leader.

"Yes," Jacob felt his heart skip a beat, "I pray it wasn't one of our people they caught."

"We all do," said Shanika, "but it's in the same area we've been using. We may have to push our schedule forward if there is any indication that our plans have been compromised."

"I think we'd know by now if something had been compromised," Jacob replied.

"Do you trust Matias?"

"Completely. I wouldn't send my brother out there if I didn't think he was with the best. Matias has more experience on moving through the fields than anyone else."

"He's too old," muttered Walter.

"Yes, he's old," replied Jacob looking into the enforcer's eyes for any sign of a threat, "but it's not speed that gets us diamonds, it's the stealth that counts. He can show my brother and nephew the hunting site. They should be quick in collecting the best stones. They're a good team. If anyone can bring in a big haul it will be Matias and those two boys."

"I'm beginning to wonder if there might be some kind of a leak to the secret police." Shanika's forehead creased.

"Shanika, we're getting quality stones," said Jacob. "The mines wouldn't let us have that many before they pounced and put us all in prison."

"Jacob's right," said Walter, "You can't bribe the diamond mines. They pay premium prices for pick-up diamonds. You know that."

"I would trust Matias with my own life," Jacob continued, "but, every time he goes out I keep my fingers crossed. This is very dangerous business."

Maria poked her head through the curtain and put a finger to her lips.

Jacob lowered his voice, "If this dead man they reported in the news is one of ours, then I agree that we need to pay for what we can and back off for at least six months to let the pressure die down."

He glanced around the room at the eyes of his comrades for confirmation. Some nodded in understanding while others seemed to be staring at him with eyes as hard as lumps of coal. Something was going on that he was not privy to. He looked down and forced himself to take a mouthful of food and a long swig of beer.

Michael took this opportunity to intervene. His smooth, deep bass voice easing the tensions immediately. "Let's get ourselves back to the business at hand my friends. We've made contact with Zambia and the arms are already on the move. The diamonds must be sent out this next week if we are going to make contact for the weapons exchange. Our friends in Zambia need the money and from the looks of things here we are going to need the weapons."

"Do you think the government will come through with a plan to share power?" asked Simon.

"Things in the Republic are turning nasty with all the riots. If things break down then we'll be going to war. If the whites decide to share power then Windhoek will follow along." He paused and looked around the room.

"Walter," he continued, "Have you checked out the places to store our new weapons?"

"Yes. Each cell will have a set of weapons. The places are clean and dry. If the police find one cache, they won't be able to find the others by torturing anyone."

"Good," Michael raised his glass in toast and made eye contact with each of the group. "Eat-up and let's get back to our jobs. We don't want anyone to think we've taken too long for lunch. Down the hatch with your beers and then get going!"

There were smiles on the faces of the men as they finished, rose from the table and headed out the door. It was only a few minutes before Jacob was pulling away from the laundry and heading into the city.

His route home passed in front of the large post office building in the center of Windhoek. He knew he'd see the blind pencil vendor on the corner. What he really hoped to see as well was a gaudy multi-colored umbrella meaning, "I'm open for business." Now, after almost a year of waiting, he was depressed, knowing they had closed the drops permanently. He would need to find a different method for contacting Washington. Time was running short. Petrov's plan was succeeding.

As he rounded the eastern corner of the post office building, the sight almost made him run off the road. There sat the blind man in his usual spot. The black umbrella was gone and in its place was a large multicolored umbrella.

Jacob drove slowly past the small desk sheltered from the sun by the umbrella's broad shadow. A cup of yellow pencils was visible next to the money box. Seated behind the desk on his low stool, white cane leaning against the wall, large sunglasses covering his sightless eyes, was the blind man. Jacob felt his heart do a flip-flop against the inside of his chest. Then he was around the next corner, turning onto the main road toward the game park.

"The Gods must be watching out for me today."

He drove a bit slower on the trip back to the game park. There was a lot to plan and he needed time to think. Everything about the future had suddenly become a bit tipsy with the discovery of the blind man. He needed to plan quickly and get a message to Washington. Then he could decide whether to stay or leave. He was brought up short by the sudden thought.

"What if the drop closes again and I haven't sent out a message? Got to figure a way to get back to town tomorrow."

He pulled over to the side of the road, took his pocket knife and cut the valve stem of one tire. The air hissed out as the tire went flat. Then he set about jacking up the vehicle and putting on the spare.

The next morning, the trip to town to get the tire repaired was the first thing on Jacob's list. He pulled the land rover off the highway, heading toward the center of Windhoek and the post office. Parking the vehicle just down the street from the main entrance he entered the main building. He walked to the postal box for the game park and checked for any new mail. There was nothing inside but he took his time, turning slightly to watch the main building door to ensure that no one was following. After several minutes, he walked back out of the building, turned in the opposite direction and walked directly to the blind pencil vendor's table.

He ducked beneath the multicolored umbrella, picked three pencils from the glass jar and spoke to the blind man in a conversational voice.

"Do you know what time it is? I have to be at an appointment at nine thirty this morning and think I may be late."

"How would I know what time it is?" replied the blind man. "Can't you see that I'm blind?"

"Oh, yes, I'm so sorry," responded Jacob. "Yes. I see now. I guess it must be almost that time. I'd better hurry."

"No, you're already too late," answered the blind man. "I heard the ten o'clock chimes just a bit ago."

"Oh, No! It was an important job interview," Jacob dug into his pants pocket. "Here, let me leave you something extra for your help. I just took three pencils from your jar. This should cover it." He placed three coins and a small folded bill with his message into the blind man's outstretched hand.

"Keep the change," he said, turning away. From the corner of his eye he saw the man tuck the note into his shirt pocket. He heard the 'clink' of the coins falling into the jar.

He drove back around the block on his way out of town. The flashy umbrella was already folded and leaning against the wall. The chair and desk had been pushed to the edge of the sidewalk. The blind man was gone.

Chapter 20
Washington D. C., August 1990

"It's Zulu!" Abe waved the single sheet of decoded message under Collins' nose.

"Are you sure this thing was decoded properly?" Jim snatched the paper and read the message.

"Did it myself," said Abe. It just came in from one of the reopened drops in Namibia."

"No screw-ups?""

"Absolutely none as far as I can see," replied his assistant. "I checked the authentication codes and sent our RS. Here, do you see anything?"

Jim Collins reread the note. His forehead creased, "No problems as far as I can see," he said. "I like the part about him having information for us, but I don't like where he wants to meet up. Petrov could still be after him."

"You're right. If he's blown, then this note gives Petrov the confirmation that he wants. He'll throw everything into hunting Zulu down."

"He expects me to arrange a chopper to pick him up in Botswana? Ha! Not likely, unless I give the ambassador enough sensitive information to share with them so they'll authorize it. We already know that Botswana wants to remain neutral in this liberation war. They have the leakiest security I've ever seen. We'd be handing Zulu's head to Petrov on a platter."

"A man can't catch monkeys without going into the leopard forest," replied Abe. "We go after Zulu and we might just get Petrov too. Don't you think it's worth a try?"

"Dammit, Abe, Petrov's in deep with every government on the continent. Sure, I'd love to have his head on a platter, but he's a very dangerous man with nearly forty years of field experience. His people cleaned Zulu's clock less than a year ago. We can't do something big like bringing in a helicopter to a remote section of Botswana. That will be a sure tip-off to Petrov. No, if we can't pick him up in Namibia, we'll have to put people in on the ground. Have we got any operators still in that part of Africa?"

"I'll check it out. How do you plan to pick him up in Namibia?"

"I want you to put out one last message through our drop in Windhoek. If we can catch Zulu in Windhoek we can have his information in under a week. If not, then I'll authorize boots on the ground."

"Sweet."

"You'll have to run it, I'm too bogged down with Libya. No matter what, we'll have to move fast before more hell breaks loose in South Africa. This church burning, the kidnapping of that lawyer from Soweto and the shootings all show an escalation of violence. We need black majority rule in South Africa. Either we get it or blood will run in the streets!"

"They postponed a whole week's worth of crucial talks because of the last set of demonstrations. It just keeps escalating."

"I'm afraid it's going to get worse sometime in the next four or five weeks."

"Ok, I'll get the message out and see if we get any response. Got a timeline?"

"Like we better have a meeting tomorrow afternoon to go over the people and the timing of our ground operation," replied his superior.

"I'm on my way," Abe was already headed for the door.

Chapter 21
Windhoek, Namibia, September, 1990

An agent gets a feeling about things in his gut and Jacob's gut had been twisted up all morning. Shanika had called an emergency meeting. Something had gone wrong. Jacob prayed it wasn't something to do with the diamond runs or himself. When operations go south, they can trigger a cascade of collateral damage.

When he walked into the back room of Tjeetjo's Café the feeling didn't get any better. Facing him were the three executive committee members. He pulled out the fourth chair at the small table and sat down. Walter, the enforcer, stepped into the room behind him and leaned against the back wall.

"Jacob," said Michael Shanika, going straight to the point, "We have some disturbing news to tell you."

Jacob took his seat. Shanika lit a cigarette, while the two other men sat, silently sipping their drinks. No one bothered to ask Jacob if he wanted anything.

At last Shanika leaned back in his chair, took a deep drag from his cigarette and blew a stream of white smoke toward the ceiling. When he spoke, his voice had a grave tone.

"My friend, you have problems. They are big problems and could hamper the success of our entire organization…"

He raised his hand slightly as Jacob leaned forward and seemed about to speak.

"No, don't interrupt me," he continued, "I want you to hear me out. Then I'll let you speak. First I want to reassure you that I have been a family friend for many years. That is why I put you in a trusted position. That friendship has not changed. This committee has had faith in your abilities. I hope this was not ill-founded."

He paused as if searching for words while folding his massive hands across the beginnings of a middle aged paunch. He leaned forward again and stared directly into Jacob's face from only inches away. His voice was now soft but the words were hard and measured like the strokes of a whip.

"The problem we see is something that Walter discovered. He shared his information with me and I have shared it with the executive group. We have decided to use you, rather than have you eliminated for recent indiscretions."

Another raise of the hand stopped Jacob's response.

"Walter has contacts in the underworld and the security forces. His eyes and ears reach into many high places. This information came from a contact in the secret police. Debbie Kotzee has been linked directly to the South African Secret Police."

The pit of Jacob's stomach felt as though a lump of lead had dropped into it.

"Debbie Kotzee," he whispered, seeing the affirming nods from the three men.

"Yes, Debbie Kotzee, your manager at the game park is a covert member of the South African secret police. This means we are extremely concerned about your previous activities in the Republic before you arrived here."

"I was working with an insurance agency."

"Yes, your story about working for an international shipping insurance agency sounds very good, although no one in the Cape Town office has ever met you. In fact, they suggested that you might have been killed in a terrorist attack on one of the company offices last year. That was all the information we could get from them except for a story in the newspaper about a bomb. Walter thinks you might be a spy." The big man spread his hands and raised his eyebrows in a questioning manner, "Are you?"

Jacob took in a deep breath. He could feel beads of sweat running down his back, despite the dryness of the desert air. He glanced toward the back of the room and lowered his voice so that it could barely be heard by the men surrounding him.

"You've taken a big chance in helping me. Yes, you might say I was a spy in the international insurance business game. We were associated with Lloyds of London and several other gigantic insurance companies around the globe. It involved investigating multinational companies who have been smuggling computers and guided missile components into South Africa in defiance of the worldwide trade embargo. We infiltrate the big corporations and gain access to their top secret records. Neither they, nor the South African Government want to be exposed. The government had some very good reasons for destroying our office.

The newspaper story is correct, the South Africans blew up our offices and burned all our records. They actually killed several of our people. I escaped but had to leave the country. I still had my Namibian documents and was registered as an office clerk under my name in the South African homeland of Bophuthatswana. Walter can check that information easily. I'm a wanted man back in the Republic. If they knew I was here, they'd arrest me immediately and send me back. I'd be executed."

The gray haired man opposite him released his breath, almost like a great sigh of relief.

"Can you supply Walter with enough information to verify what you say without compromising us or yourself?"

"Yes. You have people in high places in Zambia. The American embassy in Lusaka can verify my status. I'll give Walter a number to call and the name of the person to ask for."

"Fine, I'll let Walter and you sort that one out. He removed a small phone from his jacket pocket, dialed a number, and spoke in an African dialect Jacob could not understand."

Jacob felt as if a weight had suddenly been lifted off his chest and shoulders. He could imagine that Walter had men waiting near the laundry van for orders that would either confirm or countermand his execution. He pushed his chair backward and half rose, making ready to depart.

Shanika reached out, his broad hand covered Jacob's momentarily. "We still haven't talked about your girlfriend, Debbie," he said, dark eyes betraying no sign of friendship or forgiveness.

"Yes?" Jacob felt his chest tighten again as he settled back into the chair.

"Walter is afraid of this woman, Debbie. She may know some of the same information he found out. He thinks the entire diamond smuggling operation could be in danger. She may have you under surveillance. What do you think?"

"Me?" Jacob heard the dry crackle in his own voice. He leaned forward once more.

"Yes," Shanika continued, "You are having an affair. This white girl is an undercover agent for the South African secret police. What do you know that she wants to know?"

"My God!" Jacob let the epithet slip from his lips.

"Exactly. She visits regular South African secret police information drops here in Windhoek on a regular basis. She appears to be passing along information. Our surveillance indicates that you are the only person in our movement she has contact with. Do you know she isn't from Namibia?" The big man paused giving him time to speak,

"She said she recently came from Germany and has no family connections in the country. That's all," replied Jacob. "We've had long discussions but nothing which would compromise the group. I had thought she was just a lonely woman in a strange country."

As he spoke, his brain was screaming,

"Jesus Christ, you dupe, all these years as a spy and you don't recognize the same techniques that you use on others?"

He remembered the many times he had seen her strolling along the trails near the game park on evenings after he had met with one or more contacts. She could easily have watched his meetings through a high power scope, even filmed some of them.

"We know for a fact that her story is false," Shanika said, still watching him like a hawk. "She is from Rhodesia and definitely is working for the South Africans. One of our contacts in Johannesburg has positively identified her."

Again his brain screamed a warning, *"Petrov has been playing me!"* But the calmer side prevailed, saying, *"No, they lost you in Botswana. Petrov would have killed you outright. He couldn't risk losing Zulu again."*

"I want her dealt with tonight." Michael Shanika's voice penetrated his thought process. He made a downward chopping motion with his hand on the table. His voice, sharp as a steel blade.

"Is that clear?"

"But!"

The knife edged voice cut him off again.

"No buts! I've put myself in jeopardy by stopping a vote to have you eliminated. By tomorrow I want to have heard from you that she has been eliminated. You will do it tonight, before you leave town. Everything is already arranged. Listen carefully…"

Shanika leaned forward saying, "A message of a death in your family will arrive this afternoon. Inform your supervisor immediately and have them authorize your travel permit. You must be ready to leave early in the morning. You will be out of the area before there is any alarm about her disappearance. Once the police begin searching the game park, there will be no escape. If you are arrested, we will make sure you do not survive to be interrogated. Now, I don't care how you terminate the girl but I suggest you do it in such a manner that it will give you at least a day to get away. Is that clear?"

"Yes," said Jacob. "Who is going to take over my work with the diamonds?" he asked, seeing his world beginning to fall apart.

"That has been taken care of. Take only bare necessities when you leave the game park. You are going to a funeral. It must look like you are returning. If anything goes wrong you will be the one to suffer. You will be going overland into Botswana, carrying our diamonds to pay for the new supply of weapons. You'll be turning them over to another courier at Drotsky's Cave. I think you know where that is."

"Yes, it's due east from my village of Tsumkwe by about 200 miles. There's no surface water between the two places. You can't be expecting me to walk there?" Jacob's incredulity caused him to raise his voice.

"Quiet your voice. We have already made all the arrangements, so the answer is a definitive yes." Shanika's eyes blazed. "You have done almost irreparable damage to our cause. This isn't punishment, it's for the safety of the whole mission. The whites won't expect you to go that way. If we lose the diamonds, we lose everything. When you return to Namibia, you will be placed with a different cell group in a different part of the country."

A wave of relief swept over Jacob knowing the diamonds would be his passport to freedom. Michael would not have Walter risk killing him as long as they were in his possession.

"What about the current diamond run that's still out?" he said.

"If they arrive tonight, you'll take them. If not, they will go in our next exchange. We will be closing down all of the diamond business until we make sure nothing has leaked out."

"I'll do my best."

"Good. Now, you need to go back to your work," the big man smiled for the first time and extended a hand. "I have trusted you because of our family ties. Don't fail me!" He stood, towering over Jacob briefly before dropping his hand and disappearing through the curtains.

Despite the warmth of the afternoon sun, a wave of cold swept over Jacob as he left the café. One more trip back into Windhoek to get travel papers. What to do about Debbie? He had little stomach for field assassination work even though it was part of the training. He wracked his brain for a way out.

His speeding laundry vehicle skidded to a stop at the front gate. A chill passed through him as Debbie looked up from her desk, smiled and waved.

Chapter 22
Near Windhoek, Namibia, September, 1990

It took over an hour for Jacob to catch up on his duties with the maids and maintenance men before he could go to the main office. It was hard not to show his worries. He made every effort to keep up the usual jocular chit-chat the staff were used to. It wouldn't do to raise suspicions about his mood prior to receiving official word of a relative's death. He also needed to maintain the façade to cover up his depression about Debbie.

He entered the front lobby and collected his mail, thumbing through it with apparent idle disinterest. He found the one with his brother's return address scribbled on the rear flap. He noted the postmark from Windhoek rather than Gobabis where his brother lived. He slit it open to read the notice of his uncle's death exactly as Shanika had promised.

"My God, this was sent yesterday, but my uncle has been dead a full week. How long have you actually known about my affair? I'm being played by both my friends and enemies."

He raked his fingers through his trim haircut to make the tight curls look disheveled. Scraping a bit of dust from the door jamb he rubbed some into both eyes. The watering was instantaneous. Blinking back tears, he knocked on Debbie's office door. A big tear was beginning to roll down one cheek as he entered the room. As she looked up from her work, he blurted out the news of his uncle's death watching her face change from a smile to one of deep concern.

It took only minutes for her to telephone the Windhoek police station and arrange for his leave of absence and travel permit. Workers from the homelands always had emergencies.

"They will have your travel permit ready this afternoon," she said, hanging up the phone and walking to the window to close the venetian blinds. She then came around the desk, put her arms around his neck and looked up into his reddened eyes.

"I'm so sorry about your uncle. I can see he must have been a very important person in your life. Take the land rover down to the police station in about an hour. They should have the travel pass ready. I'm going to miss you." She reached up to brush one of the drying tears from his cheek.

"Yes, I'll miss you too," he whispered back, taking her briefly in his arms.

"When will you leave?"

"I'll try to leave as early tomorrow morning as possible," he said. "It's just... so... unexpected... so hard ... to know he's passed. He's only a few years older than me." He let out a big sigh, released her hands and smiled weakly, shaking his head.

"I expect I'll be gone the full two weeks," he said. "You know how African funerals are," he squeezed her hand.

"Take your time," she said, her hand smoothing the side of his face as he turned to leave. "Can we still see each other tonight to say goodbye?" Her own voice sounded as if she was almost in tears as well.

He stopped, gave her his best smile and said, more strongly, "Yes, we need to say goodbye this evening. I'll leave my apartment about seven and meet you at the big rock about seven fifteen. It's private. We can have a good long talk."

"Wonderful," the brightness had returned to her voice. "I'll be there." She smiled again, touching his arm before closing the office door.

The next few hours involved a whirlwind of activity. Jacob wrote up daily work schedules for the next two weeks. He met with Roberto, his assistant, to make sure he understood everything. He packed a small bag and checked that the encrypted information was secure on the lanyard around his neck. He also strolled around the apartment looking to see if everything appeared as if he planned to return.

The drive to the police station was a necessary formality. The sergeant read his message and typed out the travel pass. Then after reading him the rules for travel, gave him a card with reminders of how to behave at any military checkpoints.

With papers tucked in his front trousers pocket, Jacob thanked the sergeant and drove back to the park.

Back in his room, he stowed half his money in a leather neck pouch and the rest inside his socks. He put his clasp knife, bread, a small jar of jam, some cheese and a two liter bottle of water in his shoulder bag and set them aside for the following day.

After washing down a quick meal with a glass of water, he stepped out the back door of the apartment and casually strolled toward the hillside. It was nearly seven when he disappeared into the high brush that lined the trail heading up the hill.

The quick climb up the steep slope made him breathe heavily as he neared the meeting site. He paused to rest, looking over the precipice while listening and thinking about their meeting. He remembered meeting Debbie in this area two weeks ago and noting that she was hardly breathing. She was in good shape. If he was going to send her over the cliff, it would have to be an unexpected shove. He continued on to the top, forcing his mind to remember that this was just part of his job.

"Avoid any emotional attachment. Do it quickly and quietly. Don't let your mark suspect anything. Christ! Do the people who write these training manuals know anything about real life?"

As he came around the final curve in the trail next to the large rock, he was surprised to find her waiting for him. She was seated with her back against a large rock, gazing out over the violet hills. The orange sunset was rapidly fading off the clouds to the west. Her shoulder bag rested by her side.

"It's so beautiful up here," she said, smiling up at him, "I never tire of watching an African sunset."

He sat down next to her in the dirt. She leaned her head against his shoulder. His hand reached down to touch her bare knee. His fingers began tracing circles over and over.

"You're out of breath," she remarked.

"The hill is steeper on my side," he responded.

"You're not getting too old for these late evening pursuits on the mountain, are you?"

"I'd much rather we met somewhere with a nice soft bed and a TV," he smiled.

"Lazy boy," she laughed, "you'll have to keep coming up here if you want to catch me. No more worries about attracting attention. She leaned back against her knapsack and relaxed under his touch."

"I've been wondering about that," he replied. "Do you think we've been seen together? The girls have been making comments recently. Do you think they know something about us?"

"Really?" she cocked her head sideways, "I can't imagine they would know. Which one of the girls?" her curiosity was obvious.

"It's nothing I can put my finger on for certain," he lied. "But after I met with you in the office, I ran into Sara. She mentioned that you seem to always pull the venetian blinds whenever I go into the office."

"What did you tell her?"

"I told her about my uncle. I said that I needed to see you in private and not have snooping eyes like hers prying into my affairs. I think that put her off."

"You're just imagining things," she poked him in the ribs, allowing his hand to caress her thigh.

"One can never be sure when it comes to what people see," he replied. "We have been careful, but anyone might be out walking in the evening. Perhaps it's just as well that I'll be gone for a while. Let the rumors cool off."

"Do you really need the full two weeks? You aren't going to leave are you?"

He laughed, "I would be a fool not to stay in this job. It has all the privileges, freedoms, and money I could want. African customs on death are Christian on the outside but still African underneath. We don't just dump a body into the ground and walk away. We have old tribal customs that are very important to release the soul of the dead person for the next life. They take time. Relatives may take a week getting to the funeral from a remote village. It would be rude to send them home immediately. I need to make sure they are well cared for. They have a duty to come and pray for my uncle's spirit so he goes to heaven."

"How can you entertain all those people in a bush village?"

It's no easy task. I'll pass through Gobabis on the way home. I have to order crates of beer and food to be sent out to begin feeding people this weekend. The refrigeration for dead bodies is not reliable in the village. If there is any problem with that they may have to bury him before I get there. In that case I will have to extend my stay to placate my relatives and my uncle's spirit."

"Our worlds are so different. It's complicated. I can see why there are not many mixed marriages." she sighed, her breathing coming more rapidly as his hands caressed her body.

He took her in his arms, pulling her toward him. "Debbie."

"Oh, Jacob," she exclaimed in a choking manner, "make love to me before I start crying and ruin the evening."

Afterward they lay in each other's arms counting the shooting stars. Their close bodies warding off the cold chill of night.

Jacob felt her warmth. One half of his brain reveled in the pleasure of conquest while the other half contemplated the thought of killing her. He rolled over on his side, watching her face.

"What is it about you that makes you like black Africans?" he asked. "It's a dead end street. It will only lead to trouble. What would happen to your future if you had a colored baby?"

Her laughter greeted him, "I take the pill. I don't have to worry about babies, silly! As for your other question? My answer to that is, you're the only one big enough to give me a second climax!"

With that she grabbed his shoulders, wrapped her strong thighs around his waist, making rhythmic motions.

He could feel his body responding instantly. All thoughts disappeared as they indulged in another wave of orgasmic pleasure.

Falling back on the soft bed of grass in a state of semi-exhaustion, Jacob closed his eyes for what seemed like only a brief blissful moment. He felt her moving next to him and a rustling of her knapsack. In a relaxed voice he smiled to himself, saying, "My God! You'll kill me with all of this extra-curricular activity!"

"I don't think any killing will be necessary for another minute or two," she said, her voice suddenly cold and harsh, cutting through his reverie. Her sentence was punctuated by a small metallic 'snick,' the kind of sound guaranteed to raise hairs on the back of the neck of any trained combat veteran.

His eyes popped open, his head swiveling toward her. He raised himself to a half sitting position.

Her periwinkle blue eyes were still visible in the rapidly fading light. Now they seemed to have taken on the same steel blue-black glint that reflected from her pistol. She held the Rhodesian 9mm Mamba in a two handed grip. The muzzle was only inches away from his face.

Chapter 23
Outside Windhoek, September, 1990

Jacob felt the hard cold barrel of the pistol as she thrust it against his skull.

"Over on your stomach! Hands stretched over your head! Flat on the ground! Don't even think about bunching those knees!" Her orders were clipped, given with no hesitation or indication of weakness.

"Who are you?" He blurted. He could tell from her manner that she was well trained. He was not her first. Questions reverberated through his brain.

"Who broke my cover? What does she know? Is this just dumb blind luck? Shit!"

She didn't attempt to bind his hands but moved in toward him, placing her knees on his back. In his prone position, she was out of sight.

"Feel that on your spine?" she spat, pushing the muzzle into the base of his back. "Don't move your arms, don't twist your head or even twitch. I'm going to frisk you."

"Who are you?" He repeated the question. Her hands were moving over his lower body, probing for any weapons.

"Let's just say my employer is very interested in your meetings in Windhoek on laundry days. He is also interested in the men who come to your quarters at night."

"They're just friends. We get together on laundry days for lunch. We talk about our lives and families. At night, the people who come are from my village. They bring me news of my family. I feed them and send them on their way. I hardly ever see my family."

"So you say," she replied, coldly. "The people I work for want information, not lame excuses. I need you to fill in some blank areas. If I don't get cooperation then it ends here." She emphasized the point, jabbing the pistol hard against the back of his neck. "Just lie quietly, this is loaded and I know how to use it."

Jacob's brain was working furiously. Obviously she had insider knowledge of his meetings with Shanika. He had to come up with plausible answers.

"Get her engaged in conversation, keep talking, try to get her angry so she loses her concentration. Be patient. There will be a split second opening. When it comes you either take advantage of it or die."

He forced himself to breathe deeply for a moment, closing his eyes, relaxing his muscles, trying to regain focus and control the rush of adrenaline surging through his blood stream.

"Let me sit up," he said softly, "I'll try to answer your questions."

There was a moment of complete silence. She was thinking. A cricket began its evening chirp beneath a rock nearby.

"All right," she said.

He could feel her relaxing slightly.

"But don't move a muscle until I'm away from you. When I'm ready, I'll tell you to roll over. Roll slowly and keep your hands where I can see them at all times."

He felt a sudden decrease in pressure on his neck. She pulled away and scrabbled uphill, placing her back against a rock.

"Now, roll over slowly and sit up."

As he pushed up he could see she held the heavy 9mm Mamba solidly with both hands. Her elbows were supported on the inside of raised knees. He kept his hands high above his head where she could see them.

"Not an ideal sized weapon for a woman, but just as deadly as the snake it's named after. Probably has a hair trigger. You can't take the impact of a slug that size. Take it slowly, don't rush."

"Now, put your hands down at your sides and sit still," she commanded. "If I have to use this," she jerked the pistol, "I'll empty it. Don't give me any reason at all."

"I've seen what a 9mm does to a man during the Rhodesian/Zimbabwe war. You must be South African police or military."

"We adopted these after seeing how well they worked against the terrorists," she said. The bullets are dum-dums. Better results on impact.

He could see that the safety was off. The hammer was still at half cock.

"Scant comfort, boy, she's got ample time to thumb it back with you in this position. Wait for the chance. Keep your voice soft and calm."

"What do you want to know?"

"Let's start with where you really come from? I tried to trace your ID through your work permit card. It all came up blank. The main lead is a student from here who went to the United States on a scholarship almost ten years ago. We think he's still there studying. The only other hit for your name is a man who went to work as a clerk in the mines down in South Africa. He seems to have disappeared. So tell me about yourself. Then we'll get to your work in Windhoek."

"I'm neither of those men," he confessed, "I got these papers in Zambia. There's a man in Lusaka who specializes in ID cards. He told me the owner had been killed. The papers were guaranteed to be clean and untraceable. I'll have to talk with him next time I'm in Lusaka."

"I wouldn't count on that happening soon," she stated coldly, the pistol still steady as a rock. "So why did you sneak into South West Africa?"

"Namibia!" He shouted at her, watching her flinch in surprise at the vehemence in his voice.

"You may think you whites control this country," he continued in a softer tone," but your apartheid laws are turning the people against you. Right now this country is in a state of lock-down emergency. The revolutionaries are getting their guns from Angola and Botswana. You don't have enough men on the ground to control us if we decide to rebel. If you don't change the government we will drive you out. That's why I'm here."

"So you confess to being a terrorist."

"No! I am not a terrorist! He felt his anger rising with his voice. His emotions were taking over, impossible to control.

"I came back to see my country freed from you slave masters who have dominated us for over three hundred years! That's why!"

His voice had risen an octave. He knew he was ranting but he needed to somehow provoke her into an emotional retort.

"We have to control you people!" She shot back. "You've said so yourself! Look at Zimbabwe. Newly independent and already starving to death because they can't break out of their tribalism! Zimbabwe was better off under Ian Smith. You don't have the wits or common sense to compete in the modern world. The only hope for this country and South Africa is to keep things separate! It has to be black and white!"

Her face had become flushed with emotion, her voice raised and her eyes hard as she recited a mantra of dogma drummed into her since childhood.

"Hah!" he laughed, "those are nothing but the hypocritical words of a bunch of weak whites. You sucked on the tit of a black nurse when you were a baby. Then you spit in her face when you grew up. You're just one more fool. Why do you think you all need four or five guns in your houses? Why do you look at every black as if they are either a slave or an enemy? I'll tell you why. It's because you're greedy and afraid to share the wealth and power! I studied for five years on a full ride scholarship in the United States. I'm as smart as any one of you! You go to bed with black men but haven't got the guts to stand up and fight for their equality! You're the puppet not me, Debbie! I was actually beginning to fall in love with you!"

He saw a wave of shock cross her face upon learning the truth about the man in front of her. He had exposed her deeply held hypocritical conflicts. Her core beliefs that black Africans, no matter how smart, educated or hard working, could never, ever be equal, to whites was being laid bare by the black man with whom she had slept. He saw the blood drain from her flushed cheeks. He watched her face change, in chameleon like fashion, from livid red to an awful deathly white. Her hands began to shake with a rising inner fury.

"The system works, dammit, Jacob," she shouted back at him. "The homelands are all you blacks deserve. If you wanted them to look and produce like the Transvaal and Orange Free State you would use your brains to make them better. You'd work a bit harder. My God, you people are still evolving out of being cannibalistic tribes. You're nothing but a working stud to me!"

He felt his own anger surging to the surface. He fought down the urge to launch himself at her. Another hard push and she would go over the top. So he shouted back, knowing that it might get him killed in the next few moments.

"I don't give a damn about our sex life. You're just another easy conquest for a black man! I don't need your puppet master government or you!" His rage welled to the surface momentarily. "None of us want your left-overs. We don't want your rejected lands, the reservations with no resources or surface water. You've given us the worst places on earth to live. Places where even a Bushman would starve! All we want is to be treated like equal human beings! We want to be a part of the process of government. If we can't have that, then you whites will have to go. If it ruins the country, at least we'll be free! It's worth that price! You need to compromise now while the cards are still on the table. If not, then we will take it all, forcibly. Time and numbers are on our side!"

"Look at the other African governments!" she screamed back at him. "Look what a mess they are making of independence!" Her voice was a shriek of pent up emotion. The barrel of the pistol no longer pointed directly at him. Her hands shaking in anger as she continued.

"Sweet Jesus! Look at Angola, Rwanda and Zaire with their dictators and out of control armies killing millions of innocent people! Look at Uganda with Idi Amin! Look at how Mugabe is ruining the best fruits of Africa in Zimbabwe! Every one of them is now a dictatorship that is far worse than the colonial ruler they threw out!"

She was on her feet now, yelling, waving the pistol, moving closer into his physical space.

"Do you know why I came to South Africa from Rhodesia?" She screamed at him, her thumb moving in preparation to pull the hammer to full cock. "Do you know what those bloody, kaffir, terrorists did to my parents and sister? This is all I have left of my family, my father's pistol…"

His legs swept out, catching her off balance, sending her into the rocks and gravel further down the hill, nearer the cliff's edge.

"No!" she screamed, trying to twist back toward him. She clawed at the pistol, attempting to thumb back the hammer on the Mamba.

He was on top of her now, knocking the weapon from her hand, sending it sailing into the nearby rocks. He twisted her body grasping for her throat.

"Mmphg!" She tried to cry out as his fingers almost caught her slim neck.

Then, outweighed, outgunned, caught in a corner by a larger predator, she fought back; a little honey badger with a ferocious will to live and an incredible strength that belied her small size. Her body twisted so it faced him directly, her hands came up and she jabbed at his throat and eyes. The fury of her attack, her squirming, kneeing, scratching, biting and clawing, drove him backward.

Jacob released his hold to protect his own eyes, face and throat. In that instant she was able to break completely free of his grasp and scramble to her feet. He lunged toward her with a roundhouse swing which she narrowly avoided by taking a step backward. Then, as he watched, her heel caught a sharp rock. She staggered and stepped backward, one more time, into thin air.

Jacob was on his hands and knees, panting in shock and exhaustion. He shook his head, trying to clear it of the image of her fall into the darkness below. He listened for sounds from below. Nothing but the clatter of a few falling pebbles. He leaned over as far as he dared attempting to see her in the rapidly dimming light.

The cliff was over seventy feet high. Even if she had landed on a ledge, she was finished out here in the night. It would be days before anyone thought to look in this part of the park. By then they would only find the remains of her hyena gnawed body.

He located the Mamba between two nearby rocks. Ejecting the chambered round, he stuck the cartridge into his pocket and lowered the hammer. The thought of Debbie's beautiful body splattered on the rocks below suddenly repulsed him. He shuddered and then began scrabbling back down the gray ribbon of trail. It was steep in places and he had to go on all fours to keep from falling. At last he stepped past the final clump of thorn bushes behind his apartment building. A man's shape emerged from the bushes sending him into a frozen crouch.

High above, on a rocky ledge, some thirty feet below the lip of the cliff, Debbie regained her senses. She tried to wriggle out of the branches of the thorn bush that had broken her fall. A wave of pain surged through her body, plunging her back into the world of unconsciousness.

When she woke a second time, the pain in her head was gone but everything about her body hurt. She lay there, checking things one at a time. She could wiggle her toes and fingers so her back wasn't broken. She rolled off the thorn bush and lay on her stomach gasping in pain. Her exploring fingers found the end of the broken branch sticking out into her side. She tried to get up, but her wrist was broken and it took all her strength to come up to her knees. She could feel the throbbing of a second broken bone in her lower leg as she crawled off the rocks onto a bit of grass and collapsed.

The stars twinkled overhead in the cold black sky as she lay there curled in a ball, shivering. Movement off the ledge was impossible in the darkness. Who knew what animals might be lurking in the shadows.

The cold ate into her bones but she knew she could survive the night as long as…..Now she prayed that her tiny ledge was inaccessible to the two things she feared most in the night: roving hyenas and a man named Jacob Nkwe.

Chapter 24:

Namibia, Outside Windhoek, September, 1990

Jacob crouched in the shadows, racked a shell into the pistol and aimed.

"Psst! Jacob! It's me, Bakai," the shadow whispered.

Jacob let out his breath, lowered the weapon and leapt across the yard to embrace the black silhouette of his half-brother.

"Bakai!" Jacob whispered loudly, backing off a step. "I'm so glad you're back! Come inside. We need to talk."

He unlocked the door, shut the curtains and snapped on the lights. The stark glare of the bulbs showed lines of exhaustion on his half-brother's face.

"What happened?" Jacob asked, "You don't look like you've rested a wink in the past week."

"I just got back tonight. I met with Shanika and he had Walter bring me here. My two friends, Matias and Edward, are dead out in the desert. I just barely escaped. What's happening? Have you betrayed our cause?" The rush of Bakai's voice held an accusatory note, telling Jacob his situation had been shared.

"No, Bakai! I haven't betrayed anyone," Jacob said. "Here, sit down. I'll get you a beer and something to eat. We haven't got much time. I have to leave tonight! Tell me what happened, then I'll tell you my story. You must be starving."

He opened the small refrigerator door, pulled out two beers, leftover chicken and half a loaf of bread. Handing the food to his brother, he popped the tops off both bottles. Taking a long swig, he joined his half-brother on the sofa.

"Yes, I am starving," Bakai said between mouthfuls. "I haven't eaten in two days." He stuffed more food into his mouth.

"Walter is waiting for us. He says we can have an hour to talk. After that, we both must leave no matter what. I'm heading south for a new assignment. I won't be able to attend our uncle's funeral. Your affair is out in the open. We've closed our cells down completely and are dispersing. We are all at risk of being pulled in for questioning." He wolfed down the remainder of the chicken and washed the bread down with great gulps from the liter-sized beer bottle. His eyes were watering from the rapid consumption and swallowing when he again turned toward Jacob.

"Did you kill her?"

"Yes," Jacob nodded his head, "She went over the edge of a high cliff. Someday I'll be able to tell you about it."

"You've ruined everything for us you know," there was no missing the direct accusation and blame.

"I know. I was a fool, doing what I did. They're sending me away as well. I don't think I'll be able to attend the funeral myself. The police will be hunting me."

"You'll be on the run for the rest of your life if she was really a secret police agent. You know that," his brother said, rising from the couch, depositing the empty plate and beer bottle in the sink. He pulled another bottle of beer from the refrigerator and slumped back onto the soft cushions of the sofa. "They'll come after the whole family trying to get at you through us."

"Yes, I know," Jacob replied softly sensing how he would be branded as a traitor if he didn't complete his mission.

"I'm sorry," he continued, "I hope I can prevent that from happening once I complete my mission. Now, tell me about the diamond hunting. It sounds like it was a disaster. Did I make a mistake there? Was it my fault?"

"No," Bakai answered, "you aren't to blame for what happened. It was bad luck and carelessness on our part," Jacob's half-brother stared off into the distance as if watching a different world as he told his story.

"Matias found an absolutely spectacular hunting site for diamonds. It's small and I don't think it's ever been picked over before. The trip out was routine. Just a week's walking at night along the old dried up water courses that used to run into the ocean. When we arrived, we searched for several hours and were able to fill two small pouches with good stones. The area is loaded with diamonds but very exposed. We had to have one man constantly listening for the search planes that go up and down the coast. Then we'd take cover to avoid being seen. The big rocks nearby had lots of deep crevices to hide in."

Bakai stretched and yawned but kept speaking. "When we finished that evening, Matias wanted us to leave right then. He said we had enough stones for one run and he was afraid of the open ground around the hunting site. We should have listened, but Edward and I overruled him. That night we buried ourselves under a layer of sand to keep warm."

"The desert gets terribly cold at night without blankets or shelter," commented Jacob.

"Yes but the ground was warm from the afternoon sun and it holds the heat of your body so we were all right. Then the next morning there was a bit of ground fog. We thought it would be safe enough to get out early and hunt. Edward and I figured we'd have such a fabulous haul that we'd be able to pay for more than just the weapons we need from Botswana. It was a mistake. One of the small planes came in low under the fog bank and spotted us before we could reach shelter."

Jacob watched as his step-brother's body went almost rigid. His eyes seemed to glaze over as his brain flashed back and relived every detail.

Bakai felt the pain as he flattened his muscular body against the jagged red rocks inside a crevice. A spray of submachine gun bullets chipped off nearby fragments. He heard himself screaming to the others...

"For God's sake don't move!"

The light plane roared low overhead, its sound mingling with the chatter of the gun.

Matias, the oldest of the three, was only inches away. He yelled back, "Don't worry, those white bastards haven't caught me in six trips. It won't happen now!"

"Where is Edward?"

"Over in the shadow of that big rock. He didn't come off the beach when I gave the warning. They must have seen him." He jerked his head toward the edge of an outcropping of rocks below where they were hidden.

Then as if in a nightmare, the two men watched their friend break cover and make a wild dash across a flat open stretch of sand toward a safer crevice.

The small plane banked and came roaring back toward him. It crabbed sideways to bring the open side door to bear directly on Edward. Bullets walked across the sand and rock, splattering on the blood red stone and then ripping into Edward's body. Moments later he was nothing but a limp, oozing rag doll. The wall of lead threw another shower of rocks into their own hiding spaces.

"I watched from my niche and saw him lying there. Then I looked at my own arm. Blood was coming out of a three inch long gash. I watched the red droplets landing on the red lava. They painted a picture like a devil's face as they melted into the cracks. Then a small black beetle scuttled from a nearby crevice sucking at each red bead with its long snout. When I moved it disappeared into a crack. By then, my blood had dried to the same color of those red rocks."

"Were you badly hurt?" Jacob's voice broke through his cloud of memory.

"No. The plane came back, looking for us but we didn't move. They came back one final time and dropped a smoke bomb. Then they flew off in the direction of Walvis Bay."

"What about Matias?"

"He said he was fine. He said we had to go immediately because they would come back to find us with a tracker."

"What did you do?"

"I saw how Matias was right. The white smoke rising vertically from the desert as the fog cleared made a column that marked our position for miles around. They would know exactly where to find us. Then Matias ran over and cut off one of the two small diamond pouches from Edward's body. He had me tie it to my belt. We left the other so the trackers might think he was alone and not follow us. He headed east over the rocky crags and hills. I wanted to bury Edward but Matias said that would only waste the precious time we needed in order to escape."

"He was right," Jacob agreed.

"I never realized how quickly they would be coming after us. Matias said it would be in less than three hours. He said if we didn't make it to the main rocks, they would catch us for sure. He even had me run in his footsteps over the open sandy places so there would only be one set of footprints. That was in case we needed to split up."

"He was right about the time factor," said Jacob. "Once they radio in an alert, an armed vehicle and soldiers can be sent out in under half an hour. On the beach flats they can easily do sixty miles an hour. That means reaching your site, a hundred and fifty miles away, takes about three hours."

Bakai stopped talking, again lapsing into a trance. He stared into space, as if watching himself and Matias on their journey. Their heavily calloused feet padding along in the mile eating dog trot of their warrior forefathers, hard men of the desert who had also fought the white man for these precious sands.

"Bakai! Wake up!" Jacob's voice startled the young man back to reality.

"Sorry," he smiled, "I'm exhausted. Where was I? Oh, yes, we reached the twisted ridges of red rocks which separate coastal sands from the true Namib Desert after about an hour. Off to the east the country turns flat. Matias said we needed to stay in the ridge area which has caves for hiding. We were miles along that stony ridge by the time the land rover arrived at the place where Edward was shot."

"How many were there?"

"Matias has Bushman eyes. He can see details at distances where you and I are blind. He told me there were four of them; a white man, two tall black soldiers and a tiny brown Bushman. They also had a dog. He said we only needed to fear the Bushman. I remember his exact words."

"The white man has weak eyes but he has binoculars. If we stay on the other side of these ridges he won't see us. The two soldiers will carry the guns and follow up wherever the Bushman leads them. The dog is useless out here for the distances we have already covered. Dogs die of heat stroke after two or three hours of running in this kind of heat. It's the Bushman we need to fear. That Bushman will track us until nightfall. If we stop, he'll catch us."

"Wasn't he worried about the blacks shooting at you with their rifles?"

"Not at all. He said they were wearing big boots and uniforms. They would wear out just like the white man and his dog. All we had to do was keep moving."

"So why didn't you both escape? What happened to Matias?"

"We went on another hour or two near the top of a ridge. When we looked back we could see that they had moved the land rover much closer. The Bushman had been able to follow us much faster than we had anticipated. It was then that I saw Matias holding his stomach. There was blood all over his fingers."

"What was wrong?"

"He said it was a piece of rock or a piece of bullet that had hit him in the lower belly. He said it didn't hurt much but he could feel his energy fading quickly. He said it was time to split up."

"I only have a small wound but I can't keep running. They will catch me this time. You must take all the pouches, except this small one of Edward's. I speak Bushman. I'll convince their man that I am the only one out here. He'll tell the white man. They'll take me away. You can keep moving and escape."

"He gave me his pouches and pointed out my path. Then he took another path that would be easy for the Bushman to follow."

Jacob watched Bakai bury his face in his hands, hiding his tears.

"I ran on and then watched to see what would happen. I saw the Bushman lead him back down a gulch toward the two soldiers. They kicked him and dragged him down the cliffs to the white man," he said, shaking his head as if to throw off a bad dream.

"They drove away to the north. We'll never see him again," his voice broke.

A sharp knock on the door interrupted any further conversation. Walter stood waiting for them as they stepped outside. The black nose of his pistol was pointed directly at Jacob.

"The girl?"

"I pushed her off a high cliff. The fall was more than fifty feet. I didn't hear any sounds afterward. If she's not already dead the hyenas will finish her. They come into the camp dump site every night. They'll catch her scent."

"Good. A truck is waiting for us at the crossroads. It will take you east. I'll give you five minutes to be ready to depart. Collect whatever you need for the funeral."

He turned toward Bakai, "I have transport arranged for you at the central lorry park. You're going to the south. You'll be hidden inside the load since you don't have travel papers. Get in the car and wait for us."

Ten minutes later, Walter stopped the car at the crossroads. As Jacob exited, Walter handed him a full pouch of diamonds.

"This pouch has the exact number of carats to purchase our new weapons. Guard it with your life. When you reach your home village, you will meet with the resident party leader. He has arranged a guide to take you to Drotsky's Cave in Botswana. The trek will take you several weeks. When you arrive, wait until the Bushmen have unloaded the smuggler's truck. Then show yourself and hand over the diamonds. Not before then. Your games have almost destroyed our unit here in Windhoek. Everything is being disbanded. Is your mission clear?"

"Yes."

"We will have people monitoring your actions all along the way. If you fail us again, you and your family will pay the ultimate price. Go now before some other tragedy strikes us." The big man turned his back in final dismissal.

Jacob climbed into the back of the truck. The box was piled high with dilapidated furniture. He managed to slide through a narrow gap and curl up on the cushion of an old couch that smelled as if it had been home to a dozen rats. The truck lurched, diesel exhaust nearly smothering him.

By early the next morning, Jacob had reached Gobabis. He visited several shops and ordered boxes of provisions and cases of beer to be sent to the village the next day. Then he walked to the lorry park and found a dilapidated bus heading north before noon.

The bus was jammed full of passengers, all seated on wooden benches. Mountains of suitcases, bags, boxes and bundles were tied onto the roof along with spare gasoline tins and wicker baskets of live chickens. Smaller items and bags were stashed in the center aisle, crammed under benches and stuffed into overhead nets. Movement was nearly impossible. Everyone was sandwiched between neighbors and baggage like so many sardines in a tin.

Jacob's single bag was crammed between his legs. As luck would have it, he managed to get on early enough to have an open window. The breeze helped carry away the ripe smells of humanity, unwashed clothing and spoiling food.

His hand reached up to caress the king's ransom of uncut diamonds hidden beneath his loosely fitting shirt. An enormous sum to be exchanged for one hundred automatic rifles and sundry other weapons in Botswana. He leaned against the window frame of the bus, closed his eyes and tried to visualize the future.

It would be almost evening when they reached his home village. If all went according to Walter's plan he would not even see his family, rather meet with the guide and start his journey to the east and Botswana almost immediately. The cases of beer and other goods would arrive with his note of condolence in time for the funeral. The members of his family would know that he had done his part and forgive his absence.

He was already the black sheep of the family. His not showing up at the funeral was to be expected. He hadn't seen any of them for almost ten years. He had been the lucky one to go off to America to study. His life was now completely divorced from their ways. They would see him as a threat, someone upsetting their harsh yet comfortable existence. At least he knew that if it came to a police investigation they would be able to truthfully deny knowledge of his whereabouts.

Even more important than the diamonds under his shirt was the small disc drive which was still on its lanyard around his neck. His could only hope that his final quick note, delivered by a friend to the blind man in Windhoek would bring some sort of response from Jim Collins in the States. The best scenario would be a welcoming party at Drotsky's Cave. Otherwise he would need to find transport to Maun and then get to the embassy in Gaborone and hope for a means of delivering his information. Destroying Petrov's plans was still a long shot.

The rocking of the bus on the sand track gradually lulled him to sleep. He needed the rest. A clear head was more important than the pistol which he had secreted in his shoulder bag. Hopefully he wouldn't need it in the days ahead.

Chapter 25
Washington D. C., September, 1990

Abe met Jim Collins with the news almost before Collins could get out of the limousine as he arrived back from the Pentagon. Abe tore the small note from his clip-board and waved it under his Jim's nose as they entered the office building.

"I think Zulu is in big trouble," he said, flourishing the scrap one more time.

"It better be important, I've got my hands full with the situation in Libya. What have you got?" Collins scowled as he took the sheet and plopped down into his squeaky armchair.

"This came in about an hour ago," Abe said. "It was followed by these," he pulled several other sheets off his pad. "One's a special embassy wire from Namibia, about our blind man. He's dead. His body was found this morning near the missionary hostel where he lived. The police discovered a US Consulate contact card in his jacket pocket and notified them. We evacuated the embassy contact out of the country in case there is an investigation. The guy didn't have diplomatic immunity.

"Somebody was obviously watching the drop spot that Zulu used." Collins brushed his hands across his brow.

"Yes, "Abe said, "It looks like a clean-up job. Petrov, or someone else is still after Zulu."

"Damn it! They've certainly been more diligent at this than I would have expected."

Collins poured himself a cup of coffee from the ever ready pot. "I'm afraid Zulu's going to have to be pulled out now, or get to Drotsky's Cave under his own steam. Get the rundown on personnel available for snatching Zulu out today."

"Got it!"

"Now, what's the next piece of news? I hope you're keeping the best for last, not the worst."

"None of it's good," Abe pulled another sheet off his clip board. "This one's a flash message. It came just a few minutes before I walked in here. Zulu's turned into a hot potato."

"Oh! Shit!" Collins looked at his assistance after perusing the message. "Zulu's injured a South African agent?"

"That's kind of what it looks like," said Abe.

"The wording isn't that succinct, but," Collins read a section aloud.

"...a policewoman working undercover in counter terrorism is reported to have fallen from a cliff at a game park outside Windhoek..."

"Yes, her name is Debbie Kotzee. I'm having our people follow up on that name right now."

"I would hope so," he continued reading aloud.

"...the game park chief steward, Jacob Nkwe, is being sought by police for further questioning in attempted murder."

"That's our man," said Abe. "It was followed by this last one directly from the South African government a few minutes later." He handed a final memo to Collins.

"... wants confirmation that Jacob Nkwe is here in the U.S. as a student still working on his Ph.D. and is not sneaking around Namibia...."

Collins took a deep breath and blew it out through pursed lips. "At least we now know one thing for sure. Zulu is not among the dead and he's got something a lot of people want very badly."

"I'd add the word 'yet' after the word 'dead' into that sentence," said Abe. "We need to get him out of there."

"Yep, he's in deep doo-doo!" Collins stood up, running his fingers over his eyes and through his silver hair. "The South African government and Petrov both want him badly. Pulling him out directly may not be an option. We need a plan to put boots on the ground somewhere to pull him out. I've got to be at the Pentagon in an hour or some big General will kick my ass about Libya, so we'll discuss this when I get back. I want options, people and a timeline by then. No excuses!" He grabbed his briefcase and was gone.

Abe's "Yes, Sir!" followed him down the hall.

Chapter 26
Namibia, September, 1990

The bus was five hours north of Gobabis when Jacob woke from a doze. He was exhausted from the travel, purchasing goods for the family funeral and a night of waiting for transport on the roadside. He rubbed his eyes as a South African Army land rover sped past the bus. It was followed by a large troop truck crammed full of soldiers, each holding their rifle and kit bag.

As the truck inched its way past, the soldiers waved and grinned. The bawdy song they were roaring out, about a young man's first sexual experiences enveloped the ears of the passengers:

"Zola! Zola! Zola, na di ke batla ama, Zola!"

Several of the inebriated riders on the bus shouted back and took up the words before the truck inched ahead. Then, they were totally engulfed by choking clouds of dust.

Before he pulled a piece of towel up over his nose and eyes, Jacob saw their uniforms. This was not a band of regular army soldiers on the move but a rag-tag bunch, wearing pieces of uniforms that might have been castoffs from another unit. Their slight stature, yellow skins, peppercorn hair and heart shaped faces along with the company insignia sewn onto the side of each man's droopy bush hat identified the unit.

"*Koevoet,*" yelled one man from the window.

Pronounced like the English word "Covert," *Koevoet*, the Afrikaans term for crowbar, was the slang name for this ragtag, elite group of hunter-killer warriors. Here were the soldiers whose mission was to get up close and dirty with the SWAPO (South West African People's Organization) guerrillas in the Caprivi Strip of northern Namibia. Their job was to literally pry the guerrillas out of South African territory and send them back to Angola. By doing so, they were creating a buffer zone between Angola and Namibia. A zone of no man's land, designed to stop the smuggling of weapons and fighters into Namibia.

Without the *Koevoet*, experts in bush warfare, Namibia would have been overrun by SWAPO guerrillas, trained and led by Cuban infiltrators. Jacob couldn't blame these men for siding with the current South African and Namibian governments. Anyone who knew Bushman history, knew that the Bushmen of southern Africa had been hunted to near extinction by their larger, darker African cousins and early white invaders. The Koevoet were only taking advantage of the best option, for the survival of their families.

As the dust subsided, Jacob unconsciously reached up and felt the pouch hidden under his loose clothing. Diamonds, would be very hard to explain away if he were ever searched and questioned. His mind raced forward to consider what lay ahead on the road in his Kalahari frontier hometown.

Given the distance and the time of day, the chance of the Koevoet soldiers stopping overnight in Tsumkwe was very good. They would do patrol duty on the road checking for illegal passengers or contraband. In fact, if the knowledge of his recent activities had been broadcast to the nation, they might very well be searching for him too. What better way to get rid of a man who had killed a South African agent? Had they traced him this quickly? Had they found the body? He couldn't chance it.

For the next two hours he watched ahead on the road. Every time the bus slowed for a passenger to board or disembark, he considered his options, stay on or get off now. It was fortunate that there were a series of undulations in a small range of hills just before his village. A roadblock became visible ahead. The time for a diversion was now or never.

He took out his cigarette lighter and flicked it open. Taking out a small stogie cigar from his pocket he made a quick attempt at lighting it. Then apparently dropping the lighter accidently, he bent down toward the floor. His hand flicked the lighter again as he reached forward under the seat of a large woman on the bench in front of him. The open flame touched some exposed papers stuffed in a box under the seat. The flame flickered for an instant and then caught. It took only seconds for the smoke to rise and reach the nostrils of several passengers. The results were instantaneous.

"Fire! Fire!" the fat lady bellowed, leaping to her feet and beating at the rising flames beneath her seat. The flames caught onto the rattan stuffing of the seat.

Holding his small bag close to his chest, Jacob jumped to his feet shouting, "Fire." He pulled the emergency cord and pushed toward the rear of the bus with its emergency door.

The bus lurched to a halt, throwing boxes from the overhead baggage nets and crushing the panicking passengers toward the front of the bus. Smoke billowed from the open windows. The evening breeze fanning the flames. Eyes watered, people coughed, panic spread. Then the doors opened and the vehicle vomited forth a mass of clawing humanity. They spilled out onto the road fanning out near the first huts of the village.

Jacob pushed hard to reach the edge of the cluster of passengers as the crowd carried him toward the roadside. They were only a few hundred yards short of the soldiers' blockade. A glance told him that several soldiers had begun to run toward the bus. Villagers appeared from the nearby huts. Black smoke belched through the open windows. The rear of the bus was completely engulfed by flames. Yellow tongues licked upward toward the spare fuel cans tied on the roof.

Running away from the rear of the bus, Jacob mingled with the gathering crowd. Realizing the imminent danger of an explosion, he shouted out.

"Get back! It's going to blow up!"

As the first of the soldiers arrived, the first five gallon container of fuel exploded, showering them all with flaming debris. A billowing mass of smoke engulfed the group as they fled.

The force of the explosion knocked Jacob to his knees. Then he was on his feet, running hard for the nearest buildings in the village. There was no reason to look back. Everyone was running for their life. His hair was singed. He heard the sound of another can exploding amid the shouts and screams of bystanders. A swirling ball of flame engulfed the bus, incinerating the injured.

Jacob slowed to a fast walk as he passed through the first rows of huts. He pulled a bit of toweling from his pack and draped it over his head. With his features concealed, he appeared like a traveler who was warding off the sun.

He dared not stop near those still seated around cook fires in the courtyards. Too many people knew him from ten years ago. A chance recognition could be fatal. The village didn't need to know he was here. He reached an outlying hut on the opposite side of the village belonging to an old school friend.

"Hey! Tau! It's me, Jacob!" he whispered loudly, knocking on the wooden frame of the curtained doorway. The surprised face of his old friend appeared from the gloom. Jacob held a finger to his lips.

"Jacob! What are you doing here? I thought you were in America!"

"Psst! Quiet!" cautioned Jacob, taking the arm of his friend and turning him back into the cool shadows of the hut.

"No one must know I'm here. There was a fire on our bus. The police are looking for me. I need to speak with the party leader immediately. He knows I'm coming."

"Was that the noise in the distance? I thought I heard an explosion."

"Yes, our bus somehow caught on fire. The gasoline cans exploded. Everything will be lost."

"Why are you here? I thought you were in America?" queried his friend a second time.

"I was but I came back and was working in Windhoek. I was coming here for the funeral of my uncle but I'm in trouble with the authorities," Jacob blurted out, still trying to regain his breath.

"What kind of trouble?" The expression on his friend's face turned serious.

"I had an affair with a white woman. An army patrol is checking transport on the road. I think they're looking for me. It's the Koevoet!"

"The Koevoet!" his friend's eyes rolled showing the whites, "You're right, you can't stay here. They come through the village all the time on the way north to fight in the Caprivi. A man accused of killing a white farmer tried to hide here last month but they searched every hut and caught him. Does anyone else know you're here?"

"No, only the party leader knows I'm coming. He has pledged to help me. He doesn't know I'm here yet."

Fine, I'll find him right now and bring him back. I won't tell anyone else. The people here are country folk. They don't keep secrets. The soldiers will start by putting a curfew on the village. Then they'll go hut to hut searching for you. Take some of my food while I'm gone. Are you sure I shouldn't tell your family?"

"No! No! Don't tell anyone especially them! Better that they don't know anything at all. The Koevoet are sure to question them. The supplies for the funeral will arrive tomorrow. It can go on as planned."

"I'm going." Tau disappeared into the growing shadows of evening.

Jacob paced the small hut. It had only one tiny window. Useless in the growing darkness. He lit a candle and searched the cupboards, finding several cans of pilchards and a loaf of bread which he stuffed into his pack. Finally, he lay down on the hard cot, shut his eyes and went to sleep.

Chapter 27:
Washington D. C., September, 1990

Collins didn't return from the Pentagon that night. The two men met the following morning at seven o'clock.

"You wouldn't believe the belt-way traffic," he puffed loudly, trying to ignite his pipe. "What have you got for me on Zulu and the situation with the policewoman?"

Abe thumbed through his stack of folders. "They've got an all-points bulletin out on him with Interpol."

"He won't be dumb enough to try to get through immigration. He'll walk into Botswana. A pickup in Namibia is out of the question. What are our options there?"

"What about a chopper in and out? We've got a unit of 'Fast Company' available in South Africa."

"No way! No military crossings of international boundaries, not even into Botswana. We'd have to tell both the South Africans and the Botswanans. The secret police would be on it like ticks on a hog and Botswana's security is a sieve. It would be a death sentence. We won't know where he is until he reaches Drotsky's Cave. He's on his own for the next twenty days."

"Not even an Entebbe type strike with weapons hot in twenty days? No permission, just do it? It would make an international stink but like the Israelis, once you're back on home territory it's a *fait accompli*."

"No way! We're already drowning in FUBAR with those kind of missions."

"What about using a small mercenary unit like some of the old Rhodesian Selous Scouts? They know the territory and have the right contacts."

"They've ended up on the dark side too often for my liking. Too eager to shoot up a bunch of people. This has got to be very low key."

"Then we need to put a couple of our locals on the ground," said Abe.

"Exactly," replied Jim, puffing rapidly on his pipe. "Our friend Petrov will have to do it the same way. Nobody in the proper South African government would give him the time of day. He'll have to go in on the ground just like us. We just have to hope we make contact first."

"I kind of thought you'd say that." Abe pulled out several files. "The pickings are kind of slim out there, but we do have a couple of people. It's not going to be complete amateur hour."

"Hit me."

"Sue Ferrell, Ph.D. candidate in anthropology and linguistics, University of Iowa, linked to Western Cape University in South Africa. She's been a regular with us for nearly five years. Thoroughly field trained, top of her class. She's living in Maun, been all over the Kalahari and Okavango. She speaks Tswana, Afrikaans and more of the Khoisan Bushman dialect than any white person on the planet. The downside is that she's always worked in a reserve status."

"Hmm," Collins flipped through the file, "That means no wet ops or hot LZ experience.... This could be easy or go hot really fast." He tapped her codes into his computer, pulling her full profile up on this screen.

"Yes," he continued, "I like her location, preparation, languages, local knowledge and the fact that she's never been active enough to pop up on Petrov's screen. That could give us the advantage of surprise. Who else have you got?"

"The other guy is freelance," replied Abe, handing over the second file.

"Jacques Anjou?" Collins stared at the file. "I heard that surname years ago. French?"

"White African born and raised in the old Belgian Congo. Parents were French, his father was Foreign Legion. A hero at the battle of Dien Bien Phu in Vietnam. He also worked with a guy you'll remember, 'Mad' Mike Hoar.

"I remember Mike Hoar well, Collins' nodded his head. "He was one of our own during the war between Mobutu and Patrice Lumumba for the control of the Belgian Congo. So, what about the son, Jacques?"

"Well, it looks like the fruit didn't fall far from the tree," replied Abe. "He's an adventurer, lived all his life in every country between the Cape and Congo. He's got excellent native language skills for those areas along with French and Afrikaans. He's experienced in having to go hot when a couple of ops became SNAFUs. I'd say he knows it all."

"Is he a team player?"

"There are some downsides. He's a seat of the pants man. If it gets sticky he may ditch our plans and go it alone. Not that independence is all that bad on this kind of an op."

"I like guys who think on their feet. We can live with that. What else?"

"He's done mercenary work in a number of African countries. That means he'll be somewhere on Petrov's radar."

"How long ago?"

"At least fifteen years ago when we were working the Zimbabwe/Rhodesia conflict."

"Nothing since then?"

Watching Abe's negative head shake, he continued, "So he'll be a low profile man for Petrov unless Russia's computer data system is a lot better than ours. Where is he right now?"

"He works as a game collector out of Francistown. Shouldn't be hard to dig up."

"Excellent," Collins placed the pipe to one side and blew a final smoke ring. "Jacques becomes the point man, Sue is his backup and liaison with you as control. The West Cameroonians would say:

Jam pas die, mongi chop pepe, call-um se Njakatu."

"As in?" Abe smiled, while gathering his folders.

"Essentially, that we're up against the wall and have to live with it. Literally it translates as: In a situation worse than death a monkey will eat red hot peppers and call them sweet garden eggs."

"Oh, jeez, here we go," Abe slapped his forehead. "Go on, what's a sweet garden egg?"

"Kind of like a green tomato. West Africans use them for food and monkeys love to steal them."

"Enough!" laughed Abe. "If I'm going to be control, I better get moving on this. It doesn't sound like we have a lot of time."

"You're it! I've got my hands tied up with the Libya/Chad thing. You've worked Southern Africa before. I'll pull the file on Petrov and his SIRIUS unit. I see Petrov's signature all over that Botswana incident six months ago and now the recent police shootings in South Africa. We have to shut him down, fast."

"Why isn't this front page stuff?"

"It's a matter of top government priorities. The Libya stuff has occupied us for months. Maybe the French will finally step in. With Africa south of the Sahara, everyone just shrugs their shoulders. They just say it's the way things are in Africa: tribalism, cannibalism, witchcraft, genocide and horrible diseases. Bad stuff rules. Better to leave well enough alone."

"So this is bigger than the mining interests in Zaire and Angola that come out of the front pages but still get swept under the rug? "

"Yep, it's certainly bigger. We're all doing future thinking about world mineral and water resources. The only solution to world over population seems to be the control of the world's resources. Everyone's going after the oil, rare earths, copper and uranium."

"So it's not really about winning hearts and minds? A bit simplistic isn't it?" Abe's voice was skeptical.

"The thinking in our country doesn't seem to be to cooperate and share. It's the idea that we need to control it now or we'll have to take it by force in the future," continued Collins. "The mineral wealth of Africa may well determine the rise or fall of nations including our own. We always thought we had a lot of African influence so we've just shoved them off. Now Russia, India and China are sneaking in the back door."

"Trouble!"

"Right. We continue to ignore the fact that KGB subversion didn't die out with the Soviet Union's collapse. Russia still has some very experienced old KGB operatives in the field."

"What's their mission?" Abe sat down again.

"Same as ours," replied his superior, "get control of the African governments having the strategic wealth, namely South Africa, Zaire and Namibia."

"Domino Theory all over again?"

"More like African Chess. You want to control six or seven key countries. If you have the uranium of Niger, the oil of Nigeria, the copper in Zaire and the industrial/mineral/agricultural wealth of South Africa, Namibia and Zimbabwe, it's checkmate. You can dictate prices and strategic resources to everyone else."

"Is that really Petrov's game?"

"That's exactly what Section One, Russian Infiltration and Unconventional Sabotage does. It's been a priority mission to destabilize Africa for years."

"Has it worked?"

"Sure. In exchange for developmental money the country gives Russia a 'quid pro quo' in trade. If we aren't careful they may beat us at our own game of capitalism."

"What about South Africa? They're semi-democratic and reasonably well developed. How do they fall into this picture?"

Collins smiled, "The country has multiple antagonistic tribes. They have learned to cooperate under a very repressive government. If they can transition to black majority rule, then it will go smoothly. If not, then the shit hits the fan."

"So Petrov want to re-open the old wounds. Antagonize the black, white and colored tribes in South Africa so they go at each other's throats again."

"Exactly! Psychologists say that we revert to our old habits when under stress. SIRIUS is pushing all the buttons to bring back that intertribal stress. When that happens, the Zulu, Xhosa, Sotho, Tswana and Swazi peoples will all lapse right back into their old hatreds. The outcome will be chaos and killing. Petrov and the rigid old guard apartheid movement will be ready to take total control. Look at Zimbabwe.

"How so?"

"Well, the white tribe pretty much antagonized everyone until they got run out. Then the two major tribes, the Ndebele and Shona peoples, went for each other's throats. That let a dictator take control. He talks to anyone paying big bribes. That's how you take control of the mineral resources."

"So Petrov doesn't want to run the country?"

"No, that's old school communist thinking. Who wants to run a failed nation? Suck what resources you can out of the country and leave the dry shell for the people who live there to worry about. That's where Zimbabwe is headed in a few more years."

"So South Africa is next?"

"Right! The wealthiest best developed economy in all of Africa. Touch the match internally and the place goes up in flames. Petrov's people are in high places and they move in to make the deals that will control the violence and bring profit to the Russians rather than the west."

Abe poured the last dregs of coffee into his mug. "Looks like we have underestimated Petrov."

"Damned right we have!" Replied his superior. "We're about to lose the ball of wax."

"You act like you've seen this scenario before."

"I have." Jim Collins gave a harsh laugh. He leaned forward, his face twisted by a rictus of rage and anger.

"I've chased Petrov as long as I've been in intelligence. Every four years our country throws out any long term foreign intelligence strategies for a new set of monkey bars set up by our lame brain politicians rather than professionals. We blink while Petrov's focus doesn't waver. That's how it's been for at least thirty years. Petrov was on the scene when Nikita Khrushchev pounded his shoe on the podium and shouted "We will bury you!"

"But he didn't."

"No, he didn't. Russia doesn't want to build a Marxist empire in Africa any more. Petrov's role in this always reminds me of that movie, 'The Terminator.' He won't go away, he just keeps coming. The only way to stop him is to kill him. If we don't do it now, he or his successor will be back, out here on the veldt, licking their chops, waiting for us to make our next big African blunder."

"Sounds like a very scary man."

Collins' face became deadly serious, "Mark my words, Abe. If Petrov stays in the South African theater much longer, we'll see more blood-letting on the high veldt than we've seen in Africa since the *impis* of Chaka the Zulu washed their spears in white man's blood."

"You make it sound almost personal," stated Abe.

For a long moment the eyes of his superior gleamed again like hard chips of ice blue flint. He slowly unbuttoned the cuff of his left sleeve and rolled up the material to reveal a massive network of scar tissue.

"It is," he replied flatly, "I cut my teeth in Biafra back in the 60's. The man's a cancer. We have to eradicate that cancer once and for all. Right now Zulu is our only hope. Better get on with it!"

He spun on his chair, took a pull on the now dead pipe and began jotting notes as Abe headed down the hall.

Chapter 28:

Eastern Namibia, September, 1990

Jacob woke with a start! In was pitch black inside the hut. A whisper of footsteps padded across the packed earth courtyard. He twisted to one side, pulling his pistol and sat up, weapon hand concealed beneath his bag. Night was falling. Two shadowy figures appeared in the doorway.

"It's me, I've brought our party leader, Letebele," whispered Tau. "He was expecting you."

"Good," Jacob said.

"Yes," replied the tall thin man. "Shanika sent us a message just after your uncle's sudden death. He told us to assist you in your journey. We need to leave right now," his voice was urgent, "The Koevoet have already started searching the village nearest the road."

"Let's go," replied Jacob, dropping his pistol into his bag and standing. "If they catch me I'm a dead man."

Turning to Tau he said, "If anyone asks, you can tell them you got a note saying I couldn't make it to the funeral."

"I'll do that," replied his friend. "Now I must get back. They've called a meeting in the town hall."

"I understand you need a guide to take you across the border into Botswana," said Letebele, leading him from the hut by the hand. "I have a contact with local Bushmen who migrate across the border every year. The man's name is Quobo. He will meet you near the big Baobab tree on the east side of the village. Do you know the tree?"

"Yes. Are they looking for me?"

"Yes, they came earlier this afternoon and asked about your uncle's funeral. We told them it would occur as soon as all the relatives had been able to arrive. They only said they were looking for a man who would come from Windhoek. I take it your family doesn't know you were there?"

"That's correct. It's best not to tell anyone. They haven't seen me for almost ten years."

"Fine, Tau and I can keep a secret. You don't want them to catch you." Letebele was walking quickly. The huts became more spaced out as they reached the edge of the village.

"Here's the path to the tree."

"I know it. Thank you for your kindness. You should have someone drive a herd of goats along the path. The Koevoet are good trackers. I wouldn't want them to connect me to you, here in the village."

"Yes, I'll have Quobo do that with his children. I must leave you now. When you reach the Baobab, wait for a small boy. He will take you on from there."

"I'm sorry that I can't pay you for the trouble I've caused."

"There is no payment for what we do in this war of liberation," replied Letebele. "It is our mission." Then he was gone in the gathering darkness, rushing back toward the center of the village.

Jacob jogged down the path for a mile until the shadowy fingers of the giant tree could be seen stretching into the starry nighttime sky. He sat down at its base leaning back against the smooth gray bark, waiting.

The stars glistened in the unpolluted sky. Soft shuffling sounds of footsteps and the bleats of goats could be heard approaching. Jacob watched the trail leading back toward the village. A moment later he made out the figure of a small boy followed by ten goats and the slightly taller figure of a girl. The boy leaned down and whispered.

"I am here to take you to Quobo's village."

Jacob shouldered his knapsack and followed the boy. The girl went on towards the village driving her goats.

"She will come back this way with the goats after she takes them to water, said the boy. That way all your tracks will be covered."

They walked rapidly for an hour through the maze of paths. A woven stick fence appeared with a small hut and large thorn bush surround it to protect the goats. A man came out to greet them.

"I am Quobo," he said, "come, there is a small shelter at the back of the goat kraal," he pointed. "Crawl in there and rest. You will be safe for a few hours. When the goats come back we'll go with them to the bushman village."

The smell of goat dung was everywhere inside the shelter. Jacob pushed any fresh droppings out of the way and smoothed a place to lie down. Surrounded by the soft bleats of the goats and occasional rustles in the night, Jacob relaxed and slept. Quobo woke him from deep slumber with the first signs of the false dawn.

"We must go now, my friend," he said. "I must be back by noon. The Koevoet are checking every family. I need to be home with my family and goats. I will leave you at a small Bushman settlement. They will guide you. The Koevoet won't bother their own people."

The trip took over two hours of rapid walking through the maze of paths. Quobo led the way. Jacob was followed closely by the goats being driven by the two children.

The small, dome shaped grass huts of the settlement blended with the acacia thorn trees. Most people would have walked through the center of this ephemeral outpost of humanity without seeing more than one or two of the twenty huts. In a month's time the clan would move on. Their lives are dictated by the seasons of the Kalahari. They crossed international borders with impunity, retracing a cycle of life as old as humanity itself.

Quobo crawled through the low oval door of one of the huts and whispered softly to the occupants. A wrinkled man, perhaps thirty-five years of age appeared. His yellow skin was creased and weathered from the sun. He stood in front of Jacob, smiling shyly.

"This is X!eo," whispered Quobo, his tongue making one of the many popping Bushman 'X' click sounds, made with the middle of his tongue on the roof of his mouth. "He has family on the other side of the border with Botswana. He knows the way to Drotsky's cave. The trip to the cave will take you about fifteen days. He's done this before. You will be safe with him. He will bring you back after the weapons exchange."

"When do we start?" asked Jacob, knowing full well, as he spoke, that he had no intention of returning to Namibia.

Quobo smiled. "In about ten minutes. He needs to collect his spear and bow. Then he will make arrangements to meet the rest of the clan somewhere along the migration route."

"I wish my life were that uncomplicated," observed Jacob.

"We all have to bear life's burdens," replied Quobo. "I will leave you now. I have to get back. I don't want the Koevoet to question my absence."

"Tsamaya sentle, Rra," "Walk Easy," Jacob said as the man turned on his heel and disappeared into the brush. His children followed, the goats wiping out all traces of their passage.

X!eo was ready within minutes. He wore a leather loin cloth, and had a leather bag of corn meal and biltong slung over one shoulder. His short bow and tree's bark quiver were held across his back with a rawhide thong. A thin blanket was pinned over the other shoulder with a sharp pointed bone needle. His equipment was complete when at last he slung the two liter plastic water bottle around his neck and picked up his razor sharp metal pointed spear.

He motioned for Jacob to follow. The two set off down a goat path trailed by several members of his extended family. The family tagged behind for nearly an hour as they followed game trails through the acacia thorn bushes. They shuffled their feet along the path, occasionally selecting a piece of firewood to drag in order to wipe away Jacob's larger, heavier foot prints.

When the last of them had disappeared, Jacob felt a great weight lifted from his mind. They were gone, he was free and the rhythm of the walk was beginning to feel good. A slight breeze in the fresh morning air and the occasional surprised 'huff' of a small antelope were the only disturbances.

They covered ground rapidly. Like a homing pigeon, X!eo always seemed to know exactly where they were. His Tswana was passable so Jacob was able to ask questions about their route. As the day went on, X!eo pointed out the remnants of vines showing where tubers could be dug from the ground. In other places, near the withered leaves of dead vines, lay tsama melons. Some were partially eaten, others whole. These relatives of the gourd family were the mainstay for thirsty antelope, humans, tortoises and even lions in this waterless expanse of desert.

X!eo laughed when Jacob repeatedly asked him to repeat the names of several of the plants or got their Bushman names mixed up.

"Even my youngest children know the names and uses of these plants," he said. "A child needs to know how to survive here at a very early age. What would you do if you got lost?" Both men knew the unspoken answer to that rhetorical question posed to the city dweller.

After a while they only spoke when X!eo pointed out particular trees or rock outcroppings of significance. Then he would relate a story about the place, something that had occurred recently or several generations previously. The concept of time seemed to be immaterial in the story. The reference to a lion, a snake bite, bush fire or other event was important simply to cement the location of the site into the listener's mental map of the Kalahari.

Halfway through the second day, X!eo pointed to a large Baobab tree. He led Jacob to it and pointed near the base to two stones. Kneeling down, he dug with both hands to reveal a cache of ostrich eggs filled with cool sweet water. When Jacob asked about the location of the water used to fill the eggs, the Bushman explained that Baobabs mark areas where the water table rises during the rainy season. The empty shells were always refilled by whomever came through the area during the rains. Thus the cache would always be there for those needing it in an emergency.

That night they slept under a thorn bush with a covering of thin blankets, using cut grass as insulation from the almost freezing temperatures of night. In the morning they rose, washed down several slices of bread that Jacob still had in his pack and then continued the journey while chewing on a leathery piece of dried kudu biltong.

Near the end of the third day X!eo suddenly vanished.

Jacob had moved off the trail for a few moments to relieve himself. His guide was squatting near a rock searching for edible grubs. When he returned, X!eo was gone. It was no use shouting in this vast wilderness. If a Bushman wanted to disappear, his reasons would become known soon enough. Jacob picked out a shady thorn bush, sat beneath it and waited.

His wait lasted only a few minutes. A twig snapped back along their trail. Moments later three small yellow men, each wearing floppy campaign hats and tattered remnants of castoff uniforms came into view. Each carried his rifle at the ready. They fanned out into the brush the moment they detected that Jacob and his guide had separated.

Jacob sat quietly, knowing that it would be fatal to attempt any kind of escape. When he saw that their keen eyes had detected him, he raised his hands in surrender and allowed them to prod him upright and into the open.

"What are you doing out here?" the Koevoet corporal demanded, jerking his rifle barrel toward Jacob for emphasis.

"I have been searching for some of my cattle which strayed away from our cattle post, Jacob replied without hesitation. "It's some miles south of here,"

"Don't lie to me," came the immediate response, "we have been tracking you now for almost two days." The man's voice was harsh, "We know you came from the west. Where is the other man?" Again the rifle barrel jerked close to Jacob's face.

"He's a Bushman. He disappeared just over there," replied Jacob, pointing, recognizing the futility of lying to these rough men. They only needed one small excuse to leave his body for the hyenas in this desolate section of the desert.

One of the men walked over to the spot and cast about briefly, checking the tracks and rolled stones.

"He's gone," he stated on his return. "He was hunting for grubs. It's one of our people. We have nothing to fear."

"Good," replied the leader, prodding Jacob in the ribs with his barrel. "You come with us. There's a good place to camp about an hour's walk back. Tomorrow we can do a long march and join the others. A white policeman wants to talk to you."

An hour later, they carefully tied Jacob to a tree near a small baobab. One man lit a small fire. The other strolled off into the bush. A few minutes later there was a single shot from his rifle. He returned half an hour later carrying a small steenbok. They sliced up the liver, eating pieces of it raw and then sliced off pieces of meat.   Soon whiffs of the roasting meat wafted throughout the woods. Jacob felt his stomach growl with hunger pangs.

The three searched his pack, dividing up the remaining food. They squabbled about the two pieces of clothing in his bag, all the while keeping up an unintelligible chatter in their native click language. Jacob's pistol went into the leader's pack while the other two each got his clothing. They removed the pouch containing the mini-computer disc, and the bag of diamonds from around his neck. They laughed when Jacob protested that the shining disc was a very special keep sake. The leader replaced it in the padded pouch and put in his pocket. The other man whistled aloud when the first of the diamonds tipped from the bag into the palm of his hand.

"We'll look after all of these very carefully, my friend," said the leader. "The white man will want to know all about them. I don't think you will be needing any of these where you will be going," They all laughed again.

The leader chopped the meat into four chunks and freed one of Jacob's hands, allowing him to gnaw on the juicy roast meat. With his stomach now full, Jacob sat with his back to the tree and tried to sleep. He felt as if his world was once again falling apart. The clear starry night was terrifically cold. They refused to allow him any shelter, so he curled near the trunk of the tree beneath his thin blanket. Sleep came and went as he squirmed fitfully in the sand.

By morning his legs were cramped from the cold. He could hardly stand after the immobility of the night. The small men pushed and shoved him, in a rough manner, anticipating the interrogation, once they were back in the village.

They moved at a fast pace and were soon approaching the lone giant baobab tree where the water had been stored. A small tent was pitched in the opening under the tree. The men dropped their equipment near it, obviously having pitched it with the idea of returning this way.

Jacob sank into deep depression. It was now less than a day's march to the village. The branches of the baobab pointed their fingers to the sky like witches hands stretching above the swollen caricature of a bloated body. The three men tied his hands to a thorn bush then to his surprise fanned out beneath the giant tree, collecting the edible seeds for a later meal.

Jacob sat and waited. He could see there would be no opportunity for escape. He gazed into the surrounding forest. His eyes picking up a slight movement beyond the Baobab tree. He rubbed his hands over his face momentarily, peering through spread fingers into the deep shadows. The figure of a camouflaged man was apparent, leaning motionless across a fallen snag. Jacob looked quickly away. None of the soldiers had seen anything.

The man's automatic rifle was resting at a slant, thus blending into the brush and dead branches of the tree. Jacob could see that it would not be impeded in lateral or vertical movement by any surrounding brush. It was perfect cover for a killing zone around the area of the tent.

One of the Koevoet soldiers suddenly jerked his head upright turning to look with surprise directly at the figure of the man. His mouth began to open in alarm. Jacob saw the barrel of the rifle swing slightly. A shot rang out, shattering the tranquility of the desert evening.

The report of the rifle coincided with the explosion of the back of the man's head. The other two soldiers had no chance to mark their executioner. One man attempted to take cover by falling flat at the sound of the first shot, but he had no cover, and died as he attempted to rise and make a dash from the clearing. The other was still squatting with a baobab seed pod in his hands when a bullet took him in the chest. The bodies twisted in momentary agony, and then lay still. The executioner stepped from his concealment, the fading light illuminating his painted black face.

"Walter!" gasped Jacob is recognition of Shanika's security man from Windhoek. "How did you get here?"

"We thought you would be in trouble," a smile creased the ugly face of the huge black man. "Shanika sent me," he said. "The girl didn't die after her fall. It's not your fault, just damned bad luck that she lit in a thorn bush. The paper said she fell a hundred feet. She's in hospital, badly broken up, but well enough to tell the police all about you. We're lucky they brought you back to this spot where I could do something." He stepped forward and slashed the cords holding Jacob's wrists.

"You followed us?"

"Yes. I arrived at the village and there was a burned out bus by the side of the road. I had proper papers which was very fortunate. The patrol was checking everyone. When I asked what happened, the soldiers told me the Koevoet were searching the village looking for a tall man from Windhoek. They said he had tried to kill a policewoman by pushing her off a cliff. I knew it was you. I then went to the party leader. He took me to his man, Quobo. By then the Koevoet patrol had already gone after you. I followed their trail. When I saw the tent here at the Baobab, I decided on waiting in ambush. At least I would be able to recover the diamonds. Do you still have them?"

"They're inside the packs over by the tent. The soldiers divided up all my things. They figured I wasn't going to survive once I got back to the village."

"They were right. We need to take what we can carry and get away from here quickly. We can't risk them following you again."

"The hyenas will take care of the bodies but the vultures will be around for several days. It won't take long for the Koevoet to find their remains. What do you want to do?"

I'll stay here and bury anything we can't carry. I'll put the bodies and any food on top of the caches. The hyenas will destroy any evidence of burial. I will cover your trail and lay a false one in another direction. I'm armed well enough to defend myself against anything but a large group. I don't think they'll come past this point once they see the bodies. I'll come back here with my men in a month and possibly save the weapons."

"I'll get my things," said Jacob, already rummaging in the packs. He retrieved the diamonds, disc and his pistol. Taking as much food and water as he could carry, he stuffed everything into one of the military ruck sacks.

Walter collected a small pile of items for his own pack and then began scraping a hole with a trenching tool carried by one of the dead men. "I already have the villagers organizing a cattle drive out this way tomorrow. If the men aren't missed by then, a hundred cattle will walk through this area to graze all along your route. That won't cover the bodies but it will destroy your trail. Not even a Bushman will be able to follow you. Take one of the rifles. It may come in handy in the next week or so."

"The extra weight will just slow me down."

"Perhaps a bit, but I've been on the run in this part of the Kalahari before. That pistol won't faze a pride of desert lions. At least a rifle will give you a shot from a distance. The twenty shots might just pull you out of a very sticky situation."

"Thanks, but I'll stick with my man X!eo. He's got this whole trip figured out." Jacob held out his hand. "I owe you one." The big man picked up the second rifle and slung it over his shoulder.

"Just make sure those diamonds get where they're supposed to go," replied Walter, gripping his hand firmly. "I don't want to have to spend a year tracking you down." He turned back toward the hole and began widening it to bury the gear.

Jacob set off to the east. He'd gone no more than a hundred yards before the withered form of X!eo stepped from behind a tree.

"I was following you," he said. "I had a feeling you would escape."

"Damned lucky for Zulu's mission that I did," replied Jacob, knowing that there had been very little that the small man with his bow and spear could have done under the circumstances. He felt secure with the miniature disc and leather pouch of diamonds bouncing gently under his shirt. With renewed vigor, fed by the fear of being hunted again, he turned east following the Bushman toward the Botswana border, the Aha Hills and Drotsky's Cave.

Chapter 29:

Francistown, Botswana, September, 1990

The dusty, calf-high desert boots made almost no sound as Jacques Anjou strode in long smooth strides down the central mall of Francistown. His lean, sharp featured, hawk nosed face was partially shaded by the tan safari hat pulled down over his shock of tawny hair. The large hands, running smoothly into whipcord muscle on lanky arms and shoulders, told even the most casual of observers that this man was no stranger to hard work. The lion yellow tinge to his eyes was so striking it could freeze a man or woman on the spot much like a mamba's stare freezes its potential victim. The sheaf of papers and the bank ledger under one arm and the battered leather brief case appeared oddly out of place next to his rugged features.

It was these accoutrements that lent plausibility to his destination, Barclay's Bank Ltd. He entered the door, stepping out of the glare of the sun into the cool air conditioned office and waited while the office clerk rang for the manager.

"Jacques, good to see you back, man," the balding, black suited older gentleman said as he came out of his office. "Come in, come in, we need to have a good chat about business." He led the way back into his office assuming his customary position behind the huge hardwood desk dominating the room.

Jacques closed the door and took the hard backed chair facing the desk. He placed his papers on the mirror polished surface. A thin smile split his dusky visage as he looked into the blue eyes across the desk.

"Ben, it's good to see you again. I hope we can have a cold beer in the hotel one of these days. I've just gotten in from a twenty-one day stint with one of my best clients. I drove all the way in from Maun. Seven hours of eating dust. This is the worst drought since I began hunting and collecting animals. The elephants have dug holes down almost ten feet into river beds that would normally be full of water this time of year."

"I agree, it's the worst I've seen since my people trekked here from Serowe by ox cart and wagon back in the 20's," replied the banker. "Even the Bushmen are coming into the cattle posts and begging for food and water. I was up at Totume the other day to check with my branch manager. They've had to dig a hole twenty feet deep in the river bed to find good water for the town. Hardly enough for the people. You can forget the cattle, they're all dying like flies."

"It's the same in Maun. People are shooting their cattle and making biltong rather than let them die and rot. They've only had three inches of rain in almost two years. I saw children at the few remaining mud holes spearing the last of the trapped fish. The swamp was so low, I had to go clear up to the top of the Chitabe concession near Moremi to find an elephant for my client. If it keeps up past November, none of the hunters will be in business. The place will blow away in the wind."

"I take it you've come to see me about that possibility," the pale eyes of the banker took on a slightly harder look.

"Yes, I'll make a deposit for part of what I owe you, from my safari bonus, but I'll still need another overdraft until the end of the next trip."

"Hmm," the old man frowned and leaned forward in his chair, "let me see your order book and ledgers."

Jacques spread out the papers and opened his ledger book for the banker's keen eyes to scan. "There's one ray of hope on the horizon this month. I just got word of a special order from a client in the States. He's coming in today. Wants me to do a big collecting project. I'll pick him up at the airport and drive him to Maun this afternoon. His commission will be a sizeable bit of cash and a bonus upon completion."

"Well, your books aren't much to look at. Not much to go on for an advance."

"No, Ben, I realize that. Times are pretty rough for all of us right now."

"Have you got anything from this new client? I need to have some idea of what it might bring in?"

Jacques fished in his shirt pocket and brought out an envelope. "This is confidential, Ben. Not a word can leak out. This just came to me by special delivery from the U. S. Embassy."

"You're not going after more rhino and ivory smugglers are you?" The banker's eyes widened slightly. "Dangerous business."

"No, this is bigger. I'm helping him find a very special man. That's about all I know at the moment but you can see the deposit that's going into my Jo'burg account. It will take a few weeks to clear but it will put me back on my feet."

"Whoa!" Ben whistled lowly, "This is an enormous sum, Jacques. Governments don't make down payments like that for playing Tiddly Winks in the Kalahari. You better be very careful."

"I'm not a spring chicken, Ben," nodded Jacques, "This is an extremely important mission for the United States government. It's not just some little jaunt in the bush."

"Enough!" The banker held a finger to his lips, saying softly. "The walls have ears."

Jacques nodded.

"How much do you need to see you through to the rainy season or whenever this bonus from Washington comes through?"

"Let me have an overdraft for about fifty thousand Pula, with an extension on my current loan. Can you make the due date January?"

"If we haven't seen the cash or the Maru a Pula by then I'll bankrupt you," replied the banker. "I'll give you until the end of December. That makes my book keeping easier."

He pulled a giant bank ledger book, two feet wide and eighteen inches high out from under the top of the desk. His black pen neatly inscribed the terms and amounts in the columns. He turned the book. "There you are, sign on the dotted line," his finger pointed. "Old banking methods for old people."

Jacques scrawled his signature with a flourish. "All the computers in the world aren't any better than speaking to a man directly to discern his honesty. You can bet I'll have your money. That's a promise." He extended his hand.

The banker gave a wry smile as he grasped Jacques' hand. "We old timers have to hang together. The young bloods down in the Cape are just waiting to show an old man how to run things."

"My assistant, Grobler, will be helping on this trip. Keep this embassy stuff under your hat. He doesn't need to know."

"No problem."

"I'll be seeing you, Ben," Jacques collected his papers.

"Take care my friend."

The spring was back in Jacques' step as he went through the door and headed toward the battered brown land rover with his "Africa Game Collecting" logo on the door. Across the boulevard, he saw a passenger train pull into the station. It was full of obnoxious white school boys headed home for mid-term break. They leaned out the windows to buy sweets, bread and trinkets from the local ladies hawking their wares on the platform.

An argument broke out between one of the boys and an old woman who felt she had not been properly paid. Insults began flying in Afrikaans, English and Tswana. A stone flew breaking one of the train windows. The sliding protective wooden shutters went up in a flash, covering the windows. The conductors ran down the platform, shooing everyone back from the wheels as the train pulled out of the station. The whistle blew, answered by shouts from several of the women as it disappeared toward South Africa.

He stopped to talk to one of the Indian businessmen walking along the sidewalk. "Did you see that? It's a good thing they don't let those kids out of the trains. We could end up with a bloody riot in seconds."

"It's not good at all," replied the Indian, sadly. "You begin to understand why the blacks over there," he waved his hand toward the East, "aren't taking that guff any longer."

"The Tswana don't like that attitude brought here either," commented Jacques.

"Did you hear about the riots in the shopping mall in Johannesburg the other day?" inquired the Indian.

"Yes, I don't think the situation can go on much longer. It's bound to blow up one of these days. Hopefully it won't cause problems here."

"I lived under the Apartheid system, first in Rhodesia and then South Africa," the Indian man replied. "I'd never take my family back. Our president here is a great leader, much like his father, Seretse Khama. Sometimes I think we have it better here than in the States." With that he turned and disappeared into the cool darkness of his small clothing store.

Jacques was just about to open his land rover door and climb in when he saw a familiar Toyota Land Cruiser parked near the rear of Haskin's hardware. The back was loaded with tins, sacks of flour and a variety of staples. Jacques sauntered over. Professional hunter, Eric Ridge emerged from the store carrying a case of number four shotgun shells.

"Jacques! What are you up to man?" Eric's voice rang out. He stowed the shells behind the seat. His vice grip handshake met equal strength from Jacques. His short cropped reddish hair, a sharp contrast to Jacques' tawny coloring. He loaded the final cargo on the roof of the vehicle and secured it with bungee cords and a rope.

"How's the hunting?" queried Jacques.

"This last hunt was a bust," Eric lamented. "The guy couldn't hit the broad side of a barn. He shot up half the Kalahari, wounding three of his animals. I had to follow up and shoot them to clear his tag. He had the audacity near the end of the safari to ask me to take him out again next year. I told him where to bloody well get off. No big tip from that one. How about you?"

"Oh, I've had a couple small safaris. I just got a big order for animals that should keep me out in the field for a month or more."

"Did you get your elephant for the last client?"

"Yup, way up in the Chitabe area. A decent sized bull." Jacques chopped the edge of his left hand into the side of his upper right arm showing the length of the exposed ivory. "The tusks were about twenty kilos a side. A pretty respectable trophy considering what's been done to elephants with all the poaching."

"Great work. I hear they're going to cut back on the hunting some more next year."

"Eco-tourism is going to be the name of the game, my friend," replied Jacques.

"It'll be good for the animals. Our guiding business certainly won't suffer, but I'll miss the chase," lamented Eric.

"We all get over it," replied Jacques. "I'm going to cut out the hunting safari work and start my own eco-tours. It's the future. I'd love to see the numbers of animals we had in this country when I first came."

"Agreed," Eric smiled, giving a final tug on a rope holding the roof rack tarp. "I'm headed back to Maun tonight. Next trip goes out in a couple of days. A twenty-one day safari. Rich dentist."

"Just like the old days. Not many can afford that level of expense any more. Hope it's a good one. I'll see you in Maun when you get back," he turned to go.

"It will be. This guy has been here before," Eric held out his hand for a final shake.

Jacques strode off to his land rover and headed back toward the office. There was still plenty of time to get things ready before meeting his client's plane.

Chapter 30:

Francistown, Botswana, September, 1990

"Got a good trip coming up, Grobler!" Jacques called out as he entered the large warehouse filled with nets, snares, traps and other collecting equipment.

Horst Grobler stepped out of the back of the shed and came to the front of the building. His giant body dwarfed that of Jacques, although the two men were the same height. "What's up?"

"I have a special fellow coming in from a museum in the US this afternoon. The preliminary letter indicates it will take us all over the country."

"About time we had another big client," replied Grobler. "I was beginning to think we were going to have to close down."

"I think this will put us back on our feet until the end of the year anyway," replied Jacques locking the embassy letter away in his safe. "I'll take our man over to the hotel this evening and get the details but we're probably going to split up on this trip and take different sets of animals in order to get the full order done. I'll let you know tomorrow once I've made up the lists. Better check out the truck. I think we'll need it."

"Good, I'm tired of banging around in that tiny Toyota pick-up." Grobler disappeared into the back of the warehouse.

Jacques shut the door to his office, locked it and spun the dial on his gun safe. Pushing aside the rack holding his usual set of rifles, he pulled out a khaki backpack, an Uzi submachinegun and assorted pieces of military paraphernalia. He cleaned the Uzi, oiled the magazine and loaded it. Then he spent the rest of the afternoon making lists, sorting gear and collecting equipment getting ready for whatever his new client might be proposing.

It was nearly evening. Giant cumulus clouds that foretold the coming of the rainy season were building in the east over the Matopos Hills of Zimbabwe. Flashes of distant lightning illuminated the gradually darkening sky. Faint rolls of thunder could be heard in the distance. The rainy season for the central Kalahari was still several weeks to a month away but it finally was looking as if the gods of the desert would bring the *Maru a Pula*.

Jacques met Abe as he stepped off the plane from Gaborone. The differences between the two men were so striking that observers stared as the tall, lean, tanned hunter helped the short, pale and apparently rotund tourist collect his luggage. Other than a handshake and greeting, they exchanged almost no words until they reached the land rover in the parking lot.

"I don't think we've met before on other assignments," stated Jacques as they reached the land rover. He was mildly surprised by the hardness of the small man's grip and his attentive appraisal of everything as they set off.

"No but you've worked distantly for my boss, Jim Collins," replied Abe, tossing his bags into the land rover. "I've been in a lot of Africa, never here to Francistown or the Okavango Delta. It's a new experience but the same system." Abe's head was turned slightly toward Jacques, his eyes constantly roving, taking in the route and noting key features as they sped toward Francistown.

"I've got you booked into the Grand Hotel for the night," replied Jacques. "It's got great food and an air conditioned portion of the bar and dining room in case you find the temperatures too hot."

"Ha!" laughed Abe. "The temperatures are just fine here. Washington is sweltering under a heat wave with high humidity. Hitting this dry desert climate is just what I need. I've got a hat and suntan lotion to preserve my dainty skin. Other than that, I think I'll be quite at home with the temperatures. What's it like at night?"

"Still the end of the cold season. Temperature drops pretty fast once the sun goes down. You'll find a sweater or light jacket quite in order for the evenings. The hotel puts out extra blankets. I shouldn't think you'll be cold."

"Excellent," replied Abe as they pulled to a stop in front of the Victorian era Grand Hotel. The sparkling white exterior was offset by red trim. A porter in a white uniform and red fez stepped smartly to the passenger door.

"Welcome to the Grand Hotel, sir. May I assist you with your bags?"

"Certainly," replied Abe, following behind as the porter led the way into the cool interior and reception desk.

"I'll get your reservation sorted out," said Jacques. "Go through that door to the left and ask for one of the dining booths. I'll meet you in a moment. We'll get a bite to eat."

"Wonderful," replied Abe, handing his passport to the receptionist. "My stomach can use a bit of real food. We can talk business. Then I need to catch up on my jet lag. We had to stop off in Dakar on the way but not long enough to get off the plane."

"We can sort through the basics this evening and finalize plans tomorrow," replied Jacques. "There's nothing too urgent coming down the pipeline if your timeline is as you say."

Abe collected his passport, picked up his briefcase and strolled down the exquisitely decorated colonial hallway into the dining room.

Later over a dinner of steak, potatoes and mixed peas, carrots and onions the two briefly shared some of their past experiences. Jacques was pleased to find that Abe was fluent in Northern Sotho, a dialect of the Tswana language of Botswana.

"The locals will figure you're a South African with an American accent once they know you speak the language," explained Jacques. "That makes it easier for you to deal with them. The fact that you've been working with mining interests in the Republic means you can talk shop with the mining camp fellows. They may have information that will help you out."

"We'll see," replied Abe, "I'd much rather blend in if possible. It's hard to put on the airs of a rich hunter, when you're background is totally middle class." He fished in a pocket. "Here, I brought you a list of animals to collect. It's authentic. The Washington zoo needs all of these specimens. They will offer extras to other zoos for a bit of nongovernmental cash."

Jacques perused the list quickly. "Good, I can make two lists, one for me and the other for my assistant. That will split us up and let me do your special work on the quiet."

"Perfect. It should be a quick, easy pick-up of our man but one can never be sure. We'll pull out the maps and work out a timeline once I get settled in Maun," said Abe, finishing his coffee and flan. "I'm bushed. Think I'll call it a day and leave you to your own devices."

"Don't worry about me," Jacques laughed rising from the table. "I have plenty of company in the bar. Get a good night's sleep. I'll stop by about mid-day and we'll head for Maun."

Jacques settled back in his chair, watching the other man push his way through the swinging doors.

By morning Jacques had the lists ready to share with Grobler.

"No need for the big collecting nooses on this trip," Jacques stated as Grobler continued loading. "This will be mainly small mammals and reptiles. We'll have to split up and cover almost half the Kalahari to collect them all. We'll need two vehicles. You'll go up toward Pandematenga. I'll shoot out to Maun, get our client set up and then work the west side of the swamp. It will take us a couple of weeks to fill the complete order. I'll keep our man updated on the progress."

"It's going to take a lot of petrol to keep us running for two weeks. Have we got the cash?"

"This guy is loaded. Even if it takes a month, we'll be funded. Take a couple of extra full Jerry cans of petrol with you just in case. He made a big down payment to the bank so we're flush. Jacques counted out a stack of Pula bills into Grobler's paw-like hand.

"He wants some ostrich eggs and chicks. You can pick them up near Pandematenga and then go on out toward Kasane. You'll notice he wants two kinds of bats from Drotsky's Cave. I'll be out that way so I can pick them up. We can catch any snakes and lizards as we see them. I'll figure on meeting you in Maun in about a week and a half. We can compare notes and then pick up the remaining items. We'll save the small cats until after we meet up. I don't want to over-fill those permits. Throw in some medium sized live traps too. What do you think?"

"Sounds like a good trip," replied Grobler taking the list that Jacques had made for him. "I'll finish buying my supplies and be ready to leave tomorrow afternoon. I've got a fellow to meet over at the hotel this evening about some other business out in the Maun area."

"Fine, I'm heading to Maun this afternoon. You can leave me a message at the Sedia Hotel or Island Safari Lodge if anything comes up. Any questions?"

"Nope, I think this should keep me out of trouble. I'll finish packing my stuff and see you in Maun in about a week and a half." Grobler lumbered back into the warehouse.

Jacques sipped his coffee while watching the big man pack his supplies in the truck. Although sweat dripped from Grobler's forehead, Jacques knew there was a lot of strength and endurance in the man. He'd watched him in the field mugging zebra, chasing down ostrich chicks and performing countless outdoor tasks. All these actions ran counter to the rumor that he was slow, fat and sedentary. The fact that Grobler had a shadowy past and strange rumors often followed his disappearances into native villages didn't bother Jacques. He had seen stranger characters in the Congo and during the Zimbabwe/Rhodesian war.

Back at his desk, Jacques pulled the envelope from his safe and reread the note from the American animal collector. There would be no bat collecting at Drotsky's Cave. The collection of bats was one of the codes for locating an operation zone. He felt the blood quicken in his veins. There must be something else that Abe hadn't yet told him about the mission that called for his level of paramilitary skill. Well, he'd find out about it on the way to Maun.

Chapter 31:

Francistown, Botswana, September, 1990

By mid-morning Jacques had finished loading his equipment. The land rover and trailer were crammed with the tools of the collecting trade, including nooses, nets, live traps and a tranquilizer gun. The trailer also held an assortment of cages, water, extra petrol and various kinds of dried animal food needed to sustain any collected critters. Behind the front seat was a rack holding two rifles and a pump shotgun for emergency use. In the remote corners of the Kalahari a man needed to be able to take care of himself.

Jacques stopped by the Grand Hotel, collecting Abe and his baggage.

"Some get-up you have here," observed Abe climbing into the passenger side of the land rover. "Will you really fill all of those cages on this trip?"

"You got me the permits," Jacques said, starting the land rover and pulling out. "So the answer to your question is a simple yes. On the other hand, some of this is for show and some of it depends on your other mission for me. If it takes longer than expected to finish the assignment near Drotsky's Cave. I can still use the permits for up to a year."

"That's good. I expect it will go smoothly, but we've both seen too many bungles in the field to not prepare for the worst. What's the percentage of animals do you generally collar for your clients?"

"Oh, I'd say anywhere from seventy-five to eighty-five percent of their request lists on any one trip."

The land rover bumped off the good pavement at the outskirts of Francistown and onto the white gravel-like calcrete surface of the main Francistown to Maun road. A cloud of dust rose behind the speeding vehicle.

"So you keep a backlog of animals to collect for other clients on any particular trip?"

"If it's a client who can afford to pay for more than one expedition or for a new annual permit, then yes. If it's a one-time operation, I get as many animals as I can, they pay me and we start all over the next time. With the big zoos like London, I keep renewing the permits automatically. That way I can watch for their special animals and bill them accordingly each year."

"What about your partner?"

"Grobler? He works on contract for me when I have a big order. The rest of the time he comes in part-time, fixing equipment, helping keep the animals and minding the shop if I'm out of town. He's a bit of a queer bloke, lives alone, likes his beer and keeps to himself. I hear he worked up in Uganda during the time of Idi Amin, years ago but don't know a lot about it. He's pretty closed mouth about his past, the way a lot of guys are out here."

"Hmm, maybe I'll have the office do a bit of checking."

"I'm not sure he's a type you want to get close to," replied Jacques. "There are rumors about him associated with poaching. Nothing confirmed but enough so that I've had to warn him. He also binge drinks and has blackouts. When he comes back into town he sometimes looks like he's been dragged through the swamps. I'd steer clear of getting him into the intelligence business."

"Good point. We don't need a loose cannon."

"So tell me what you have in mind for this little trip. I drop you in Maun and head straight to Drotsky's Cave or what?"

"First I need to link up with a lady named Sue Ferrell out in Maun. She'll be working backup with me."

"Sue Ferrell?" I know her. "We date whenever I get time off in Maun. She's working with the Bushmen on their cultural stories and history. What do you mean by backup?"

"She's one of my Africa Division people. Trained in operations by us, top of her class, but in a reserve status while she does her PhD." said Abe. "Nice that you know her."

You must be kidding!" replied Jacques, "My girlfriend is going to be my backup?

"No, I'm not kidding," said Abe, watching Jacques closely. "She'll be in Maun with me while you're out in the bush collecting our man. If something goes belly up she and I will come in and bail you out."

"Maybe we better get down to the nitty gritty of this mission a bit more." Jacques' voice was hard with emotion. "I'm not about to get my girl shot up in a wet op if that's the way this could go."

"Keep your shirt on," Abe raised a placating hand, "Sue goes out in the bush all the time. She can manage as well as either of us, maybe even better. I don't think you have much to worry about because I don't see this mission as one that will go hot.

"Famous last words. You need to tell me more about this guy."

"OK. His code name is Zulu. He was head of our South African intelligence unit collecting data on a subversive movement by the Russians aimed at starting a racial blood bath and stopping the transition to black majority rule.

"What's he doing out at Drotsky's Cave?"

"He's coming in from the cold after a year of running from the Russian unit that blew away his op nine months ago. He got away. You probably heard about an attack on an insurance company in the middle of Pretoria? That was his unit."

"A pretty sophisticate operation."

"Yes, very professional. Zulu was the only survivor. He managed to get to Namibia and linked up with some kind of group that was involved in smuggling diamonds. The South African Secret police got wind of something and went after him. Zulu evidently injured a police woman in trying to escape. So he's also on the run from the police. His final message indicated that he was headed for Drotsky's Cave. We need his information to stop a move that will push South Africa into total racial chaos." Abe paused for a moment.

"So," responded Jacques, "we have a blown agent, trafficking in blood diamonds, being hunted by both the Russians and South African secret police. You are asking me to waltz out to Drotsky's Cave to pick him up? You're nuts! I'm out, man!"

"What you're telling me," shot back Abe, "is, that I should send Sue Ferrell in to do this because you're afraid to go." Abe's voice was icy. "That's the mission. She's the backup. That's what you want?"

"No! God Damn It!" shouted Jacques. "You know that's not what I mean!" He slammed on the brakes and pulled to a stop near two giant baobab trees. "I need to take a leak!" he said, jumping from the land rover, slamming the door, and walking to the nearest tree.

Abe joined him. "That's not what I meant either," he said as they climbed back into the vehicle. "What I've told you sounds nasty if you run everything together in a string like you just did, but that's not the way it's playing out in the real world."

"I'm still listening," said Jacques.

"The international complications are going to prevent this from becoming a large scale operation by either side."

"How so?"

"The South Africans are only connected to him by the incident with the policewoman. They think he's still hiding out in Namibia. The Russians may know where he is, but we aren't sure. They want to kill Zulu but keep it low key. The diamond smuggling across Botswana is a clandestine weapons smuggling operation perhaps with Russian involvement. They don't want to blow that either. So the scenario calls for a small one or two man operation. No choppers, nothing fancy. The sketchy part is when Zulu arrives with the diamonds. When he meets his contact who has the weapons, they may exchange goods and go separate ways. That's what we hope is going down. If you get there first, you pick up Zulu and skedaddle. By the time the opposition shows up and blows the whistle, he's long gone."

"But, Zulu may be walking into a trap. Right?"

"Right. If there's been a leak, the gunrunner will have orders to terminate him. Or, the Russians may have their own man out there instead, we don't know. But it won't be gunships or a platoon of men. The extraction could go hot, but it will be a one on one situation. That's why I'm trusting you. You have the experience to react on the ground. We'll be in Maun. If you and Zulu go down in the field, our hope for South Africa dies too."

"Who's the Russian?" Jacques asked, "He sounds like a real winner of a guy,"

"Not someone you want to meet. He's old KGB and now Russian Foreign Intelligence Service, the SVR. His name is Colonel Petrov. I shouldn't think he'll actually be in the field."

"The puppet master sending in his man," Jacques said.

"Exactly. Zulu's saving grace may be his lack of a timetable. He's somewhere in the bush. I'm hoping by the time Petrov locates him, you'll have Zulu headed for an embassy with enough information to sink Russia's mission."

The two men drove on in silence toward Maun.

Chapter 32:
Maun, Botswana, September, 1990

Five hours later, Jacques pulled up in front of the business office of Maun Safari Outfitters Unlimited, having just left Abe at his Island Safari suite. Sue Ferrell would be waiting for him after the long drive from Francistown. His anticipation grew just thinking about spending time with her again.

He remembered their first meeting out in the bush several years previously. He had been sent to deliver a month's worth of supplies to her camp. Upon seeing her in tank top and short shorts, his image of an academic anthropologist had been shattered. He still remembered the voice in his brain that day, saying:

"Wow! What happened to horn rimmed glasses, tight hair buns and pith helmets?"

Now, Jacques' soft desert boots made almost no sound as he approached the large umbrella-shaded table covered with papers and yellow notepads. He could see her bent over, bikini clad, shapely figure. She was thumbing through a series of files. He watched from a distance, then strode silently up behind her and poked her in the ribs.

Sue jumped and swung around, right hand high near her face, left hand lower covering her throat.

"Whoa!" he shouted, laughing and stepping back in surprise at her reaction.

"Jacques!" her smile blossomed immediately. "You're lucky I didn't slosh you, poking me that way." She stepped forward and gave him a quick hug and a peck on the lips. "What a pleasant surprise. I thought you weren't due up here for another week or two."

"I came into a lucky new contract and thought you'd like to hear about it," he replied, smiling. His eyes locked onto hers, "Any parties coming up?"

"This is Maun, silly," she laughed. "Of course there are parties coming up." She showed her even white teeth and rolled her eyes seductively, "There's a big one in just over a week and then of course as we get closer to Christmas the number increases exponentially."

"Do you have a date yet?"

"I've had three invitations already," she raised her eyebrows, "from a couple of the really eligible safari guides and hunters…," her eyes focused on his, watching for a reaction.

"I guess that pretty well cuts me out then," his faced showed the disappointment.

"…and I turned them all down, because a little bird told me you might be coming this way," she said smiling brightly, eyes sparkling.

"You apparently already knew I was coming," he replied, his demeanor brightening. "I should be back from my little collecting trip by then."

"Wonderful!" she stepped forward and gave him another big kiss. "I've also heard a rumor that you and I may have a week or so to work together. That also came from the same little bird."

"I had heard that rumor too," remarked Jacques, casually breaking free of her grasp.

"We need a beer to celebrate," he said, signaling a bar waiter. He plopped down on one of the chairs under the umbrella, watching in silence as she collected her papers, neatly stacking them before leaning back in her chair and raising her eyebrows.

"So," he began, taking a sip from the glass of ice cold Lion beer, dripping with condensation. "The faster I connect with Zulu, the less chance that he'll be compromised. I get the feeling the opposition already knows about some of our moves."

"Right. When we start using old drop boxes, we have to assume that somebody out there knows it." Jacques saw a shadow of concern cross her face.

"Luckily I know that part of the country well," he said. "It's pretty hard to keep track of me out in the bush when I'm collecting. Anyone following will either have to anticipate where I'll be or wait for me around Drotsky's Cave. I don't want you to worry," he grasped her hand.

"I'll try not to, Jacques. You know I worry about you whenever you go off alone in the bush. It's not like there are good radio connections if something bad were to happen." She leaned over and kissed his cheek.

"It will all work out just fine," he smiled reassuringly. "The best medicine right now is to distract ourselves. So, I'm going to change clothes and cool off in this fabulous pool. Want to join me?"

"I'll be waiting right here." She smiled at him in a beguiling way, "I'm already dressed for the pool in case you hadn't noticed."

"Oh, I noticed, all right," he replied, smiling. "Don't go away, I'll be right back!"

"Wouldn't think of leaving," her cheerful voice followed him down the shaded hallway.

After their swim, they dried each other off in his bedroom.

"How about a walk along the river," he suggested, as they pulled on fresh shorts and t-shirts.

Minutes later their sandaled feet were following a sand track toward the almost nonexistent river.

"I love evenings along the Thamalakane," she said as a Saddle-Billed Stork rose into the air and soared low over the marshy shallows.

They watched it finally put down its long ungainly yellow and black legs and land on a tiny island. A beautiful black and white Pied Kingfisher dropped off a tree limb and splashed into a smooth pool, returning to its perch moments later with a silver fingerling clamped in its needle sharp bill.

"This is the life," Sue said, taking his hand.

Ahead of them, children and women waded out from the shore with water containers, filling them and then trudging back into the village, carrying the precious liquid home for cooking. In the distance at one end of a finger-like peninsula, a group of men bathed. A hundred yards away a group of women bathed themselves, their children and washed clothing. Sue sat on a fallen log near the bank and pointed to the groups.

"Look at how peaceful it is with the sun going down and the water so smooth and clear. Everyone bathing and carrying water. It's been like this for thousands of years. Now it's all beginning to change so fast, with the increased tourism and money coming into the country. They're opening new mines for copper and diamonds. There are even rumors of oil under the middle of the swamps. If they aren't careful, it will be all gone before they know it." She squeezed his hand and sat silently.

"Yes, I love it this time of the year," replied Jacques. "When the rains come in another month it will be like spring. All the desert flowers will shoot up and bloom. The veld will green up and the animals will migrate back out into the Kalahari. It's like paradise."

"Paradise with hidden thorns though," she reminded him. "Don't forget how deceptive that clear water is near these villages. Ninety percent of the locals here have Schistosomiasis from wading in the water. It may be fine to go for a swim up in the middle of the swamps, but down here it's another matter. Maun is in need of a really good hospital."

"Sounds a bit overrated to me," Jacques laughed. "I've swum here in the middle of the river from a motorboat whenever I've been out waterskiing. I've even been swimming along the Shashi River numerous times and never picked anything up."

"You're just one of the lucky ones," she replied. "Don't get cocky. The long term effects of the Schistosoma flukes around your bladder or large intestine can be debilitating as you get older. That reminds me. Did you go in for your rectal snip with the doctor this year?"

"My God, isn't it amazing," Jacques laughed, hugging her. "Where else but in Africa can one sit on the edge of paradise with their girlfriend and talk about their latest bowel movements and rectal snips for parasite eggs, just as naturally as if they were discussing the latest party or dance. Yes, I did go in and see Dr. Mpho last month. No parasites in this fellow."

"Good," she smiled. "I suspect the middle of the river is safer because you're farther away from the weeds where the vector snails live. Over on the Shashi, the water runs pretty fast during high water so again it's not ideal for weeds and snails. I wouldn't go wading out here or where those folks are bathing. One of our hunters just went down to Jo'burg for the full treatment. By the time he gets back I suspect his hair will have fallen out."

"You just converted me right there," smiled Jacques, running his fingers through his wavy hair. "I don't want to lose these locks any sooner than Mother Nature has it programmed for me. Certainly not because of some bug."

The sky began to take on the brassy look of evening. A woman and small boy with his dog came down to the water's edge and pulled lily pad roots. The mother filled their two buckets with the starchy stems to be pounded into a mashed potato like meal while the boy threw sticks for his dog in the shallows.

Jacques' quick eye picked out a swirl in the water some twenty feet off shore. He saw the eyes of a medium sized crocodile poke briefly above the water. He was on his feet in an instant, running toward the boy and his dog, shouting!

"Hey! *Kwene!* Crocodile! *Tlhokomela!* Look out!"

His dash took him into the water next to the boy. He picked up a handful of the mother's roots and tossed them into the pool near the dog. The splashes decoyed the swimming dog which immediately grabbed one and swam back toward his master. Jacques threw another handful of roots into the smooth water beyond the dog.

As Sue watched, the blackish green snout of an eight foot crocodile sliced upward in an open arc to catch the nearest moving object. Then in a swirl of water it disappeared into the black depths of the river with one stroke of its powerful tail. The small dog swam past Jacques, now standing over knee deep in the water. It growled at him as a perceived threat to his master, then splashed ashore tail wagging.

The woman stood frozen near her basket, hands still raised toward her face in a gesture of half fear, half surprise. Then a smile creased her face as it dawned on her what had just transpired.

"Ke itumetse thata, Rra. Thank you so very much," was all she needed to say for Jacques to know she understood how his quick action had likely saved her son's small dog and possibly that of the boy himself.

Jacques dug in his pocket and gave her a handful of coins.

"Go reka dijo, Mma. To buy food," he said smiling and walked back to Sue, still sitting on the log. He took her hand.

"So much for my recent rectal snips" he grinned as he pulled her upright, "I just got exposed to Schistosomiasis."

"I think you're lucky you were wearing shorts, hero," she laughed.

"Come on," he said, turning back towards the lodge. "I've worked up an appetite and I can clean off any mud or bugs in the shower."

"I'll help you into something warm before dinner," she said, "I think you just did something wonderful."

"That was an eight footer. I'll call the game department tomorrow and have them hunt it down. It's big enough to take a boy that size quite easily. Humans and crocs don't mix."

She stretched up and gave him a solid kiss.

Chapter 33:
Francistown, Botswana, September, 1990

The next morning, Grobler finished filling up with petrol and stopped back at his dilapidated house in Francistown to find Col. Petrov waiting outside in the shade of a Frangipani tree.

"You're late," Petrov's tone indicated his displeasure.

"I couldn't load up and sort my equipment until Jacques was gone yesterday, plus, I needed to fill up on a lot of petrol," replied the big man. "Jacques should be in Maun by now with his client. This way I can do your business while I'm bugging around supposedly doing his." He opened the door to his tin roofed shack.

Petrov noted the unkempt nature of the house. The window glass was cracked, a red shutter hung by a single hinge. The paint was peeling off the sun-bleached door, mimicking the inside walls. He stepped from the brightness of late morning into the relative coolness of the dim interior. His nostrils were assailed by a peculiar odor, not unlike that of an old gymnasium after years of accumulated sweat and grime. He stood in the doorway momentarily, allowing his eyes to adjust to the dimness.

"Have a seat," Grobler waved his hand toward a padded rocking chair. He sank onto the tattered cushions of a sofa on the other side of the room.

"I got your telegram last week," the big man said. "I didn't expect you until next week. As it turned out, it's just as well because of this new trip Jacques was planning. I'd have been gone in another day and been hard to catch up with in the bush." He wiped his hand across a perspiring brow and rubbed it down the front of his already grubby T-shirt.

"I've pushed our dates forward. The American spy is coming in with information about my plans in South Africa. I want him stopped." said Petrov.

"How can you be sure he's coming through Botswana?" the big man leaned forward on the dilapidated sofa, pausing.

"Want a beer? I've got plenty in the fridge."

"Sure."

Petrov's eyes followed the big man like a hawk as Grobler entered the tiny kitchen. He opened the fridge, selected two Lion beers and tossed Petrov a can as the Russian began speaking.

"We intercepted a contact he made with Washington about a week ago," said Petrov. "We followed up and found that he's been designated as a diamond runner by the Namibians who are buying weapons from us." He paused, popped the tab on his beer and took a sip.

"It's queer, how in this business, the paths of opposing intelligence groups seem to cross. He's somehow linked up with the Namibian liberation front and has become the front man in the exchange of diamonds for our weapons. The exchange will happen near Drotsky's Cave. I want him captured if possible. If not, then I want him removed."

"So you need my help?"

"Yes, I had another man designated for the job, but the plans changed. You're on site and know the ropes. I want you to help me finish this off."

"Any others involved? You know I like to work alone."

"Not directly. I have two men flying into Maun this week to act as support. If I need to send them into the bush, I'll make that decision from Maun. I think you can locate this man fairly easily. With your collecting truck, nobody will pay attention to you in that part of the country."

"I've got a problem with Jacques," Grobler shook his head. He's got a client with a giant order. They're in Maun now. Jacques is supposed to be working the Drotsky's cave area while I do the east side of the swamps. That could muck things up."

"Your job is to bring in this man," Petrov handed over a small picture. "If anyone gets in your way, even your boss, you are to kill them. All my agents in Southern Africa are in those files, including you."

"So he's a spy," Grobler fingered the passport sized photo.

"He's top level CIA. Don't underestimate him."

"And the diamonds?" Grobler's eyes showed his keen interest.

"I want them too. You'll deliver the weapons after we have the data. It's probably on some kind of a small computer disc like this," Petrov unbuttoned his shirt pocket and produced a shiny disc.

"I'll get them. What's our timeline? I want to avoid my boss if possible."

"I understand," Petrov's eyes bored into the big man. "In a pinch, you will eliminate him as well. Understood?

"Perfectly. I can make it look like an accident." Grobler's facial expression confirmed Petrov's suspicions about the man.

"Good. You already know how to collect the weapons in Pandematenga to take to Drotsky's Cave. I need to get back to my hotel. I have to coordinate another action in South Africa. Can you give me a ride?"

At the Grand Hotel, the Russian climbed out, dropping his room key as he descended from the vehicle.

"Damn, dropped my key. Hold on a second," he said, slamming the vehicle door and bending down momentarily. His hand reached under the lip of the door to affix a tiny magnetized GPS transmitter.

"Aha! There, got it," Grobler heard the voice say from beneath the side of the vehicle. Then the Russian was standing erect, smiling.

"I've got it. Thanks for everything. I'll be in Maun at Riley's Hotel. We'll meet briefly when you get there about any change in plans. After that you'll be on your own until you've taken care of the American." He gave a one finger salute, watching intently as the truck pulled away.

"Don't even think about going off route after you collect those diamonds. I'll be watching you all the way big man."

Petrov turned, smiled to himself and handed a small tip to the red hatted doorman.

Chapter 34:
Francistown, Botswana, September, 1990

Grobler's route out of Francistown followed the same track that Jacques and Abe had taken the day previously. At the Dukwe gate he turned north off the main road, skirting the hills separating this section of Botswana from Zimbabwe.

Grass had grown up in the middle of the bush track. Fine seeds clogged his radiator several times despite the extra screen over the front of the land rover. He swore each time the temperature gauge indicated the engine was overheating. The removal of the feather like seeds from the radiator took fifteen minutes.

At one of these stops he almost stepped on a small black-necked spitting cobra. He was leaning forward over the radiator cleaning out the vents with compressed air when he felt drops of liquid strike the back of his calf. The surprise of feeling moisture made him step backward and look skyward searching for the source. A second spray of liquid made him whirl and jump in time to miss being struck by the fangs of the three foot snake. The head of the serpent hit the sand with a thump where his foot had been moments before.

He laughed, stepped to the side of the land rover, retrieved his snake stick and pinned the neck of the offending cobra to the ground. Picking up the hissing three-foot reptile behind the neck, he carried it to the back of the trailer and deposited it in a snake box.

"Don't accuse me of not collecting things on this trip, Jacques," he smiled to himself.

Three hours later he pulled past the baobab tree marker near the guerilla camp. A guard took him to Makwatsine.

"You're back." Makwatsine's hostile stare pierced him.

"I've come for the fire."

"You brought the inventory?"

"Yes," Grobler handed over the list of weapons and ammunition.

"Fine. You're taking them directly to the border to hand over to our comrades?"

"Yes, I'll make the exchange and be back within the next ten days with the diamonds."

"It took a long time for them to make this delivery. What was the problem?"

"I think the police found out about their smuggling ring. I saw something in the news."

"We only hear the BBC out here," boomed the African. "Come, let's get this done, I need to have those diamonds so I can go back to Zambia and order another load. The locals are getting suspicious and starting to talk to the police. We'll chose another spot to camp next time."

The boxes came out of the storage shed in a conga line. Grobler checked off each item or box as it was stacked into the back of his truck.

"Let me check out a couple of the boxes," he said, climbing into the back of the truck. He pried several tops off the boxes.

"We've already test fired several to make sure we were getting the real thing," said Makwatsine.

"Good, then it won't take us long to confirm that I'm also getting the real thing as well," smiled Grobler. He selected several of the rifles randomly from each of the boxes and pulled several cartridges from random boxes.

"Get me a blanket. Have one of your men load up these magazines."

With experienced hands he disassembled each weapon checking the parts including the firing pin. He slapped magazines into each weapon and fired several automatic bursts from each into a nearby Mopani tree.

"Fine," he said, dropping the empty magazines into a box and stowing the rifles. He examined the remaining boxes. Hey! What's this? Grenades?"

"Yes, they weren't part of the agreement," replied the leader, "but our commander said to give you a few to try out. We have more if you find them useful."

"Excellent," Grobler's smile gave his face a diabolic appearance in the gathering evening shadows. "We're done. I'll leave now."

"Come sit by the fireside and have a beer with me," replied the black leader, turning his back on the weapons and striding toward the firelight.

"How good are your men against the South Africans?" Grobler asked, after taking a seat near the crackling blaze.

"Not as strong as I would have hoped. They talk tough and are eager for a fight but they aren't regulars. Very few militias can stand up to professionals. If we ever met them in a pitched battle, we'd be slaughtered."

They shared several more beers, both pretending not to notice that Makwatsine's men had removed one entire box of ten rifles from the truck.

"Better to let them think I'm ignorant of their thievery," thought Grobler. "I only need these weapons long enough to get my hands on that shipment of diamonds."

The African rose from the fireside, "They're finished," he gestured with his hand. "It would be best that you take your leave while they are playing with the new toys you have gifted us." His eyes were like chips of black obsidian. "You understand, I'm sure."

"I understand," replied Grobler, glad to get away from what might become a murderous situation. "We can arrange for further deliveries when I come back with the diamonds."

"My man will be waiting," the black giant strode toward the truck. "Until then, *tsamaya sentle,* travel easy."

The truck engine fired on the first try. Grobler was glad to have them behind him. He took a compass course straight out to the sand track that angled toward Nxai Pan and drove deep into the night.

Chapter 35:
Maun, Botswana, September, 1990

Three days later, Col. Petrov was sitting at the cutoff road to the Sanmedupe Bridge just east of Maun when Grobler arrived. He flagged the animal collector down.

"I don't want you staying in Maun," the Colonel said bluntly as the big man walked up to him. "Your boss, Jacques Anjou is still here in town with his client. I want you out at Drotsky's Cave ahead of him. I think you'll be able to nab our quarry without any fireworks. He is counting on being met and you look just like the kind of man he'll be expecting. We can't afford to let him slip through our hands with the project so close to completion. Here, have a beer while I fill you in on the next stage of our plans." He gestured toward the cooler in the shade of his rental car.

"Fine," Grobler said, taking an ice cold beer from the cooler, popping the top and tilting his head back. "Aha, Heineken!" he sighed after the first long swallow. "All right, I'll go straight across the narrow bridge, fill up with petrol and keep moving." Grobler stared into the distance to keep from looking his superior directly in the eye.

Petrov watched his man's stance and reactions carefully. He had worked in the field with enough operatives to know about hidden agendas.

"What is this man planning? His background has been double-cross, torture and murder for over twenty years. He wants those diamonds so badly, I can smell it. He won't look at me squarely. Where will he go? If he slips away into Namibia or Angola, I could lose him for ten years. The SVR isn't omnipotent."

"I suggest that you keep a very low profile until you have Zulu," he said. "Then I need to meet you immediately afterward and collect both him and the diamonds. I need to know where you are at all times, so I want this small locator beacon on your truck. That way I can follow your progress and know when you start heading back toward the main road and Maun.

"That way I'll know when to send in my clean-up team if you try anything. You won't slip away from me."

Petrov raised his beer in salute as he pulled the small locator from his pocket. Handing it to the animal man, he said, "It's magnetized so just put it on your dashboard."

"Fine," Grobler smiled, walking to his truck and placing the locator near the windshield on the metal dashboard, "How's that?"

"I'll ditch this thing on a lorry headed for Shakawe in a couple of days. Then I'll be long gone."

"Perfect."

"So I'll be off then," he replied tilting his head back one more time to finish off the last drop of his beer. "Got another Heineken for the road?" he grinned. "They sure beat a Lion for flavor."

"Help yourself," the Russian waved toward the cooler. "There's a full case in there, take it all. I won't be having any more today."

He watched the big man scoop up the box of green cans, tuck it under one arm, and climb into his truck.

"You know what to do if your boss Jacques gets in our way," he reminded as the engine turned over.

"Don't worry. It will be my pleasure." The toothy leer on Grobler's face left no doubt as to his intent. He pulled away, heading toward Maun and the setting sun.

Grobler stopped at the single petrol point on the west end of Maun. The air conditioned office was refreshing and he bought a bag of chips while the attendant filled his tanks and cleaned the dirt off his windows. He didn't notice the man filling his petrol tank stoop to place one small magnetic locator under the chassis of the vehicle and another behind the mud guard on the collecting trailer

Across the road a small crippled boy noted the animal collector's size and the markings on his truck. As the truck drove off toward the west, the boy hobbled back through the grass roofed huts to the witch doctor's house.

"The man you have been waiting for has just left Maun, *Moloi*," said the boy. I heard him tell the station man he was headed out to Lake Ngami on a collecting trip."

"You have done well, son," said the old man, placing several coins in the boy's hand. "Go home and I'll call you the next time I need to watch for someone."

The old man turned away and disappeared into the back room of the rondavel. He unrolled the massive python skin, placing it on a pedestal. Then almost as an afterthought he donned his threadbare suit coat and he went out into the warm afternoon.

An hour later, he was seated in the courtyard of the police chief, discussing the matter in the cool of the evening.

"So, Hector, you are absolutely sure of the truth of what the woman told you last month?" asked the chief, listening intently to every word.

"Yes, Chief," replied the wrinkled man. "This is the white man who not only committed murder but committed a sacrilege against all of the old spirits whom we no longer worship. He has done something that is against the laws of our country, our tribal values and our Christianity."

"If he has done something wrong, then he must pay for it, my friend," counseled the police chief. The important thing for you to remember is that Botswana is governed by laws and the man must be tried under those laws."

"Yes, Chief, I understand. That is why I came to you now instead of four months ago when the woman from Pandematenga came to report the incident. The police in that area know about the crime but they have done nothing. Now that he is in Ngamiland, we must try to remedy the situation."

"I thank you for your information, Hector. I will follow up on it with my friends to the east and see if we can arrest him but I must warn you we cannot take matters into our own hands. The law will prevail if he is guilty."

"Only an evil person would try to use the old rituals," replied the old wizard. "What is this man trying to do? He is not one of us. All that can come from him is black magic. Who could possibly think a human sacrifice would work? Why would a white man use this old ritual? It was used many years ago to try to bring the rains and make good crops. It was outlawed by the British years and years ago. This thing he has done is the work of a devil. He is not a normal human being. It cannot be left unpunished. This man needs to die a most painful and horrible death!"

"Hey, Hector, *Moloi,* Wizard, my Friend,*"* cautioned the chief, laying a calming hand on his friend's shoulder. "We've been through a lot, you and me. I have never heard you so upset. If this man is truly a murderer, then he must be brought to trial. If he is found guilty, then he will surely hang. I don't want you to commit a crime because this man has done something evil. I will contact my supervisor in Gaborone."

"I agree, Chief," the old man's red-rimmed eyes were moist but his gaze was calm as he addressed his superior. "The Old Chief Moremi and I were at the top of our grade six level class years ago. I have been an educated man since then and studied many things. I have no intention of taking the law into my own hands. This man is a murderer. The spirits will not sit by and let such a man go unpunished. I will call on them to tell them about this man. If they bring justice it will be swift and terrible. I can assure you that no man will lay a hand on this evil person because of my prayers."

"You make my heart glad to hear that, Hector. Now, I want you to go back home. Don't worry yourself about this again. After I call Gaborone, I will be in contact with the constable in Pandematenga. I want to hear the story from him. Then I will send out a patrol to look for this man. You say he went east?"

"Yes, Chief. He told the gas station attendant that he would go past Lake Ngami toward Mwako Pan, then out near the Goat's Tit Rocks, the *Mabele ya Pudi*. After that he will stop in Ghanzi, and then travel up toward Tsau. I am sure a patrol will be able to find him."

He rose slowly and shook the policeman's hand. "I must go back home to my wife. This is Monday, let us hope everything is settled by the time we meet at church next Sunday." He said his good byes and strolled off into the swiftly falling darkness.

The old wizard trudged past the morgue and then on through the village until he saw the darkened tower of the church silhouetted against the sky. He pushed open the old door and entered the blackness of the church. Feeling his way to the nearest pew, he knelt and prayed, asking forgiveness for what he planned to do. Finally he rose and hobbled back home. His wife was seated in the courtyard, dutifully stirring a three legged black pot of stew over glowing embers. She dished him a bowl of stew and placed it next to the plate of yellow mealy-meal.

"You were out late. I was worried." She handed him the bowl and watched as he lowered himself stiffly onto a chair.

"I needed to talk with the Chief about some serious affairs that need my attention," he replied, taking a glob of yellow cornmeal in his fingers, dipping it into the thickened stew and popping it into his mouth. "Hmm, very nice, tender goat," he smacked his lips in appreciation.

"Will the business take long?"

"Less than a week," he replied, continuing to eat. "I will make my preparations tonight. Tomorrow morning you must go to stay with our son on the other side of town. When you return all will be well."

His wife's eyes widened in understanding.

"Ah," she said and a shiver of fear ran down her spine. She rose, entered the rondavel and hastily placed a few things into a small suitcase. When she came back out of the hut he had almost finished eating.

"I'm ready for the morning," she stated quietly, collecting his dishes and rinsing them under the nearby tap. "I had hoped you would not have to become involved with these things anymore."

"I am sorry for this," he said quietly. "If the woman had brought an ordinary problem I would have sent her away. The spirits have many ways of taking vengeance on those who defile them and the lives of others. I will be speaking with them on her behalf. Whatever they decide will happen, I am only the informant. I take no action on these things myself."

"I understand," she replied placing the dishes near the warmth of the fire to dry.

"Good. We will sleep well tonight after that delicious meal. I will need my strength in the coming days."

The crowing of the neighbor's rooster woke them well before sunrise. After a cold breakfast, the old man watched his wife depart with a haste brought on by a fear of the occult. A thin smile creased his face as he watched her walk to the road and turn toward their son's home several miles away.

"Let their old tongues wag," he muttered, "the spirits will have their revenge."

He bent down to the small morning fire and scooped up a shovel full of coals and placed them into a metal pot. Then filling several containers with water, he carried them into his second room, sealed the door and opened a large chest containing aromatic herbs and woods for the sacred fire.

As smoke filled the hut, the old man's voice rose and fell as he stroked the skin of the giant python, chanting words of songs so ancient that their meanings were known only to a few trained ears. For two days he would fast and meditate, while invoking the ancient African spirits which the missionaries had worked so hard to exorcise from the culture. On the third day he would utter a curse of death. A curse so powerful that his own heart quailed at the thought. A curse that would follow the murderer into and beyond the grave.

Chapter 36:

Maun, Botswana, September, 1990

On the other side of Maun, in a luxury room at Riley's Hotel, Colonel Petrov pounded his fist on the writing table.

"Damn it!" He flipped off the shortwave radio and encrypted computer and stormed out of the room and down to the main dining room for dinner.

His two assistants had arrived only yesterday. They were already eating. He poured himself a large glass of deep garnet colored South African Cabernet and glared at the menu. The 'British', lamb chops, tatties and neaps with greyish overcooked peas looked decidedly unappealing. He ordered the American rack of barbecued pork ribs with a heap of French fries and a tossed salad. His companions knew better than to comment on his tastes. The scowl lines creasing his forehead indicated a possible massive eruption of temper.

"It's moving too fast in South Africa," he stated, taking a deep swallow of the red wine. "We have to finish up here this week and get down to Pretoria to finalize plans. Everything must be in place. Zulu's information will be useless to the Americans once we get past the celebrations and assassinate the old guard leaders. Once that happens, we only have to release our damning evidence against the president. Then, our people will step into power as this government collapses."

"I understand the president attacked the hardliners last night," volunteered his second in command.

"Yes, Mr. Botha is not the man I had hoped to see take South Africa's reins. He's a moderate. Even though we can destroy his credibility with our information, it has to be coupled with our assassinations. Once we have anarchy, President Botha will have no choice but to back the hard liners and clamp down with the full force of the police and army. We can't let him pull apart the last vestiges of Apartheid and secret police powers. We need to divide that country now. Warfare between blacks and whites needs to become a reality. We have to get our hands on Zulu and those diamonds this week. Buying power in South Africa right now, is much more important than keeping a warlord happy on the Botswana border.

"When will they release Mandela and the other old men from prison?"

"Early next week. When that happens, there will be euphoria in the black homelands. They were martyrs for the cause of Black Liberation back in the 60's. Now they will be living legends of survival. The people will flock to them. Our assassinations will set off a reaction the likes of which has not been seen since the Hutu and Tutsi genocide in Rwanda. Life for whites in South Africa will get sticky very quickly. We're going to blow the whole country apart and then come in and pick up the pieces."

"Do you want us to take out Zulu before Grobler, gets there?"

"No, I think we've got a couple of American operatives here in Maun who may need our attention. Zulu is desperate to get out of Namibia and share his intelligence data. He'll be careless. He'll believe Grobler is picking him up. It should be easy. As for you two, I want you to deal with the American girl, Sue Ferrell. She's lower level CIA. We can use her to control her boyfriend, Jacques Anjou. If we neutralize Ferrell and Anjou, her stateside control will be useless."

"What about Jacques?"

"Anjou is a different matter, he's freelance. The CIA hired him to pick up Zulu. I think he's going to get quite a surprise when he meets Grobler at Drotsky's Cave. I've given orders to eliminate him."

"Fine." Replied the cold faced Marina. "We've already seen the file on the girl. It shouldn't be difficult to spirit her away. Do we know what she looks like?"

"We don't have her in our files. She's never been on an operation before. I expect you to find that out in the next few days."

"I'll keep an eye on the fat American," said Dimitri.

"He's another one we haven't got data on. I want photos and full descriptions of both. Whatever the two of you can get. You'll work on those things this week while we keep track of Grobler. He's my key worry. He wants those diamonds. So far the tracers have worked perfectly. I want to see what he does when he gets Zulu and those diamonds. If he runs, you two will have to go after him."

"And the girl?"

"She's secondary to Grobler. Don't let him get away!"

He finished his steak, signed the hotel chit and pushed back his chair, "Enjoy the luxury of this place for another few hours, tomorrow morning our work starts."

Back upstairs, Marina checked the tracking device on her screen, comparing it to the topographic map spread out on her bed. She knocked on Petrov's door.

"It looks like Grobler is right where we expected him to be, Commander. I have two blips from the truck and one from the trailer. He hasn't tried to ditch anything."

"Excellent," Petrov walked over from the desk, "Now let's hope Zulu arrives on schedule."

"You think Grobler is going to run with the diamonds?"

"That's my guess," replied Petrov. "Just wait, his true personality will take over when he gets those diamonds."

"What makes you so sure he's going to run?"

"It temptation. It always happens sooner or later with the hired help, Marina," Petrov laughed while watching the computer screen and map.

"I know everything about Grobler's past," he continued, "He has been with us for a number of years now. He's incurring some big debts due to drinking and gambling. There are rumors that he's indulging in some of the things he learned from Idi Amin in Uganda. The man's becoming a liability. When this operation ends, he has to go. Understand?"

"Perfectly, Comrade Colonel," Marina smiled.

Chapter 37:
Maun, Botswana, September, 1990

Sue came back to the room later that evening, having worked as a substitute waitress in Riley's restaurant. She met Jacques and Abe sitting in an isolated corner of the bar near the splashing pool's fountain.

"How'd it go?" Abe asked as she pulled up a chair and sipped on a cold beer.

"Almost everyone there is in tour groups, it was pretty easy to pick out our strangers," she said.

"What have you got?" Abe looked up from the metal table where he and Jacques had been pouring over a large map of the swamp area.

"Looks like there are three of them, she said. One woman and two men. I checked with one of my friends at the front desk. She says they came in day before yesterday. Three adjoining rooms on the third floor."

"Names? Descriptions?"

"They're registered under their company name, Federofsky Hybrid Seeds. Apparently here working with the Botswana Department of Agriculture on introducing new drought resistant crops. Unintelligible scrawls for signatures."

"So they look like farmers? Big hands, ruddy faces, like they would be out in the sun working with the locals?"

"Hardly," Sue laughed. "More like they all just stepped out of Ranger school uniform and tried to shrug on civvies. I didn't wait on their table but got close enough to get a good look. The older man, who I'd say must be pushing mid-fifties, appears to be the leader. Looks about like an aging version of the big Russian guy who fought Rocky in the movies. Blue eyes, blond hair, heavy broad shoulders like a bouncer. Someone you wouldn't want to meet in a dark alley."

"Could be Colonel Petrov himself if the old profiles on him are correct, said Abe. "We'll try to pull up something off the computers. See if there's an old picture. What about the other two?"

"The woman is slender, but muscular. She's got relatively narrow hips, well developed shoulders, and big veins on the forearms which probably indicate weight training or other heavy arm work. I'd say she's about thirty five, dark eyes and hair. I caught her eye once. Her face could be pretty but when she looks at you it'd completely emotionless. Like looking into a dead person's face. She gives me the willies."

"The third one?"

"He's the most human of the three. He's still big, probably as tall as the leader but lighter in build, although he fills out his clothing pretty nicely," Sue paused, rolled her eyes an smiled, remembering the man. "He's also mid-thirties, black hair and eyes with a five o'clock shadow."

"OK. Good description," replied Abe. "We'll see what comes up later tonight on the computer. I'm not too optimistic about us getting much help with this new internet stuff. It comes in over the telephone lines pretty slowly. I'll also try faxing some stuff to the embassy and see what comes back. It would be good to make a positive ID."

"I'm worried that these guys are hanging out at Riley's Hotel," said Jacques.

"How so?" replied Abe.

"If Petrov really is in town, then something big is going down here. This is the jump-off to Drotsky's Cave. We could be one step behind already. I've got to get out there tomorrow!"

"Come down to my room," said Abe folding the map and rising. "I'm glad I moved here from the other lodge. Better to be with the two of you."

Abe dug into his suitcase pulling out a case apparently containing a custom three piece fishing pole. He handed it to Jacques.

"You'll want to take this along to the cave," he said.

"No fish there," said Jacques, pulling the three sections from the felt padded case. "No surface water."

"Check it out," Abe stood there smiling.

"What's the deal?" Jacques started to assemble the pole, but stopped as Abe shook his head. "Any tourist might have one of these for fishing up in the swamp. I certainly don't need it for cover. I'm a collector, complete with truck and equipment."

"Nope," said Abe, taking the three pieces from him. "It certainly looks like a nice stout rod. Something you might use for tiger fishing, but this," he hefted, the lower section, "is the important piece."

"Not a sword cane," remarked Jacques taking it back. "I suppose I might beat a man to death with it. What are you suggesting?"

"Something a bit more technical," said Abe with a thin smile as he unscrewed the chrome end of the butt. "This is a miniaturization of what the old guard military would call a LAW, for Light Anti-Tank Weapon."

"Pardon?" Sue reached out, took the rod and held one end up to the light while peering through the other. "Looks hollow to me, although I do see a couple of little nubs sticking up inside that could be electrodes. How does it work?"

"Here," Abe smiled, pulling a box of .458 Winchester shells out of his bag. He began unscrewing what appeared to be the slug.

"This won't actually take out a tank but it's powerful enough to bring plenty of pee." He tipped the open brass casing upside down over his palm. Instead of powder, out came a small white shaft. He unscrewed a second and third cartridge to reveal a red shaft with furled dart like wings and a blue tipped cone with small wings. He screwed the three pieces together.

"Jesus," said Jacques, "it's a damned miniature rocket!"

"Precisely," replied Abe, adding two sights to the tube and snapping a small battery pack in place.

"It's called a WIGLAW, a Wire Guided Light Armor-piercing Weapon. Very accurate to a hundred yards. Just hold on the target for one second after firing. Once the laser brain locks onto the target, it never misses."

"Whoa!" exclaimed Jacques, sighting it out the window toward a palm tree. "What would it do to that palm?"

"Pretty much blow the top off the tree," remarked Abe. "These are great for detonating gas tanks and penetrating light armored cars. The head has a thermite shape charge. It just came out of combat field testing about a month ago."

He pushed a button, popped out the rocket and folded down the sights. Slipping the weapon into its case and handed it to Jacques.

"Put this ammo box where it won't get mixed in with your real shells. It wouldn't do to slip one of these dudes into your chamber." He laughed, tossed the box to Jacques and pulled more small boxes from his suitcase.

"This connects to our new global positioning system" he said, handing it to Jacques. "It tells us to within fifty feet where your land rover is. Connect these wires to your radio antenna, switch it on and you're all set. Computer tracking."

He handed Sue a quarter sized object. "This may help us follow our Russians if you can get it into one of their bags. The battery lasts for ten days."

"You're going to want me to get this into one of their rooms at Riley's?"

"That's the idea. Tomorrow and the next day you get to play hotel maid, waitress and anything else you want to get into those rooms. We need to know everything we can about these people."

"You'd really like to get Petrov as well as pick up Zulu, wouldn't you?" said Sue.

"You bet! From what I hear, Colonel Petrov has caused enough grief on this continent for one man. It's time for him to go. Now, I think we better call it a night. It's almost midnight and we have a lot to do in the coming week." Abe shooed them out into the hall.

"Coming in for a drink?" asked Sue, face upturned, as they reached her door.

"Sure as long as I get to have my forty winks," smiled Jacques giving her a long kiss.

In the end it had been a short forty winks. When his wrist watch buzzed, Jacques dragged himself reluctantly from beneath the warm blankets. It was four thirty in the morning. He had a deadline to meet. He kissed Sue's sleepy face, leaving her to sort out the situation in Maun with Abe.

"A short night, but certainly restful, my man," Jacques reflected, smiling to himself as he sped out of town.

After the pavement ended, the road gradually got worse and worse as Jacques headed westward past Lake Ngami and then northward around the southern tip of the Okavango Swamp. The last section into the Aha Hills and Drotsky's cave was deep sand. He drove the final twenty miles in four wheel drive. It was after dawn when he finally pulled off into a dense grove of Mopani trees, and hid the land rover, several miles from the cave entrance.

A high section of the Aha hills still obscured any view of his goal. He had already noted recent dual wheel truck tracks in the area and had no intention of driving into a hornet's nest. He sat quietly for the next hour, assembling more of Abe's tiny rockets and dozing slightly. As the sky lightened further, sun streamed through the shading trees. Jacques finished checking out the Uzi and buckling on several ammo pouches. Then with the WIGLAW over one shoulder, he slung on his hunting pack, and headed into the brush. His route to the south, contoured the wooded hillside, climbing up and over the Aha Hills.

****

A few miles south of Jacques' position, Jacob had also watched the jagged rocky teeth of the Aha Hills change from pink to limestone white with the first glow of dawn. Now the night sky had fled leaving a deep purple covering of clouds, through which, the sun sent golden streaks, like ladders ascending into the sky. The rains would soon be coming to this section of the Kalahari.

"We're almost there," said his wizened Bushman guide, pointing ahead. "We must be careful, I thought I heard a vehicle. Someone may be waiting for us. You want to make sure it's the right man."

"I will," replied Jacob, stepping out more quickly toward the brightening hills. He was still amazed at the sharp senses of the small yellow-skinned man, who had guided him unerring through the scrub thorn desert for fourteen days.

"What a pity we have to spend our lives imprisoned in our stinking exhaust and noise polluted cities. Why are we so dependent on money?"

As they approached the open camping area near the cave, X!eo became restless.

"I will leave you here," he said quietly. "A small camp of my people is just to the north of the hills. I will go there and wait. When you are ready to unload the truck we will come and help. Then I will travel back to Namibia with you." He turned and started to walk away.

"Wait!" Jacob stopped him. "Tell me about the cave."

The old man sat on a fallen log, where he could see the distant rocks and hills ahead.

"This is a very old place for our people," he said, pointing. "Up on those high cliffs are the hand prints and hunting pictures of many of my ancestors. Even inside the main entry you will find their pictures. The entry is right near those dark rocks." he pointed. "Our people hid in the caves long ago when they were being hunted by the tall black men from the east. The black men were afraid of us in the darkness. They finally left us in peace to live in this part of the desert. Inside you will find rooms and in one place a small pool of good water."

"Is there another way out of the cave?"

"Yes, there are two ways in and out. Look at the dark rocks where the large entrance is. Now look to the left of that and you can see two bushes all by themselves. The small opening is directly below those bushes in a small bush covered gully. It is difficult to see but if you know it's there, you will find it."

"Can I reach it from the inside easily?

"Yes, but be careful. We are a long way from any help out here."

"What about animals?"

"The locals say a leopard sometimes uses it but I've never seen any sign. Anyway, you have your pistol. If I hear shooting, I'll bring some men to help."

"Good, then I will say goodbye until the truck comes with the rifles. I don't see any sign of other people at the moment." Jacob raised his hand in salute, "Go well. *Salang Sentle, mong wa me*." The small man disappeared into the bushes giving an answering wave, indicating he had heard.

Alone for the first time in two weeks, Jacob surveyed the slopes ahead of him. He needed a firm understanding of the terrain in case things didn't go as planned. If his message had gotten through, there might already be someone there to take him to safety. If Petrov's men had intercepted the message, then the opposition might be waiting. Alertness and caution were a high priority.

He saw the sparse hill covering. The rocky areas were wide open. A man holding the higher ground would have a great advantage. He chose a small brushy ravine which angled upward toward the cave entrance. He moved slowly, searching for any human sign. His eyes roved the bush, watching ahead and to the sides for any movement. Nothing. He fingered the pouch of diamonds around his neck.

"How stupid to get stuck out here on foot carrying this fortune in diamonds. If the opposition controls the road out, I may need to control that cave entrance."

He climbed nearly to the summit. Surveying the whole of his surroundings. Nothing moved in the forest below. After watching for fifteen minutes, he was convinced it was safe. He dropped down to the main cave entrance, pausing briefly to examine a ghostly ochre handprint. At the corner leading to the entrance was a crude stick man shooting a long necked giraffe. The testament of some long dead artist.

Because his eyes were riveted on the drawings, he missed the shadow that broke cover briefly in the nearby gully. By the time he looked up, it was gone.

The cave entrance was large. Scattered cigarette butts and the scuff marks of shoes were everywhere. Tourists visiting the site during the rainy season hadn't picked up their trash. Nothing appeared to be new. He entered the passageway, stooping low to get through into the cathedral room with columns and flowstone. He shown his small torch on the wall, admiring the formations.

"Wow, too bad this cave is so far from a good sized population center," he murmured. "I could settle out here and make a fortune just charging admission to tourists."

He continued downward along the main passage that spiraled into the core of the hill. The cave leveled out near a final dead end. He turned off his flashlight and waited until his eyes became accustomed to the blackness of total darkness. Turning slowly he picked out a faint glow coming from the direction of the small secondary entrance.

He flicked on his light and searched for a place to hide the pouch of diamonds.

"Can't expect to have time in an emergency. Can't bargain if you have them slung around your neck."

He stuffed the pouch and pistol beneath a large flat slab of broken roof debris. Then placing the torch to one side, he made several practice runs, diving over the rock in the dim light and grabbing the pistol. Replacing it carefully next to the gems, he turned toward the small exit hole.

The shaft to the outside was narrow necessitating his doing a belly crawl. A wall of brush greeted him at the exit. He surveyed the surroundings and then backtracked. He checked his watch as he arrived back at the main entrance. Walking to the edge of the entrance, he looked out at the valley below. A rolling rock on the opposite side of the entrance caused him to spin around.

A large white man stepped out from behind a boulder. His rifle was aimed directly at Jacob's chest.

Chapter 38:
Maun, Botswana, September, 1990

"Don't do anything stupid now," Grobler's tone was deadly. He moved swiftly across the flat entry way. The rifle's evil black muzzle never leaving its target.

"Looks like I walked into that one," said Jacob smiling and raising his hands slightly to show that he was unarmed. "You must be Prometheus the bearer of the fires of freedom. I'm…" He took a step forward still smiling.

"I'm not in the habit of telling people twice," the giant's face scowled, jabbing the rifle barrel toward Jacob. "I can't imagine that you've been down that hole for the past half hour just sightseeing. Where are the diamonds I'm supposed to receive? Keep those hands way up!"

"I hid them between here and the Bushman camp just over between those two hills," lied Jacob, suddenly sensing something was going awry. "I'll take you to them once I know the weapons are here and ready to be delivered. I've been waiting for you for several days. I got bored and came up here to reconnoiter and look around."

The big man stepped forward quickly and swung his rifle. The butt took Jacob in the belly doubling him over.

"You lying black bastard, I saw you arrive! I'm the one who has been waiting!" The barrel of the rifle crashed into the side of Jacob's skull sending him sprawling unconscious onto the cavern floor.

Consciousness returned in waves of pain and nausea. Jacob tried to pull his hands up to check the side of his aching head but both were secured to small bushes. His throat was parched. His feet were free, so he was able to twist around enough to see the mouth of the cavern above him and the truck and animal trailer in the open area below.

A vehicle had been pulled to within a hundred yards. From the vantage point he could see a small group of Bushmen working to unload boxes. On a nearby tarp they were unpacking each box and laying the weapons out in neat rows. There were also boxes which appeared to be labelled as explosives or ammunition. He was about to call out when his captor came striding up the hill.

"Well, well," he said smiling down at his prisoner. "Did you sleep well?" He severed the cords binding one of Jacob's hands and held out a bottle of water.

"You see how well my part of the bargain is being kept," he pointed to the truck. "Drink up, I don't want you dying of thirst before you fulfill your part of the bargain or," he paused, "I get to have a bit of fun." He leered, pulling his hunting knife and stroking the razor sharp blade up and down his bare arm.

"I need to check that you brought what we bargained for," replied Jacob, feeling a chill of apprehension sweep through his body. "After that I'll give you the diamonds. I'm no threat to you with all those men working down there. Just cut me free."

"No, you'll be just fine right here." laughed the big man. "You'll give me the diamonds and a lot of pleasure as well, before I'm done with you." He lashed Jacob's free hand to the bush again and turned to go.

"You stay here like a good boy. I need to finish counting the weapons. Then, after I've had a few drinks with the boys, I'll be back." He walked off down the hill.

****

High on the hill above, Jacques watched the events below from his position of concealment.

"Damn you Grobler," he muttered to himself, "You've sold out to the terrorists or someone even nastier. You're running guns. I should have known something was up from the rumors circulating in the district."

Jacques checked the safety on his Uzi and laid it aside on a rock.

"This won't do much good at this range. Let's see if Abe's little fishing pole will do the trick?"

Unslinging the WIGLAW case from his shoulder, he removed the light metal tube and one of the assembled mini-rockets. Sliding the rocket into the rear of the cylinder he heard a satisfying click. Then he wormed his way down the hill until the piled boxes of ammunition and grenades were well within range. On the hillside above, he could now see a lean black man staked out to a bush near the cave entrance. He had seen Grobler's menacing knife waving only moments earlier.

"Shit! That's my man, Zulu, on the ground! My God, what a predicament!"

Jacques crept closer and settled in to wait as Grobler handed beers to the workers, quaffing two for himself, in rapid succession.

The weapons and boxes had obviously been checked to everyone's satisfaction. The men were now seated in a circle leaning on the boxes, chattering away in their strange click language while they chugged the beer. Grobler headed up the hill.

As Grobler approached Jacob, he drew his knife. His voice carried to Jacques across the open boulder strewn slope.

"All right big boy," his mouth wore an ugly smirk, "let's find out how much you'll tell me."

"You're not the man I'm supposed to meet," Jacob said flatly. "What happened to the guy I'm supposed to meet?" The unholy gleam in the other man's eyes nearly made him sick to his stomach.

"Oh, Jacques?" Grobler laughed, "I don't see him anywhere, do you?" He laughed. "I suppose he'll be along sooner or later. I have a welcome arranged for him too," the big man laughed wickedly and leered at Jacob. "Right now though, it's just the two of us. So, let's get down to business and see what we can negotiate."

"What's to negotiate?" asked Jacob. "I can get you the diamonds in a matter of minutes and you can be out of here. I'm on foot and supposed to take those weapons back to Namibia. Just untie me and we can both be on our way."

Grobler squatted down near Jacob's head. "I won't let you go, so you're just going to have to tell me. Otherwise…," he paused, jamming his knife deeply into the sand next to Jacob's side.

"Otherwise, what?" Jacob asked.

"Otherwise, I'll take back just enough identifiable evidence to show that I've completed my mission," said Grobler.

"So! What's it going to be?" He laughed. "Your choice!" He drew the blade of his razor sharp knife along Jacob's leg, cutting through the trousers. A line of blood welled up through the fabric.

Jacob winced in pain, jerking his leg away. Sweat was running off his brow. He could hear the fear in his voice as he said again, "Cut me loose. I'll show you."

"I see it in his eyes, this man is not going to let me out of here alive."

On the opposite slope, Jacques held the mini-rocket launcher to his shoulder, peering down at the small band of Bushmem. The sight was centered on the box of high explosives.

"This thing had better work the way it's supposed to."

"No, you're just going to tell me," laughed the killer, moving closer, the knife blade now lying flat on Jacob's arm.

"I used to perform an interesting operation on Ugandans when I wanted information," he continued loudly enough for Jacques to hear from a distance. "Let me show you how it's done. They always told me where the money was hidden," he giggled, "even when they didn't have any money."

Jacob lifted his head and spat directly into Grobler's leering face. He brought his legs up at the same time, pulling them into his body and kicking Grobler in the chest with all his might.

The giant man, squatting next to him was caught off guard and fell downhill backwards into a thorn bush. Jacob thrashed with his legs and wrenched with his arms trying to free himself. He saw the transformation on Grobler's face. It was no longer that of a playful cat toying with a mouse, rather it had become a rictus of killing rage.

"You!" The giant man screamed, leaping forward...

"Here's one for all those Ugandans." Jacques squeezed the trigger.

Grobler's angry yell coincided with a "Whoosh" as the small rocket, surged out of the tube toward its target. Jacques held the sights steadily on the box of explosives. The backwash of the rocket left a black splash of soot on the white limestone cliff behind him.

"WHOOM!"

The explosion was deafening. The concussion wave, coinciding with Grobler's angry charge, propelled him beyond Jacob. He was on his feet in an instant, turning toward the scene of carnage. Below, his Bushman crew writhed on the sand in their final death throes. He abandoned Jacob and raced down the hill toward the rubble of his trailer and the pile of shredded bodies.

Chapter 39:
Maun, Botswana, September, 1990

A pop-up warning light flashed on Dimitri's computer.

"Got something!" Dimitri called through the open door leading into the adjoining room.

"What do you mean?" Petrov and Marina raced in to look over his shoulder.

"I'll let you know as soon as it opens up and I can see…." Dimitri opened the file showing minute by minute transmissions from the locators on Grobler's vehicles. "Something has gone funny with the trailer transmitter. It just winked out."

"Must be a battery or electronic glitch," replied Petrov. We can still track him?"

"Yep, just fine. Either the transmitter malfunctioned or something just destroyed it. There wasn't any signal power decrease like you see with a battery."

"Well, keep an eye on things. It's possible he's found the transmitter and destroyed it. If he ditches the others, you two are going to have to intercept him. Marina, I want you to check on flying up to Shakawe. If he's going to run, it will be in that direction."

"Yes, comrade," Marina said, "and while I think of it, that blond waitress is poking around on this level. I saw her in the hallway earlier today."

"You got her photo?"

"No, she saw me and disappeared. From her looks, she could be a sister to this Sue Ferrell who works for the CIA. Same height and hair coloring."

"If she's connected with the Americans, we'll deal with her in due time. When you're down checking on the flights, ask about her."

"Yes sir!"

****

The roar of the exploding ammunition and grenades had barely faded before Jacques was on his feet racing toward the cave entrance. He dropped onto his stomach next to Jacob, pulled a knife from his desert boot and sawed at the ropes. As the bindings gave way, Jacob jumped to his feet.

"Into the cave!" shouted Jacques, racing up the hill behind the freed man. The report of a rifle sounded behind them. Jacques heard Grobler's curse. Several rifle bullets ricocheted off the entrance walls above their heads. Jacques pulled the Uzi off his back, flipped the selector switch and sprayed a magazine of bullets back toward the scene of carnage.

"Not going to hit a lot at this range," he said, "but it will make him think. Slow him down."

"Thanks," replied Jacob, rubbing his numbed wrists.

"He'd have gotten those diamonds out of you." Jacques spoke as he exchanged magazines. "You know that don't you?"

"I'm still shaking," Jacob replied, shuddering as if from a cold wind. "He said he worked in Uganda."

"Probably under Amin," replied Jacques, pulling a small flashlight from his pocket. "I think we better get your diamonds and keep moving. He's not going to let us go easily. I don't want to be inside this cave if he gets his hands on a couple of grenades." He handed the light to Jacob. "Lead the way."

They crouched and stooped through the maze of tunnels. Reaching the slab of rock, Jacob swept up the pistol and bag of diamonds from their hiding place.

"Let's get out of here," Jacques said, turning toward the opening. "I don't think this is end game yet."

"There's one more thing," Jacob's voice had suddenly taken on a harder edge. Jacques turned. The light partially blinded his eyes but he could still make out the pistol leveled directly at his midsection. The African's eyes shone like two bright coals.

"Whaa…?"

"If you're really the man sent here to collect me, then you must know someone or something that will verify that fact. If not, then this is where we say goodbye. Don't even think about twitching with that Uzi. This is a nine millimeter Rhodesian Mamba. Just tell me what I need to know. It's been a rough day, so far."

"I'm Jacques Anjou, hunter, game collector and occasionally work for the US government. My control here in Botswana is a fellow named Abe who flew in from Washington a week ago with your particulars. I'm supposed to bring you out to Maun. They will take you from there."

"I am Jacob Nkwe," Jacob replied. "Abe must have told you something no one else knows about this mission. I need more." The black pistol never wavered.

"Abe told me your code name was Zulu," Jacques replied, keeping his eyes on the other man's face. "He said you'd recognize these words from your last clear message before you went ghost. *'The Indaba is over, see you with the Maru a Pula'.*"

Jacob pocketed the deadly instrument and stepped forward.

"Then I should be thanking you, Jacques Anjou." He stuck out his hand. "You saved my bacon back there. It was going to get sticky in another few seconds."

"I'd say you're a very lucky man. Now, let's get the hell out of this hole." He motioned toward the entrance of the cave.

"I don't think it's smart for us to use that exit," said Jacob. "There's another exit. It won't be visible from his truck. You think he knows about it?"

"I doubt it. I've been here several times but never found it myself. If you know where it is, let's go. My land rover is on the other side of this hill. Let's move!"

The two men wormed their way in total darkness out of the narrow lower exit of the cave. Evening shadows were spreading across the hills. They cautiously contoured down to the flatter ground. Now, completely out of sight of Grobler and his truck, they dropped into a swinging lope, following the sand track toward Jacques' land rover.

"We need to keep moving. It won't be long before he realizes that we're gone. Then he'll come looking for us. One high powered slug in my petrol tank and we'll be walking home."

"I don't fancy another hundred miles," replied Jacob, close on his heels.

"That's my land rover up ahead, glad it isn't pitch dark out here or we might have missed it coming from this direction." Jacques opened the bonnet of the land rover, searching for the wire he'd removed as a precaution against theft.

The distant whine of a truck engine told them the pursuit had begun. Jacques stopped his search and quickly unlocked the rifle rack. Jacking a round into the chamber of his .458 Winchester, he handed it to Jacob.

"Go back down over that little dune there and give him something to think about. I need to reattach that wire and get this bugger cranked up. Stop him permanently if you can."

Jacob raced to the top of the nearest sand ridge. As the truck jounced around one of the sand track corners, he placed a bullet through the wind screen. The bobbing lights disappeared as Grobler slammed to a stop, hitting his light switch. Jacob threw one more round at the truck's after-image, knowing that it probably didn't do a lot of damage. Then, hearing the rover start, ran back down the slope and piled into the passenger's seat.

"I don't think I did anything but scare him," he panted. "The truck was bouncing so badly I was lucky to hit the windscreen."

"Anything that slows him down," replied Jacques, slamming the vehicle into gear and spinning the tires as they caromed onto the main track.

"I'll try driving with the lights off. It will make it harder to get up to speed but he won't be able to follow us quite as easily. Once we hit the road junction ahead we may lose him."

The vehicle jounced across a dry pan pockmarked by old elephant water digs. Jacques flicked on the lights. "Can't afford to hit one of these damn holes," he shouted over the racket and roar of the engine.

He swerved wildly to miss a three foot hole in the rock like surface. "I just hope we have a good enough lead to get back into the forest before he breaks cover."

His answer came moments later as they neared the tree line and slowed for a sharp bend. A "whump" on the back of the land rover indicated that Grobler had them in his sights. Two more faint "Bwah's" of the elephant gun reached their ears as he slowed again. Another slug slammed into the rear of the vehicle and they heard it strike metal behind them.

"I hope that wasn't my radio," shouted Jacques as they made the corner and swept out of sight. "I had hoped to check in as soon as I'd picked you up. Then they'd come meet us."

"How do I check it?" asked Jacob.

"Climb back there and turn the lower right hand knob. If a light comes on we're probably in business."

Clambering over the seat in the rollercoaster ride of the vehicle, Jacob twisted the knob. "Nothing!" he shouted in Jacques' ear.

That means we're up the creek as far as communication. "I'm keeping the lights on. We'll make better time through this twisty stuff. Maybe we can put some distance between us by the time we hit the main road. He knows we're headed to Maun."

"How's the petrol?"

"Got a full t... Whoa! We've got trouble pal. Our gas gauge is dropping like a rock. He got lucky. Got a hole in the tank."

"Can we plug it with a quick stop? Have you got any epoxy putty?"

"Yea, it's right there in the tool box at your feet," Jacques flipped on the cabin lights while Jacob rummaged in the box. He came up with a packet of cellophane wrapped double colored epoxy putty. He cut off a piece and began kneading the two compounds together.

"It sets in five minutes," said Jacques, "we're going to have to be fast at this before it starts to turn solid. When I stop, you head around the back of the land rover and I'll dive under with the flashlight. As soon as I see the leak, hand me the putty and I'll try to work it in. Then we're going to jump back in and be on our way. You know how to use that Uzi?"

"Part of the requirements for my job."

"Good, take it when we get out. I don't think he'll catch us but if he does he'll be right on top of our tail before he stops. You can work a tattoo on the front of his vehicle and maybe finish it once and for all. Here's the corner. Go! Go!" He swooped around the curve, slammed on the brakes and cut the lights.

Both men were out of their doors and racing to the back of the vehicle. Jacques went flat on his back and pulled himself under the vehicle, flashlight in hand.

"Hand me the putty! I've found one hole, there's another up top where I can't reach it." He crammed the warm soft putty into the hole plugging the flow of fuel.

"Ok, that should do it! Let's go!" He rolled from under the vehicle and listened for the sound of the approaching truck. Nothing.

"He's not back there or he's stopped," said Jacob climbing into the front seat as they accelerated forward.

"Damn, he took the cutoff just where we turned into the bush. It goes higher over the open hills. I didn't take it because it would put us too much in the open. He may be hoping to cut us off. We're pretty low on petrol. There's an Angolan refugee camp on the edge of the swamps before we hit the road to Maun. It's run by a Roman Catholic priest. He has a radio. We can still get out a message."

The land rover ride smoothed out as they hit a deep sand area and Jacques had to put it into four-wheel drive. He continued with his thoughts.

"A friend of mine, named Malcolm, lives about a mile beyond the priest's place. It's just this side of the junction to Maun. He has a big motorboat in case his rover packs up. If we can get a message out to Sue and take his boat, she can have a light plane pick us up on Chief's Island."

"Sounds like we're about home free," said Jacob.

An hour later the land rover sputtered to a stop. Jacques poured in his spare can of gas but the gas ran out in a few minutes through the hole which they didn't seem to be able to plug again.

"Looks like the putty isn't holding. We aren't even going to get to the priest's place," said Jacques as they sputtered to a final halt. "Grab that grub box and a couple of canteens of water off the back seat," instructed Jacques. The walk won't take us more than half an hour from here.

"Almost made it," commented Jacob, noting that Jacques had left the rifles behind. "What's with that fishing pole you never let out of your sight? Why don't we take the rifles?"

"This pole is a present from Abe," replied Jacques, shifting the weapon to his back. "It saved your skin back there. It's a techy remodel of a hand held rocket launcher used by infantrymen. It's reduced in size and essentially now looks like part of a heavy duty fishing rod. It's a lot lighter than a big rifle and can take care of anything we might run into in the swamps. This baby will stop a charging elephant. You saw it in action back there on the ammo dump."

"Pretty good stuff, I'd say. So, why not ambush him here on the road?"

"He's already way ahead of us and planning something. Grobler's pretty cagey. My bet is that he figures he holed the gas tank. He'll wait ahead someplace and be prepared for us to dodge off into the swamps. If he's already at Malcolm's place, he has the option to ambush us on the road or take the big motorboat. We'll see what the priest says."

Another ten minutes of walking brought them to the Priest's tin roofed, rondavel. Jacques rapped on the wooden door of the hut.

"Father Flynn," he called, "open up, this is Jacques Anjou. It's an emergency!"

"Coming!" A clatter inside the hut was followed by the sound of a striking match. A lantern flared and a bleary eyed man with a shock of disheveled white hair peered out at them.

"Jacques, what's the problem?"

"We've got to get to Maun. The land rover is broken down. I need to borrow your motor boat to get to Chief's Island and have a plane pick us up."

"The motor is on the blink. I had to send it to Maun for repairs. If you can wait until tomorrow there's a lorry coming through about midday. They would get you there by midnight."

"No way! This is national security stuff with gun runners. Grobler is involved in it. He shot a hole in my petrol tank. I think he's trying to cut us off from reaching Maun. Is your radio still working in the dispensary?"

"Sure, I'll take you there now if you like."

"No, I'll just leave you with the message to send. We need to keep moving. Is there any kind of water transport at all?"

Malcolm's got a boat."

"Yes, I need to get to Malcom's place if his boat hasn't already been commandeered."

"I have a good *mokoro,* a dugout canoe. You're welcome to it. It's an hour's pole through this part of the swamp to Malcom's place from here."

"That's just fine! Grobler will start wondering where we are and maybe pull out. In the worst case, we can take it clear to Chief's Island. You've got to get my message to Sue at the Safari Lodge by morning time. She'll make arrangements to have us picked up." Jacques walked to the priest's desk and scribbled a message.

"No problem," remarked the priest glancing at the paper. "Now, let's get you into that *mokoro.* There's a single channel down to Malcom's so you can't miss it. I'll start up the generator and send this message immediately." The priest collected a flashlight and walked around his hut toward a small dock on the edge of a watery inlet.

"Wait until morning to send your message, Father," cautioned Jacques, "If Grobler knew you had a radio, he could bring in reinforcements. Sue will notify the police as soon as she gets this message."

The two men clambered into the narrow dugout. Jacob sat in front leaning back on the grub box. Jacques stood with the fifteen foot pole in the rear. The priest gave them a push-off into the blackness.

"Not to worry about us, Father," said Jacques, his voice floating back across the water. "We can handle the swamps. Grobler will be gone by morning one way or the other. Right now you need to go back inside, shut off your lights and don't answer the door. He's a nasty piece of work."

"Will do," replied the priest. *"Tlokomela dikubu e dikwena, borra.* Watch out for the hippos and the crocodiles, guys."

Jacques poled for an hour until they sighted Malcom's large dock. Lights were on inside the house. Grobler's animal collecting truck was visible in the drive.

"I think we better stay in the shadows and keep moving," whispered Jacques. "He's probably inside spinning a yarn about poachers and the need to borrow the boat. We need to put some distance between us and this place before morning."

They glided silently past the lights along the opposite shore. The blackness of the swamp enfolded and swallowed them up completely.

"You think he'll hurt your friend?"

"I doubt it. If we can push it all day tomorrow we'll reach Chief's Island. By then the Father will have talked to Sue. We need to survive the night and evade him tomorrow. He wants your diamonds so he'll come looking for us. We'll have to stick to the back channels."

Chapter 40:
Maun, Botswana, September, 1990

Petrov watched the path of Grobler's truck moving across Dimitri's computer screen.

"Aha! It looks like he's moving, he said. "I'd say he's coming our way."

"We'll know once he reaches the junction that either takes him to Shakawe or back here to Maun," replied Dimitri.

"I'm going out to see if Marina's found out anything about the girl." Petrov strode out the door.

Half an hour later he was back. "Any changes?"

Dimitri's finger pointed to the screen and then to the map. "I think he stopped for the night at a village near this crossroads. There's a refugee camp there, probably some people he knows."

"You could be right," said Petrov, perusing the map. "If he was planning to run, he wouldn't be stopping."

"My guess is, we'll see some movement in the morning. If not, then he's abandoned the truck there."

"Tomorrow we're going to need someone out there if he doesn't head south. Zulu knows our timetable. We can't let him get to an embassy."

"You want to send me up there?" asked Dimitri.

First thing tomorrow morning I want you to contact our man in Shakawe. Then if Grobler's truck is still stationary, it means he's probably trying to ditch us. In that case, I'll want you to find a flight up to Chief's island. It's in the middle of the swamps. I'll stay here with Marina in case Grobler actually decides to come in and turns up with Zulu."

Marina walked in the door.

"What have you got?" snapped Petrov.

"Sue Ferrell doesn't have a twin. That was her working part time as a waitress."

"That means we have compromised. We need to remove her from the picture. I want you to plan on attending the Friday party. We'll question her and find out how much that chubby American knows."

"There's a new message from our embassy in South Africa," said Dimitri. "It says the government has agreed to a referendum. Whites will vote on allowing blacks to participate in a unified government. The white extremists, Weerstandbeweging, are threatening civil war. They're drilling in public with weapons."

"Our timing is going to be perfect," said Petrov. "We'll keep things riled up for another week and then do our last push. That will sway the vote to the side of the hard line apartheid conservatives. When the blacks realize they have no hope of getting to govern, the tinderbox will ignite. Boom!" he laughed.

"You really enjoy this work, don't you?" Marina said.

"Of course, in a few years one of you will be in my shoes. Then you will understand how supreme power can become totally addicting," he smiled. "Now, let's make our plans for Sue Ferrell"

****

In the darkness of the swamps Jacques listened to the splash of water and the grunts of a hippo only yards away. The two men remained motionless, lying flat in their mokoro. The black shape of a huge hippo surged out of the water and up onto the open grass of the island. Another followed only moments later, grunting and snuffling as it moved with extraordinary speed into the deep swamp grass. A heavy odor of steamy dung hung like a blanket over them in the still air. Jacques nudged Jacob.

"It's a good thing we didn't meet those two in one of the channels back there," he whispered, "we'd have been mincemeat."

"How are we going to get any sleep with this going on?" Jacob asked, referring to the audible grinding of the giant beast's molars, the rumbling of its digestive tract and the sucking sounds made by its platter sized feet as they pulled out of the muck with each step.

"Shhh, they have very good hearing. I don't want him to come over and investigate us. A smashed pile of mud and human gore won't make your government happy. Just pull your blanket up and pretend he's the wind." With that, Jacques rolled on one side, covered his head and promptly went to sleep.

The first light of dawn brought the distant whine of an outboard motorboat to their ears. They watched a black cloud of Marabou stork rising in the distance beyond several islands.

"Grobler's over in the main channel," Jacques observed casually. "That's what sent the birds up. At least we won't have to worry about him sneaking up on us."

"Where do you think he's headed?"

"He hasn't a snowball's chance in hell of finding us in all these small back channels. So he's headed down the main channel about twenty kilometers. There's a place where we have to come out into the main river in order to reach Chief's Island. It's a kind of lagoon area. He'll wait there hoping to surprise us. He still wants those diamonds for himself and he wants us both dead. All the same, he doesn't want to go swimming to find them at the bottom of the drink. He wants to find us, run us ashore, and then kill us. After that, it will be mission accomplished with no witnesses."

"Nice thought."

"Yep, but no use us worrying about it. I think we can fend for ourselves. Here, have some groundnuts for breakfast while we push off. We'll hit that lagoon by late afternoon. He'll be a bit drowsy from sitting around all day. My guess is he's got a crate of beer with him. That may soften up his reflexes and thinking."

"How are you expecting to get around him without having our heads delivered to some Russian for his trophy room?"

"I expect he figures we'll take at least a day and a half to reach that lagoon so today is our day to show him how well we can pole this damn canoe. If we surprise him at the bottleneck, then my little fishing pole toy should be enough to pull us through unless we're ambushed. I know a lot about the man and a lot about the swamps. I think we can outwit him."

"Let me have a turn at that pole when you get tired," remarked Jacob.

"There's plenty of time. Think you can do it?"

"No time like the present to learn."

The endless expanse of papyrus was broken by an occasional island covered with palm trees or creeping mangrove bushes holding giant rookeries of storks. The giant birds clacked their beaks, jumping and hopping off their nests as the two men poled past.

Glassy pools in wider channels were covered with the yellow, white and purple blossoming water lilies. Swarms of dragonflies, bees, wasps and colorful butterflies fluttered through the air. Brown-bodied, splay-footed Jacana birds walked gingerly from lily pad to lily pad sampling the bugs. Their outlandishly wide yellow feet distributing their weight evenly on the floating rafts.

"Looks like a natural smorgasbord for those Jacana birds," observed Jacob.

"I can imagine dying and going to a heaven that looked like this," replied Jacques.

"Keep your thoughts of heaven to yourself, please, said Jacob. I'm much more interested in seeing this stuff from above ground."

"Amen," Jacques' voice was thoughtful as he poled to shore. "Here, take over the poling. I'll see if I can catch us a fish for dinner. I'm getting tired of biltong and groundnuts. We'll want good food if we have to stay out another night."

"Good idea."

By nightfall they still had not reached the main channel. Jacques pulled into the shore of a small island through an old unused hippo channel. They roasted several large-mouthed bream over a small fire. A million chirping frogs surrounded them, swelled their throats in anthem to the stars.

The evening concert was shattered by a rifle shot not far away.

"Sounds like our man is out there waiting," said Jacob.

"Let's hope it was a floating log and not some poor bugger trying to get home to his wife and kids," said Jacques.

"Cut the chatter and let me get to sleep before the frogs start chirping again," said Jacob. "They're worse than the mosquitoes."

"Good idea, we'll be starting way before first light. Should be able to slip through. The island's not far now."

Two more shots ripped through the night, briefly silencing the celestial chorus and reminding the two that the game was still deadly serious.

Jacques shook Jacob awake just after midnight. "Have some groundnuts. We need to get moving." He slipped the mokoro into the river, wading out in the water up to his chest.

Jacob followed suit, feeling refreshed by the water. The early morning chill would pass quickly with the morning sun. The stark white of the pale moon overhead sent a shiver of fear down his spine.

"Crocs should be drowsing now and hippos will still be ashore feeding with this moonlight," said Jacques. We've got as good a chance as any right now."

The maze of channels became wider. A slight current could be detected in the still waters. A large crocodile slipped noiselessly into the black pool ahead of them.

"I thought those guys were asleep," said Jacob.

"An early riser," whispered Jacques, shifting to the paddle as the lagoon became deeper.

"I think this is about where I would have placed last night's shots," he whispered, keeping as near to the edge of the mangroves as he dared.

"I see ripples on the river just ahead," Jacob pointed to the channel in which they could see swirls of current.

"Yes, it doesn't run very fast so I think I can angle us toward that far side. Keep as low a profile as possible."

Another splash sounded to their right and both men watched another long sinuous crocodile tail swirl the water before disappearing into the depths.

"Another pretty good sized croc there," observed Jacob,

"That one was about fifteen feet long and three feet across the back," whispered Jacques. "It could rip you to pieces. Fortunately there are plenty of fish here. I doubt it's hungry."

"Sorry I asked," Jacob whispered back.

"Remember, I've got our little rocket launcher ready for any party. If he comes at us in the motorboat, sit up and paddle directly toward him until I yell. Then I want you to turn to the right. That will make the rocket back blast go out over the water and not in your face. Got it?"

"Got it. Any guidance if we tip over?"

"Just pray it doesn't happen," Jacques swatted at a mosquito. "If there's an angry hippo or a mother croc nearby, they'll attack the boat. In that case, go underwater and try to swim a hundred yards away, out of the danger zone. Best not to dwell on it. We'll have no control if it happens."

"You just made my..."

"Whump!" A bullet splintered wood off the mokoro. The impact sound preceded the bellow of the rifle by a fraction of a second.

"Ow! Jesus that hurts!" came Jacques' ragged voice. "He missed me but I've got one heck of a big splinter in my leg."

"Anything I can do?"

"No, just don't move. He may think we're a log. I'll pull out what I can without moving a lot."

The buzzing snap of a second bullet passing overhead was followed by another rifle report which echoed across the water.

"We're past him and getting further away by the second," said Jacob, "I saw the muzzle flash on that last shot. He's on the shore."

"Ugh," grunted Jacques, pulling one of the splinters from his leg. "I'll be lucky not to wind up in the hospital with a massive infection."

The cough of the starting outboard motor reached their ears. Jacques sat up and swung the small rocket launcher up to his shoulder.

"Damn! He's coming for us! Paddle toward him and turn when I yell."

The powerful engine revved several times and a white wake gleamed in the night light as the boat left the shore. It planed across the water at a frightening pace, straight toward them.

"Ok, magic fishing pole, do your thing," muttered Jacques groaning in pain and twisting himself upright to watch the rapidly approaching speedboat. "Right turn! Now!" he shouted at the top of his lungs.

"Steady, steady," Jacques spoke under his breath as the prow of the mokoro swung to his right. He twisted to align the sights.

The speeding boat lifted its prow out of the water, rapidly closing the distance. The big man stood in the back, a wide grin on his face, feet braced, one hand on the steering, the other holding his rifle.

"Like shooting ducks on a pond in another few seconds."

Grobler swerved slightly to the left, planning to swamp the mokoro in his wake. He cut back on the throttle, bracing his feet.

The "Whoosh" of the rocket launcher was followed by a pencil like flame that traced a curved line directly toward the prow of the speedboat. The downward motion of the boat, coupled with the swerve accentuated the damage as a sixteen inch hole opened up along the waterline. The prow went downward, instantly swamping the craft.

Grobler staggered forward. His momentum propelling him into a nosedive over the center of the boat. He landed in the bow, dropping his rifle and struggled to regain his footing. The prow of the aluminum boat dove in deeply and the boat settled rapidly into the lagoon. Moments later he was alone, thrashing in the water.

The wake of the motorboat travelled along the side of the mokoro nearly swamping it. Jacob back-paddled furiously.

"Want to go after him?" he asked Jacques.

"No, keep paddling. He'd sink us. We can't subdue him. Crocodiles are a consequence in the swamps. He's going to have to live or die with them.   We'll push on to Chief's Island and Maun. Your mission is a lot more important than catching a killer. The rangers and police will follow up with him if he survives. They enjoy a good man-hunt. Keep moving. I'd still like to make that Safari Lodge party tonight."

"You are a real piece of work, my friend," Jacob smiled paddling with all his might.

Chapter 41:
Maun, Botswana, September, 1990

Sue was about to go snooping. She had watched the man in room twelve and his two assistants for nearly a week. She'd taken pictures of them at Riley's Hotel and Abe had sent them back to Washington. He was ecstatic about the feedback from Jim Collins.

"Those are the first good pictures of Col. Petrov since the 1970s," he said to Sue upon reading the message. "Congratulations! You could be up for a promotion. Do you want to go on activate duty full time?"

"Not a chance, Abe," Sue laughed at the older man's enthusiasm. "I like working part time at the moment. Maybe later on in my career after I get tired of sitting in an office at some university teaching freshman students basic anthropology. But now is not the time."

"What do you think of our Russians?"

"They seem pretty confident. I don't see them scurrying around trying to play catch-up. They don't seem to care if we're here or not. I'd say they're ahead of us on information about Zulu's return. It could spell real trouble for Jacques."

"I'm worried too," replied Abe. "I definitely want you to get into Petrov's room and set some microphones."

"I can probably do that about lunch time," she said. "They all eat together. I'd have about a half hour for a good snoop. The rest of the time they always seem to have someone in the rooms. They're all adjoining you noticed."

"Yep, sounds like a good plan. Let's go down to my room and I'll fix you up with the electronics. Are you sure you'd say 'no' to going active duty?"

"I tell you what," Sue responded, placing a hand on Abe's arm, "I won't definitely say 'no' right now. I'll talk it over with Jacques. He's going to have to make some decisions about our relationship pretty soon. In six months I'll be done here and back in the states. I may not get back to Botswana for years." She said this almost forlornly.

"I understand. I'm fine with that response and we can put things on hold for a while. We need to concentrate on our mission right now. I'm headed up to Chief's Island this afternoon. I got the last seat on the plane. Paid a bundle for it. "From the priest's message, it sounds like our boys are on their way home!" His face lit up as they entered his room.

Half an hour later, Sue was stowing the tiny electronic bugs in her small shoulder purse.

"I'll do my best with these bugs," she said. "The Russians spook me. Definitely not tourists. I mean, this is Maun. It has gambling, safaris, hunting, fishing and all sorts of adventure sports. They don't seem to be interested in anything fun. The girl is the spookiest of the three of them."

"Hey girl, they're Soviet spies. It's the way they're trained." Abe tried to placate her.

"I know," she went on, "but after almost a week in a resort town you'd expect a few beers in the bar. You'd think they'd loosen up a bit, laugh with the locals, visit the casino. You know, do something. None of them has given a wink or nod to anyone outside of their three-some. I hope they aren't on to me."

"Sue," Abe reassured her, "You aren't on their radar. They are totally focused on this mission. That's the way they get trained. They have blinders on. You don't figure into the picture so you get ignored. Being Russian carries its own cultural baggage."

"I'll say!" she shook her head. "I saw them out running the other day. Two men of action and the Amazon woman keeping right up with them. When I waited on tables near them, they seemed to be appraising everyone but it was almost clinical. Anyway, I promise that I'll get into room twelve today for a really good snoop. When you get back from Chief's Island we'll share adventure stories. OK?" She gave him a winning smile.

"Just you be careful, young lady," Abe patted her hand. "Stay under the radar. I don't want you worked over by either the gorillas or that Amazon. If you sense any problem, get out and stay out until I get back. You know too much about this mission to get into the wrong camp. Have you got your cyanide tooth job yet?"

"My what?"

"Sorry graveyard humor, as in 'Break a leg' with the theater. Just be careful. I'll send you a message when we're headed back. I want a plane standing by to whisk Zulu off to the embassy in Gaborone as soon as we get back. Understand?"

"Yes sir!" she smiled, leaving him to finish his preparations for the afternoon flight.

Sue got to Riley's Hotel at noon. Shelly, the receptionist, had already stepped out for her lunch break. She was lying next to the pool, sunning herself and showing off her figure to the world. Everyone's eyes seemed to be focused in her direction, even those of the Russians. Sue simply walked behind the counter and nicked the key. Then she headed down the hall to the maid's cleaning closet and picked up a packet of clean bed linen and a maid's white head scarf.

Walking back past the dining room, she saw the three Russians still seated at their usual table eating their meal.

Room twelve had the typical guest room layout with a giant double bed in the center, engulfed under a full mosquito net dangling overhead. The coffee maker, television, desk with telephone and computer access were top of the line as one would expect in a five star hotel.

She walked straight to the computer and tapped the return key. A request for password popped up. She walked away and toured the rest of the room looking for anything that would give her some kind of information pertaining to their mission. Nothing popped out immediately, so she placed the linen on the bathroom counter and set about installing the electronic bugs.

Abe had given her two types. The first was a telephone bug which required her to open the receiver of the phone and insert it between the line and the microphone. Following that, she slapped a magnetic microphone onto the bottom of the lampstand and placed another along the metallic frame of the bathroom mirror. Finally she started another slow search of the room.

The neat pile of papers by the computer revealed only that they were written in Russian with a few in English. Nothing jumped out as she snapped pages with her camera.

She stayed clear of the briefcase and suitcase which would certainly have alarm systems. Through the open door into the next room she saw a map on the table. She entered, snapped a picture, while noting a line running from Maun across the center of the Makarikari Salt Pan to the border of South Africa. She was about to check the computer again when she heard movements outside the door.

She quickly slipped back into the main bedroom, picked up her linen from the bathroom counter and began stripping used towels off the rack, replacing them with clean ones. She was exited the bathroom, clutching the laundry to her breast as the main door swung open.

Colonel Petrov dropped his center of gravity the moment he detected her standing next to his bedside.

"What in the devil are you doing here?" he demanded, stepping forward to block her path.

"Just picking up the used towels in the bathroom," she explained, smiling and moving toward the door.

His arm shot out, blocking her way again. Then his hand moved upward, stopping just beneath her chin. He used one finger to tilt her head back so that her eyes met his. She found herself looking directly into the coldest ice blue eyes she had ever seen. A knot of fear cramped her stomach. Her eyes widened and a chill swept across her body.

"I've seen you too often around this building and my rooms of late," he stated coldly. "From now on you and the other maids are to stay out of my room unless I am here and answer the door. Is that clear?"

"Yes," her voice came out in a whisper.

He dropped his hand, stepped to one side and walked toward his computer table. She hurried to the door, stepping into the hall. If she had looked back, she would have seen him staring after her. His flashing blue eyes boring into her back with the same intense look of a predator gives before striking its prey.

She fled down the hall, instinctively knowing he had seen her in the hotel other times that week. She stopped by the maid's closet, dropped off the dirty towels and strolled down to the office desk. Shelly was back on duty.

"I found this set of keys on the floor near room twelve," she said, dropping them on the counter. Before Shelly could comment, she was out the door and headed down the street.

"Oh, God! What a disaster!"

She had calmed down a bit by the time she got back to her room, deciding that it wasn't such a big a deal as she had thought. They didn't know where she was living and the smallness of her hotel would make it very hard for anyone to accost her without witnesses being present.

That comforting thought evaporated when she unlocked her room and stepped inside. A jumble of her clothes and papers were spread across the bed and desk top. The smell of a woman's perfume lingered in the air. It was blatantly obvious who had searched her room. The Amazon Russian woman had been there and pawed through her clothes and private items. The thought terrified her.

She turned to her computer, which had been left on standby. The screen opened directly to her email file without asking for her password. Alarms in her brain went off again.

"She's been messing with my computer too. They must have seen me go up stairs in the hotel. I was spying on them while that woman was here spying on me!"

Her fingers flew over the keyboard sending messages to everyone who might need to know that her system had been compromised. Then she quickly wrote out her observations of Petrov's room and described the map she had seen. All the while she was wondering:

"Did they put a keystroke tracer on the computer? A forwarding bug? God, at least they didn't go in and reformat my whole hard drive. My PhD thesis is on here!"

She slipped in a disc and started a backup. When it was done she made another and then a third. She stuffed one drive into a padded envelope and addressed it to her major professor with a note saying that someone was messing with her computer. She sealed her camera and another backup in an envelope and took them to the front desk of the hotel where they were locked in the safe to be held for Abe. The final disc she placed into the special money pouch she carried while travelling and taped it to the bottom of one of her dresser drawers.

Feeling better, she sat down and wrote Jacques a note. She explained how much she missed him, saying she would be going to the Safari Lodge Party and hoped he would be able to make it back in time for the final dance. She closed, saying how much she loved him and hoped he was safe. This went into Jacques' hotel mailbox.

She ate a small afternoon snack, showered and slipped into a light sweater and slacks for the cooler evening air at the outdoor bar. No need to dress up formally for a Maun party. It was definitely a come as you are place.

"Ok, all prepared, just let them try to do something to me while I'm out dancing and ten macho safari hunter are watching."

Chapter 42:
The Okavango Swamp, Botswana, September, 1990

The swim to shore had been no real problem for Grobler. He swam breast stroke, smoothly and slowly to keep down any splashes. There was no way he was going to do any rapid kicking movements which might attract crocs or hippos. He was angry with himself for having bungled the sinking of the mokoro. Still, there was a good chance he could catch them if he moved rapidly during the day ahead.

"All I have to do is beat you to Chief's Island. Then I'll have a rifle. What the hell was that rocket thing Jacques used? It must have been what set off the ammo back at the cave."

The first island had been a piece of cake. Mostly high sandy grassland with a few Makolwane palms. It had no marshland or mangroves. As he crossed and left that island, he was tempted to follow the hippo and elephant canals to the next high ground, but the water in them was over his head which meant swimming. That was a no-no. The only path led through a thick tangle of mangrove roots.

By late afternoon Grobler's heavy scowling face showed the strain of clambering over thousands of tangled mangrove roots. He had used his long hunting knife to hack through thick papyrus marsh areas. The rough hairy stems of the plants cut into his knuckles like tiny knife blades. His muscular legs felt like leaden weights as their strength was sapped by muck or high stepping over mangrove snags.

He knew his goal, Chief's Island. It was the same goal that Jacques and his black spy had in mind. He needed to reach it before they could escape his clutches. The diamonds, once a dream leading to independence and wealth, were now an imperative. Colonel Petrov was his boss. The man would never tolerate failure. It was now a race to save his own life in a game of winner-take-all.

He was constantly tempted by shortcuts. The cool smooth-surfaced pools of open water where only fifty feet wide separating one island from another. What a temptation it was to know that a five minute splashing swim across that open water would avoid another thirty minutes of slog, razor-like grasses and tangled mangroves. The craving grew but only until he spied the next giant croc's tail or toothy cavernous snout. Thinking one could sneak past a basking crocodile was pure foolishness. The outcome was certain. Gut wrenching fear kept up his firm resolve to avoid taking the easy route.

He knew from observing other creatures mistakes in the swamps that any misstep, or splash would send out vibrations, alerting the giant scaly monsters. In a few short seconds the sleepy basking croc would be off the beach and in lightning quick pursuit. Massive jaws would clamp onto warm, soft flesh. Churning tails would roll the gigantic bodies with a force capable of tearing off whole legs. Finally, twenty pound chunks of warm quivering flesh would be gulped down a monster's gaping maw.

He didn't want it to end that way. His furtive eyes planned each route from one island to the next. He avoided all but the shortest exposure to the dark waters and their lurking dangers. It was taking longer but he would reach Chief's Island. He wasn't about to become a rotting corpse, slowly digesting inside the guts of a giant saurian.

Approaching the next waterway he made out a mound of stork nests, towering like a small hill above the papyrus. He clawed his way upward, ignoring the squawks and rustles of the colony. Moving cautiously, he made his way around each nest, startling only the closest birds. The main flock was off feeding. In another hour the entire rookery would be filled with clacking, gabbling birds, settling in for the night.

His hand moved a clump of papyrus revealing the black scaly sheen of a snake as thick as his wrist. He froze and his brain screamed the warning. *"Black Mamba!"* With wide eyes he watched as an eight foot long snake worked its head slowly over a stork egg. When finished, the shiny black serpent slithered down a hole into the depths of hell. His eyes roved the nearby area knowing that Mambas tend to mate for life. Another black coil lay directly ahead. He retreated, seeking a safer path some hundred feet to one side.

The cold sweat of tension dripped into his eyes as he lowered himself again into a narrow hippo trail to swim to the opposite side. Then once again he pulled himself up onto the land, and staggered forward, safe for the moment. He knew he could still arrive well ahead of the men in the boat. They needed to stay in the wider channels. All he had to do was reach the survival hut where a rifle was stored. Then he would sort them out, once and for all.

****

"Grobler made it to shore and he's ahead of us," Jacques stated, pointing to the deep footprints where the big man had plowed along the muddy edge of a mangrove swamp and then cut into the papyrus wall to cross onto the next island.

"Is that a problem?" asked Jacob.

"It definitely is. He wants to reach the emergency survival hut on Chief's Island. There's a rifle there. If he gets to that our only hope will be to skip the island and try for Maun directly. That's another three or four days of poling. He'd be hunting us all the way. I'm only hoping the water is up enough to allow us to take a shortcut up ahead. We still have a chance." Jacques leaned into the pole once again pushing the mokoro along the hippo path.

"What about Sue and Abe? From everything you've told me we should have someone waiting for us on the island when we arrive."

"That's if we get there. The hut is about a mile away from the airstrip. They land on the south east end of the island. I'm more worried about Sue right now," Jacques' voice cracked a bit under the strain and pressure. "If Abe leaves her in Maun, she'll be all alone. I think Petrov knows a lot more about our operation than we do about his. She will be a sitting duck if Petrov believes we've messed up his plans."

"You're right. Snooping around could get her into deep trouble. Hopefully she isn't anywhere in Petrov's files. Let's hope he's short on resources right now. We're making him rush his timetable. Murphy's Law is likely to kick in and he will make a mistake. The outcome for both sides is hanging in the balance." Jacob dug his paddle in a bit deeper.

"What do you see as his options?"

"If the S1RIUS group succeeds while we're out here in the bush, we can kiss South Africa good bye. In that case we may as well stay here, enjoy ourselves and go tiger fishing. If we get out, Petrov will have to rush his game. He can't afford to let us leak all we know."

"What about Sue? What if they kidnap her?"

"Then we'll definitely need these." Jacob shook the bag of diamonds hanging around his neck. "Petrov needs these diamonds to finance his operations. He'll make a trade."

"I could use a couple of those for my own operations," Jacques said, eyes gleaming.

"We'll talk about rewards if we get out alive," laughed Jacob. "Right now, you're earning your full pay. A bonus might be in the offing. So put your back into that pole, big boy!"

"Ha," laughed Jacques. "I can pole all day. Can you keep paddling? Got any blisters yet?"

"Nope, I'm as tough as nails."

"Good, we may need some nails. I think we're gaining on him, if I read the birds correctly."

"Why is there an emergency hut all the way up here?"

"It was set up in the 1970s when roads were nasty and transport was minimal all over the country, not to mention, here in the swamps. If there was a plane crash, mauling or a snakebite they wanted to have a place to call for help. It was set up after old man Van Doorn died out here after being bitten by a Mamba.

"Has the hut been used recently?"

"No but it is well stocked and checked by the rangers on a regular basis. A couple of years ago some adventure kayakers got in trouble when a croc ate one of their party. They called out on the crank-up radio. Grobler wants the supply of food and that rifle."

****

Ahead of them, in the final section of mangrove swamp, Grobler felt a new tightness in his legs.

"Cramps, I'm going to cramp up just as I'm about to reach the hut!"

A lightness surged through his head and body. He stopped and stood, legs quivering, hand grasping a mangrove branch. He was near total exhaustion. He could see the edge of the island ahead. His final goal was just across a smooth languid stretch of water. He only needed to reach the narrows and swim across. It was a matter of a few hundred more yards to success.

New energy surged through his body as he saw a troop of baboons on the opposite bank. They had spread out, eating nuts, berries and grubs. Baboons on the ground generally meant no big predators. The thought spurred him forward. A warning bark from the lookout baboon in the giant Motsintsela tree sent them scrambling. A moment later the entire troop had retreated into the high branches. They screamed down insults at Grobler, their ancient enemy.

He laughed at their fear and approached the water's edge cautiously. Again, although nearly exhausted, his instincts told him he was approaching hysteria. He stopped himself from dashing out into the black waters and swimming for it.

"Careful, old boy. You're not home free, yet."

The baboons shook leaves and small branches into the lagoon. Grobler reached the narrows and gazed from the high bank across to the sandy shore. He swung himself down through the overhanging mangrove branches, into the cooling waters of the Okavango. Water lapped up to his armpits. He relaxed momentarily, the cool water reinvigorated his system and soothed his tired muscles. His gaze instinctively travelled upward and back toward the dappled shadows of the overhanging bank behind him.

****

In Maun, the evening temperature inside the witchdoctor's rondavel was oven-like. The old man sat motionless, concentrating on the giant skin draped across his lap. His hand caressed the watery gray ripples and tan camouflage patterns that once coated a mighty beast's body. He took the remnants of the head in one hand and an ancient rattle in the other. His voice croaked out an ancient song. The tempo of the rattle increased. The wizard's high voice rang out.

"You have waited so long, for this meal.
You have waited so long, to feed your hunger.
Now strike with the power of the ancient gods.
Destroy this man who has broken your laws."

The strength of his voice grew and the tempo of the rattle increased. The chant was repeated again and again. A group of women passing along the road heard the witchdoctor's rattle and crossed themselves, fearing for their very souls.

****

The form of a gigantic python registered in Grobler's exhausted brain with the impact of a lightning bolt. He staggered backward in surprise. His hand groped along his thigh, seeking the hilt of his bush knife.

The primitive instincts of the massive snake were primed. A combination of ground vibrations, mammalian body warmth and motion had cocked the spring behind the mighty arrow shaped head. Now as the man descended into the water, the head of the snake was drawn back in an arch. The muscles were as tense, as a fully drawn crossbow, waiting for the trigger to release the power of steel springs into the bolt. The body of the beast was frozen..., waiting..., watching... the tired baboon-like man-creature below. A vulnerable land animal he was totally at the mercy of this watery swampland predator.

For what seemed like an eternity, man and beast were frozen statues. The man, crouched in fighting stance, neck-deep in the water, eyes wide, staring, hair raised in fear, adrenaline surging into his warm blood. His fingers were clenched white on the hilt of his knife. The snake, its head angled slightly to one side, the neck curved like an 'S' shaped spring. The heat sensors beneath the snake's eyes were homed in, its slit eyes focusing intently on the man's head, the black tongue dangling from the mouth, tasting the man scent in the air. Both animals waiting for the triggering movement that would start the dance.

Grobler raised his left arm more out of instinct than thought as the beast's head shot forward. His shoulder took the full force of the strike meant for his head. Inch long teeth drove home to the bone as giant coils writhed from beneath the mangrove to encircle him. He staggered backward toward deeper water, bowed almost double by the enormous weight of the coils.

Grobler knew the sandy beach on the other side of the channel was his only hope. As the snake's coils swept around his body, his head went beneath the surface. He staggered, rising up and frantically charging toward the opposite bank. His partially encased right arm working frantically to stay free of the entwining crushing coils. His ham like fist, still clutching the knife, slashed at the constricting bands of snake muscle encircling his chest. His powerful legs lifted and drove hard through the muck seeking the firm sand of the shore. To remain in the water was to die.

He panted with exertion. Each exhaled breath allowed the steel coils to massage his straining chest in an ever tightening vice. Grobler's florid face changed to bright red and then to a distorted purple as life sustaining oxygen was cut off. The eyes bulged and capillaries popped under the intense compression. He gained the beach and sank to his knees, consciousness fading and strength becoming feeble.

Working its needle sharp teeth free of the man's shoulder, the snake transferred its gaping mouth to the top of the man's skull. The distended maw slipped down over his head covering the back completely, lapping over onto his forehead. A nightcap, straight out of Hell.

Grobler's legs collapsed. He rolled onto one side as the point of his knife found its mark in the monster's spine. Separated from the primeval brain, the coils no longer writhed with intent. The suffocating wrap loosened from his chest. His breathing reflex not yet extinguished, prompted him to suck in air with rattling gasps. Life giving oxygen again flooded his body. Consciousness returned. He felt no pain, only an enormous sense of exhaustion, a desire to sleep within the encircling blanket of coils. His left arm was still completely trapped. His right hand flexed on the sand. It found and gripped the reassuring hilt of his bloodied knife. He had survived.

A brain reflex as old as time itself still controlled the head of the dying snake. Its urge to feed and swallow had not yet been extinguished. Slowly, inexorably, the terrifying jaws began to inch forward, gliding over the top of the man's trapped skull. With each swallowing contraction, the mouth and dagger like teeth advanced down over the man's head.

The stark realization of the meaning of those gently creeping jaws sent another surge of adrenaline into the big man's bloodstream. His body arched and twisted. The jaws held fast. He wrenched his head back and forth. The shadow of the scaly lips moved past his eyebrows. His high pitched screams disturbed the nearby baboons. The sound rippled across the deaf waters of the swamp having no effect on the cacophony of clacking Marabou Stork. It swept over the papyrus, reaching the ears of Jacques, Jacob and the rangers, all converging on the emergency hut.

Did he hear voices?

"Oh, God! Let them find me!"

The powerful right arm rose, bringing the razor sharp blade down, again and again, slashing at the armor plated snake skull. The unrelenting forward motion of teeth covered his eyes, then the top of his nose. The naked blade rose and fell, slashing, piercing, striking, any skull, man's, beast's, they were as one.

The splashing of a mokoro pole and voices reached his nearly smothered ears.

Screaming! Panting! Listening! Screaming!

The knife rose again as another frantic surge of strength swept through Grobler's body. At last the point of the knife drove home. Glancing off the jaw of the snake, it passed beneath Grobler's earlobe and drove deep into the groove along the side of his neck. Warm blood spouted, pumping freely, out onto the white sand. The powerful hand relaxed. The bloody knife fell to rest on a now crimson beach.

In the silence of the moment, the mokoro came ashore. Jacques leapt into the shallow water, dashing forward, only to recoil in revulsion. A macabre mask rested on what he knew were Grobler's shoulders. As he watched, the head inched forward one final time to cover the dead man's chin.

****

The witchdoctor's rondavel was silent. The old woman knocked..., no answer. She pushed the door wide open. The fire was out, the smoke gone. The old witchdoctor lay as if dead. Wrapped tightly around his body was the skin of a massive python. She shuddered, closed the door and went outside to kill a chicken. As the night turned pitch black the old woman cooked their dinner and went in to nurse her husband back to health.

Chapter 43:
Maun, Botswana, September, 1990

The sun was almost down. It was almost time to leave for the party. Sue felt her heart jump when Willy, the radio operator, knocked on the door of her room and called out.

"We just heard news from Jacques!"

"Is he...?" She snatched open the door.

"He's fine. We just got a message from Chief's Island. He's there with that American guy, Abe. There are several rangers there and a fellow from Namibia. The message was garbled, but they said something bad had happened to Jacques' partner, Grobler. He's dead. Something about a big snake."

"What about them coming down tonight?" Sue asked.

"They're sending the body down tonight on a fast boat. Jacques and the other two will also be on the boat. It's all confusing, the message was disjointed and interrupted by a lot of static. Anyway, I'll be glad to give you a ride out to the party this evening. Jacques won't be here until at least ten tonight," Willy looked at her expectantly.

"Sorry to spoil your dreams, Willy," Sue laughed, "I've already got a ride with Keith and his wife. They're my chaperones for this evening."

"Ok, I'll see you out there then, right? What about a dance or two?"

"Of course. You know how I love to dance. There are too many guys and never enough girls to go around. I'll just enjoy myself until Jacques arrives."

"I wouldn't want to make him jealous."

"Don't worry, Jacques can take care of himself," Sue laughed. "See you tonight, Willy."

She closed the door to the room and pulled out the small oval makeup compact. Flicking open the top, she removed the eye shadow container and slid a new watch sized battery into the slot beneath. Closing it, she set the time on the digital watch nestled in the front. The tiny locator chip in the bottom of the compact was now fully functional. Tucking it into her pocket she walked out on the patio to wait for her ride.

The party was in full swing by the time Sue arrived with Keith and his wife. The married couple went off to dance. Sue was left to wander toward the barbecue area on the patio. The water of the lagoon glistened in the fading light. A resident hippo splashed ashore in the distance. She watched the barbecue wishing that Jacques were already there to enjoy the fun.

A group of rowdy hunters surrounded the cooking fire, chugging cold beers. The volunteer chefs were doing their best to shoo tasters away from the roast pig hung over the spit. Next to the spit was a large grill covered with sizzling sausages and steaks. The smells made Sue suddenly remember that she'd forgotten to eat any lunch. Her mouth watered.

Rumors about Grobler's death were swirling through the tiny community. Willy was the center of attention as the recipient of the radio messages from Chief's Island. He elaborated on his scant news to a crowd of rapt listeners. Within seconds Sue found herself drawn into the excitement of the festivities.

"Come on Sue, grab a beer and relax."

She smiled at Larry, one of her many suitors, who suddenly appeared and took her hand.

"I'm starving," she replied, "Let's get something to eat."

"Great!" shouted Larry above the din of the crowd. "Jacques will be back later tonight. Loosen up, have some food and dance until then." He led her to the large food table and grabbed a couple of paper plates. "He'll be here before you know it."

Sue smiled at him. Larry was always her second choice for a date whenever Jacques was away. He was a hunter with a wide range of interests. He didn't waste her time with endless tales of derring-do in the bush.

"Let's play darts after dinner," she said. "There's a doubles tournament starting up. The good dance music won't start until later."

"I'll go pay the entry fee," volunteered Larry. "Be right back."

Sue loaded her plate, grabbed a large cup of beer and settled into a chair to wait.

"We're in," said Larry, returning with a mountain of food on his plate. "The prize, will be the entrance money so we won't really be out anything."

They both knew that according to local tradition, the champions plowed their winnings back into rounds of drinks for the rest of the players. It was hard for losers to have bad feelings when they got to drink up a good share of the winnings.

An hour later, their turn to play in the tournament finally arrived. Larry was good, having grown up playing darts all his life. Sue wasn't bad, but they didn't make the cut into the final round, so chatted and danced instead.

Sue saw the three Russians in the crowd as the evening progressed. They mingled with the locals and seemed not to pay any attention to her. She watched as they actually seemed to be socializing, eating, smiling and talking to others. Marina, the Amazon, even managed to dance, although Larry said she looked like a storm trooper. Despite their nonchalance, Sue was sure they had her under constant surveillance.

"Let's go over to the other side of the bar for a bit," she said. "Someone said a couple of guys were going to climb the pole."

"I definitely want to see that," said Larry, leading her through the mass of dancing revelers.

The crowd's attention near the bar had been drawn to two young men challenging each other to shinny up the central support pole of the safari lodge.

The pole, as thick as a telephone pole, rose some thirty feet straight up to a crosspiece that supported the thatched roof of the large building. The bartender calmly took bets, writing amounts on a sheet of paper. The two prospective competitors joked and downed their beers while waiting for all the bets to be placed.

"I'll put my money on Rick, the headmaster of Maun Secondary School," Sue remarked to Larry. "He's sober. Besides, I like the looks of his body. It's whipcord like my Jacques. He'll be fast!"

"You're no judge of men," replied Larry, handing his money to the bar keep. "Look at those shoulders on Ulf. He's a builder. His arms are like ropes. He'll go up the pole like a monkey."

"Too much belly fat," remarked Sue, smiling, "I'm into stamina and staying power."

"That's not what this is about, my sweet girl," Larry's eyes sparkled. "How much did you bet?"

"Two Pula."

"Ha! Then I'll be getting your money back for you when you lose, that's what I bet."

"Since you're a gentleman, if I lose, you'll have to buy me a drink to soften the loss," Sue smiled taking Larry's hand.

"Perfect. When I win you'll get your drink and I get the last dance of the night. A deal?"

"You'll only get the last one if Jacques doesn't get back in time," she replied. "I'll guarantee the second to last one. OK?"

"OK. But, since you won't let me have the last dance, how about something like…," he thought momentarily.

"…like the loser pays for a dinner out here, one evening next week, just you and me," finished Sue.

"Perfect, but it will break your bank to buy me a full meal deal," Larry sounded as triumphant as if he had already won.

"I go mad for lobster tail," said Sue rolling her eyes. "I'm sure the cook will pick out a big one for me when I tell him you're treating." She glanced up the pole leading to the roof rafters. "Oh! Look! They're starting!"

They both turned to watch the wiry headmaster take a vertical leap and grasp the pole. His bare legs and feet clamped onto the round surface while his arms shot upward, over and over, straining to climb the pole. One hand stretched upward for the last two feet, touching the high crossbeam. He grinned downward at his audience.

"Who says man isn't related to the apes?"

"Thirty-seven seconds!" called out the bartender as the climber shinnied down.

Sue noted that the top of one of his feet was bleeding from friction against the pole.

"Not easy, is it?"

"You better bloody well believe it isn't," replied Larry. "I tried it a couple of years back. Just about fell and broke a leg. This is a concrete floor."

"Next!" shouted the bartender.

Ulf stepped forward.

"Ready… Steady… Go!"

The builder was off up the pole like a monkey, using the inner soles of his feet to clamp the pole, allowing his brawny arms to reach up and pull. For the first twenty feet his speed was such that it appeared obvious he would win. Then gravity, the weight of his paunch and the extra beers began to take their toll. The crowd below could hear his ragged breathing.

"Hang in there Ulf!" yelled one of the hunters. "You can take him!"

Sue jabbed Larry in the ribs with her elbow and grinned, "What did I tell you about stamina and staying power?"

With his arms and legs wrapped around the pole, the builder was still two feet short of the crossbar. He no longer had the strength to extend an arm that far above his head. He inched upward. At last touching the cross bar he slid back down. His descent was accompanied by cheers. Upon reaching the bottom, he received a slap on the back and a cooling drink from the smiling victor.

"Forty-eight seconds!" called out the bar tender. "Three cheers for Rick! Hip! Hip! Hooray!"

The crowd went wild, buying drinks and cheering. Several others attempted the pole, but failed to get anywhere near the crossbar.

"I told you so," trumpeted Sue, bestowing a kiss on Larry's deflated countenance. "I'll go tell the cook to save me that lobster. What day should we do it? Tuesday?"

Larry groaned. "Tuesday it is. The pleasure will be mine even if it costs me a week's pay. That's a damned hard climb. I was picking splinters out of my crotch for weeks afterward."

"Must have been hard on your love life," beamed Sue. "Come on, the music's better now. Let's have a dance."

They set off across the large open hall towards the dancers.

"I'm going to run to the loo," said Sue. I'll meet you out on the floor in just a second."

Sue had just entered the ladies room when she heard someone outside shout.

"I hear a motorboat!"

By the time she had finished her business everyone had disappeared from the dance floor. She could see the crowd near the landing site. A police van had backed down to the water, its blue lights flashing. She hurried toward the sounds.

Ahead she saw one of the Russians on the walkway. She swerved into a small clump of trees. As she entered the shadows a gloved hand reached out and pulled her into the darkness. She got a glimpse of Marina's hard face as a second gloved hand covered her mouth. Then she felt the prick of a needle in her arm. A cloud of fog seemed to spiral out of the center of her brain and envelope her thoughts under a shroud of gray. In the distance she recognized Petrov's voice. It seemed to be coming from very far away, echoing down the spiraling tunnel.

"You're about to go on a long trip, young lady."

Then everything was black.

Chapter 44:
Maun, Botswana, September, 1990

The flood of relief that had surged through Jacques' brain as he sighted the crowd on the landing was short lived. He expected Sue to be right up front when he set foot on the pier. She was nowhere in sight. Moments later, when she didn't appear as predicted by Larry, he felt a stab of angst in his chest.

"Where was she?"

The situation became worse when the police captain ordered him to accompany the body to the morgue.

"I need you to officially identify the body and then answer some questions," he said.

As Jacques departed in the police van, the search for Sue was full-on.

****

Long before morning Abe, Jacques and Jacob gathered together to review Sue's computer notes. With bleary eyes they read her description of her encounter with Petrov at his hotel. The cause of her disappearance was obvious.

"Petrov has her," stated Abe, running fingers through his sparse hair.

"We're lucky to have her computer at all," Jacob replied. "After what they did to my people, I'd have predicted they'd put a torch to her room and the hotel."

"I think they want us to know who they are," said Abe, shutting down the computer. "We've still got something they want very badly."

"The diamonds," said Jacob, fingered the leather bag still hanging beneath his shirt.

"No deals!" Jacques stated flatly. "She wouldn't have wanted that. They have a head start but it's a long way to the border we can still stop them."

"I don't think they'll fly" Abe said. "We've had a couple of US and South African spy planes along the borders. I was hoping they'd try something like that. Petrov knows that a plane would trigger alarms. I'm sure they're taking her overland. Jacques is right we can still intercept them."

"We'll mobilize all the bush pilots and do a search," said Jacques tracing his finger on the map. "The main roads north toward Chobe and east toward Francistown can be covered pretty well from the air."

"We'll have to move fast to extract Sue. Petrov wants to blow South Africa wide open," said Jacob, pacing the small room like a caged leopard.

"Jacques, I want you to head up the search for Sue after Jacob and I leave for Gaborone this afternoon. We've got to get him debriefed and push his information out to the people who can stop Petrov." Abe's bulldog face was grim.

"Petrov knows my information will be in government hands by the end of the day. He'll push up his timetable. There's a big African celebration coming up in South Africa. He may use that to touch off the race riots." Jacob said, slapping his forehead. "Damn, why didn't I think of that beforehand?"

"What's that?" Abe was rapidly typing on his computer.

"September 24th is the beginning of Chaka the Zulu Days. It's less than a week away," replied Jacob. "I had thought he'd wait until October or November. But with us pushing him, he's going to move now."

"What's so important about Chaka the Zulu Days?" asked Abe.

"It celebrates one of the bloodiest periods of South African history. Black Africans celebrate their near wiping out of the white colonists. The old guard of British and Boer patriots celebrate their military victories that prevented the annihilation. It's a perfect time to stage a racial confrontation. The government sanctions four days of speeches, parties, parades, games and tribal dancing. It's a big blow-out for everyone meant to defuse tensions, all thrown into one drunken week of whoop-tee-do."

"You're right, it's a gigantic festival," agreed Jacques. "The celebration is going to be massive this year because of the push to suspend apartheid. Several of the old members of the outlawed ANC are being let out of prison. They will be giving speeches. A couple of assassinations would change everything. They would plunge the country straight into chaos."

****

Sue felt consciousness returning slowly. It was pitch black. She could hear the whine of the land rover's engine as they sped over sand tracks. She felt dizzy, sick to her stomach and her brain felt as though someone had driven a nail between her eyes. She shook her head and tried to sit up. Then a prick on her arm sent her back into unconsciousness. Her next impressions were of the smell of coffee, voices and the crackling of a campfire.

"Jacques?" she asked groggily as a dark shadow bent over her.

"Ha, you're dreaming young lady!" Petrov's voice sent shivers up and down her spine. She closed her eyes tightly.

"Time to wake up!" The voice came again.

This time she opened her eyes, looking skyward through the overhanging white spines of a *Mosu* bush. The sky was the light pink color of dawn. She groaned and sat up, rubbing the sleep from her eyes.

"Here! Drink this, it will help your headache." Marina thrust a mug of coffee into her hands. Sue took it, throwing off her blanket and feeling the intense morning cold.

"Burr!" she said, sipping her coffee and warming her hands on the cup. "Where am I?"

"We're headed north to Zambia through Savuti and Chobe," replied the tall Russian. "You are our insurance policy in case your friends have ideas of intercepting us."

"I haven't any idea what you are talking about," she lied, staring down into her cup. The hot bitterness of the coffee was bringing her back to reality very quickly. "Why would you kidnap me out of a dance?"

"Never mind for now," replied the Russian, "You've had a rough night. Everything will become clearer in the next few days. There's clean water in that jerry can. Wash your face and have a bite to eat."

She splashed water on her face and tried to rinse the fuzzy taste out her mouth. Her headache was disappearing. She ran her wet fingers through her hair, thankful for a pageboy cut.

She scanned the surrounding area for predators and a place to do her business. She stood up and walked out of camp. The three Russians were busy eating and ignored her. They knew she wasn't going anywhere, yet.

"That's better," said the oldest member of the group as she returned to camp. "Allow me to introduce myself. I am Colonel Petrov of the Russian Embassy's SIRIUS group. These are my two assistants, Dimitri and Marina," he gestured. "Have a plate of food and pour yourself another cup of coffee." He waved toward the bubbling pot on the fire. "You may join us or eat by yourself, as you wish."

"What is this all about?" Sue tried to keep her voice calm while eating and watching the three. "I'm a graduate student in African Studies at Harvard. I'm out here on a grant studying the language of the San people. Why have you kidnapped me?"

"I think you already know the answer to that question," replied Petrov. His icy blue eyes bored into her. "Let me just say that you have nothing to fear as far as your personal safety is concerned. Your friends will soon be negotiating for your release."

"You mean Jacques? What's he got to do with all this?"

"Jacques and the man you know as Abe are working with the American CIA. You're one of their agents as well. You got yourself noticed by spying around my hotel room."

"Spying? I was helping one of the girls change the linen. I'm no spy," Sue tried to sound injured by his remark.

"Finish your breakfast and don't waste my time," Petrov said, getting up and pouring himself more coffee, "We leave in five minutes. If you need to use the bushes one more time, you had better do it. We'll be on the road for a long time now. Oh, and by the way," he turned back toward her. "I know you are well versed in African bush survival. This would not be a good place to try to escape. We glimpsed a pack of wild dogs just before we pulled off. They aren't as discriminating as lions about what they eat. It could be messy."

Sue watched his back as he turned and strode away. His assistants kicked sand onto the fire and loaded up the equipment. Scraping the last bit of food off her plate, Sue filled her mug and placed it on the hood of the land rover.

"One last potty stop. Head's clearing. I wonder what drug those guys shot me up with last night. I'll wait a bit before I dump them. Don't want to mess with wild dogs. I'll know where I am in an hour. Bide your time. My tracking device is on. Abe will locate me if we aren't out of range."

She walked around the vehicle. It was packed full of equipment.

"Four jerry cans of gas on the roof rack. We're in for a long trip. Rifle butt looks like an automatic weapon, everyone has pistols. This is a nasty bunch to tangle with."

"Time to go," announced Petrov, slamming the rear door of the vehicle and climbing into the shotgun seat. Dimitri took the driver's position. Marina and Sue were relegated to the back.

"You won't escape from Botswana in this direction," stated Sue, recognizing their northward heading from the sun's position. "There are police checkpoints with radios. They'll expect you to sign in, pay fees and show your papers before lifting the barrier."

No one responded.

She spent the next few hours bracing herself as the vehicle jounced over the rough road. An occasional bump would send her crashing into the metal ceiling. Eventually they left the calcrete and the road turned into the soft gray sand of the northern Kalahari. Giant ruts left by transport trucks slowed their progress. Dimitri had to shift down into low range to pull through. Sue got tired of staring out the window at bands of elephant. The behemoth animals seemed content to stroll through the Mopani forest, breaking off limbs and stuffing them into their mouths like so many sticks of broccoli.

As they pulled up to the Savuti Ranger Checkpoint, Sue received another lesson in the cold efficiency of the Russians.

A young corporal stepped from the guardhouse, smiling broadly with clipboard in hand. His eyes widened in surprise as Dimitri stepped from the driver's seat and pushed his pistol into the man's stomach. As this was happening, Petrov and Marina climbed out and walked toward the guard house in a relaxed manner.

"Don't move, just pretend we are talking and nothing bad will happen," Dimitri said. "Is there anyone else inside?"

"O-o-only my t-two p-p—partners," stammered the young man, taking a step backward, He eyed the pistol fearfully.

"Call them out, in English please. Tell them there's a big snake out here and they need to come help kill it."

"Hey, Letso! Molife! Come quickly! There's a big snake!"

The other two young policemen came running. One carried a rake and the other an Enfield rifle. As they passed, Petrov and Marina, both Russians stepped smoothly to one side, and extended an arm to catch their man across the throat. With one leg they swept the men off their feet. Landing flat on their backs, both men had the wind knocked out of them. A pistol materialized in each Russians' hand. They jammed the weapons up under the rangers' chins.

"Don't move!" commanded Petrov.

The Corporal near Dimitri suddenly twisted around and swung his clip board at Dimitri. It was no contest. Dimitri parried his blow and almost carelessly brought the barrel of his pistol down along the man's temple. He slumped like a rag doll.

Marina picked up the rifle and herded the other two men into the hut. Taking plastic zip ties from her pockets, she firmly secured their arms around the central lodge pole.

"That should hold you," she stepped back smiling.

"Do the same with their aggressive partner here," said Petrov, dragging the barely conscious third man into the building. "Put that water can within reach. That way they can get a drink in case no one comes by for a day or so. By then we'll be long gone into Zambia."

He swung the heavy butt of the rifle twice, demolishing the radio transmitter on the counter.

Marina pushed down on the counterweighted pole gate, allowing Dimitri to drive through.

"What if a lion comes along tonight?" asked Sue.

"My dear girl," replied Petrov, "if three strong men can't figure out how to get out of some nylon ties by nightfall then they deserve to be eaten. I should imagine they will be free in a couple of hours. By then we'll be far away."

Chapter 45:

Maun, Botswana, September, 1990

"Any word of a sighting?" Jacques asked as he returned from his visit to the police station.

"Not a thing so far," replied Abe, standing up from the map spread across the lodge dining room table. "We've got more planes in the air and have alerted the South African army. He won't escape that way. We'll concentrate our search in the Northern sector of Botswana."

"We've got to find her," the emotion in Jacques' voice made it clear how special she was.

"We will," Jacob rose from the nearby bed and spilled his bag of diamonds onto the center of the map. "Petrov won't consider this project closed until these beauties reach their final destination and I'm out of his hair forever."

The men's eyes were drawn to the pile of double pyramid crystals glistening in the morning sunlight. Sparkles of blue, white, yellow and reddish brown radiated from the heap like a small fire burning on the map beneath.

"My God," exclaimed Jacques, seeing the stones for the first time. "It's a good thing you didn't show me those until now. Only one man might have come out of the Okavango."

"I'm glad we didn't have to decide who that one person would be," laughed Jacob. He gathered all but five of the multicolored stones together and put them back into the pouch.

"Those five stones are yours," he said. "An exact accounting won't be made until I log them in at the embassy. Abe and I decided you should get this bonus. You got me out of one big jam at Drotsky's cave. I doubt I'd be here without you."

Jacques' hand trembled as he picked up the stones. He tucked the stones into a zippered pocket on his shirt.

"Thanks," emotion crackled in his voice.

"We're the only ones who know of this," said Jacob. "It won't leak out."

"They'll go into my safe deposit box for a while," replied Jacques patting the pocket. "I can't waltz into the nearest bank and ask for cash. Fortunately, I manage to find a pick up diamond occasionally on my collecting trips. They appear along some of the ancient alluvial deposits out in the desert. I'll turn one stone a year into the official Botswana Diamond Exchange of DeBeers. They'll credit my bank account directly. I'm already on their known list of finders. They won't be at all surprised. This project and these stones will keep my head above water. I'll be able to turn my cattle post into a true ranch and ..."

He paused, as if embarrassed to be sharing his inner dreams. "We better get our act together if we want to locate Sue before Petrov gets her out of the country. I'll put you two on the plane to Gaborone. When I get back, I'll follow up on a few hunches of my own."

"Be careful with those guys," cautioned Abe. "They're ruthless."

"So am I when it comes to Sue's welfare," replied Jacques. He turned toward the door. "I'll take you out in about an hour." He headed for the bar.

Jacques took his beers to the back patio and sat watching the distant clouds through the branches of a large Fever Berry tree, a *Motsebe.*

"One of the Kalahari's miracle mystery trees," he thought, remembering how the bark of the tree can be used to poison fish or cure malaria.

He needed to concentrate on a plan to rescue Sue, but couldn't get her out of his mind.

"My God, man, you're totally infatuated with the lady! You love her bright personality and infectious laughter. You've become attached to her golden yellow hair and blue eyes sparkling like dancing ripples of water."

He watched a kingfisher dive off a branch and splash into a distant black pool on the river.

"Damn you Jacques," he cursed himself, sinking into self-recrimination. *"What an idiot you've been with her. You've kept her on a string for the last two years. You always expected her to be waiting for you when you showed up. Now you're on the verge of losing her. You better start planning to settle down on that ranch. You need to start a family. She can do her Bushman work while you herd cattle and hunt to your heart's content. All your friends have settled down with wives and have kids. Why can't you?"*

He shook his head, downed the last beer and stood up, breaking out of the reverie by saying aloud, "Get cracking old man or you'll lose it all!"

When he returned from the airport an hour later he was met by a breathless young houseboy.

"Mr. Jacques! Sir! We have a message from one of the search planes! Mr. Willy wants you in the radio room."

Jacques burst into the radio room. Willy was on the radio with one of his hunters. Switching off, he turned toward Jacques.

"I just got a call from Dave," he said with a grin. "He landed up near the Savuti Ranger Post that leads up to Chobe. He found three game scouts tied up and their radio smashed. The description sounds like Sue and our three friends. I told him to fly a search pattern along the northern track to the border. The guards said they talked about going to Zambia. "Let me see if we can raise him." He switched the band knob to Dave's channel.

"Dave, this is Willy, can you read me? Over."

A crackle and faint signal came back,

"Dave here. Your CQ is weak but I read you, over."

"Any news? Over."

"That's a negative. According to the guards they left the gate well before noon. They must have cut off the main road and gone on a covered bush track in the forest area. I'll circle back over the area. They could be as far south as Nxai Pan, or all the way up north near Kasane. Any suggestions? Over."

"Refuel at Kasane and then fly a pattern from there headed south east along the Zimbabwe border. I'll have Jacques look at the map and get back to you with more ideas. Over and out."

Jacques, standing in front of the Ngamiland map shook his head.

"No, he won't go out by Kasane. It's a tourist area. The good road is too easy for the police to cover. He could cross into Zimbabwe or he may have decided to cut back and try to make it out by air."

Jacques turned toward the radioman. "Willy, where could you or another good bush pilot land a five or ten passenger plane within a six hour bush track run from the Savuti Ranger Post?"

Willy came over to the map looking at it closely. He used his hand to estimate the distance to the border of Zambia, Zimbabwe and South Africa.

"It's over four hundred miles to the South African border in a straight line from where he was last seen," said Willy. "Most of the decent small airports are a hundred or so miles east of the Limpopo River. Let's figure the plane needs a range of a thousand miles to come in and out without refueling. He'll want a two engine turboprop, something like a Cessna F406. His big problem will be finding a bush airstrip that can take that size of plane. Most of our bush camps have strips that are good only for short takeoff and landing planes, STOL's. He can't use a proper airport near here or Francistown, so he's got to use the bush. It's got to be one big flat area but still out in the bush away from any people. By pushing it for six hours through the bush tracks he could make, Nxai Pan or a dry place on the Makarikari Salt Pan, although that's farther."

"You're right. He can ditch the vehicle but not his assistants. He's got a deadline to meet in South Africa. Sue is his security blanket only if he can get her to a safe place from which to negotiate. Yes!" Jacques' eyes lit up, "They'll pick him up at Nxai Pan."

"There are a couple of other places," Willy pointed to several other locations, "but unless the pilot flies this area he won't know about them. Nxai Pan fits the bill perfectly. It's not rainy season, so there won't be any tourists out there. The animals are all up in the swamps."

"Have we got a bush pilot and a plane available?"

Willy shook his head. "Not for at least an hour and a half. They'd have to turn around, fly back here and refuel. You going out there?"

When Jacques nodded, Willy continued, "Take my Toyota Land Cruiser. It's new. You can drive it at sixty or seventy on the pavement and fifty on washboard. With luck you'll make Nxai Pan Cut-off in a couple of hours. The keys are in the hallway by the desk."

He turned from the map. Jacques was already gone.

****

Petrov stood on the low ridge above Nxai Pan using his binoculars to scan the entry road into Nxai Pan. It was easy to pick up the dust cloud coming off the main road to Maun.

"I don't think that's a lorry raising that dust," he said, handing Dimitri his binoculars. "It's moving too fast."

Dimitri raised the glasses, watched momentarily and grunted in affirmation. "I'd say you're right, Colonel." He looked over at Marina and Sue, seated in the shade of several thorn trees. "How long before the plane arrives?"

"Less than an hour," replied Petrov. "One vehicle shouldn't cause us any problems unless it's a troop transport, which I doubt. They're certainly doing their best to stop us." He chuckled and walked over to the shaded area where Marina was seated.

"A vehicle is coming. When it crosses that ridge over there," he pointed. "We'll blow the C-4 on the trees. With the road blocked, I'm hoping they will take a hint and stop. I'd prefer not to have to kill someone just to get out of the country, but you never know. I want you to be ready."

Marina walked over to the land rover and pulled out a rolled tarp. She spread it neatly on a flat section of ground. She returned to the vehicle and extracted a rifle bag. Its contents revealed a long barreled Belgian FN FAL battle rifle. She snapped in a clip, arranged the tripod and dropped down into the prone position to sight down the barrel. Satisfied, she unpacked her sniper scope. She carefully attached it to the weapon and then placed two large cushions beside the rifle butt. Again lying prone, she squinted through the scope and wiggled her body, folding and adjusting her cushions.

"Looks good, commander," she said. "I've got the target area acquired, ready to fire."

"Excellent," Petrov turned to Sue, "I'm expecting your friends will stop at the road block. If they decide to come this way by going around or coming on foot, Marina will fire a single warning shot. She was on our world championship military pentathlon team. This will be like shooting ducks on a pond. You can watch." He handed her a small pair of binoculars.

Sue sat quietly, watching and praying that Jacques would stay out of harm's way. She could hear the whine of the Land Cruiser as it pushed over the low dunes on the sand track. She saw it clear the last dune and descend into the wooded area encircling the pan. It picked up speed along the harder pan surface, entering the final clump of Mopani trees, three hundred yards away.

The sound of explosives thundered across the pan. Sue felt the concussion wave. Trees fell in the distance forming a tangled mass across the road. There was the sound of metal hitting a solid object. The vehicle stopped. It was partially obscured within the mass of broken trunks and branches. It was obviously blocked both in front and behind. It would take a day's work with saws to reopen the road.

Sue could see Jacques emerging from the trapped vehicle. His silhouette was clear. He ran toward the edge of the woods. Through the binoculars she could see what looked like blood on his face. His hand held a rifle. He ran across a clearing, then cut back into the trees.

"Give him a warning!" snapped Petrov.

A single shot rang out. A plume of sand sprayed up directly in front of Jacques. He didn't stop, but swerved back into the trees. Through the binoculars, Sue could see a shadowy ghost of a figure running from pillar to pillar within the trees.

"The fool! He's not going to stop! On my command take him out!" spoke Petrov, pacing back and forth.

He whirled around as Sue jumped to her feet, throwing herself toward Marina's prone position. She kicked at the scope and screamed at the top of her lungs.

"Jacques, it's a trap! Look out!" Her body collided with Marina's as the woman pulled the trigger.

Sue's impact knocked over the tripod, sending the shot wide of its mark. She swung the binoculars with all her might, striking Marina on the head.

Marina rolled to one side, her hands releasing the rifle as she clutched her head. Sue's right hand chopped downward, striking Marina on the left cheek and neck. She lept on top of Marina's now prostrate form. Her eyes were blazing in fury."

"Enough!" shouted Petrov grabbing Sue's hair and lifting her off the prone woman as if she were a rat in the mouth of a terrier.

Sue tried to twist and bite at Petrov, but he jerked her backward, clapping a hardened hand over her mouth while saying viciously, "If either you or your boyfriend is going to live through the day, you'd better do exactly as I say!"

Tears of frustration and anger welled up in Sue's eyes. She nodded in acquiescence.

"Let's go!" shouted Petrov.

Dimitri grabbed up the rifle. Marina tossed the tarp and cushions into the back of the vehicle. Petrov forcibly threw Sue into the back seat and followed to sit next to her.

The snap of a bullet and its impact on a nearby tree, left no doubt that Jacques was not backing off. Dimitri gunned the engine and sped off down the narrow tree-lined track. He cut down the sandy slope and accelerated out onto the concrete-like surface of the pan. Then he sped eastward, toward the broad center of the pan. In the distance a light plane landed in a swirl of dust and taxied toward them.

They circled the now stationary airplane. The whirling props produced an ugly whine. It took only moments for the pilot to lower the steps. Petrov jumped from the land rover and spoke with the pilot while Marina and Dimitri wrestled Sue from the vehicle. They half dragged, half-carried her aboard.

Handcuffed to a seat, Sue watched as the four Russians formed a human chain, tossing equipment into the plane's cargo hold.

Petrov emptied a five gallon can of gasoline onto the back seat of the vehicle and set two open cans in the front. He set a small explosive timer. He scrambled aboard the plane. The whine of the props increased to a scream as they taxied across the pan, and took off.

"Circle back," commanded Petrov. "I want a quick look."

They banked and flew back across the pan. Sue saw a rising mushroom-like ball of flame erupt from the land rover. Then as they continued over the western edge of the pan her heart went out to the tiny ant-like figure, far below, emerging from the edge of the forest.

The pilot waggled his wings in farewell, banked back to the southeast and sped low over the vast Mopani forest. Ahead lay a sky of rose colored clouds, brilliantly illuminated by the setting sun behind them.

Chapter 46:

Outside of Pretoria, South Africa, September, 1990

Debbie Kotzee was also watching the slowly setting sun as she led her military cadet group toward the targets at the far end of the old gravel pit. She still limped and had one foot in a special boot-cast to hold her broken ankle in place. It was a constant reminder of her mistake in Namibia. The fall into the bush had saved her life. The injuries, demotion in rank and assignment to a youth training division meant her career in the service was very likely finished.

"Check your targets with your partner," she commanded. "Total up your scores. Have your partner sign your card. I'll collect them when we get back to the range house. Anyone who qualifies for their marksmanship badge will still get the award before the parade."

"Do we all get to carry our rifles in the parade?" queried one cute girl.

"Only the cadets who are over sixteen get to carry rifles in the parade," replied Debbie. She patted the girl on the head. "You'll have a hard enough time just marching for two hours through Pretoria in your uniform with those heavy boots and your Billy-club. That will be plenty of weight, honey."

They crowded around their targets. She began the slow painful walk back to the rifle range house. The sunset made her think back to those idyllic days in Namibia when she had been a free agent for the secret service on a special assignment.

"Oh, Jacob, what a wonderful time we had together in that illicit interlude of our lives. I wonder what happened to you and all your plans. By now you're probably locked up in a cell for the rest of your life or buried in an unmarked grave out in the Kalahari. What a waste of a good man...and body." Her subconscious jabbed at her.

They all caught up with her at the range shack. She watched as they cleaned their rifles and stored them in the special locked cupboards. She tallied up their shooting scores and wrote them on the large chart behind her desk.

"I'm starving," groaned one of the gangling teenage boys.

"No complaining! We'll have snacks on the bus. You can eat on the way back into town. Right now we have time for about half an hour of marching practice. Then we'll head home in time for your parents to pick you up."

Later in the warm evening air she watched them marching proudly in step around the central park square commanded by their own junior officers. They looked so fine in their desert tan uniforms with red epaulets on the shoulders. Her one task, other than daydreaming, was to continually encourage them to, "Look Sharp!"

"Remember," she reminded them at dismissal, "We have to show those weak kneed politicians that we are ready to make a stand for our country. They have to know that we're ready to fight for our beliefs. We can't let a bunch of wild tribal blacks take over our lands. They'll kick us into the sea!"

Practice was almost over. They would all be going home and she could concentrate on the next phase of the Chaka the Zulu celebrations. She brushed her light strawberry blond hair from her eyes and watched the final exit to the bus area. They were led by two seniors from the local school.

The troop came to a halt in front of her. The two flag bearers presented their flags, first the new national flag, followed by the red ultra-conservative Weerstandbeweging banner. The three sevens at the center of the conservative flag, arranged inside a white circle, gave a Nazi swastika-like appearance to the red flag.

As a salute, the troop all pulled out their Billy-clubs, raised them at a forty-five degree angle toward the passing flags and broke into a cheer.

She dismissed them to the bus. Turning back toward the setting sun one last time, she saw Dirk Van Zyl.

"A nice bunch you've got there, Debbie my girl," he smiled, taking her hand. "Keep them at it. One day soon we'll all be back in the laager picking off screaming blacks as they charge down upon us."

"Hi, Dirk," she smiled at him. "I don't think there will be a shooting war. It's a political battle now. Our numbers in the big parade will show the government how strongly we support the apartheid system. They need to pay attention to us."

"They will, Debbie," he placed his arm around her shoulder. "One day you'll be able to go back to that farm in Rhodesia because we're making this stand. I just received a very important message from our Colonel Petrov."

"He's back?"

"We only have a week before Chaka the Zulu celebrations begin. He has to be here to pull everything together if we are going to win this secret war."

"What's the message?"

"He's got a CIA hostage, a woman they captured in Botswana."

"What's that got to do with us?"

"He's bringing her here to the farm. We're going to hold her until after the celebrations to make sure the Americans don't interfere. She's a link to someone you know," He smiled, giving her a mysterious look and a wink.

"I don't have any contacts in Botswana," she replied.

"I know, this is a link to a man named Jacob Nkwe. I think you know him."

"Jacob!" Debbie felt her heart leap. The problem was, she didn't know whether her feelings were hatred or relief.

"Yes," said Dirk, "He escaped to Botswana. He has information Petrov doesn't want leaked out. The girl is our insurance that the CIA will hold its tongue until after the celebrations."

"He's the man who pushed me over the cliff," said Debbie, still struggling with her inner feelings.

"I know," he took her hand and squeezed it. "You're lucky to be alive. I'm certainly glad he didn't succeed. Petrov wants you at the farm to help keep an eye on the girl while she's in our custody. You'll be playing the part of a nurse, one of your old jobs in the past as I understand it."

"Yes, I was in nursing before I entered the police force, said Debbie. "I'll be glad to get away from this kid training stuff. It's definitely not my cup of tea."

"You've done an excellent job of it. You can't march with that foot anyway. It's much better that Petrov and General Breytenbach want you doing some other job. My inside information tells me the police will be setting the marching route a bit differently than last year. The distance between the two parade groups will be at a minimum."

"I'm sure the parade will go just fine," she looked off to the west. "Wow! isn't that a wonderful sunset? Sometimes I'm almost glad I broke my foot so I get to stay around with you." She turned to face him.

"Careful, there might still be some of your students around," Dirk gave her a brief kiss on the lips.

"I really don't care," she replied, returning his kiss with more enthusiasm.

"Let me take you out to dinner this evening," said Dirk. "Colonel Petrov arrives later tonight. We have to be at the farm by ten. Then I'm on special details for the next week so we won't be seeing much of each other until after the celebrations."

"Let's stop at that nice overlook on the way back into town and celebrate a bit before we have to get down to business and hard work," she smiled up at his face.

"A splendid idea. After that I'll drive you home so you don't have to take the bus. You can sort out your nurse uniform and medical kit. You may need some drugs to keep her calm. I'll drive you to the farm and we'll drop things off. Then we'll go out to that nice pub just down the road and have a bite to eat."

She took his hand as they walked toward his car.

Chapter 47:

Nxai Pan, Botswana, September, 1990

Jacques stood beneath the rapidly darkening skies of the desert watching the lights of the plane disappear into the distance, lost in the few evening stars. His rifle shot, fired at the fleeing aircraft was a sign of desperation rather than having any chance of stopping Petrov's departure.

"What if you actually hit the plane? What if it crashed and Sue were killed? Idiot!"

He sighed, taking stock of the situation, noting for the first time the clotted blood on his face. It would take most of the night to get the Land Cruiser out.

"Well old boy," he said aloud, *"you've got some spunky girl there. She must have done something to mess up that sniper. About time I popped the question. Now, I better find some grub."*

He turned and began walking west toward the park entrance gate.

"I'll bet there's a pot of porridge and stew at the ranger's camp fire. I can at least calm his nerves about the shots and send in a radio message. Got to save Sue."

****

The touchdown of the light plane on a small back runway just outside the Pretoria airport woke Sue from her restless sleep. She struggled to sit upright and remove some of the pressure from her bound arms. Her movements brought Petrov to her side.

"You'll never get away with this," she said defiantly, seeing his face in the dim light.

"That's where you're wrong," he laughed. "I've already gotten away with it and you too."

"Don't think you can escape from Jacques here in South Africa," she hissed. "He has contacts everywhere."

"Oh, I'm not worried about your boyfriend," he replied. "He was lucky. Don't try to push him into doing anything here, especially if you value his life and friendship. Lady Luck doesn't dance twice with the same partner in this business. Don't ever try to get between me and my mission again."

He turned to Marina, seated nearby. "When we get to the farm, put her in isolation in the stables. If she acts up just call in the nurse, her name's Debbie. She can give her something strong enough to calm her down until we make contact with her CIA friends. I'm sure they'll pay handsomely to get her back in one piece." The glare of distant airport lights enhanced the sinister look on his face.

Dimitri hoisted Sue like a sack of potatoes over one shoulder and boldly descended the plane's stairs. It was as if she weighed no more than a feather. They didn't pass through any immigration. The high chain-link fence had an open gate with a large black car waiting beyond. Marina opened the trunk. Dimitri deposited Sue unceremoniously into the padded vault and slammed the lid.

Sue felt a wave of helplessness sweep over her.

"They can do anything they want with me here, even in the middle of this city. What kind of people has Petrov linked up with?"

As they sped off into the night, Sue initially tried to keep track of turns. After a few moments of swerving corners, she realized it was hopeless. The best she could hope for was to not get physically sick from the ride. They seemed to be on a highway. The humming of the tires gradually lulling her to sleep.

The car jounced off the pavement and down a gravel driveway, waking her from a drugged slumber. The trunk popped open and the bright lights blinded her. Dimitri again threw her over his shoulder. Sue could clearly make out the farmhouse, stables and barn. Dimitri carted her toward the darkened stables. Marina and a woman dressed as a nurse followed.

The scents of a farm, manure, horses and hay assailed her nose. She read the sign on the door, Quarantine Area! Keep Out! Authorized Personnel Only! On the other side was a corridor. Down the hallway was another door, also marked quarantine. Behind that door was a well furnished apartment. Dimitri set her down on the bed. His knife cut the ties binding her hands and feet.

"This is our resident nurse, Debbie," said Marina, watching Sue rub the circulation back into her hands and feet. "I'll leave you here until morning. If you need anything, either Debbie or I will be right outside the door. Don't make us have to come in and knock you out again."

The young nurse limped forward in her walking cast. She handed Sue two small white pills and a cup of water. "These will relax you and give you a good night's sleep. If I have to give you an injection of tranquilizer you'll have a dreadful hangover for a full day afterwards. Don't make me do it." The cold blue eyes and muscular arms told Sue that she was probably capable of doing it without Marina's help.

The nurse watched Sue swallow the pills, then pointed to the bed. "Get some sleep. We'll bring breakfast when you wake up."

She paused as she was about to close the door. "You heard what Marina said a few minutes ago. I won't repeat it. I just want you to understand that I follow my orders to the letter. Is that clear?"

Sue nodded, lying back on the bed. The nurse flipped off the light and closed the door. Mental and physical exhaustion, along with the pills took effect almost immediately. Sue curled up on the soft mattress, and slept soundly. The morning light woke her.

It was at least midmorning. Sue scanned the walls and high windows for any obvious weaknesses. Seeing none, she prowled the room, testing and pulling on everything that might be useful as a weapon. Seeking any opening leading to a possible escape route. The room was an impregnable prison.

The only portals to the outside were the open skylights more than twelve feet above her head. There were no objects to climb on. She searched the closets, noting the variety of clothing for both sexes. She wasn't the only person to have occupied this room. The bathroom had a shower, clean towels and new toiletries. The bookshelf contained a variety of reading materials. The television brought in only one local Springbok channel. At least she could keep track of time in the outside world.

"I may be safe now but I've got to find a way to let the outside world know I'm here. Otherwise, they can do anything they want. No one will ever be the wiser."

Debbie arrived with a late breakfast of eggs, ham and toast. "I hope everything was satisfactory," she said, smiling. "Let us know if you need anything. That button on the wall is connected to Marina's radio. She'll be on guard. Commander Petrov has said he will eat his dinner with you this evening."

Debbie's eyes were cold and watchful. Marina had obviously told her about Sue's interrupting the shooting in Botswana.

After eating Sue lay down on the bed and surveyed the room. Getting up, prowled like a caged cat, reassessing her search of the confines, reexamining everything. The lock showed numerous scratches indicating previous failed attempts to pick it.

As the day rolled on, she decided to take a quick shower and freshen up. As she was undressing and removing her bra, an idea popped into her head.

"Elastic can be used to make a slingshot. What can I shoot? Spit wads! It won't hurt to try. If they catch me, Debbie will just drug me up until Jacques eventually bails me out. Right now, I've got nothing to lose. Nothing ventured, nothing gained. I'm not just one more ball for Petrov to bat around."

After the shower she pulled out her compact, highlighted her eyes and made herself ready to go to dinner with her captor. She looked at the lines of tiredness on her face, patted her cheeks to give them some color and gave herself an encouraging smile in the mirror.

"May as well go to dinner looking like a good bargaining chip."

****

Jacques finally joined Abe and Jacob in Gaborone just long enough for them all to catch the next flight to Johannesburg. They arrived at noon. Diplomatic passports gave the three quick passage through customs. An embassy car whisked them into Pretoria.

The safe house door was opened by a tousled white-haired man, whom Jacob recognized instantly.

"My God! Jim Collins!" he cried, embracing the older man. "This is the man who dreamed up the Zulu operation," he explained to Jacques. "He had enough faith to keep a drop open even after I'd gone 'ghost'."

"Surprised the hell out of me when something actually came down the pipeline," laughed Collins, chewing on his pipe stem, a gleam in his eyes. Then his face became serious and they got down to business.

"Abe, we've got to break Sue out of her hostage situation and prepare for what may be dooms-day at the end of the week. We're going to put off any further debriefing until a later date. I want you, and Jacques to work on pulling Sue out. Fortunately she still has her little tracking transmitter. We've got a fix on her now. Our Fast Company commander can provide you with the details. I want her out ASAP. We can't afford to have Petrov work her over with truth serum."

"Got it!" Abe replied, "Hopefully they don't know her full status. As long as she's just a weak pawn, Petrov will hold her until we deliver the diamonds. If they find out she's a computer crypto person and that Bushman languages are just a hobby, then we have trouble." Abe and Jacques disappeared into the next room with three men wearing smartly pressed tiger fatigues.

"Jacob," Collins continued, "I need to get a better picture of what has you so fired up about Chaka the Zulu Days."

"Sure," replied Jacob, "Let me give you a bit of history. First of all, it commemorates one of the greatest African warrior kings of the nineteenth century, Chaka the Zulu. He was the illegitimate son of a small Zulu clan leader, who through sheer military prowess rose to become king of the Zulu nation."

"So what?"

"You might say Chaka was the Napoleon of southern Africa. His dream was to unite all the Nguni peoples from Rhodesia and South Africa into a single fighting nation. Although he failed to achieve that fully, he drove the hostile Ndebele out of South Africa into Rhodesia by defeating their paramount chief Mzilikazi. Then he subjugated all of the northern Zulu tribes and formed an empire covering a million square miles of territory. At the peak of his power he commanded over fifty thousand warriors. His forces controlled all the lands from Bulawayo to Johannesburg. He did it all through sheer force of personality and terror."

"Doesn't Bulawayo in Zimbabwe mean, 'the killing place'?"

"Exactly. Bulawayo was Chaka's capitol for a while. The scenic Matopos Rocks near there were the sacred grounds for the tribe. If a group within the tribe opposed him, he sent his *impis*, or warrior bands, out to fight and subdue them. Any warriors captured alive had their necks broken. The bodies of those paralyzed rebels were then stacked in piles awaiting final death. It served as a gruesome reminder to others not to stray from the fold."

"Not your mister nice guy."

"Nope but he was no worse than many European generals of the same period."

"What happened to him?"

"Chaka managed to alienate a lot of his constituents after the death of his mother. When she died, he decreed a two year mourning period and decreed that any woman who became pregnant during that time should be put to death."

"No consequences for any male making that woman pregnant, I presume," Jim Collins said. "How little we humans have changed."

"Yes. Because of the anger over his decree, his own warriors plotted against him." Jacob smiled wryly. "Chaka was assassinated in 1827."

"So why celebrate a tyrant who succumbs to the Machiavellian principal of absolute power corrupting absolutely?"

"Because his wars united the Zulu Nation to the point that they never again became feuding clans. Since then, the Zulu peoples have identified themselves as one nation, with great warriors, good speakers and level headed rulers. He gave them a sense of national identity, purpose and ownership of much of this land."

"So why aren't they still the rulers of this country now?"

"Because fifty years later the Zulu peoples made the mistake of trying to throw out the British Empire. Fifteen thousand British troops fought twenty-five thousand Zulu *impis* to a standstill at the battle of Ulundi on July 4th, 1879. That battle ended Zulu domination of the Transvaal and much of Rhodesia."

"Subdued."

"But not beaten or broken. Today they are a driving force behind the independence movement that Petrov wants to undermine. If he can turn them to the dark side of feuding and anarchy, this country will go to hell in a hand basket very quickly."

"Genocide?"

"Just as nasty as in Bosnia, or Rwanda. Blacks against whites, blacks against blacks and all the other combinations you can think of in the polyglot nation. That's why it's so important to stop Petrov. This whole thing will come to a head in a couple of days. We have got to break up Petrov's plans. It's the only way to give the moderates enough time to finalize a coalition government and organized elections."

"What can he pull off to cause this kind of eruption?"

"It has to be something big. I think he's planning the public assassination of several well-known ANC leaders. A group of those iconic old revolutionaries from the 60's have just been released from prison. It has taken years of negotiations by the current Chief of the Zulu nation. The assassination of one or more of those famous men would bring on massive riots. If that were coupled with a confrontation during the big parades next Saturday, we'd see open rebellion and civil war."

"What about the parades? Anything there?"

"Probably not, although we need to look into that too. The parades happen in different parts of the city at different times. The VIP's get to see both groups but the times and routes are coordinated to keep the groups separate. I think our first priority should be the assassination theory. Several key ANC men are going to speak here in the big stadium along with the Zulu Chief. A single shot could change South Africa's history."

"I see where you're going. If something comes up on the parades, we'll have to be ready to react. But until we have something concrete, we're shooting in the dark. It would be a waste of manpower." He paused, thinking for a moment and then questioned Jacob directly. "Should we tell the South Africans about Petrov?"

Jacob shook his head, "Their security forces and army are riddled with Petrov's people. We couldn't trust that Petrov wouldn't get a tip off. What kind of help can we get from our American embassy?"

"I have a couple of deep cover people inside the South African government." Jim Collins said, running his fingers through his white hair, "Help will only be on a very small scale."

"That's all we need if there's a mole in our own system. Give them just enough to see if Petrov reacts. Our goal is to make Petrov, and S1RIUS disappear."

"I'll have the Fast Company guys look at the security plan for the big stadium. We should be able to put a couple of counter-snipers inside to keep an eye on their people during the speeches."

"The parade happens the morning after the speeches. If we stop an assassination, then Petrov will go to a backup plan. Someone needs to check all the parade routes," said Jacob fingering one of the maps. "Ten or twenty thousand people marching through a city could turn into a flaming massacre if something went wrong."

"Good. I'll carry the ball from here," stated Collins. "It's getting to be late. You need to get together with Abe and Jacques. I want Sue out of this mess before any blow-up happens. Our intelligence says she's at a farm north of here. We only have a few hours to pull off an extraction."

Chapter 48:

Near Pretoria, South Africa, September, 1990

Sue was extremely tired after her shower. She curled up on the bed thinking about the slingshot idea. The next thing she knew, a hand was shaking her awake. She started up, hands reaching for the throat of the woman leaning over her.

"It's just me, your nurse," the sound of Debbie's voice stopped her. "No reason to beat up on an innocent person."

Sue dropped her hands. Her eyes coming into focus on the face of the young woman. Marina was standing back from the bed, observing, but obviously ready to move in and subdue her if help were required.

"You must have drugged me!" Sue shook her head, trying to clear away the fog.

"No, it's probably just depression at having no chance of an escape," the nurse replied. "It's almost dinner time. Colonel Petrov would like you to come down and have an early supper with him. We'll be back in ten minutes to escort you." The two retreated through the doorway. Sue heard the snick of the magnetic lock.

Sue wasted no time in changing her rumpled blouse for a nice clean one from the closet. Then, after quickly rinsing her face and checking her eye shadow again, she gazed briefly at the overhead skylight. The sun was past high noon and it would soon be evening. She rapped on the door to indicate that she was ready. It swung open. Marina stood waiting.

"Just like a bunch of depraved Russians to have a peep hole for observation," she thought.

They walked from the stable to the veranda of the main house. A table had been set up in the shade overlooking a large pond filled with Koi. Petrov was standing by the pool watching the fish.

"Quite a mansion you have here," Sue said, noting that Petrov was dressed like a gentleman farmer. He wore a gray safari suit, matching shorts and high socks, rounded out by suede desert boots.

"It's good to see you looking so refreshed," Petrov gestured toward a chair, stepping ahead to pull it out for her. "Help yourself to the fruit salad and then Maria will be here to serve us our supper. I have a long evening ahead."

"What do you want from me?" Sue went directly to the point.

"I am the head of a Russian organization known as Section One of the Russian Infiltration and Unconventional Sabotage unit. You Americans call us by the acronym S1RIUS. We wish to take control of the natural resources of Africa. The Republic of South Africa is our current target."

"I don't understand," Sue feigned ignorance.

"I'm sure you know more than you are letting on," Petrov smiled, "but that will be for later. Let me just say the world is about to see me take control of the politics of South Africa. After that, I will help some key leaders form a new government. They will make special concessions to Russia by trading with us for certain strategic minerals." He leaned back in his chair, snapping his fingers at the nearby maid.

"Maria, check if our supper is ready. The young lady is almost done with her fruit. I don't want her to go hungry."

"What do you mean by saying you will form a new government? The negotiations are proceeding very well already for black rule." Sue felt a gnawing in the pit of her stomach.

"His attitude is so self-assured. Can we really stop him?"

"Today is the beginning of the Chaka the Zulu celebrations throughout the entire country. We expect ten thousand blacks and the same number of whites to be attending rallies and preliminary celebrations all over the country, including here in Pretoria. On Saturday, there will be massive parades with around twenty thousand people marching here and an equal number in Johannesburg. All told, there will be half a million people celebrating their cultures and history."

"So, it happens every year. The country always celebrates Chaka the Zulu Day. Why is this different?"

"Because, my dear," Petrov dished himself a large helping of potato salad and a variety of small sandwiches from the platters now at the table, "Black majority rule is never going to come to South Africa. I am about to touch off a massive rebellion by the black people of this country. By the time they finish, apartheid will certainly be gone, but not due to peaceful negotiations. The gutters are about to run deep with blood. You are about to see how a Marxist revolution can tear a capitalistic, apartheid country apart. After that, my people will start over here."

He paused, looking at her intently, then said solicitously, "Here, here now I'm upsetting you. Please don't let your dinner get cold."

Sue dutifully tried to tuck into her food. She concentrated on chewing slowly. She watched the humming birds buzz around the red feeder only a few feet away. When she sat back, leaving a few scraps on her plate, Petrov continued.

"We'll all go into hiding for a few days until my provisional government takes over. After that, we should be able to discuss the terms of your release."

"What terms?" She was instantly back on guard.

"Your people have a commodity of mine that got lost when one of my workers died in the Okavango a few days ago." He sat back, watching her intently.

"You mean Grobler? Jacques' assistant? He worked for you? What did he have that was yours?" She didn't have to lie about her ignorance on this one.

"Grobler was carrying a quarter of a million dollars-worth of high grade uncut diamonds." Petrov paused again, watching her closely. "I sincerely hope your side thinks you're worth that much. What do you think?" His cold eyes and smile nearly stopped her heart.

"I have no idea what you're talking about," replied Sue, feeling a chill ripple down her spine. "Grobler was just a part time worker for Jacques. Are you sure about all this?"

"I suspect you're ignorant of the diamond smuggling going on across Botswana," the Russian laughed, seeing her genuine surprise. "At the same time, I know your boyfriend and the man he collected out at Drotsky's Cave know exactly why I brought you here. He'll follow up the way I expect him to. If not, well then…," He laughed.

Her face went white. Her breathing came in several shuddering gasps.

"Oh Jacques! How did I get myself into this situation? Why haven't I told you how I feel about you? We should be getting married, living out in the bush and having babies. We should be far away from this madness."

This was followed by an even more awful thought…

"What if I'm not worth a quarter of a million dollars in diamonds to him? What if I'm stuck with this… this monster?"

"Marina!" Petrov's voice rang out, "I think it's time our guest went back to her room. She is obviously quite upset and needs a rest."

****

Throngs of people came into the cities by the thousands that afternoon and then toward evening by the tens of thousands. Their bodies swelling the giant football amphitheaters, bloating them to full capacity with seas of black, yellow, tan, brown and white faces in undulating, bobbing and chattering oceans of humanity. They had come to hear speeches by the living martyrs of the black African liberation movement, and their leaders.

The assassin watched from high above the swirling mass of black faces. He was nestled into his cozy nook with his sniper rifle. Waiting like a predator for the appearance of his unwitting prey. Below him, individuality was lost unless viewed through his scope. The drums of the fledgling nation, the rhythm of sticks beating on ceremonial shields throbbed through the rapidly falling night and reached his ears, high above. All of them, him included, were waiting expectantly for one man, soon to be coming to the podium. The noise grew to a crescendo!

The aged politician far below was not in sight but he too felt the surge of human spirit and power coming from the crowd. His depression from the years of solitary confinement faded. The rheumatic aches in his limbs, which had been tortured beyond belief, fled from his bones. The fatigue in his brain, deep-seated after years of harassment, lack of sleep and drugs was washed away. Here were his people, his body of support. They were waiting for him to step forward, to claim his rightful position and fulfill their dreams of his mission.

"What power! What glory! To be standing in front of my people once again as a leader!"

The giddiness of the thought almost went to his head, making him dizzy. He realized the hidden potential within that sea of humanity.

"I can take them with me tomorrow into the streets of the cities and we can rid ourselves of all these whites and their oppression forever. Shall I ask them once again to take up their spears against other people? Shall I ask them to help me drive them out forcibly? Shall we send them packing?"

His hands began to crumple the sheaf of papers that made up his speech. A speech forged within his mind by years of experience in prison and abuse at the hands of the rulers of the nation.

"Am I capable of forming a nation from this mass of humanity or will it all crumble around me?"

His eyes picked out the solid shape of the podium erected at center stage. Surrounded by bullet proof glass it was a safe haven for his presentation. Beyond the stage his gaze took in the forms of his own personal army. Over two thousand men, creating a human barrier between the stage and the crowd. The red head-banded warriors standing in the warm spring of the evening, their shoulders draped with ceremonial animal skins. Their glistening muscles bore the welts, scars and wounds inflicted by that other nation's army, also present in large numbers but standing well back in the shadows. Towering head and shoulders above all others, at the front of his troops, stood the magnificent gigantic form of Eli Gkozo, a true son and heir to the Xhosa and Zulu nations. A man who would follow him with his troops into the very heart of hell if he chose to take that route.

A shudder of cold fear wracked his frail body. His assistant stepped close, a look of concern on his face.

"Are you well sir?"

"I am being tempted in the wilderness tonight," mused the old man straightening the wrinkles out of his papers. "By the grace of God we will survive the coming days. Tonight is our one chance. We must move our country on to greater things."

"There are thousands of people here, sir," responded his aide, "How can this be a wilderness?"

"You see people and believe we are with friends, William," replied the old man. "I see people and recognize the awesome political power within them. They are pawns in the winds of a gale of political intrigue. Here is the true wilderness. Tonight we must control the power of that wilderness, or South Africa will descend into a nightmare of violence.

Tonight we must take the steps proposed by our Bishop Desmond Tutu to gain peace. Tonight we must somehow find a way to move away from a platform of violence that I espoused through the A.N.C. some thirty years ago. Tonight if we are to have a country that is truly a home, I must shape my people into a power above and beyond a simple black nationalistic movement. Tonight I must make them believe in something we have only imagined. We must become a truly multi-racial nation as envisioned by Gandhi so many years before in this country. If I fail, then we will certainly all descend into the hell of a racial revolution. We will see the chaos and anarchy of genocide and civil war. Tonight I must make us all winners in the struggle for freedom and equality in our country."

"You will succeed, *mong wa me*, my owner," reassured his assistant. "I have faith and your people love you."

"Will they accept that I am no longer the man they dreamed me to be thirty years ago? They loved another in ages past and it led to a cross. What will happen here tonight?"

"But how can you preach about love and reconciliation on Chaka the Zulu day?" Doubt had entered his assistant's voice.

"In the same way that I can accept my old friends of the A.N.C., also recently released from prison. Men like me who refused to renounce violence when they felt young and immortal. Now we are all old men, now we must have the wisdom to join together to lead this nation. Tonight the spirit of Chaka will be God's tool for showing us the way. The men of *Umkhonto we Sizwe*, The Spear of the Nation, will rise again and be great. But this time they will rise in a different manner than they had envisioned. If only they will heed my words."

"Yes, my leader. Now, sir, they are ready for you to go out. The Bishop has given his blessing and the Chief is just finishing his speech."

And so it began, with television cameras, floodlights, the chanting mob of thousands and a lone white-haired black man walking toward the podium.

Chapter 49:
Outside Pretoria, South Africa, September, 1990

Across the city, Jacob stepped from the limousine now parked in the secluded shade of a tree covered lane. He removed the chauffeur's jacket and cap revealing his camouflaged outfit.

"Ride's over fellows." he said to his three camo garbed passengers.

"This will take us to the horse farm?" Abe pointed to the narrow pathway leading off into the nearby trees.

"Yes," replied the unit commander, shouldering his automatic weapon and leading the way. "I have three of our Fast Company standing by near the front gate. They only need my word and they'll be in the front gate in a flash. We'll have them in a vice. No escapees."

"Allow me," Jacques stepped past the man once they were beyond any visibility from the road. "I will lead tonight. I've worked a lot of South African farm areas. These old riding paths are probably not used anymore but they're a good screen for other activities. He will have lookouts at some of the trail junctions. I know you're a pro, but I'm used to spotting them on my own turf."

Jacques held the small PSE Tac-Elite Crossbow at port-arms across his chest. "This will cut down on any noise. We don't want to use that thing except in an emergency," he nodded toward the commando's rifle.

"Right, it could bring a pack of hornets down on us. Take point," said the unit commander."

The last shreds of light washed off the tree leaves. The sun fell to the west. They high stepped forward, toes touching ground first to feel the terrain underfoot, slowly, carefully moving forward. The shadowy shapes of the buildings ahead barely visible as total blackness obscured their vision. Jacques flipped down his night-scope eyepiece and viewed the trail ahead, one eye seeing the greenish image superimposed on the other eye's sight with his native night vision.

"Nice view."

A few moments later, Jacques, still on point, dropped to one knee. His shadow companions followed suit.

"A smoker stinking in the night, Easy prey!"

A whiff of tobacco on the breeze reached his nostrils. He remained motionless, barely twisting his head as his roving eyes searched for his quarry.

"Aha! Movement! Good night vision gear!"

In the silence his ears picked up a *"Click!"* ahead on the trail a lighter flared momentarily. The sudden white glare through the night vision scope nearly blinded that eye. He shut it and waited, watching the trail and the orange lighter flame with his naked eye. He heard the lighter click shut. Opening his scope eye he watched the tip of the cigarette glow as the smoker pulled in a deep drag. The man exhaled with a slight sigh."

"Now I've got you!"

Jacques eased forward bringing the crossbow up slowly, crosshairs centering on the shadow.

"Wait! Breathe slowly! Wait!"

The next drag on the cigarette produced a white dot in the night scope. The crosshairs centered on the silhouette of the head. He gently pulled the trigger.

"Pfsst!" Followed by a 'thud' and total silence.

"Good! Hardly audible! Now, wait! Take your time and watch for movement!"

The silence was deafening. A minute passed, no sound of any movement. He used the lever to gently cock the bow and fit another bolt.

"OK! Go! Softly, Softly!"

Jacques lifted his hand and motioned two men forward. Abe bent over the body, expertly frisking it. They pulled it off the trail between several bushes.

Abe signaled 'OK' as a flare of headlights cut through the trees ahead. Two vehicles pulled into the driveway at the front of the building. Jacques stopped again.

"Looks like company, whispered Jacques."

"Maybe he's having a party. Let's hope he isn't calling in reinforcements because of us," replied Abe.

"No, they just turned on the yard lights on that side of the house. Must be motion sensors. Let's wait a minute and see what happens. Then we crawl off to the left behind what looks like a big barn," Abe commented.

Again they waited.

****

Sue drew back on the elastic shoulder strap of her bra one more time. It had taken a while to figure out how to make a slingshot. The upright back of a folding chair had been the best she could do. Stretching the bra strap between the two uprights had given her the necessary rubber band. Then, when seated on the floor she could aim toward the open skylight. She released the stretched elastic. Another folded note flew through the gap of the open window into the darkness of night.

"Yeah! Two in a row! My God! How frustrating! You've been at this for ages. What are my odds that this will work? A one in ten chance of getting something through the hole? A one in ten chance that the message will make it off the top of the roof? That's already a hundred to one odds against me! Then there's maybe a one in a hundred chance that someone helpful will pick up the paper, read it and do something about it. What am I thinking? That's a one in ten thousand chance of this working. Pretty puny, but better than nothing. So here goes another nothing!"

She pulled back again on the strap, fitted another message between her fingers and shot it into the night.

****

The three-man team leap-frogged now, moving faster with the cover of night and the apparent concentration of people and cars at the front of the farm house.

The Fast Company commander took a stand where the parking area was clearly visible and centered the crosshairs of his sniper rifle on each license plate. Whispering each number into his phone, he transmitted the information back to headquarters.

Then Abe wormed his way with Jacques toward the barn and stopped at a main trail to cover their rear. Jacques crawled ahead around the back of the barn. A man came out of the stable door dressed in hunting gear. Through the half opened door Jacques could read the quarantine sign. He clicked once on his radio transmitter and received a two click from Abe.

"Nothing urgent. I think they have a safe house behind a quarantine barn for horses!"

He began to slide closer and then saw the guard appear to suddenly have a change of mind, reverse directions and start down the bridle path toward him. The man's flashlight played off the trees and bushes as he came. Jacques froze. He brought up the crossbow and tensed himself. When the guard reached the corner of the path, his light would shine directly onto Jacques' prone shape. Five more steps and there would be another dead man.

A shout came from the front of the house. The man stopped, turned and disappeared back around the corner, entering the building. A light snapped on inside the stable and Jacques could see a skylight. At that moment a white object shot through a more distant skylight, rolled down the roof and bounced on the ground only a few feet away.

"What the .... Spitballs?" Then it dawned on him and he grinned to himself, *"That's my smart girl!"*

He took a chance and crossed the open area near the building picking up several of the white objects. As he had surmised, they were tubular shaped, folded in the middle. Any middle school teacher in the world could describe them. The supposed secret method of passing messages across the classroom by shooting them with a rubber band.

He heard voices approaching. He ducked into the bushes as three men with bodies like dance hall bouncers passed, entering the stable. Moments later the light through the sky window was extinguished and the three exited, bodily carrying a fourth person.

It was all that Jacques could do to hold himself back as he recognized the body shape and blond hair. Sue was being hauled away one more time. Caution told him it was better to wait. Follow the trail to the next location. Her release was important but so was smashing Petrov's cartel. He turned and wormed his way back to Abe.

"They've got Sue and are taking her somewhere," his voice was no longer a soft whisper due to his emotion.

"We're on it," replied Abe, "I saw them bundle her into the trunk. Just called in the vehicle plate number of the car. They seem to be flying the coop. My bet is, the final phase starts tomorrow and they want to be on site to view the fun. We'll follow."

"What about our dead friend?"

"The men have already dragged him back to the vehicle. The embassy will dispose of the body. Nice shot with the crossbow. We don't want to draw attention by leaving a cadaver with a crossbow bolt between the ears. We need to get on the road. You ready to move out?"

"Let's go for it!" Jacques followed the other black shadow. Noise was no longer an issue with all the car noise. They raced down the paths.

Jim Collins was ecstatic. He took them directly into the war room when they got back to headquarters.

"I can't believe the names attached to those license plates at Petrov's farm!" he was almost dancing around the room. "With what we've got, along with Jacob's earlier intelligence, we can nail the majority of the main players in this scheme. Our final problem is figuring out who we can trust with the information once we turn it over."

"Sounds like the original Zulu data wasn't far off the mark," observed Abe glancing briefly at the names and photographs. "You've got a real brew of traitors here.

"Yep, all the way from the hard core military to top right and left wingers."

"An odd stew of political agendas," Abe's voice held a note of skepticism. "Do you really think the military would work with communists? I can see them with the apartheid right wingers but not the commies."

"Communists, neo-Nazis, radical white militants and radical black groups, they're all in on it. The mission is to create anarchy and overthrow the government." Jacob explained. "After that, they will throw out current alliances and blow each other away. Everyone wants control. It's going to be one bloody mess."

"Just like old Hitler and Stalin. All smiles in 1939. Then as soon as the ink is dry, go for the other guy's jugular. You figure it will start tomorrow?" Jacques asked.

"If not tonight at the stadium," replied Jim. "We've got a man in place. Sue's note confirms it. We have at least a part of their plans. Let me show you what I think is going to happen." He picked up a pointer near the large street map of the center of Pretoria.

"Here's the parade route for the Black Nationalists and the ANC tomorrow. Straight up Ben Schoeman Avenue onto Potgeiter. Then a right turn here," he pointed to a junction, "taking them on to Klerk and past Parliament and the dignitaries over here. When they finish, they turn right onto Paul Kruger, another right onto Skinner and are back on Potgeiter taking them straight out of the city."

"Looks like a good route," observed the Colonel. "So what's the problem?"

"I've been wracking my brain on this one," said Collins. "There must be some flaw to the route that the anarchists can exploit."

"Troops will be stationed all along the route to keep the parades from straying," said the Colonel. "The crowd won't even have to look at street signs, they just follow the barriers into and back out of the city."

"Sounds foolproof," observed Jacob. "Who's in command of the troops?"

"The whole operation is overseen by General Breytenbach..." Collins paused looking owlishly at Jacob.

"Breytenbach!" Jacob glanced at the list of commanders. "He was one of the main military leaks. He's in cahoots with..."

"Petrov!" Collins interrupted Jacob in mid-sentence. "Guess where he was last night?"

"Oh, Shit! With Petrov at the farm?" The incredulity in Jacob's voice was shared by the others.

"Damn right! Unless you made a mistake with the license plate numbers. I'd say he's being groomed for a big role in Petrov's new government!"

"Where will he be tomorrow?" growled Jacob.

"Somewhere in this area I've circled red," Jim pointed. "We'll have a better fix tomorrow morning when I get together with a general who's been working with me since Angola."

"Something about the names of a couple of those commanders rings a bell," said Jacob sliding his finger down the list. Aren't these guys all in charge of units of the Thirty-second battalion?"

"Right, that's the main group doing the parade management. What's the problem?"

"The Thirty-second is made up of Koevoet. Those guys aren't street patrol soldiers, they're hunter killer units. They're used to pry guerillas out of hiding in Namibia. These men are Bushmen trained to work on the Angolan border. They aren't military police versed in crowd control."

"Wait, Jacob," Jim raised a placating hand, irritation showing in his voice. "Aren't you being a bit over-dramatic on this? They could be rotating back into South Africa for peacetime duty. Who better to control black marchers than black troops?" "We're all tired. I need to get a bit of shut-eye before dawn. Tomorrow is going to be a long…"

"Wait!" Jacques held up a hand, interrupting the exchange between the two men. "You just said it! Blacks controlling blacks! That's not what you've got here. These little guys aren't recognized by other black Africans as black. These are battle hardened warriors of a minority group. They've been disenfranchised, hated and even hunted. These guys aren't friends with the Zulus, Xhosa and other black tribes any more than they're friends with the whites!" His own voice had risen in pitch. "They don't like either side. If a commander says 'Shoot!' They'll do it! These guys are already outcasts in this society. What better scapegoats for the start of genocide!"

"You must be kidding," said Collins, but his eyes were shining with interest at the idea.

"There has to be a trigger," Jacob interjected. "There has to be a justifiable reason for troops to open fire. Something needs to push the crowd into violent action. Something has to happen to menace the city, or whites, or government officials. That way the order to shoot is justifiable!"

"He's right," Abe spoke up, "The ANC has backed away from violent means. The Bishop and other ANC leaders are all giving speeches tonight. If an assassination occurs tonight, then tomorrow the people would be on edge. Another incident during the parade, could push the crowd over the top to become a mob. If cars get overturned, windows broken, fires started, the populace will be endangered. Someone will give the order to open fire. After that the outcome it will depend on who the Koevoet shoot."

"There has to be a trigger," said Jacques.

"We don't know what that is," Collins shook his head. "All we can do is deal with tonight's mess and hope something pops up tomorrow to give us a heads up in time to stop mayhem."

"We've got the best sniper in our unit in position as a counter sniper tonight at that stadium. He's in position to put a bead on any of the four South African snipers guarding the leaders. If they make a wrong move it will be curtains."

"I hope so for all of our sakes tomorrow," Collins said.

"Before we quit, I need to see last night's list from the horse farm," Jacob said.

"It's everyone we expected," Jim Collins now sounded completely worn out and even more irritated that they weren't closing down for the night. He handed the list to Jacob.

Jacques peered over his shoulder as he read the names aloud.

****

Inkatha – Radical leftist militants of Zulu origin: Willy Bengu, Lucas Mncwango, Mabongi Magope.

Umkhonto we Sizwe – Left wing militants of the African National Congress: Joshua Tona Mbeki, Eli Gkozo.

<u>Wit Wolves</u> – Neo-Nazi white militants: Jan Treurnicht, Lisa Marie Kotzee.

<u>Military, Police and Secret Service</u> - South African Government: Gen. Breytenbach, Col. Dirk Van Zyl, Agent Deborah Kotzee.

****

"Are you kidding me?" Jacob shook his head in disbelief, "Van Zyl and Kotzee! Are you sure of these names?"

"We have positive visual ID on everyone on that list." stated the Colonel emphatically.

"What's the problem with Van Zyl and Kotzee?" asked Collins.

"Two names from my past," said Jacob, sitting down in a chair. "We now know our sniper and probably the name of the person who is watching Sue."

"Tell me," Jim Collins' face turned red as he glowered down at the other man.

"Captain Van Zyl is a career officer with one of the special units we were tracking. The ones who were close to Petrov. He was attached to our US Embassy as a liaison and worked with my cell before it went down."

"We already know that, so?"

"So he was playing us. He's a double agent. He sold out the Zulu operation to Petrov."

"So what do we need to bring him in and put on the thumb screws?" said the Colonel.

"Even more than that," stated Jacob. "We need to inform our man inside the coliseum Van Zyl's operational specialty if he were a sergeant in the US infantry would give him an 11B4 prefix. The '4' means he's a qualified sniper! Van Zyl has an officer's commission. He has placed his men to guard the speaker from assassination. They are all watching the crowd. But Van Zyl is free to will pick his own position to supervise them. He's our assassin! He's going to nail the speaker! We've got to stop him now! The main speaker is a walking dead man!"

"Shit! I'm on it!" Yelled Collins, racing across the room and grabbing his field radio.

"Mongoose! We've got a snake in the grass…"

****

High above the thundering crowd the assassin lay prone and secure in his special cranny above the press box.

The Bishop had finished his speech and taken a seat to one side of the stage. The national anthem was being played.

As it finished, the MC, dressed in native robes began his eloquent introduction of the main speaker for the night. The man the assassin had come to see. The man who was to be eliminated during his brief walk to the bullet proof podium.

"Bahaetsho Wa Me! My Peoples!" shouted the MC drawing everyone's attention. His introduction rang throughout the coliseum translated simultaneously into Tswana, Zulu and English for his mixed audience. It raised more cheers, more thumping of sticks on shields and the stamping of tens of thousands of feet.

The curtain to the side of the stage parted and the figure of a short man could be seen standing in the shadows. A shiver went through Van Zyl's body as he centered the crosshairs on the man's chest and waited. He remembered General Breytenbach's words.

"Wait for the shot that will give the greatest emotional impact! Let him get almost to center stage. People will rush forward to help. At that point you can take out two or three of the others. I want this to be a proper blood bath on stage. Then get out! Fast! Before they can shut the whole place down."

The white-haired man stepped into the spotlight.

****

The Fast Company sniper's earpiece crackled.

"Mongoose!" The urgency of the voice was palpable even through the electronic ether, "Target's moving! Acquire the snake! He's above the press box!"

Mongoose swiveled his body slightly, bringing in the top of the press box.

"God dammit! Where are you? Why didn't our quartermaster have a wide angle scope? Not my proper rifle. At least it's got a trued in laser. Where is he? This is taking too long. Concentrate!

"Mongoose! I give him fifteen more steps. Acquire! 13, 12, 11, 10..."

"Ah! There you are, you white racist son-of-a-bitch! Relax... right arm pressure on the sling... left arm take up slack... breath, squeeze..."

****

Across the stadium Van Zyl's eyeball peered through crosshairs at the black man crossing the stage. His finger began to tighten on the trigger...

"Now I've got you cold, you black bastard! Five more steps, 4, 3, 2... Wha...? Red Lase...?"

****

"The radio next to Collins crackled.

"Control, this is Mongoose. Contact made, snake down. Out!"

"Congratulations, come home! Out!"

The thumps from the two silenced rifles were drowned out by the cheering crowd far below. The zip and thump of a single bullet impacting the wooden stage was lost to all but the closest security man. By the time he moved, he realized his leader was inside the bullet proof podium. Speaking softly into his radio, he sealed off the stadium, letting the speaker begin his speech.

Raising both hands to the sky the heart-faced, white-haired, yellow-skinned man who had suffered thirty years of imprisonment for his beliefs, shouted out over the roar of his peoples for all the world to hear.

"Umkhonto we Sizwe...!Ukuthula!"

"Spear of the Nation.....!Peace!"

Chapter 50:
Pretoria, South Africa, September, 1990

Moments after being escorted from her room by the nurse, Sue found herself again trussed and bundled into the back of the black limousine. She had no way of knowing where they were headed. She sensed only the rapid stomach-churning turns along the country road. She snoozed once they hit the long straight highway stretch but awoke to more swerving on smooth pavement. She decided they must be inside the city. A final downward slope with sharp squealing turns told her they had arrived somewhere with an underground parking lot.

The trunk popped open. Marina produced a wicked looking sheath knife.

"I'll cut the bonds on your legs," she explained. "You'll walk between Debbie and me. We'll put Debbie's nurse cloak over your shoulders. It will be covering your hands as we pass through the hotel lobby." Debbie adjusted her garment so it hung naturally over Sue's bound hands.

"Show her the syringe, Debbie," said Marina.

Sue watched as Debbie opened a small black shoulder bag and extracted a syringe with a needle already attached. She removed the sterile cover from the needle. Sue noted that Debbie was wearing her full nurse uniform. It had been concealed until now by the cloak.

Debbie stepped forward with the syringe.

"I'll be walking next to you the entire time with one hand on your arm." She slipped the hand with the syringe through one of the arm holes of the cloak. Sue felt the needle slightly prick her skin.

"See that you keep a good eye on her, Debbie," remarked Petrov, coming over from another vehicle.

"This system never fails," Debbie replied. "If she makes one false move I'll inject the entire contents. She'll go down like someone's just hit her with an ax handle."

Sue's stomach churned at the touch of the needle on her skin. It made her want to throw up. "What's in the syringe?" She asked, knowing that she really didn't want to know.

"It won't kill you," explained Debbie, "but we won't have any trouble explaining away anything you might shout out. The hotel administration has been told that we're transporting a demented person who might need sedation. Dimitri will be on your other side in case you collapse. Trust me, the hang-over is nasty."

"Thanks, sounds consoling." Sue smiled grimly at her own graveyard humor. "I hope I don't barf all over the lobby. Needles make me squirm."

"We'll walk slowly to get the rhythm," said Debbie, guiding her with gentle pressure toward the service elevator. The door was opened by a man with a suspicious bulge under his sweater.

The elevator stopped at several floors on the way up. Sue watched helplessly as several cleaning and security personnel got into and out of the elevator, riding part way with them. At each stop Debbie's hold on her arm increased and the needle pricked a little deeper into her skin. Sue closed her eyes.

The elevator stopped on what appeared to be the top floor. Sue felt Debbie relax her hold slightly as they stepped off. The cleaning man who had stayed behind jammed the door open with his mop and bucket and hung an "Out of Service" sign over the mop end.

"They must own the whole floor," thought Sue. She felt Debbie withdraw her hand. She saw a tall man in fatigues standing near a door down the hall.

Dimitri stepped ahead of the group. He held the door into what appeared to be a giant suite of rooms. A large florid faced man in military fatigues approached, smiling, "Ah! Colonel Petrov, Comrade Dimitri, ladies Marina, and Debbie, so glad you could all make it to ringside." His hand swept wide to indicate the large picture windows. Two broad avenues stretched into the distance, running at right angles to one another.

"General," Colonel Petrov gave a perfunctory salute while Dimitri and Marina clicked his heels and saluted smartly.

"Oh! And who is this pretty lady with our nurse?" The general turned toward Sue, "Not another convert to our side I suspect by the dour look on her face, eh?"

"She's our insurance policy against any interruption," replied Petrov. "I'm planning to cash her in for some very valuable merchandise in the few days."

"There's plenty of space in the spare room over there," the general pointed. "It's secured and soundproof. So, she's your collateral for the diamonds?"

"Yes. I'm convinced that her presence will ensure quick delivery. Her boyfriend and the CIA would love to have her back in one piece."

"Excellent! I hope we can manage that. Are we expecting other visitors tonight?"

"I doubt it but we'll keep the guards posted just in case."

"I was sorry to hear the party at the coliseum didn't turn out as planned."

"Van Zyl was an excellent officer. One of our best operatives. We've already checked out the other snipers. None of them fired a round. Someone leaked information and Van Zyl paid the ultimate price. I've already put out several false leads. We'll track those and see if a mole surfaces."

"Good! Put the girl in the other room and then let me show you what's going to happen in the morning. I have a street map over here."

As Debbie led Sue off into the side room she saw another group of men in military uniforms, wearing blood red berets. Leaning against the wall were two long barreled rifles with wide angle sniper scopes. The map to which the General was pointing, was obviously a blow-up of the central streets in Pretoria.

Debbie shut the door, cut the bonds on Sue's wrists and turned on the television.

"It should be quiet in here for the rest of the night," Debbie said. "If you get bored tomorrow, look out the window. It's one-way glass so no one can see inside. When the action starts, you'll have a bird's eye view of the parade and then the mob." She walked out, locking the door, leaving Sue to contemplate her fate.

Sue made a quick reconnaissance of the obviously normal hotel room. The window to the outside wasn't locked and opened only a small gap. Nowhere near large enough for a person. The cool breeze from the street helped clear her head.

The thought of attracting anyone below got thrown out when she realized that the angle on the building allowed her captors a view of the window opening.

"OK, TV time. Relax and wait. See what happens."

She lay down on the bed with some pillows, flipped the channels and promptly dropped off to sleep.

****

Morning found the CIA command center still in turmoil, trying to relocate to the center of the city following the departure of the Russians from the farm. Sue's tiny locating transmitter had been virtually useless for tracking the kidnap car.

It was nine when the computer operator called from his terminal.

"Got a fix!

Collins rushed into the room. "Where do you have her right now?"

"She's in a hotel on the corner of Skinner and Potgeiter, right in the heart of downtown," said the computer man. "We don't know which floor but that shouldn't be hard to figure out once we're on site."

"How's the signal?"

"Her battery is way down. If they move her again I'm not sure we can pull her back up."

"Fine, I'll see if I can pull some high level strings to get us in close to that site."

Fifteen minutes later their contact in the South African Army had found a spot in a nearby athletic club which was closed for the holiday.

"Let's go, guys!" Collins headed for the door. "Jacques and Jacob, you take the telephone repair van. Put on the coveralls and look the part. By the time you get there we'll have the location of the utility entry box. Abe and I will set up on the upper floors of the health club which is kitty corner across the street. Our South African security people will clear the health club using the excuse of a national emergency. I don't think the opposition will suspect anything."

It took Jacques and Jacob half an hour of weaving through mid-morning traffic to reach the hotel. The junction box in the maintenance tunnel under the hotel was easy to locate.

Jacques parked the van on the opposite side of the underground lot while Jacob entered the tunnel. Opening the phone cable box, he followed the conduit of wire down a tunnel and around a bend. His heavy cutters sheared through wires. Then he sat in the entrance to the tunnel and waited.

It took another fifteen minutes for two repair men from the phone company to arrive. They parked near the tunnel entrance in the basement. One man stayed near the truck while the other entered the tunnel, opened the junction box and began testing wires.

A scuffing noise behind the repairman barely attracted his attention. "Is that you Peter?" he said, continuing to check all the connections. Jacob hit him in the temple with a lead filled sap. He slumped to the ground.

Jacob then walked out of the tunnel and waved to the man inside the truck, yelling, "Hey, Peter!" He waved again. The man climbed out of the vehicle to be taken silently from behind by Jacques.

They dragged the two men into the tunnel entryway. Injecting each with a drug dose sufficient to keep them sleeping for two or three hours. Jacob turned to Jacques.

"Here's the company card, we'll take the truck up to the front of the hotel and park it there. If anyone tries to stop us, we say we'll move in about a minute. By the time they know we aren't coming back we'll be headed upstairs. Collins will see the van and know we're in business."

"Got it! I hear the sound of drums. The parade is getting close!"

"We better move!"

"I could use a drink right now," said Jacques, "I keep thinking of Sue!"

"I thought you were all steel, man," Jacob gave him a slap on the back.

Moments later, Jacques pulled to a stop in front of the hotel. A husky army sergeant approached him and shouted angrily, "Get the hell off this street! Didn't you see the barricades?"

"What's the problem, sergeant?" Jacques' voice was calm and nonaggressive. "We'll be here just a second to check in and then go down below to fix the telephones that went out in the hotel."

"I just had two other telephone guys here doing that same thing. What's going on?"

"A bigger break than we had thought," responded Jacques.

Well you can't stay here!" bellowed the military man leaning in toward the window aggressively. "We've got a parade of ten thousand people coming by here in a few minutes. I've been told to keep the streets clear to prevent any problems. Get it off the street or I'll do it myself!"

"Damn it, sergeant," yelled Jacques back at the bull faced man, "the parade isn't on this street. We know it's going past on Potgeiter. That's around the corner. This is Skinner. The blacks go past the hotel but not on this street. I'll be back out in just a second. Jacob will take our equipment inside." He opened the door and pushed past the sergeant, who, although bulkier, was by no means as tall.

The sergeant reached out and grabbed Jacques by the shoulder, "Don't be a fool, man," he whispered in a hoarse voice, "I'm not worried about the blacks coming down Potgeiter with their parade, I'm supposed to keep this street open for the whites."

"What?" Jacques' voice sounded outraged. "The white parade has finished its review. It's headed out of the city four blocks away. They're over on Andries Avenue. There's a whole battalion of military between them and us. The two groups are always kept apart. You're screwed up, Man!" Jacques pushed him again.

"No!" the sergeant's voice was low but clear, "Listen to me man. I'm trying to save your white ass! The white parade is being diverted from Andries down Skinner to this corner! Don't you get it? They'll be marching through here in just a few minutes. You and your black friend need to be long gone unless you've got body armor. Those whites are armed. They're going to march right into the center of these black bastards!" He laughed, "I can see it already in tomorrow's headlines. Big slaughter on the streets of Pretoria. It's going to happen right here. Zulus versus the Boers." He laughed and slapped his thigh then shouted directly in Jacques' face. "Now you and your black boy get your asses off my street or you'll both be just another statistic!" He backed away unslinging his weapon. "That's an order!"

Jacques jerked away, turned to Jacob, saw the grey ashen color of his dark face and said, "I'll take the van down to the basement, park it and use the elevator to come back up. You carry the equipment inside. I'll let Collins know. Meet you inside."

Jacob grabbed his satchel, opened his passenger door and ran.

Jacques gunned the motor, pulling the van around in a 'U' turn. He keyed his radio and was shouting into it as he barreled toward the parking lot entrance. As he turned the corner he looked back. Four blocks away at the junction between Andries Avenue and Skinner Street he could see the military already clearing away cars and removing barricades.

He shouted into his radio, "They're opening a corridor to channel the white marchers straight into the middle of the black parade! The white parade is marching down Skinner Street!"

The first black marchers were just reaching the intersection as he pulled over, partially blocking the entrance into the parking lot. Grabbing his own satchel of equipment! He clicked his radio to speak again.

High above him, Collins laid down his radio and peered out the window. He could see Andries Avenue four blocks to his right and Potgeiter Avenue, running parallel, just below to his left. The first marching band followed by vehicles full of black government officials was passing below. Four blocks away looking up Skinner Street, he could just make out the goose stepping youth group followed by hard faced white adult marchers. He pulled up his binoculars and watched the military men remove more barricades. His radio screamed at him from the table.

"Jim! Jacques here! Petrov has Sue upstairs. Jacob is inside handling that. I'm headed up the street! I've got to find something to divert the parade off this route!"

"Go! Go! Go! Do whatever it takes to stop them! We'll have a blood bath!" Collins shouted back. He watched the white parade come down the street.

"Shit! Here they come! Kids first, Billy-clubs whirling, swastika-like banner waving proudly, followed by..." He squinted, *"men carrying shotguns? Oh Christ! They'll claim they were protecting their own kids!"*

Jacques keyed his radio again, "Jacob! You're on your own! Get Sue! I've got big street problems! The van is in place. If you need it, take off!" He raced up the street toward the marchers.

"Got to do something to prevent this!"

A gasoline truck was being diverted off into a side street. As it began to turn, Jacques leaped to the running board, jerked open the door and climbed in. His pistol came up level with the driver's head. He saw the man's eyes widen.

"Stop! Now!"

Jacques was literally on top of the man, yelling in his face!

"Out if you want to live!"

He pushed the man hard as he opened the door and pulled on the emergency brake. Then he jumped to the ground himself. A rifle brandishing guard was approaching from the center of the street.

"Halt! Wha…"

Jacques shot him between the eyes with his silenced pistol and raced to the rear of the truck. He reached into his satchel, pulled out a programmable timed explosive charge attached it to the rear of the truck with its magnetic base. He pulled a small wrecking bar from his utility belt, twisted it through the padlocked petcock, twisting and snapped the lock. Yanking the handle, he opened the valve. A golden yellow stream of gasoline shot out and splashed onto the street running toward the gutters and storm drains. He punched the thirty second button on the timed charge and ran for his life.

As he ran he yelled at the pedestrians still on the street, "Run! The gas truck's going to explode!"

He heard the cry taken up by others as he ducked into the side entryway of the Loreto Convent.

The grenade exploded igniting the flowing gasoline. Moments later, the "Whump" of the igniting fumes in the storm drains shot flames fifty feet into the air. Then a conflagration engulfed the rear of the truck, igniting the tires and flaring up around the still intact body of the tank car. The intersection was now completely blocked by intense heat and flames.

No one was paying any attention to Jacques as he raced back toward the hotel. Bounding down the parking lot ramp he reached the telephone junction box in the basement.

Chapter 51:

Pretoria, South Africa, September, 1990

Jacob stepped out of the elevator on the tenth floor. He flipped the "Stop" switch and proceeded up the fire stairwell. As he opened the doorway onto the upper floor he saw two uniformed soldiers and a cleaning man. He walked up to the cleaning man.

"Why isn't the service elevator working? I'm supposed to be fixing the telephones that got knocked out. There's some general who keeps calling us. Wants them fixed up here like right now!"

The man eyed him suspiciously and then pointed down the hallway to the two guards in front of the doorway.

"It's probably not the general," he said, "only some damned colonel. Get on it boy!"

"Yes Sa!" replied Jacob, in his best submissive tone. He turned away smartly and trotting down the hallway toward the two guards next to the door.

"Massa! You got a broken telephone line inside?" He flashed his ID card.

"About time boy," answered the larger of the two soldiers while giving Jacob's telephone ID card a cursory glance.

"What's in the bag?" said the other.

"Just my equipment, boss" Jacob dropped the bag and stooped to unzip the top.

"Nay, I don't want to see it lad," replied the big man. "What kept you so long getting here?"

"Traffic and those damned parades," he replied as the man knocked on the door, "I had to detour all over town. Working on a holiday is sad times."

"Know what you mean," replied the army man as an officer pulled open the door.

"Get in here, Boy!" he bellowed. "The Colonel has an army to command. Something's going on out on the street!"

"Nothing happening when I came in," replied Jacob observing the crowd of men in front of the window and a black column of smoke in the background. "Looks like a fire."

"Some kind of explosion up the street. The phone is over there," he pointed. "Get on it!"

"Yes Sa!" Jacob's heart sank as he noted that Sue was nowhere in the room. He picked up the phone and unsnapped the cord.

"This shouldn't take but a couple of minutes," Jacob spoke as he worked. "My partner's down below. We can localize the problem and get it fixed quickly." Jacob snapped on his tester and punched several buttons as if doing a check. He spoke into the phone, all the while observing the positions of the two snipers overlooking the black parade on the street below.

The voice of the commander could be heard clearly.

"We didn't get that black bastard last night. I'm not going to let this opportunity slip by me again. Do you see the old man?"

"He should be coming into view any moment now, sir," responded one of the snipers.

"What's going on up the side street? I see smoke."

"I'm not sure, sir. It looks like a gasoline truck is on fire. The white marchers had to turn back."

"Dammit! Boy!" The officer raged at Jacob, "Get that telephone fixed! I need to find out what happened, you hear?"

"Sa!" Jacob plugged the telephone back in and pretended to listen.

"Be ready men!" A captain with a spotting scope shouted out. "He's coming."

"Once the old man is down, it'll be open season. Take out anyone who looks important," stated Petrov. "They'll be the ones standing up in the vehicles. Then pick out some of the whites in the crowd over there. This is going to be an equal opportunity moment!" he laughed.

"Sa! Have you got another phone in this apartment?" Jacob shouted out. "This line still has a glitch and my partner thinks it's in the second phone."

"In here," said a large man opening the main bedroom door. The bulge of the man's pistol was visible under his open jacket.

"Good, this should be quick," Jacob approached the door.

The big man stepped aside so Jacob could enter.

Sue and a woman in a nurse's uniform were standing in the room. The television going. Both women were peering out the window at the scene below.

For the briefest moment Sue's blue eyes locked onto Jacob's. She looked away feigning disinterest. The nurse didn't bother to look at him.

"Sorry to bother you ladies," Jacob apologized, heading for the telephone beside the bed. The guard turned away and shut the door as a commotion erupted in the next room.

Debbie turned around at the sound of his voice.

Jacob was on his knees, bent over the satchel. He unzipped it, pulling out a stun grenade and his pistol. As he stood, his eyes met the wide eyed look of recognition on Debbie's face.

"Jacob!" His name came out of her mouth in a gasp. Debbie started toward the door.

Jacob shook his head, "No! Debbie!"

At that moment, Petrov's shout came from the adjoining room. "Dimitri! Get the girl. Something's stopping the parade. We're clearing out! Assembly point three! All of you! Now!"

The guard stepped into the room reaching for his weapon. Jacob placed two bullets from his silenced Glock into the man's upper chest. He stepped to the door, pulled the pin from his stun grenade and flipped it into the main room.

He had just time to slam the door and stick his fingers in his ears before the grenade blew, shattering the windows of the other room and immobilizing its occupants.

Sue, seeing him, followed suit and was also able to protect her ears. She turned on Debbie, punching her in the nose, and then following up with a vicious karate chop to the neck.

Let's go!" Jacob yelled and grabbed her hand. He jerked open the door of the room.

Taking a quick look, he noted several of the officers were completely down and out. Others sat or were slumped over furniture, moaning, holding their heads. Blood trickled from their ears and noses.

The two guards from outside the room came through the door and meet two more of Jacob's well placed bullets. He pushed Sue toward the door. "Run!" he shouted, turning for one last scan of the room. Debbie appeared in the doorway, her nurse uniform was streaked with blood from her nose.

"Jacob! Don't go out! They'll kill you!"

Jacob turned and stepped through the door. Petrov's pistol barrel caught him on the side of the head, dropping him like a rock. The Russian grabbed Sue's arm. He dragged her toward the service elevator. Turning back toward the fallen man, he raised his pistol.

Debbie appeared at the doorway. In a desperate effort, she threw herself on top of Jacob's prostrate body, screaming at the top of her lungs.

"No, Colonel! Leave him! He's too valuable to us as an information source. I'll immobilize him with a drug. You can send men back to get him!"

Petrov's silenced weapon spoke twice with the hiss of an adder! Debbie's body twisted in a spasm of agony, then lay still, draped across Jacob's inert body.

Petrov dragged Sue into the elevator, slamming her against the wall. "I should have killed that man just now," he raged, hitting the descent button. "He's alive because either he or his hunter friend knows where my diamonds are. As long as I have you, they will eventually come to me. I'll get them back. Once that happens, all bets are off. I'll keep my word that you go free. Nothing else."

Sue, still slightly dazed from the force of impact with the wall, asked, "Why did you kill her? Why?"

"She was nothing but a pawn," replied Petrov in vicious anger. "She picked the wrong side back there."

They've ruined your plans haven't they?" Sue smiled thinly, knowing that his killing rage might overflow onto her.

"We aren't done yet," Petrov replied grimly, squeezing her arm tightly. "I've been through worse situations than this. Anarchy always wins once you pass a certain point. Ethnic and racial equality can't be maintained even in America. It's going to fail here in a catastrophic manner." He twisted her around, drawing her face to within inches of his own.

"Now pay close attention! When we get to the basement we'll wait in the maintenance tunnels. My men will come to pick us up. If you so much as make a move to try to escape or thwart me, I'll injure you severely. I've said I won't kill you. That's because you're valuable to me alive. Don't think for a moment that I can't incapacitate you if I have to. Your injuries will be permanent. Don't cross me again. Understand?"

"Yes," she nodded, looking downward. His strength was far superior to hers. He was in control again. Only patience, determination and stealth could win against odds such as these. Direct confrontation was not an option.

The elevator door opened, Sue stepped out in front of Petrov who held her arm firmly up behind her back. Her body was his shield. A shadow moved to one side and two bullets zipped past her. Sue heard her captor grunt. Then Petrov raised his own weapon. It spat a bullet into the shadows.

He dragged her toward one of the service tunnels. The smell of blood hit her nostrils. He flicked on a small flashlight, pulling her further into the gloom.

"He's bleeding. Now it's only a matter of time. Someone on our side knows he's here. Oh! Jacques, be careful!"

In the dim light of another alcove not far away, Jacques sat quietly and listened.

"Come on," he muttered, "can't let Petrov win."

****

Jacob sat up. He crawled from underneath Debbie's body to the door of the elevator. His head ached. He still saw stars. He replenished his magazine, pulled several stun grenades from his utility bag, stuffing them into his baggy uniform pockets. When he tried to stand he realized that his lower leg had a nastily flesh wound.

"You are one lucky bastard, Jacob. He must want you or the diamonds very badly. That was Debbie? How did she end up here? My God, what a strange twisted world!"

He leaned against the wall of the elevator and hit the descent button for the basement. The door opened at the lobby to reveal a chaotic scene. Groups of soldiers were clustered near the entrance of the building watching the panic in the streets.

Several men pushed into the elevator next to Jacob, not noticing the blood or the weapon held firmly against his leg. Jacob pushed several buttons for the upper floors and stepped out the door. As the elevator door closed, he flipped a concussion grenade inside. Then he staggered down the hallway towards the fire door. The grenade detonation made his ears ring as he slipped through onto the stairs leading down to the basement.

Jacob crashed through the basement door. Jacques was nowhere to be seen. His pistol and eyes tracked the parking lot. Nothing.

"Jacques!" he shouted.

"Here in the phone box tunnel," came the echoed reply.

"Someone banged me on the head and shot my leg," said Jacob. I've lost Sue." He staggered into the tunnel and slumped to the floor.

"What happened to you?" Jacques said, pulling a bandage from his satchel and going to work on the wound.

"Petrov nailed me just when I thought I had Sue home free. Did they come this way?"

"He's got Sue in the tunnels," replied Jacques. "I may have winged him with a snap shot as they came out of the elevator."

"Badly?"

"A bit of blood but I don't think it's fatal. He shot back at me, then pulled Sue into that big tunnel. I'll go in after them down the parallel tunnel.

"Go ahead," said Jacob, "I'll stay here until I feel functional. Then I'll take the tunnel to follow up behind Petrov. We'll have him in our crossfire at one of the side tunnels." He slumped down with a groan. "Find me a couple of pain pills before you go. I need just enough to dull the pain but not put me to sleep."

"OK," Jacques dug into the satchel. "What's our plan? We just can't expect him to give Sue up for nothing."

"Here, take the diamonds," Jacob slipped the pouch from around his neck. "Make him trade Sue for the diamonds. If he's still playing by the rules, he'll take the bargain. She's definitely worth it."

Jacques handed Jacob the pills and a bottle of water. "Swallow these," he said. "Are you sure you're going to be all right?"

"I'll be just fine sitting here for a while. I'll cover this end of the tunnel in case he gets reinforcements. Eventually he'll have to go through one of us unless there's an exit we don't know about. You better get a move on, this guy is smart and tough. He'll have called for support."

"What about us? Any word from command?"

"I think something must have happened up there to take them out of the picture. My radio doesn't work anymore. What about yours?"

Jacques keyed his radio. "Nothing."

"Ok, we will go it alone. I'll be seeing you in a bit."

Jacques turned and walked toward the second tunnel. He stooped down briefly and ran his finger through a dark shining droplet. Bringing it to his nose he sniffed it.

"Humph, blood. Let's hope it's a nasty wound. I hate hunting wounded leopards. No quarter given or taken. But, there's no choice when the client's in danger."

He sat down and removed his boots. Then, checking to make sure the safety of his pistol was off, he entered the tunnel. Silently, like a cat stalking its prey in darkness, he began the slow, cautious hunt.

****

Sue, now completely exhausted from her four day kidnapping ordeal, allowed Petrov to drag and push her deep into the dark tunnel. They crept forward leaving the light off. Occasionally, Petrov would give a quick wink with his flashlight to illuminate the passage ahead.

She could smell rancid scent of fear that emanated from both of their bodies. Petrov's hot breath was on the back of her neck. The barrel of his pistol brushed against her back. His left hand gripped her shoulder. His closeness in the dark terrified her. She was utterly under his control. Her only hope of leaving the tunnels alive was complete obedience.

Petrov moved slowly. Time was on his side. His men would regroup and begin looking for him. The black American agent was unconscious or dead on the floor upstairs. He might even be a prisoner by now. His buddy was somewhere back in the shadows behind them hopefully wounded or dead from his one snap shot. One of them still had the diamonds.

Petrov pulled his hand away from Sue's shoulder momentarily and touched his own shoulder. The stickiness was still there, the blood wasn't flowing badly. It was probably just a flesh wound.

"Still a chance to win," he told himself, *"I can bargain with the girl's life. Concentrate on the tunnels. Fight off the pain."*

Sue could smell his blood. Her other hand reached into her pocket and felt the electronic tracer and her small cigarette lighter.

"Is he getting weaker? My tracer won't work down here. What can I do with the lighter?" Hope resurged as she heard a slight wheeze to his breathing.

He flashed on the light again, revealing a low passageway off the main tunnel. He pulled her into that tunnel. They were both forced into a stoop. He was leading her now, his fist gripping her upper arm. He turned on the light as they advanced. Their clothing brushed against overhead cables and pipes. When they reached a small pocket in the side of the wall he pulled her down and sat next to her, shutting off the light. They sat in total darkness.

"We may be here for quite some time," his whisper was next to her ear. "I want absolute silence now. If your friends hadn't mucked things up, we'd be negotiating your freedom."

"They beat you, didn't they," she smiled to herself in the darkness.

"We have contingencies for this. My men know where I am," his whisper was harsh, the wheeze from his breathing more definite. "We will win, in the end. Now, I want silence!"

****

From hiding, Jacob watched three red bereted soldiers approach the tunnels. He struggled to his feet and slipped back into the darkness. The pain in his leg had eased somewhat.

"Ah! The miracle of drugs. They're going to see my blood trail. Things are going to get messy.. Just give me an opening where I can see all three at once."

On the street above them, the surging yellow stream of gasoline fueling the gigantic fire gave a final belch as the tank level neared empty. Air entered the open valve spigot mixing with the vapors inside the tank. In milliseconds, a licking flame followed the pocket of air into the confines of the nearly hollow tank. The resulting explosion was cataclysmic. The concussion wave travelled for blocks, knocking out windows a mile from the scene. It picked up vehicles and slamming them against buildings.

The three soldiers reacted instinctively to the concussion, dropping low, spinning and raising their weapons. Two of them ran out of the parking lot. Jacob stepped from his concealment dropping the third man in his tracks. The pistol slide stayed back following the shot.

"Out of ammunition? No! A jam! How in the hell?"

He hobbled back into the shadows working at the weapon, seeing nylon fibers caught in the slide.

"No time to disassemble this thing. Nothing to do but hope I don't need you. That rifle won't help me in the tunnel." He patted the useless weapon, dropping it into his utility bucket.

Chapter 52:

Pretoria, South Africa, September, 1990

The sound the fuel tanker explosion echoed throughout the underground parking lot. Inside the tunnel the noise was deafening. Sue felt Petrov jump reflexively. His pistol knocked against a pipe. The 'clank' reverberated down the passageway.

"Sue!" Jacques called from down the side tunnel in the ensuing silence.

Petrov covered her mouth with his hand, jamming his pistol into her ribs as he shouted back.

"I'll do the talking," his voice had a hollow ring to it. "She's here with me. I presume she's worth something to you. Do you have what I want?"

"Right here around my neck," responded Jacques edging forward slightly in the darkness. He felt a slight breeze coming from the smaller shaft where Petrov and Sue were hidden. "Send me Sue and I'll leave the diamonds here or throw them to you."

"I want you to turn on your light and throw the diamonds into this tunnel as far as possible," ordered the Russian. "I'll have the girl retrieve them while you leave the light on. Once she brings them back here to me, I'll release her."

"Can I trust you to send her out?"

"What's your choice? This young lady is in the safest position of the three of us. I didn't drag her in here intending to kill her." He paused momentarily, "But don't get any ideas in your head and think I won't hurt her. If you play games with me she will suffer. Now, do exactly as I say and it will all work out fine."

Jacques flipped on his small flashlight, keeping his shooting eye shut to preserve its night vision. Placing the light so the beam shown directly into the smaller tunnel, he peered around the corner and lobbed the leather pouch into the tube.

Sue, also with one eye tightly shut, saw the bag fall just ten feet away. Petrov released his hold and gave her a slight push signaling for her to go. She scuttled forward and picked up the bag. Then she looked at Jacques' light only some twenty feet away. An awful urge swept through her brain.

"Go for it girl! No! Wait! You will be safe if you follow orders! Jacques is so close! You can make it!"

Petrov's voice echoed from behind her. "Don't try it! From this angle the hunters in Botswana would call it a Portuguese heart shot. I might miss a bit, so as not to kill you, but you'll be maimed and probably paralyzed for life. Just turn around and bring me the diamonds. Now!"

The strength of his voice forced her decision. She turned and crawled back toward the nook, placing the bag in Petrov's outstretched hand. In the dim light she could see the dried blood on his shirt. A dark red splotch was gradually spreading out from his shoulder. His breathing was ragged.

He took the bag, untied the thong holding the top and spilled a diamond into his other hand. The whiteness of the tetrahedral crystal sparkled in the dim light. He tied the top and slipped the sack inside his shirt. Then he aimed his pistol down the shaft and shot out Jacques' flashlight. They were plunged back into total darkness.

"Hey!" shouted Jacques angrily, "we've got an agreement!"

"I didn't say I'd deliver her to you," Petrov replied laughing loudly. "You wait right there, I'll take her part way up this tunnel with me and then let her crawl back to you. I'll keep going my way, you go yours and everyone stays alive."

He groaned slightly as he began to crawl back down the tunnel, still holding onto her wrist.

Hope surged in Sue. His grip no longer felt as strong and commanding to her weary body. She crawled behind him and prayed silently that he would abide by his agreement with Jacques.

Suddenly there was no longer a tug on her arm. Her wrist was free. She stopped crawling hearing his movements ahead. He was going on alone. Tears of relief swelled in her eyes.   She turned and scrambled back toward Jacques. Back toward safety! Back toward the man she loved!

****

Jacob had seen the glow of Jacques' flashlight and marked the end of the side tunnel. Then the shot from Petrov's pistol had sent the passageway back into total darkness. He inched along slowly, listening to the scrapings of Sue and Petrov along the side tunnel as they came toward him.

The sounds changed. The rapid scrabbling of Sue back down the tunnel indicated that Petrov was alone. Jacob hobbled forward, fingers feeling the entry into the side tunnel. He listened and heard the approaching heavy breathing of his nemesis. There could be no turning back. He crouched slightly, feeling the pain shoot up his wounded leg.

"Don't go into shock! Concentrate on the man you are going to kill! This is end game. You are the only man standing between him and anarchy for the Republic of South Africa! You are Zulu! You don't ever give up!"

He concentrated on listening to the telltale movements, the rustle of clothing and the rasp of breathing as they came closer. Sweat dripped from his brow. The grunts of pain told him his quarry was badly wounded. He tensed his muscles.

Somewhere near the far end of the smaller tunnel Sue's cigarette lighter glowed. Light flickered down the tunnel, backlighting Petrov's figure. He was at the tunnel's mouth, twisting to bring the pistol back around and point it in Sue's direction.

Jacob lunged forward striking the arm of the man who had hunted him for nearly a year. A scream of rage and pain tore from his throat. Petrov grunted in pain at the impact of Jacob's body. The pistol went off uselessly as it was torn free and sent clattered into the darkness.

Then, fueled with a surge of adrenaline, Jacob grappled with his opponent. Mortal combat drove any feelings of pain or weakness from his mind. Like his namesake, the leopard, the *Nkwe of the Kalahari,* he focused only on the kill. He twisted his body to position himself behind Petrov's back. His arm encircled the vulnerable neck. His wrist centered over the Adam's apple.

Petrov twisted sideways, momentarily freeing his neck from the sleeper-hold's pressure. His voice rasped out in the darkness, "Here are the diamonds, take them. We can call it even."

Even as he spoke the vice-like grip of Petrov's hand bit deeply into Jacob's wounded leg.

Jacob could feel his own consciousness beginning to slip. His teeth cracked with exertion. He reared back, straining and snarling like a wounded animal. Tightening the hold around Petrov's neck.

"Never! I am Zulu!" he muttered through clenched teeth.

With all of his remaining strength, he arched his back, bore down on the choke-hold while mentally counting to one hundred.

Chapter 53:
Hospital in Pretoria, South Africa, October, 1990

Jacob opened his eyes to a view of light mint green walls. The smell of disinfectant permeated the room, almost making him sick to his stomach. A small counter, topped by a vase of purple and white dahlias could be seen toward the bright light of the window. He fought down the urge to vomit, struggling to sit up.

"He's coming around," said a familiar woman's voice.

He reached up toward the dangling button overhead and raised himself to a sitting position. The dizziness and torpor of the operating room disappeared. Then his eyes focused on the figures of his two friends seated on the nearby couch. Sue met his eyes and smiled.

"My God! How did I get here?" Jacob shook his head again. "The last thing I remember was squeezing the life out of Petrov in that black tunnel."

"Jacques did a one man fireman's carry to get you out of the tunnel," said Sue, standing and coming over to the side of the bed. "I drove the van like a mad woman. We managed to get you here with a couple of pints of blood still remaining in your veins. It was a close one."

Jacob let his head fall back onto the pillow, "We got Petrov at last," he sighed.

"He was dead on the floor when I got to you," said Jacques, coming to the other side of the bed. "But his body was gone by the time the police security team got there. We think his own people pulled his body out and took it away."

Jacob lifted his head again, peering at his friend through the fog in his brain with narrowed eyes. "You think they got him out? Does that mean he's still alive?"

"Very doubtful. I saw his eyes when I picked you up," said Jacques. "They were glazing over."

"The embassy says we'll have to wait for confirmation," said Sue. "They say it will probably come later on this month when the Russians hold a hero's funeral for Petrov."

"Damn! We might have failed! What's happening outside in the country and government?"

"We won," replied Jacques, smiling. "Several of the old Africans who were released from prison addressed Parliament yesterday,"

"I hear Mr. Mandela is having private talks with the President. They're going to form a new multiracial government," said Sue. "Apartheid is on its way out."

"My God," replied Jacob, smiling for the first time since sitting up, "We finally licked Petrov."

"We helped but it was really you who licked him, Jacob," replied Sue. She placed a cool hand on his still feverish forehead. "It was you. Your years of collecting information when everyone else denied that S1RIUS and a 'Third Force' existed. It was you returning from exile when the cards were stacked against you. You beat Petrov at his own game."

"What about my information on the traitors inside the South African government?"

"That's not a complete win for our side," said Jacques. "The government wants to avoid big scandals. So we expect to see a lot of resignations or early retirements. They'll come up with plenty of good excuses. Then, of course there will have to be new appointments, taking into account tribal and racial groups. The system will need a lot of TLC."

"What about the two of you?" Jacob asked, noting the glittering stone on Sue's finger.

"I finally made a decision about our future," said Jacques. "I've asked Sue to marry me."

"And I said, Yes!" exulted Sue. "We'll spend our honeymoon in Chobe watching animals and getting to know each other better. My parents are going to fly out from the States."

"I hope I'm well enough to come. I'd love to see the two of you get hitched," said Jacob. "What about a wedding present?"

"I think you've done more than enough for us already," replied Jacques winking at him.

"Then you two love birds better let me get a bit of rest," said Jacob. "I couldn't have done this without you."

Sue leaned across the bed. Jacob felt the touch of her cool lips on his forehead.

Jacques spoke over his shoulder as he walked toward the door with Sue on his arm, "When you get out, it will be, as my father used to say when he talked about Foreign Legion celebrations, *Un bouteille de vin pour la fete.*"

"I'll take you up on it," Jacob said, smiling and closing his eyes.

Acknowledgements

To my wife, Jill, the light of my life and my greatest fan. She's supported me through hours of writing, and been a wonderful companion as we have travelled and adventured across Africa and much of the rest of the World.

To the readers of the early drafts of this book: Geneil Hammermeister, Ken McCarty, Roger Blashfield and Myrin Bentz. You gave me invaluable early feedback on the characters, grammar, wording and plot which allowed me to pull together the diverse strands of this tale and make it a whole.

To my editors, Melissa Meeks and Lisa Pottgen of Black, White and Read Author Services at <http://bwrtours.net> for your detailed reading and corrections of my final draft, without which, this novel would not have become a finished product.

To my daughter, Gigi, the professional artist who worked with me to develop the splendid cover for the book depicting the struggle between ideologies for the soul of South Africa.

To the hundreds of African acquaintances, students, missionaries and friends from my years in Africa who have guided and influenced my attitudes and writing on the struggle for African liberation.

Thank you all!

To My Readers

Thank you so much for taking the time to read **The Ghosts of _Ukuthula_**. I sincerely hope that you will take the time to review my book and make comments about what you have read on Amazon.com, Goodreads.com, Barnes and Noble.com, your blog or wherever you feel it will further my book being read by your friends and others. Please feel free to express your thoughts both positive and otherwise as I read my reviews and try to improve my writing skills with every new publication. If you visit my website and leave a comment, I will make every effort to reply to it and keep in touch.

My next book, **_Sendero Rojo_, The Path of Blood**, will spin a tale of South American action and adventure in a novel which again plays off of the idea of odd bedfellows brought about by the vagaries of politics, drugs, war, liberation and money. Until then, enjoy your reading and share your ideas with others.

Rick McBee, May, 2016

http://www.richardhmcbeejr.com

About the Author

Rick McBee, full name Richard H. McBee Jr., has been in love with Africa from an early age. Rick's father read aloud many African classics including: I Married Adventure, by Osa Johnson, Hunter, by John Hunter and African Game Trails, by Theodore Roosevelt. These books stimulated Rick's imagination and desire to work on what was known as the Dark Continent.

Rick's many experiences in Africa have influenced his writing. These began in the 1960's when he taught Biology as a Peace Corps Volunteer in West Cameroon. He later worked in the 1970's as a teacher and headmaster for Maun Secondary School while serving as missionary in Botswana. This work, at the height of the liberation movements in Zimbabwe, Mozambique and Angola greatly influenced his writing of this book. His latest visit to Botswana, Zambia and South Africa in 2015 inspired him to complete the book after seeing the many positive changes occurring under African governments.

Hood River, Oregon is now Rick's home where he lives with his wife Jill in the beautiful orchard covered countryside surrounding that town. The social and emotional atmosphere of Oregon allows him to pursue his passion for writing while still allowing him to participate in many outdoor activities, gardening and reading.

44486216R00224

Made in the USA
San Bernardino, CA
16 January 2017